Bedtime Stories For Grown Ups

Vol 1.

Praise for Bedtime Stories for Grown Ups

"Peggy Hill is a magical storyteller. What a pleasure to inhabit the 'worlds' she created with such compelling detail and clarity. I was transported – to a cold cave trying to escape a human trafficker, to a slightly magical antiquarian bookstore, to the wilderness, face-to-face with wolves. Her ability to describe the physical environment is only exceeded by her characters' depth, their emotional connection to one another, and their very real struggles and triumphs. I wanted to read one Bedtime story each night. I failed. I hope you are better able to space them out. I devoured them and now I want Volume 2 of Bedtime Stories for Grownups! Hurry up, Peggy!"

Karen Blase Fixsen

"Wow. Wow. And WOW. I Truly loved this book.
With her remarkable debut, Peggy Hill delivers profoundly human stories across multiple genres. You will care deeply about her characters who are filled with resiliency and hope, often in the most difficult of circumstances. At times mystical, haunting, suspenseful, funny, and sweet. This book is, quite simply, a beautifully written, rip-roaring good read."

Lauren Baker

"What a wonderful gift you've provided.
Peggy's writing makes it easy for the reader to become part of the time and place of the stories . . . . and not want to leave."

Ric Durity

*Prais*e **for Bedtime Stories for Grown Ups**

"Peggy has a talent for creating very engaging characters that the reader comes to care about in very short order . . . If I ran across these people in the real world, I would recognize them immediately."

Robert Phillips

"Bedtime Stories is a delightful and exciting collection of tales that transported me to other times and new places. Each story was a wonderful mix of enchanting, exciting, joyous, thought-provoking writing all wrapped up in excellent prose. I found the main characters to be charming, well-crafted and believable. Each tale is a gift to the reader to carefully savor while being transported to a new time and place. I regularly re-read my books. I look forward to re-reading these stories to enjoy them once again."

The Rev. Diane Moore

"Peggy's ability to weave any topic, any location, and any character into gripping short stories is a true talent."

Ray Merenstein

Bedtime Stories For Grown Ups

Vol 1.

PEGGY HILL

Word Binders Publishing

Word Binders Publishing
An imprint of Journey Institute Press
A division of 50 in 52 Journey, Inc.
journeyinstitutepress.com

Library of Congress Control Number: 2022938655

Names: Hill, Peggy
Title: Bedtime Stories For Grown Ups, Vol 1.
Description: Colorado: Word Binders Publishing, 2022
Identifiers: ISBN 9781737359142 (hardcover)
Subjects: BISAC: FICTION / General |
FICTION / Short Stories (single author) |FICTION / Literary

First Edition

Printed in the United States of America

Set in Baskerville URW, Cansu

To my mom, who encouraged me to play as well as to work; to Julie, who steadfastly supports my creative compulsion and continues to welcome first readings; to Nancy, my first editor; to the Reverend Michelle Danson, whose broad-minded spiritual direction has been lifegiving in every way; and to Dafna and Michael, for taking a chance on new authors.

Table of Contents

INDICTUS BOOKS   13

LILY'S CURIOS AND COUTURE   37

A FAMILY OF BROTHERS   43

DANI'S WOLVES   75

HELEN THREDGOOD'S SURPRISE   83

JONATHAN'S UKULELE   109

FINDING GRACE   121

AUNT CATHERINE'S FIREHOUSE   189

MYSTERY ON LITTLE DUCK ISLAND   205

RABBIT VALLEY WATER   235

NATHAN'S DILEMMA   269

HENRY'S FRONT PORCH   279

WORTH A SHOT   295

INDICTUS BOOKS

Mariana had a weakness for antiquarian bookstores. In a pinch, when traveling, she would dive into a more pedestrian used bookstore in hopes the shop's owner might have some overlooked gems, or a cabinet hidden away with a selection of valuable acquisitions. It was a grounding ritual for her. She was an advertising executive focused on digital marketing. But when she walked into a shop and breathed in the dust of old books, with their distinctive scent of threaded bindings and old glue, she felt immediately connected to the history of people who loved language. Just like her.

At the end of a long day of meetings in Sacramento, she was ready for a good walk. She headed for an Indian restaurant about eight blocks from her downtown hotel. One block short of her dinner destination, her eyes drifted toward a rather anonymous, dimly lit shop across the street. The entry was set back a bit from the sidewalk and covered by a short gray-and-white awning with the number 721 on the front.

She slowed her pace, turning to face the door. There was something about it. Entirely nondescript as it was, it drew her in. Crossing the street, Mariana peered under the awning to see the name of the shop—and a slow smile spread across her face.

Dinner be damned, she thought, as she whispered it aloud: "Indictus Books." In Latin, it meant "the untold." What an intriguing name for a shop full of stories. Mariana pushed the door open slowly, enjoying the satisfying tinkle of bells hung from the inside handle on a braided gold rope.

She closed the door behind her and waited a moment for her eyes to adjust to the low light.

"Hello. And welcome." A softly resonant male voice drifted toward her from some place deep in the shop.

She walked forward, idly picking up volumes from their stacks on a dozen antique tables while she took in the full dimensions of the bookstore. There was a large central room, but along both sides, a warren of smaller spaces extended and connected with one another through short hallways. All were lined with heavy, dark wood bookshelves that reached within a foot of the high tin ceilings painted white. Mariana thought they might have been 1880s vintage ceiling tiles, disturbed only to add recessed can lights. Each room and corridor had a sturdy stepstool, and motion-sensing lights popped on as she entered the space. It was magnificent. She could not stop smiling.

A tall, older gentleman appeared, polishing wire-rimmed half-glasses with a small white cloth he pulled from a pocket in his unbuttoned sweater. He smiled at her, and she couldn't help but find his blue eyes arresting. They were the color of…a lagoon. Or the edges of blue iris, freshly unfurled. Mariana shook her head to refocus on a normal response to a shopkeeper's greeting.

"Good afternoon, sir. Your shop is, umm, much larger than I expected."

"It is a peculiar layout, but it works for me. Though I have to reorganize absolutely everything when I acquire collections that need to be kept together," he said as he strolled toward the small rolltop desk near one of the two front windows. "Are you looking for something specific?"

"No. Well, yes. I'm always on the hunt for fine printing, unique illustrations, eighteenth century or earlier, ideally."

"Why?" The man turned to face her and stilled himself, giving Mariana the intense attention she hadn't experienced since the last time she was in therapy.

"Why? Why…what, why," she stumbled.

"Why seventeenth, eighteenth-century work?"

"Not sure, just drawn to some of the stylistic patterns, I suppose." Mariana frowned slightly, and brushed a suddenly damp palm against her slacks, taken aback by the need to explain herself.

The man nodded, waiting, offering Mariana a gently curious smile. She felt he expected her to continue. And after composing herself, she did continue, much to her own surprise. Mariana had told no one about her search.

"I have a great-great-grandfather who was a printer in Boston in the mid-1700s. From what little I've been able to learn, he specialized in illustration as an art form."

"Closer," he said, after another pause. "But there's more, isn't there?"

Mariana felt a chill. He was right. Much more.

"Who are you?" Mariana could not shake the feeling that she was in the presence of someone who read far more than books.

The man chuckled, finally breaking his kind but penetrating eye contact. He extended his hand, offering to shake hers.

"Martin Laurent. Collector of stories told and untold. I believe you might enjoy some time in Room six. Back left. Take your time."

Mariana nodded and thanked him as she briefly took his hand. She turned to head toward the back of the store and bumped into a table. Inanely, she apologized to the table, then shook her hand in the air, trying to dismiss her clumsiness. She was flustered.

Martin said nothing, smiling to himself as he walked to the old rolltop desk and pulled out his accounting book. He still preferred his credits and debits on paper in neat rows. He would go and check on her in half an hour or so, after she'd had some time to explore.

Mariana found the room numbers in Roman numerals, high on the framing of each doorway. Room VI did not have shelving like the others she'd seen, but rows of pale oak cases covered in glass and latched, but not locked. Each had its own low LED lighting. Some contained very old books, and some contained artifacts of various kinds. She paused to appreciate the plans for assembling a nineteenth-century rotary printing press and a case of cast metal type pieces organized into sentences in a composing stick. They were used in printing processes in Europe for hundreds of years following Gutenberg's invention in 1450. She was astounded that a nondescript book-shop in California had been able to acquire such things.

Although fascinating, Mariana was looking for something else. She was looking for a part of her family's story. And most of it had been lost for gen-erations. More accurately, it had been carefully excised. She had only the tiniest pieces of its fabric and she had clung to those as if they contained the genes that mapped her soul.

Mariana Perrot was born into a family that had a gift for creating wealth. Proud of their history and proud to trace the expansion of their wealth across generations and continents, she had grown up hearing tales about her fore-bears' talents and political influence. She had great-grandfathers who had shaped nations, uncles who established international trade routes that wound from Ireland and France to the nineteenth-century provinces of Canada. They found there was money to be made in everything, from lead mining to fine textiles to commercial finance and investment. And much of it wove synergistically together, creating exponentially more wealth.

Mariana had no interest in any of it. The Perrots were notorious for their devotion to making money, and from a young age, she had developed a dread of its reach and power over the lives of her siblings and cousins. Marriages had all but been arranged to connect families from industries that one visionary or another saw as opportunity. She herself had grown up dividing time between a vineyard in France that had been passed down on her father's side and a hilltop property in southern Virginia that had been her mother's childhood home, overlooking the town of Roanoke. Her mother's family had owned much of the town since the 1800s, when they invested in establishing the railroad routes connecting Virginia and the Carolinas to Maryland and points north.

Mariana's mother had been introducing her to acceptable young men in both countries from the time she turned 16. Five months after her 18th birthday, Mariana put a flaming, gas-soaked torch to a towering family scandal of her own creation by moving into a tiny sublet carved out of the attic of an old Victorian in a neighborhood of Columbus, Ohio where none of her suitors and absolutely no one in her family lived.

She was thinking about the Victorian house back in Ohio as she paused again by a case displaying a set of quills and intricately etched glass ink pots. Those writing implements might have occupied the corner of a desk in a study in that home when it was first occupied and in its prime. After she had secured its modern-day attic apartment online, she had fantasies of furnishing it solely with period pieces she would acquire from antique furniture shops. Pieces just like those in the case at her fingertips.

But in the end, she left Roanoke with only the belongings she could load into the used Honda Civic she had bought with her own money her senior year at the Kentwood School. The money was thanks to a ridiculously profitable Etsy shop she started with one of her friends making specialty cosplay costumes on commission for major conventions. Her parents didn't even know about it. She landed a job in Columbus as a digital illustrator's assistant based on a portfolio she had quietly created while finishing high school. Then she enrolled in Columbus Community College, paying her own way toward the start of a degree in art history and beginning the process of accumulating a raft of Adobe digital photography and illustration certificates. She was focused and determined to be independent in every way. She had serious artistic talent as an illustrator in both digital and traditional media, and she came by her entrepreneurial instincts honestly.

Her skills, quick mind, and interpersonal sophistication led to quick promotions. At age 25, she advanced to regional director and had been pressed into a position on the board of directors of the Museum of Fine Arts in Columbus. She had little interest in hobnobbing, but understood the need to represent her company in community service. She also agreed because it gave her access to some other things that mattered to her a great deal.

What mattered was acquiring a network for researching the provenance of old illustrations and the books in which they were found.

It was a privately held obsession. She was looking for traces of a particular and eccentric branch of her family tree, which had long ago been ripped out of the encyclopedia of family stories. They were reportedly mad, often short-lived, probably alcoholic artists. They married or didn't, sometimes several times, had children from each relationship, parted ways, and took offspring with them, or didn't. They traveled. They rarely put down roots. Most supposedly died in abject poverty, which in Mariana's family was high crime, not just misdemeanor. A few had achieved a bit of notoriety as artists within a literate circle of publishers and writers. Mariana knew at heart she was one of them. And she felt certain that if she could ever find these relations in the present day, she would have found her real family line.

But they were very hard to track.

Mariana had a feeling there was something there in Room VI that would matter to her search. She frowned in concentration as she pulled a small notebook from her purse. In the notebook was a small set of annotated names that Mariana had determined held the most promise for reconstructing the lineage of her spirit. Some were Perrots. There were also Greens and Greenes, descended from an Alexander Greene, one of the first printers in Boston and the father of 19 children by three wives, many of whom also became part of a family network of printers and publishers and booksellers in the growing English Colonies. Some wealth had emerged in that business, so Mariana's mother didn't write them out of the Perrot tree entirely. That's how Mariana knew to look for them.

She stepped over to another glass-topped cabinet at the very back of the room. It contained a single enormous book, the cover open. Her eyes locked onto the intricate artwork of the frontispiece, and a particular feature along the edge of the drawing.

Arthur Bartholomew Greene. The name was in faint blue-black ink, woven into a complex trellis shape that framed a wild garden of botanicals. It was opposite the title page of a book of botanical illustrations published by Harvard College. In 1725. She tried to lift the top of the glassed case to look for more information. But this case was locked.

She spun on her heel and made for the front of the store, looking for Martin Laurent.

"Mr. Laurent, sir, there's a book in one of your cases I must see. Could you please come open it for me? I have questions for you. Please, if you would."

Martin looked up from his ledger and studied her face. "Of course, one moment," he said. He quickly opened a tiny drawer in the desk and pulled out a set of small keys. He nodded toward the back of the store, inviting her to return to Room VI. Mariana strode quickly back with him to the case and pointed to the book.

"Ah, Franz Bauer's commission to the colonies. You have an interest in botanicals, I presume? He was the Queen's illustrator, employed by the Kew in the mid-eighteenth century. But I expect you know that already." Martin was smiling as he looked up at her over the top of his glasses. He hadn't met anyone in a long time who cared about this work.

"It's not the botanicals themselves that I need to know more about. It's the artist who did the frontispiece here." She pointed to the page. "Arthur Bartholomew Green, see the name? In the vines that frame the illustration."

Martin peered again and nodded. He had never noticed the signature before. Interesting. He quickly unlocked the case and pulled a pair of white cotton gloves from a plastic envelope on a shelf beside them. Gloves on, he opened the case and carefully lifted the book out and carried it over to a wide, softly padded oak lectern, and switched on a small bank of lights to illuminate the book.

"So, tell me about Mr. Arthur B. Greene," Martin said quietly.

"He is, I'm pretty sure, a relative of mine. In a line of artists my family wishes hadn't been born to sully the family tree of famous politicians and wildly rich and successful entrepreneurs," Mariana said, unapologetically.

"I see," Martin said. "And you'd like to find out what happened to these carriers of sullied genetic material? Your people, perhaps?"

"Precisely. My people. I'm an artist. An illustrator. And I don't care about money, though I'm making enough, which I know makes it far easier not to care. I may be rejecting my family and their money, but they've made me privileged and I'm trying to be grateful. Long story, sorry. I have a great-aunt on my mother's side who understands and has helped me a bit. My name is Mariana Perrot. I have been looking for a family of publishers and illustrators named Green, or Greene, with an 'e' on the end. Again, Boston area. Or at least Northeast."

Mariana knew she was babbling. Martin Laurent listened and seemed more than able to sift wheat from chaff.

"Well, it appears you've found one. This book was published in the right period, and it wasn't unusual for publishers to have a short list of highly trusted artists and illustrators they would turn to for particularly important pieces. If it was a family member, all the better. Kept the revenue closer on commissioned work."

"Yes, exactly my thought. Mr. Laurent, do you by any chance know if there is still a publishing house associated with that name today?" Mariana turned to face him, trying hard to keep hope from seeping through her eyes.

"There is. Greene and Wollman. In Brookline. Still has an association with Harvard University." Martin met her eye, a conspiratorial smile on his face. "Sounds like you have a trip to Cambridge in your near future, my dear."

"But how on earth will I make these connections without calling down my clan of inveterate interferers? I don't know a soul in Boston, or at Harvard, much less in book publishing or the art scene there. All my work is in digital media."

Mariana leaned in to scrutinize the book more closely, shifting her handbag higher on her shoulder. When she glanced up to ask Martin another question, he had a funny look on his face and was staring past her right shoulder. She turned, thinking someone was there. The room was empty but for the two of them. She raised an eyebrow quizzically, suddenly wondering if he was a bit daft.

"Mr. Laurent?"

Martin didn't respond right away. He still didn't know how to explain to new customers that he had certain capabilities that other collectors of historical objects didn't have. It had served him both well and badly during his previous career as an academic, with appointments in both anthropology and literature at the University of California.

Martin Laurent could see and chat with dead people. Over the years, they had sought him out when they wanted him to find something of importance to them. It had taken him decades to get used to the sporadic appearances of people from the other side of life as we know it, but he had learned to accept them with curiosity and interest. Unfortunately, his inability to cite traditional sources for some of his discoveries and subsequent publications ended up getting him relieved of his university position. As a result, he was now just a collector and seller of old books and other treasures.

Gazing over his customer's shoulder, he suspected one of Mariana Perrot's lost artistic relatives had shown up and asked him to help her. The presence was female, a robust and interesting personality with a devil-may-care attitude who in life probably suffered no fools. She was insistent, obviously full of care for Mariana, and quite interested in connecting with her. Martin couldn't engineer that exactly, but he could pass on a message. He relaxed his shoulders and nodded to the vague form in early nineteenth-century dress standing behind Mariana and waited for the words to become clear in his mind. When he thought he had it, he turned his attention back to Mariana. All of this had taken no more than four or five seconds.

"Mariana. You are worried that you'll not be able to make the right connections out in Boston, am I right?"

Mariana nodded, confused.

"Well, all I can tell you is that you'll have help. You needn't worry. But you need to stay alert and responsive to unexpected opportunities or invitations. They might not connect directly with your aim, at least it won't seem so at first. But say yes. For example, I believe there will be a gallery opening soon at the Boston Museum of Fine Arts. See if you can get an invitation to attend the first night's celebration. You will meet someone there who will help you."

And with that, Martin fished one of his business cards from his pocket, handed it to her, told her to call him anytime, and left the room to answer the phone, which was ringing from the top of his rolltop desk at the front of the shop.

Mariana watched him walk away, struggling to make sense of his advice. Then she turned back and gripped the sides of the padded lectern to look at the amazing book of illustrations a final time. She stared at the name, Arthur Bartholomew Greene, until it swelled and shifted. She blinked and refocused her attention. She could feel the animation of his life, his pace down an old street on the way to work, his concentration on a new piece of artwork done in dim light as the late afternoon sun faded. His patience. The fact that he hated it when his feet got cold. Just like her. She had a soulmate. A brother, a cousin, somewhere in history who was as real to her as anyone she might ever hope to have beside her at a family gathering today. She had to find him. And his descendants.

She snapped a photo of the open page with her phone before leaving Room VI, walking back through the shop. Martin was still on the phone, cradling the old-style handset between his ear and shoulder while he wrote something in a notebook. She waved to him as she reached the door, then stopped. Turning to a nearby table, she set down her purse and extracted one of her personally designed business cards, which she only used for her creative enterprises. She added a quick "thank you" to the back and signed her name. With a flourish, she underlined the words, complete with a quick sketch of vines that grew up to circle her name. She slid the card beneath Martin's elbow. He met her eyes and smiled while still talking to his other customer. Mariana stepped back out into the Sacramento evening and continued walking toward the Indian restaurant she had selected for dinner.

***

Mariana was scheduled for an early flight back to Columbus the next day. On her ride to the airport, she ignored the list of work calls related to the regional meeting she'd just finished. Instead, she searched "Museum of Fine Arts, Boston" on the internet. Navigating to "Exhibitions" in the menu, she was only slightly surprised to see a new opening advertised for later in the month titled "Fugitives from Europe: Lithographs and Engravings from North America, 1700–1860." It was part of a year-long series focusing on the role of art and artists in political rebellions from different parts of Europe, driving immigration to the colonies. Last month's showing featured work related to the Netherlands. This month would be France and Germany.

Her ride pulled into the terminal, and she shoved her phone back in her purse to collect her belongings. Once at the gate, she told herself she had paid work to do and checked for texts and voice mails. There were several. She started with a text from the chair of the board of the Columbus Art Museum, Anne Fontaine, telling her to check her voice mail. Typical of Anne, she thought, impatiently texting her about a voice mail, which probably told her to look at an email from the day before, which would be pages long and detailed. Mariana sighed. They were starting a capital campaign. It would be like this for months.

She was right. The voice mail was about an email about the capital campaign. She tackled the email, reading about a prospective donor who had graduated from The Ohio State University 20 years ago and now lived in Boston. Boston? Mariana read on.

Johannes Scholler has lived in Back Bay for years and has been a generous donor to Boston's Museum of Fine Arts. But his passion reportedly lies elsewhere, given his family's ties to Ohio. He has been researching German immigration from the Northeast into Ohio and Michigan using both the usual ancestry documents, but also tracking the appearance of historical painting and lithographs. He's still got ties to OU and has been in conversation with the dean of the College of Arts and Sciences about one of their collections. We'd like to forge a partnership with OU around the topic of immigration and art as part of what the campaign could accomplish, but we need someone to build a relationship with Mr. Scholler. Any chance you could go to the opening of the new exhibit on European lithographs at the MFA in Boston? I know it sounds rather dull, but he'll be there as one of the exhibit's funders. Think six digits. Let me know, okay?

Mariana read the email again. She felt a buzzy excitement that had nothing at all to do with the capital campaign. She texted Anne a brief message: "Yes, I'll go to the opening in Boston."

She looked up the date of the opening. A Thursday night, October 21st. Her next calls cleared her work calendar for four days and booked flights to include a weekend stay in Boston following the opening. Well, Cambridge, to be specific. She'd figure out what she would do with that time later, but she hoped it would be fruitfully spent in Boston or Cambridge library archives hunting for references to a certain Arthur Bartholomew Greene. Or perhaps in a meeting with some executive at the publishing house of Greene and Wollman. Where was it that Martin Laurent had told her their offices were located? Somewhere near Cambridge.

Mariana opened a search engine and typed in *Greene and Wollman, publishers.* There was a business listing with a website, which turned out to be a paltry landing page with a succinct company history in a cursive script she found slightly annoying in terms of readability. No phone number listed and no physical address. Just one of those maddening online forms as a contact option. As a rule, she refused to use those. Clearly, these people did not do business with the public. Frustrating.

Her flight was boarding. It was 7:20 a.m. She didn't think antiquarian bookstores opened until far more reasonable hours, particularly those that were open later, during dinner hour. Martin Laurent would still be at home, and probably in bed, not hovering around his rolltop desk at Indictus Books in not-quite-downtown Sacramento. She needed to talk to him. It would have to be later.

Mariana arrived home in Columbus that evening, hungry for a real dinner and lamenting the spare contents of her refrigerator. Yogurt, a plastic container holding three boiled eggs, a few limp carrots. A half bottle of pinot held promise. She pulled out the bottle and set it on the counter. There wasn't even pasta in the cupboard. She poured herself a substantial glass of wine and left the kitchen, switching on the light above her comfy reading chair. She called her favorite Middle Eastern restaurant, which was her favorite not only because it was good but because it sat on the corner, a half block from her apartment.

"Hello, Shish Kabob Syria, can I help?" It was a familiar male voice, thickly accented.

"Aadeez, I'm starving. I know it's late, but do you have any chicken shawarma left? And maybe some tabbouleh? It's Mariana."

"Ah, habeebti, for you? Of course, we have shawarma. And tabbouleh. Just come over. I'll have it ready for you. Another late flight from somewhere?"

"Exactly. Thank you. This is why I love you so much, dear man. I'll be right over."

Mariana threw on a jacket and stuffed her feet into a slouchy pair of black-and-white checkered sneakers she used as slippers and headed down to the lobby of her apartment building. She walked to the restaurant, tossed $30 on the counter, and waved off Aadeez's offer to make change as she picked up her bag of food. It was hot and smelled of cumin and garlic and smoky paprika. Her mouth watered. She opened the bag as she left, just to inhale the aroma more deeply, and noticed that Aadeez had plunked a large piece of baklava on top, thick with green pistachios and wrapped in parchment. She snagged it out of the bag and nibbled happily, licking pastry flakes off her fingers as she shouldered her way back through the door to her building. Life was about to get much better.

After partly working her way through Aadeez's delights, Mariana opened her laptop to see if her ticket purchase to the Museum of Fine Arts exhibit opening had gone through. It had. Still wanting to talk with Martin Laurent at Indictus Books, she checked her watch and did the mental math to make sure it was a reasonable hour in California. It would be seven there. Perfect. She pulled out Martin's business card and dialed the number.

"Indictus Books, Martin Laurent here." His calm, pleasant voice made Mariana smile.

"Mr. Laurent? This is Mariana Perrot. We met just last evening. I was the one..."

"Of course, Mariana, I remember. The frontispiece illustration in my valuable book of botanical illustrations, which interested you not a whit. And call me Martin, please. How can I help you? Was your trip home uneventful, I hope?"

Mariana chuckled. She was becoming quite fond of this slightly peculiar, unassuming man with the quick wit. "Yes, Martin, I am safely home in Ohio. I'm calling to thank you for your slightly unnerving tip about the MFA in Boston."

"Oh, really? So soon? Well, that's lovely. Sometimes one must wait for these things. Hard to say about timing. But tell me more. Was it a gallery opening of some sort? Did you say yes?"

"Well, close. An exhibit opening. Three weeks from now. Lithographs and etchings from Colonial New England. French artists in America, I think. But how did you know this would be relevant to me?"

Martin sighed. Oh, well, he thought. Nothing left to lose, really. "In short, I see and hear things from people who are no longer with us in this life, but still have business to transact of some sort. Sometimes they, well, get in touch."

"You're a *medium?*" Mariana didn't even try to hide her shock.

"Well, I've never pursued it professionally. But yes, I seem to be able to communicate with those who have passed on. Not everyone, mind you, and I don't go looking for them, ever. But sometimes they come to me. In your case, it was a rather demanding woman with a large personality in dress that suggested she was last with us sometime in the eighteenth century. She is quite fond of you, apparently. And wants to help. She is the one who suggested you attend some sort of art exhibition in Boston. Are you going, by the way? To the opening?"

After a pause to absorb all of this, Mariana hauled her mind out of its brief seizure. She'd never met a medium, and whatever she thought they looked like, it certainly wasn't anything resembling the distinguished and unassuming Martin Laurent. She took a breath, collected herself, and, realizing she had no intention of turning back, replied.

"Yes, I said yes. I have a ticket. Actually, I bought two. But I don't have a date. I was wondering if you might like to fly across the continent to attend an obscure and probably dull art history opening at the MFA in Boston in three weeks? With me?"

A ripple of deep-chested laughter filled the room from the iPhone speaker. It was a total whim, she realized, but she smiled just to hear Martin's laugh. She didn't say anything, took another bite of her shawarma, and waited. Nothing ventured…

"You are quite something, Mariana. You remind me a bit of one of my nieces. Brilliant, audacious, and I must say, always on the verge of trouble, escaping only by virtue of wit and swift thinking. Are you serious?"

"Quite serious, kind sir," Mariana responded, digging her fork into her tabbouleh and taking another sip on her wine. There was a long moment of silence, which felt considered rather than uncomfortable.

"What's the date?" Martin asked. Mariana told him. "Yes, Mariana, I would be delighted to join you at the opening in Boston. Might I treat you to dinner afterward? With anyone you happen to meet while making rounds at the event, of course. Because I'm quite sure it will happen if you pay attention." Martin's voice was both amused and entirely serious.

"I remember your counsel about being open to unusual invitations, and yes, that would be delightful. I don't know Boston well, so you pick the restaurant," she replied.

"I know Boston quite well. My French and Scots relations all seemed to settle in the area. Rhode Island, northern Vermont, Boston itself. I just lost all affection for winter 20 years ago and accepted a position teaching in California to escape it. I'll enjoy being back for a bit. Call me when you have the details about where you'll be staying. I'll meet you for a civilized libation before we look for your Arthur Bartholomew Greene wherever he may be lurking amongst the etchings."

Mariana hung up, feeling very satisfied with herself for lunging after instinct and folly. It's genetic, she thought to herself, still smiling.

***

The next few weeks flew by as Mariana kept herself busy with work. Anne Fontaine was beside herself with gratitude to Mariana for agreeing to make the trip to Boston at her own expense to find Mr. Scholler, their prospective donor, and make his acquaintance. Mariana would arrange a time for a follow-up meeting with scholars at OU when Mr. Scholler was next back to see his parents, who still lived outside Columbus at the family's large estate. Other than that, she didn't expect to need to do much more on that assignment. The rest, she thought, would simply have to unfold. If nothing else, she was sure that a dinner conversation with the owner of Indictus Books of Sacramento would be delightful. She always enjoyed exploring unfamiliar cities, and she looked forward to seeing more of Boston than she had on previous brief visits.

October 21st arrived, and Mariana caught an early flight to Boston. She wanted to make sure she got to her hotel in Back Bay with plenty of time to spare. Right on time, Martin appeared in the hotel lobby, trim and handsome in a well-tailored dark suit. He extended his arm to her as she neared, the click of her black heels on the marble tile echoing in the grand open space of the atrium.

"You look lovely, Mariana; welcome to Boston," Martin greeted her, giving her a gentlemanly kiss on both cheeks.

"Thank you for coming, Martin. It's truly a delight to see you again," Mariana said.

"Shall we?"

Martin rested a hand on top of Mariana's where she had slipped it through his elbow. At that moment, she was grateful for her upbringing among gentlemen. She knew she looked good. She had worn her favorite black cocktail dress. Its elegant, angled hem travelled from left mid-thigh to below the knee on the right and swirled gently as she walked. The neckline held a parallel line from one shoulder to a marginally conservative but interesting place beneath her other arm, exposing her long collarbones. She wore a silver necklace that hung asymmetrically, a string of gleaming citrine stones punctuated with onyx forming a long, slender triangle resting against her bare skin. The pale-green stones picked up the lighter shades in her eyes, which were hazel green. She carried the look well, and unselfconsciously.

Martin led her to a quiet corner not far from the atrium bar. The table he chose was backed by tall green potted plants, which softened the sounds of the lobby and marked the outer zone of the seating area. He waved to the bartender as he pulled out a chair for Mariana.

"What would you like to drink?" Martin asked.

"The house white would be fine. A pinot if they have it," she replied.

Martin took his seat as the bartender arrived, and they greeted each other briefly.

"What can I get for you both?" the bartender asked.

"Do you still have the Giatl, Alto Adige Riserva, in your pinot grigio? It's been a few years since I was here," Martin said, nodding toward Mariana to show he was asking on her behalf. His Italian accent was perfect. The man continued to intrigue Mariana.

"Of course, sir. And for you, sir?"

"I'd like a martini. Chopin or Belvedere, if you have either one for the vodka," Martin said with a nod.

"We have several of the Belvedere. Infused or single estate?

"The simpler the better, thanks."

"I'll make it with the Heritage 176," the bartender said with a wink as he retreated to the back of the bar.

Mariana and Martin chatted, getting acquainted in a conversation that was at once polite and familiar, befitting the odd juxtaposition of their status as near-strangers now sharing a quest for Mariana's very personal artistic lineage. An hour passed quickly, and it was time to go to the museum.

Martin paid for their drinks and asked for a cab. He preferred taxis to Lyft and Uber. They walked to the wide revolving doors that led to the street, where a bellman ushered them into the waiting cab. Martin gave the driver their destination and sat back, offering Mariana a smile.

"This will be fun," he said as the cab pulled into the rush of one-way Boston traffic.

The greeter at the reception area in front of the exhibit opening watched as the interesting couple approached. A beautiful young woman on the arm of an older gentleman. They looked familiar, but not intimate, and completely at ease in themselves and with each other.

"Martin Laurent and Mariana Perrot, of the Greenes and Perrots," Martin announced to the greeter. Mariana looked at him sideways, wondering at the reference to her historical familial names. He seemed to know what he was doing. The greeter, whose name was Beatrice, nodded respectfully.

"Of course, Mr. Laurent, Ms. Perrot, welcome, and thank you for joining us this evening. I hope you'll enjoy the exhibit. Mr. Greene, when last I saw him, was over by the Letourneur waterfront lithograph, back right," she said, waving generally toward the back of the exhibit area.

"Thank you so much," Martin replied. He turned to Mariana and winked.

"Well, you wanted to meet someone from the esteemed publishing house, did you not? Let's go find him. We'll loiter and eavesdrop until we can pick him out. On the way, you can look for your Johannes Scholler, and we can get that out of the way. Stay bright, my dear, there's someone else here for you to meet as well. I have no idea who it is. Your visitor from the shop came back last evening and insisted that you should look for someone tall and male. Probably dark-haired, but that might have been a hat. Can't be sure. The specifics fade in the translation from the other side sometimes, but I'm sure you'll figure it out." Martin met her startled stare with an impish grin, then set his features in distinguished respectability and set out into the gathering with Mariana at his side. He knew she would recover quickly.

Halfway across the room, Mariana spotted Johannes Scholler. She squeezed Martin's arm and nodded in the man's direction. She had shown Martin a photo of Scholler so he could help her find him. Martin nodded and released her with a gentle nudge.

"Go, do your thing," he said. "I'll admire some art and look for obscure, nearly invisible signatures along the sides of book illustrations."

Mariana made her way over to Johannes Scholler, who was gazing at one of the framed lithographs on the wall. She glanced at the artist's name on the tiny wall plaque beside the piece.

"That looks for all the world like a section of the old German shops along Deshler Street in Columbus from the early 1800s, am I right?" Mariana's opening drew Scholler's attention immediately.

"Why yes, exactly! How did you know?" Mariana introduced herself and deftly navigated their conversation in a perfect balance of polite interest, respectful curiosity, and the lightest dappling of information about her work with the Columbus Museum of Art. Johannes Scholler responded beautifully. In under 15 minutes, he agreed to meet in Ohio and they graciously exchanged their respective cell phone numbers. She placed her phone back in the pocket of her clutch and shook his hand appreciatively. That was done. Now, to the heart of it.

Mariana looked around and spotted Martin locked in a slightly uncomfortable conversation with an older woman wearing too much makeup and dripping in gold jewelry too heavy for her outfit. It was quite a display. She recognized the messaging. *I'm rich*, it said, *and you're attractive.* She made her way over to Martin and caught his eye, which met hers with relief. He bowed courteously to the woman in gold and stepped aside to join Mariana.

"Over here," Martin said. "I've found Richard Greene. The fourth. They've all owned the publishing house in their generational turn. It's a Boston thing. They never left the banks of the Charles."

Martin led Mariana over to a short, slightly rotund gentleman in a vested suit revealing, of all things, a gold pocket watch on a chain that draped across his belly and disappeared beneath his lapel. How very 1800s, Mariana thought to herself. This should be good.

"Mr. Greene," Martin said, placing his hand gently on the man's shoulder. "Martin Laurent. We met some years ago over my search for a book published by your great-great-grandfather. I don't expect you to remember, but there's someone I'd like you to meet." Martin turned to Mariana with a broad smile, as though he knew that meeting Mariana would become a turning point toward joy in the beleaguered-looking man's life.

"Mariana Perrot, I'm pleased to introduce you to Mr. Richard Greene, the fourth, publisher of fine books from authors throughout the world and associated with Harvard since it was merely a college. Mr. Greene, Ms. Perrot is descended from a long line of illustrators and lithographers, including one of your own forebears." Martin took a half step back after grasping Greene's hand in greeting, leaving Mariana looking Greene in the eyes. They were about the same height.

"I'm very pleased to meet you, Mr. Greene," said Mariana.

"A Perrot, you say? The old mining family?" Greene asked, one eyebrow raised.

"Yes, mining and textiles, and finance and importing. But more important to me, sir, is someone related to you that we have in common further out on a thin limb of our family trees. Are you aware of someone in your background by the name of Arthur Bartholomew Greene? An artist and illustrator of mid-eighteenth-century books commissioned here in New England from Europe?"

She knew she was being very direct, in the middle of an event where being circumspect was an art form all its own. Richard Greene looked at her a bit blankly, then blinked.

"Arthur Greene is related to the Perrots? He was famous in his time, rarely accepted commissions from anyone outside of our family. And yes, he was at his prime in the 1750s and '60s. A long career for an artist."

After only a brief hesitation, Mariana opened the door to her family's darker side of biases and exclusion. She lifted her chin before she spoke, determined to press on. "He was a relation on my mother's side, though she'll barely acknowledge it. There are stories my family doesn't tend to tell about the artistic line in our family. They're far happier to claim the wealth associated with their business ventures."

"Yes, yes, that fits. The Perrot clan was—is—notoriously arrogant about their wealth. No offense meant, personally, I mean you seem quite nice…" Greene was stumbling. Mariana rescued him.

"None taken. I find most of them unbearable myself, and I still get invited to holiday dinners." Mariana laughed lightly, waving off his discomfort. She saw Martin nod encouragingly in her peripheral vision.

"That's partly why I'd hoped to meet you, Mr. Greene. I think there are more of us. The artists and illustrators and writers who've circulated with esteemed publishing houses here in the Northeast, for generations. I feel somewhat more akin to them than the Perrot side of the family. I'd like to find them. Any of them, really. If I can."

"Well, I'll be…" Richard Greene shook his head as if to clear a bit of fog, and seemed to relax a little, with actual smile lines appearing in the corners of his eyes. He nodded and looked past Mariana's shoulder, out across the room, then lowered his balding head closer to Mariana's ear, as though he expected to share a secret. "You're serious, aren't you," he said.

Mariana nodded and whispered back, "Yes, I am. No agenda."

Mr. Green straightened and pointed vaguely across the room. "My nephew is here. Bartholomew Nathaniel Greene. Goes by Nate. He's about your age, I think. Hopeless romantic. Poet, artist, chronically underemployed, but a good kid. Fascinated by obscure art forms with no future whatsoever, like paper making. Got a master's degree with a thesis reflecting his obsession about the qualities of interaction between ink and handmade paper using techniques from the 1500s. You might like him. And God help you, you might be related somehow. Or not. Some of the family on our father's side are a bunch of drunks. Educated, world travelers, but crazy."

Mariana looked at Martin, who was silently laughing at the ceiling behind his hand. He met her eyes as she whispered to him, "My people!"

Richard Greene stepped up on a nearby bench to get a better look across the crowded venue. He looked absurd, and clearly didn't care. He was grinning now. His scanning stopped close to the bar that had been erected against a wall by the entrance. He waved his arms like a referee, trying to get someone's attention. Then he stepped down, craning his neck in that direction. He waved again, encouraging someone to come over.

Mariana followed Greene's gaze. Making his way through the crowd was a young man with a thick shock of soft brown hair that kept falling forward every time he looked down to avoid stepping on anyone's foot. Tall with dark eyes, he was wearing a plain white button-down shirt with what looked to be a borrowed jacket that was a bit snug through the shoulders. His movements were gentle, and Mariana could tell he was softly apologizing to everyone he nudged as he made his way to his uncle. The planes of his face were sharp and handsome. Everything else about him seemed soft and kind and just a bit sad, or perhaps just overwhelmed. She noticed an ink stain on top of his left shoe when he arrived.

"Yes, Uncle Richard, do you need something?"

"Nate, thank you for joining us. I've just met someone I think you might enjoy talking to. Mariana Perrot, please meet my nephew, Bartholomew Nathaniel Greene. Nate, Mariana. She's here from Columbus with her friend Martin, who owns an antiquarian bookstore in California. Delightful people. None of you quite belong anywhere. You're perfect for one another. Now, chat. I have to get some business done at this dreadful little affair, so if you'll excuse me?"

And with that, Richard Greene vanished into the crowd. Martin shook Nate's hand, then leaned over to speak directly into Mariana's ear. "You've found him," is all he said.

Martin bowed slightly to both Nate and Mariana, then made his apologies. "I'm afraid I need to make my way to the gentlemen's club, but I'll circle back around to find you in a bit. Go on then." Martin waved in the direction of a slightly less occupied space in the room, past a collection of cases that looked remarkably like those in Room VI, back in the dim light of Indictus Books.

"Hello, Nate, I'm Mariana. How are you?"

Nate's eyes were wide with unabashed admiration as he took her extended hand and clasped it in his. "I'm well. But you're...better. Who *are* you, really? Have we met before? I feel like we must have, but that's the lamest line invented by any man in 10 centuries. My uncle, he just met you? Here? Shut up, Nate, you're babbling."

Mariana laughed, her eyes full of delight. This man was beautiful, inside and out. She took his hand again and led him away from the crowd. She acknowledged the outrageousness of the extraordinarily warm and fuzzy sensation she was feeling, and happily plunged toward what felt like destiny. She spoke to him over her exposed shoulder, shifting her necklace slightly with her free hand.

"Nate. Come talk to me. I've got all night, and from what your uncle told me, I'm in luck, because you do, too. We have things to discuss."

***

Sixteen months later, Perrot and Greene, purveyors of fine art, held their new gallery's opening in Columbus, Ohio. The event was catered by Shish Kabob Syria, and Aadeez and his lovely wife, Bassma, joyfully served everyone who came with plates full of more delicious food than they could possibly eat.

Nate and Mariana placed tables and chairs all around the space so people could sit and chat, comfortably enjoying a meal rather than delicately balancing appetizers and trying to converse around the gallery's first acquisitions. It was an eclectic collection of oils and watercolors, sculpture, lithographs, and very old books, some of which had been purchased at auction solely for their illustrations.

Martin Laurent was a member of the gallery's new board of directors, and a steady supplier of new and extraordinary items, found through connections both material and ethereal. How he found each fabulous piece didn't matter to Nate and Mariana, and neither did the irregularity of his sourcing practices.

Johannes Scholler had invested in the start-up, as had Mariana's Great-Aunt Martha. Scholler's funding came with the condition that a branch of the gallery would open in Boston. His preference was somewhere on the prestigious streets of Back Bay, but Mariana and Nate negotiated. There was a perfect location in a nondescript building with a wide glass storefront right next to Greene and Wollman's Publishing offices in Brookline, just up the road from Harvard Square.

Nate handled most of the art business, and Mariana had transitioned into a digital marketing and design business of her own, with clients throughout the United States and in Europe. They both made time for their personal creative work, which sold in their gallery almost as well as the pieces they collected. Mariana had a talent for finding buyers for each distinctive type of art. She was discovering that the personalized matchmaking between what they had procured for the gallery and the people those items would delight was an unexpected joy.

Nate and Mariana brought their baby, Julien Martin Perrot Greene—Jules for short—to the gallery opening, and he played happily by himself with a trio of brightly colored balls in a big, open playpen in the corner. Nate had hired a licensed babysitter to remain with Jules through the event, but he was such a good-natured child the woman was barely needed. Jules smiled readily at anyone who approached to talk to him, and eagerly offered a drool-slicked hand holding a ball to those who expressed interest.

Nate and Mariana had not gotten around to talking about marriage. They'd been busy and were having way too much fun.

The Perrot side of the family did not approve.

LILY'S CURIOS AND COUTURE

When Tony Rostanzo died of a heart attack right in the kitchen of his own delicatessen, his last three regulars were there to take care of business. Danny Costa, Marlin Moretti, and Roger DiMaria were old friends whose backsides had worn individualized dents in the vinyl seats of the corner booth by the window.

Roger was a retired and currently unlicensed attorney. He had moved back to the old neighborhood in Philly after his career folded in on itself and perished. This slow vocational death followed a year-long tumble of only partially mitigated disasters resulting from Roger's lost ability to keep his thoughts to himself. He blew his last case to glorious smithereens when he told the district judge in Schenectady exactly what he thought remained of the old man's *testicoli*, hiding beneath his black robes. He chose unfortunate timing for this display of pique, as the courtroom was full and included members of the media lining the back wall in preparation for the start of a murder case that was slated to begin right after Roger's drug-running case concluded. Roger was tired of seeing drug dealers get off easy. His ambivalence about ending his career resolved with the help of the state bar association pulling his license and bluntly suggesting that he find another line of work.

The following weekend, Roger packed up what little he cared about in his tiny apartment in Schenectady, loaded it in the back of his old blue Ford Taurus station wagon, and went out to dinner. On Monday afternoon, he dropped off his work laptop at the law office, came home, and left a note for the landlord on the kitchen table with the keys to his front door and mailbox. He drove home through the night to Allegheny West in

Philly, where his two oldest friends still lived a few blocks off the Schuylkill River. He hazarded a guess that they still met for coffee at eleven o'clock on Tuesdays at Tony's deli.

Roger was already at their old corner table drinking coffee at eleven when Danny and Marlin walked in within three minutes of each other. They resumed their decades-old conversation like Roger had never left.

When Tony dropped out of sight with a loud thunk behind his glass-fronted counter full of hams, salami, and his daughter's pastries, all three of them looked at each other for a second before reacting.

Danny was the first to get to Tony's crumpled body. A Korean War vet, he knelt stiffly beside Tony's shoulder in the cramped space and checked his vitals.

"KIA," came the pronouncement, Danny's head shaking with a grim look that carried the sudden presence of so many other old friends who had already passed on.

"Damn," said Marlin.

"Oh, *merda*," Roger muttered in Italian from where he remained seated by the window. "Call the fucking cops. And we better put him in the cooler. They won't get here in a hurry."

Roger rolled up his shirtsleeves and got up from their table, his chair scraping against the broken green linoleum. He walked back behind the counter with a deep sigh and leaned down to pick up Tony's legs while his buddies came around and grabbed Tony's thick shoulders.

Danny and Marlin nominated Roger to take possession of the keys to the deli, since he was a lawyer and they figured he could talk himself out of any trouble that might result. No one complained, including the cops who trailed out after the coroner's deputy finished up.

A couple of days later, Roger got a phone number for Tony's daughter in Jersey by looking through Tony's file cabinet in the jumbled section of unpaid invoices.

"Joanie? It's Roger DiMaria. How the hell are ya?"

"Uncle Roger? Haven't heard from you in a hundred years! I thought you'd died in New York or wherever you disappeared to," Joanie said. The three old friends were in the deli so often while she was growing up, she called them all uncle.

"Yeah, well, I'm back. Got lousy news for you. Me and Danny and Mar were in the deli on Tuesday." Roger paused, steeling his nerve.

"That's not news, Uncle Roger. What, did the old man finally drop?" Joanie said this as matter-of-factly as if she had just learned that PECO, the Philly electric utility, had turned off the power to the deli again.

"Yeah, Joanie. He did. Dropped right behind the cash register, staring at your pastries."

Joanie let out a sigh. "Figures. His last thought was probably how much he'd stiffed me for cannoli."

The two chatted for a little while. Roger said he hadn't been able to find a will, and Joanie just laughed affectionately. She told Roger that Tony had expected to both live forever and see the deli back into the black and had achieved disappointment on both counts.

The next week, Roger helped Joanie go through her dad's apartment, leaving with a plastic grocery bag containing a few things of sentimental value. Those included pieces of her mom's jewelry that were still in the bedroom bureau's top drawer, likely last opened when Joanie and her sister Lucia were choosing clothes to bring to the undertaker for their mom's wake and funeral.

Joanie gave Roger a hug and her grateful permission to deal with the rest of the business of her father's sudden departure. She had four teenage boys still at home back in Fairfield, and a catering business to run. Roger became Tony's pro bono executor.

Together, they decided to empty the deli and close it down. The three old friends brought scrap lumber and tools and boarded up the front together. While they were at it, Sarah Rossi stepped out of her wedding dress shop next door, accompanied by the tinkle of her door chime. Leaning against the weathered wood of the door frame and scratching the back of one arm on the warm red brick, she shook her head sadly.

"I'll sure miss listening to him cuss through the wall," Sarah said, a little misty.

"Hey, Sarah, how's business?" Danny asked, standing up slowly, hammer in one hand while he clutched his lower back with the other.

"Not bad, not bad. Changing neighborhood, you know. Not so many big weddings."

"Tell me about it," Danny said. "Pretty soon, Father Dougherty is gonna be doing special collections just to buy communion wafers."

"Hmph," Sarah replied.

At that moment, Sarah's 19-year-old daughter Lily popped out of the shop behind Sarah. A free-spirited thing, she did her best to embody a different decade in history, depending on what flamboyant scraps of vintage attire she found in Philly's thrift shops. Today she was wearing a sleeveless, dropped-waist burgundy dress weighted with rhinestones along the hem, black tights, stocky heels, and black gloves that ended above her elbows. All she needed was a foot-long ivory cigarette holder, Roger thought, and he would see West Philly thrown back into the 1920s through Lily's sheer force of stylistic intent. He just grinned and looked over Lily's shoulder to give Sarah a sympathetic roll of the eyes. Lily had to have been a handful growing up.

Lily was also one of the most wildly gregarious young women ever to stay in the neighborhood after graduating high school. She made friends with everyone, picking up on the dialects of African immigrant mothers as easily as she exchanged jibes and greetings with the dealers and hookers who took up residence on the street corners in the vicinity every night. She was an Allegheny West native and determined to remain so.

"Hey, guys! So, what's going to happen to Tony's shop?" Lily posed the question to all three men with curiosity and the gilded edge of a little something more.

"Dunno, Lily. The landlord will likely try to rent it to some other fool," Roger replied.

Lily grabbed the giant, gold-toned yin-yang symbol she had hanging from a braided metal chain around her neck and began to twirl it in response, a broad grin spreading across her face.

"Crisis and opportunity, gentleman, the same thing at the same time. All depends on what you make of it," Lily proclaimed cheerfully as her mom rolled her eyes and turned to go back inside.

Lily stepped around the three men and up to the front door of the deli as Roger, Danny, and Marlin continued pounding boards over the windows. She peered in through the glass, cupping her hands around her eyes to cut the glare from the sun. She could see it already. Her vision was taking form, right around the tables and chairs piled against the wall and the heap of deli paper that had drifted to the floor from the counter. She smiled with the wily ambition of a scrappy Philly teen and the burgeoning ambition of a young entrepreneur.

"It's *perfect*," she said, waving off the confused frowns of the three old men that she, too, had grown up thinking of as distant uncles.

And that is how Lily's Curios and Couture was born. Lily wrangled a business loan with her mother and talked an old boyfriend into helping her gut the inside of the deli and do some rewiring. She attacked the work of installing new flooring, upgrading the deli's bathroom, and scrounging second-hand racks and shelving with fierce joy. Then she assembled Allegheny West's finest and most wildly diverse collection of resale thrift shop gleanings, arranging it all with creativity and artful whimsy.

She opened her shop next door to Miosa's Bride and Beauty in a little less than a year. And a whole new generation of locals began to congregate, catch up, tell stories, fall in love, sip coffee and even turn up with the occasional treasure from their own attics to help keep Lily's bottom line favorable.

Roger, Danny, and Marlin tended to drop by on Tuesday mornings to check on Lily's progress. The door still had the same bell that had chimed customers into Tony's deli, and somehow that always made them feel comfortable loitering over a coffee and sitting at the little red bistro table and chairs that Lily had marked for sale in one corner but that somehow never sold.

Roger watched one day as Lily helped an older woman shop among the vintage dresses for something her granddaughter might like to wear for her quinceañera. Proprietor and customer were a sight to behold. There was Lily, with her half-shaved head and dragon tattoos, gently lifting a pale-blue dress to display its lacy bodice to the admiring Latina matron. As the two talked together in quiet Spanglish and laughed, Roger stepped back out into the West Philly sunshine, content and smiling.

Allegheny West had some good in its future after all.

A FAMILY OF BROTHERS

Mark had gone to his room right after school and hadn't come out. He had snagged an extra apple in the lunch line at school and stole a candy bar from the vending machine by surreptitiously kicking it in just the right place while holding the delivery button. Dinner was served.

He was glad the adults in the house were ignoring his existence. The TV had been blaring from the living room for hours, and above that noise, Mark could now hear his dad yelling at his most recent girlfriend, Denise, about some atrocity she had committed related to the remote. He didn't want to get in the middle of it.

Mark was mentally keeping track of how many times his dad called to Denise to get him another beer. The total was growing. His dad was a mean drunk. When the number crested twelve, he would have to decide whether to stay in his room for the night or leave. He knew other kids at school whose parents were sloppy, sleepy drunks who failed to take care of tasks like laundry or grocery shopping. Mark was jealous of them, but never chimed in. It seemed stupid to compete for "worst parent" status. He preferred not to think about it when he didn't have to.

Nine years old and skinny, Mark knew that if things got bad, he could always lever himself over the windowsill, jam the toes of his sneakers into the rough brick of the outside wall of the apartment building, and drop the 10 feet to the ground. His older brother, Chip, had taught him how to do the tucked roll in the dirt beneath the window. It was a skill Chip had developed for the same reasons before he had left home for good when he was 15.

Mark finished his book and did a little homework, then reached up to turn off the lamp beside his bed. He scrunched down under the covers and pulled his pillow over his head. He had lost track of the beer count at 10. But he was too tired to keep sifting the relevant data out of the background noise of alcohol and hostility. He drifted off, wrapped in his own familiar insulation of dull resentment and stoicism.

A particularly loud thump woke Mark from what had miraculously turned into a deep, exhausted sleep. He was instantly wide awake, his heart beating fast as he tried to figure out what was happening based on what he could hear through the walls and his still-closed door.

He looked at his little bedside clock, shaped like a baseball glove with the hands in a white circle in the palm of the glove. Almost two in the morning.

The sound of shattering glass, a fist hitting flesh, and Denise yelping made Mark sit up in bed and untangle his legs from the covers. He thought he heard Denise's body hit the floor, and then he didn't hear her say anything else. Mark's dad just kept yelling profanities at her, laced with crazy accusations, from the side of the living room where a big mirror was hung. Or used to hang. Then silence, but for his father muttering angrily.

Mark reached for his jeans and pulled them on, then felt around on the floor for his sneakers. He never took his socks off. He quickly laced his sneakers and pulled a sweatshirt over his head. Kneeling on the floor beside his bed, Mark debated heading out the window, but then realized it was too late.

He could hear his father coming down the hall toward his room, the soft scraping sound of his knuckles dragging along the wall for balance. That was how Mark could tell how close his dad was to his bedroom door. He guessed he had about the count of four before the doorknob would turn.

Mark shoved open the window then dropped back down to the floor and rolled quickly under the bed, pulling everything he could grab with both hands after him. If his dad looked, he would see the stuff and not Mark. Clothes, toys, books, and a dropped pillow were what he had snagged. Now he lay flat with his head lifted just enough so he could glean sound from both ears. He tried not to breathe.

He heard the doorknob turn and the latch let go as his father shoved his way into Mark's room.

"Where are you, you little bastard?!" Mark's father bellowed. The noise reverberated in the tiny room and floated out the window.

Mark's father stumbled over something on the floor and caught his balance by grabbing the dresser. Then he angrily swept everything from on top of the dresser to the floor. Mark winced as he heard all his favorite things strike the wood floor and scatter. He feared that the shattering glass was his one picture of his mother, who had disappeared right after his sixth birthday. He closed his eyes and listened to where his father was moving.

Two steps over to the windowsill. That's right, Mark thought, I've gone out the window, I'm not here, you don't need to keep looking. More baritone mumbling and swearing. Then he heard his father take a swing and punch the window frame, leaning out and yelling.

"If you left this apartment without my permission again, I'm gonna find you and you're gonna pay!!" The big man's voice was loud in the night quiet, and Mark noticed the crickets stop chirping outside. The sound dissipated into the woods behind the building.

Mark's heart was pounding, and he was sure his father could hear it, just a few feet away. Peering out from under the bed between a pair of books and a mechanical robot that didn't work anymore, Mark could see his father's bare feet and baggy gray sweatpants in the dim light. He watched as the feet took a step back from the bed, then another. On the third step, his father stepped on the broken glass and howled in anger and pain, hopping toward the door, grabbing on to the doorframe, and bellowing profanities again. Mark prayed he would keep going.

The man left the room and headed down the hallway toward the bathroom, slamming his fist into the wall on his way. Mark heard the click of the light switch and could see a wedge of pale fluorescence reach into the hallway from the bathroom. He waited a bit longer to make sure his father was occupied.

Carefully, silently, Mark slid objects out of the way so he could crawl out from under the bed on his belly. Just a few inches at a time, he moved an object, then pushed his body toward the edge of the bed. Move things a bit, shift a leg or arm. Then wait. And listen.

It felt like an hour, but probably only took a couple of minutes. He heard his father turn on water in the bathroom sink, open the medicine cabinet and pull things out, kicking them across the bathroom floor when they fell. Mark thought he had at least a few minutes while his father was distracted by whatever he had done to injure his foot.

He scanned the floor and saw his mom's photo in its broken frame. He quickly pulled it free, sliding it into the pocket of his sweatshirt. He grabbed his coat, turned, and shoved half his upper body and one leg over the windowsill.

Mark looked back into his room just as his father's body filled the door-frame, backlit. The man's hand was lifting a .45 caliber handgun. Mark didn't take time to think. He slung his other leg out of the window and pushed away into a fall. It was an awkward landing, but he rolled as soon as he felt the ground, bounced up, and sprinted for the woods.

Mark heard a single shot ricochet off a tree to his right, so he dodged left. The one good thing about it being a 10-beer night was that it meant his father's aim was lousy.

Mark kept running.

***

The school custodian, Aloysius Cousins, carried a large ring of keys on a retractable chain in a circular aluminum case clipped to his belt. Chip listened to the familiar clinking of the keys fade into the distance.

As a savvy homeless teen, Chip had learned to track the direction and rate at which the sound faded to guess where Mr. Cousins was headed. The sound dropped quickly if he turned the corner to his tiny office next to the boiler room and lingered if he was walking further down the hall to another destination.

Mr. Cousins was tired, based on the slow rate of the clinking as he walked.

The old Negro spiritual he was humming reverberated in the empty hallway as though he was in the company of generations of exhausted old Black men. The man's voice receded into his office.

It was a quarter to ten at night. Chip knew he had about an hour to slip into the boys' locker room next to the gym and get a shower. After he finished cleaning up, he hid his damp towel in the bin under others that were already dry. Then he quietly returned to his sleeping spot on a pile of high jump mats the physical education department kept stashed inside the doors closest to the track behind the high school.

In another two hours, Mr. Cousins returned to double-check that he had locked the doors, and then headed out to his old blue Dodge Rambler to go home. Chip settled in for a few hours of sleep.

Before dawn, Chip got up, left the school, and did a slow jog back to the apartment complex where he no longer lived with his father. But his little brother, Mark, still lived there. Faithful as the sunrise itself, Chip met his nine-year-old brother every day at seven in the morning to walk him to his elementary school.

Their meet-up spot was a cluster of rangy evergreens off to the side of a faded green sign marking the entrance to the apartment complex. The facing that had once framed the wooden sign had long ago broken off, and the paint was peeling; but the irony of its bold and promising name remained strong: Knollwood Estates. You'd think it marked the entrance to a small grouping of faux-Tudor mansions, set back on three-acre properties, staff bustling around four-car garages built to look like horse barns. Not so much. Everyone in the county who needed subsidized housing lived there, and the property manager didn't think the residents cared much about paying for landscaping, paint, and signage.

Chip waited, checking his watch, expecting any moment to see Mark walking out of the entrance to the second building on the right. If Mark emerged at seven, plus or minus 10 minutes, it meant the night before had been quiet.

When Mark didn't appear, Chip grew concerned. Mark might have forgotten to set his alarm. He was only nine, and those things happened. Or maybe he was in a funk and had rolled over and gone back to sleep, hoping the world would disappear and leave him alone. Totally legit. If either of those explanations proved true, Chip would just get him up and dressed and drag him to school. What worried him was that Mark had said their dad lost another job, was drinking non-stop, and that he and Denise (or was it Darlene?) had been fighting a lot about money lately. Chip knew it wasn't always possible to stay out of the way when that kind of rot was boiling. Mark might not be okay.

Chip slipped stealthily into the woods that ran along the back of the complex. That narrow strip of trees created a visual barrier for residents who would otherwise be looking at the back of a cement factory. The dope dealers in the area had also made those woods ground zero for a healthy heroin economy. Supply and demand both seemed strong, Chip thought, as he stepped around one unconscious but still breathing body and noticed various forms of drug paraphernalia as he scanned the ground.

At the far end of the woods, Chip could approach the back of the building where his father lived. The first floor had balconies that hung off the building about 10 feet off the ground, cutting off all hope of natural light reaching the barred windows of the "garden level" apartments beneath. Chip had spent most of his childhood in one of those basement dwellings, before his mom had disappeared.

Chip looked at the first window to the right of the balcony of his father's apartment. That was Mark's bedroom. The slatted white blind was cock-eyed, the window half open. It was a cold October morning, and the sun was still low. It was hard to tell if Mark's room light was on.

Nearby, Chip kept an old empty oil drum stashed as a makeshift ladder. He quickly stepped back to the tree line and found it right where he had stowed it the last time. Chip hefted it above the thick brush and carried it quietly over to the wall under the window, then hopped up on top with the agility of a long-limbed, six-foot-tall cat.

He rested his hands on the windowsill and peered in. The room was dim, and he saw no movement. He balanced his weight on either edge of the top of the barrel and cupped his hands around his eyes and looked again. He could see the rocket ship-themed comforter on Mark's bed, pushed down halfway. But no Mark.

Chip jammed his fingers under the window casing and tried to raise it further to get a better look inside. Just then, he heard a sharp whistle behind him, coming from the woods. He turned quickly, almost losing his balance.

It was Mark, signaling him from behind a big tree. Chip hopped off the barrel and jogged over to his brother.

The kid looked exhausted and had a twig with a couple of leaves stuck in his hair, his green camo hoodie twisted sideways under his winter coat.

Chip bent down and placed his big hands on either side of Mark's head, peering into his eyes. Tears had made tracks through the grime on the boy's face.

"It got bad," Mark said simply. The weighted energy of all that went with the words hung about the two boys like electrified sewer gas.

Chip dropped to his knees and wrapped the younger boy in a hug, pulling him against his chest for warmth. Mark leaned in, resting his head.

Chip took a deep breath, looking out past the trees, searching for sky. He wanted to tell his little brother that everything would be okay, but he knew he couldn't promise that. Instead, he said nothing.

In the lengthening silence, Mark reared back in Chip's arms, fierce determination slapped on over fresh tears.

"I'm not going back there," Mark hissed. "I don't care what anyone says. I'll run. I know how to get to the train yard, like the hobos did, I read about it! I can hop on a train and be gone from here. Forever!"

Chip made himself breathe slowly and let Mark spout. He had to think of something he could do to keep Mark safe. Mark was getting angrier with every cycle of their father's violence, and less sad. Chip placed good odds that Mark would try to run soon, and he was way too young to be out on his own.

Chip dropped his chin to the top of Mark's head as the younger boy began to calm. He wished he could turn his entire body into the kind of shelter Mark needed.

"Mark, don't run. I know you can, and I know you want to, but it wouldn't be safe. Believe me, okay, buddy? Besides, I need my brother. I don't want to lose you," Chip said, quietly.

Chip was working hard not to lose it himself, remembering what he'd experienced last year when he'd bolted for the last time after a particularly ugly fight with their father.

Mark sniffed and rubbed the sleeve of his coat across his face. He squirmed away enough to look up at his brother, his face a perfect blend of anxiety and defiance.

"So, what are we gonna do?"

Chip didn't want to say what he was thinking, which was that he didn't have a clue. He needed time to think.

After Chip had left home a year ago, he had stayed in school, kept his grades up, and avoided attention in every way. Though he'd dropped off the track and field team, much to Coach's disappointment, Chip had stayed close to the safe world of his high school. Without anyone finding out, Chip had figured out how to use the school building as his home base, faked his father's signature to get a work permit, and solved a host of other logistical problems like mail and money and phone calls and where to stash some clothes. He had established a workable routine for doing life.

Bottom line, Chip was bright, street savvy, and painfully mature in his decision-making. He had converted his anger into a dead cold resolve to keep his own life on track until he could claim adulthood on his 18th birthday. He would turn 17 soon. Just one more year on the frayed edge of everything. He knew he could do it. But his certainty depended on his ability to be agile and self-reliant, accepting whatever difficulties arose, knowing he had a high tolerance for discomfort.

With Mark as a dependent, all that would change.

But Mark was still staring at him, waiting for an answer.

"Right now, we're going rafting," Chip proclaimed.

Rafting was one of Mark's all-time favorite adventures, and Chip thought the river would be soothing and a good distraction for them both. It would also burn some daylight hours.

They could both skip school today.

Together, the two boys walked wordlessly through the woods, away from Knollwood Estates, listening to the sound of their footsteps scuffing through soft leaf litter. Every so often, Mark would pick up a rock and throw it at a tree.

They made their way to where the woods connected to a county forest preserve that bordered both sides of the Fox River. A mile or so in, away from the well-tended walking trails and bike path, Chip had a hand-built raft stowed up the bank at a bend in the river. There, the water was shallow and had about four feet of sandy beach frequented only by raccoons and deer in search of a drink.

The raft was a bit clumsy, but sturdy. Chip had built a quarter-size prototype in shop class that floated beautifully, as did this larger one. It was just heavier than he had anticipated.

Mark helped Chip pull the raft free of the brush and down onto the sand. Chip retrieved the two mismatched oars he had bought at garage sales and gave the smaller one to Mark. The water was calm, flowing slowly downstream in front of them. Chip noticed that Mark already appeared to be in better spirits, caught up in the tasks of a familiar adventure.

The day passed easily, and Chip had money in his pocket from his part-time jobs to get them both a meal to go from Maria's, a tiny family-owned Mexican restaurant near the forest preserve. Since Mark was a bit of a mess from his night of camping in the trees, Chip had him stay out of sight in the woods and brought him the food. They sat cross-legged in a patch of weedy grass and wolfed down burritos and tortilla chips.

"Okay. Here's what we're going to do," Chip started, mustering all his confidence to reassure himself and Mark of the viability of his plan. "I'm going to show you how I've been living this past year, but it's dangerous, okay?"

Chip stopped and stared his little brother in the eyes to make sure his seriousness registered.

"Okay. I'm cool," Mark replied, sounding like he'd just turned 25.

"We cannot be discovered. You have to be super quick when I tell you, and super quiet," Chip warned.

Mark looked at him with a wry, sideways quirk to his lips.

"I think I've got 'super quick' and 'super quiet' pretty much down," Mark said, full of the dry sarcasm that always cracked Chip up. Both boys burst out laughing.

"Okay, got me there," Chip said, tossing another tortilla chip over into Mark's lap.

Chip explained how the back door to the gym stayed open until eight at night, when the last of the coaches left after team practices ended. The maintenance door by the dumpster stayed open after that. He walked Mark through the path Mr. Cousins took through the building on his nightly rounds, and how they would use the boys' locker room for showers. He explained how to steal only a couple pieces of bread and lunch meat from the big cooler in the cafeteria kitchen so no one would notice; and how the thick, heavy high jump pads stored in a heap in the gym's foyer made comfortable beds. They just had to be out of the building by 5:20 a.m.

Mark listened carefully, taking in everything Chip said. But Chip could tell that Mark was imagining this would become their new life, together, for as much of the future as a nine-year-old could envision.

"We should be okay tonight," Chip said, "but we both have to stay in school, and we need a better solution for the long term."

"No! I can be quiet! This will work fine," Mark protested.

"Yeah, I know you think so," Chip said, his tone guarded, "but I'm not so sure."

Mark looked like he was going to ratchet up his argument, but saw how worried his older brother looked and backed down. He chewed the the last of his burrito, a pensive expression on his face.

"I am not going back to Dad's. Ever," Mark stated flatly. "He'll kill me. He shot at me last night as I was bailing out the window."

Chip inhaled sharply. He had been telling himself that their father would never pull his gun on skinny little Mark, like he did a year ago in the fight that was the final straw for Chip.

"Damn it, Mark. I can't believe he pulled his gun on you. I mean, I believe you, absolutely. I just didn't think he'd do that. Was he drunk? Never mind, that doesn't matter."

Chip watched Mark fiddle with a couple of stones on the ground by his knees and didn't say anything more. Now he was feeling grim and scared. If their father was that out of control again, it really was dangerous. But he also knew that there probably would not be enough evidence for the state to relieve their father of custody. Sober, the man could be charming and manipulative, and he would make Mark out to be a conniving, budding delinquent who just needed discipline.

A faint plan was forming in Chip's mind. At 17, a court could declare him an adult.

***

Later that week, Aloysius Cousins leaned his shoulder into the heavy double doors leading out from the high school gymnasium and stepped through, bringing his large push broom with him. The sun was setting. A shallow plaza at the top of wide concrete stairs gave him a pleasant view to the west this time of day. Resting here for a bit was one of the small delights of the job of head custodian. After savoring the last of the orange and pink light, he took his time sweeping. It was quiet. Cousins had taken the late shift so his staff custodian could be home for evenings with his family.

He swept the steps slowly, glancing from time to time toward the far end of the fields for the two figures he'd been watching for the last few evenings.

Al suspected the boys were using the school at night for shelter, but it had taken him awhile to figure that out. They were good at it. He had never seen them enter the building. But there were still signs. A bit of water around the shower drains in the boys' locker room after he'd already cleaned and mopped, a sandwich wrapper or empty bag of chips shoved deep in the bottom of a trash bin he'd already emptied. He still had not found where they slept, but he knew they were here somewhere.

The old man was torn. He knew he should report his suspicions, but he felt for the kids at the same time. When Al was 13, his father had thrown him out of the house when he was caught shoplifting at the mini-mart down the street. They had taken him home, and his father had beaten him badly. Not for shoplifting—Al's parents regularly sent him to do that to help feed the younger kids. The beating had been for letting the cashier catch him pocketing a jar of peanut butter in his sweatshirt. Al's father had grabbed him by his belt and one arm and physically chucked him out the door, telling him not to come back.

He, too, had tried hiding out at his school. Al would never forget the awful night a teacher caught him when she was working late on props for the school play. Al's hideout was the little theater at the front of the cafeteria that doubled as an auditorium. What came next was a whole ugly series of bad foster care placements, runaway attempts, and eventually a street life in another city for the longest and ugliest chapter of his life.

Al had eventually got himself sorted, joined the military, and served two tours honorably. The army discharged him, and Al slowly built a life for himself. But he would never forget. He was 67 years old now, but seeing those boys in the distance, waiting for him to disappear back into the school, brought it all back.

Later that evening, Al noticed a small strip of clear packing tape placed low on a side door between the gym and a foyer where the track coach stored the high jump mats. He guessed that the boys used the tape to secure the latch so it wouldn't lock after he'd checked the area. So that was where the boys were sleeping. He didn't see them.

Al decided he needed to catch the boys and talk with them. It wasn't right, what they were doing; and further, it wasn't right that they had to. There had been nothing on the news about a frantic parent searching for two lost boys, so he figured his instincts were right. The two kids were on their own with a parent or parents who didn't really want them back.

A little after eleven o'clock, Mr. Cousins decided to see if he was right. He quietly walked back across the gym from the west hallway of the school and slipped out to the foyer. The tape was in place over the door lock, just as he'd suspected.

He peered over the railing at the top of a short flight of stairs and waited for his eyes to adjust to the deeper darkness. Sure enough, behind the nearest stack of high jump mats, he saw the younger boy curled up against the older one's back, his thumb in his mouth, sound asleep. Al stood there, breathing quietly, looking at the two kids in the dim light. He guessed that one was about sixteen and the other eight or nine. He thought he recognized the older boy from last year's track team. He shook his head at the whole sad situation and then coughed quietly.

The older boy's head flew around and they locked eyes. Al lifted one hand and beckoned the older boy over. He placed a finger across his lips, trying to tell the boy not to wake the younger one. The older boy slowly scootched over to the edge of the mat, slid his feet into his untied sneakers, and walked over, looking defeated.

Mr. Cousins motioned to the boy to follow him back through the door and into the gym where they could talk. The teen was silent, and the old man spoke first.

"I don't want to get you in trouble, son. You've obviously got plenty of it already. I'm Mr. Cousins, the custodian. And who, good sir, are you?"

"I know who you are, Mr. Cousins. I don't want to get you in trouble, either. I tried really hard to keep you from finding out, so you wouldn't have to do anything," Chip said.

"I know that, and you've done a darn respectable job of it, too. How long have you been using the school building as home?"

Chip thought about it a second and decided there was no point in lying. "My brother got tossed out by our dad a few days ago, and I just brought him along with me until I could figure something out. He can't live like this. He's too young," Chip said. "I've been sleeping at school since last year, though, to answer your question." Mr. Cousins' eyebrows shot up in stunned surprise.

"A *year*? You've been here at night for a *year*?" Al couldn't believe his ears. He hadn't seen a single sign of the teenager before this week. Then the teen's statement about his brother being too young for this kind of life struck him in the heart. "And you think you *are* old enough?"

The boy just shrugged in response, as though to say, *Well, it's worked so far.*

Al just shook his head, looking at the boy with a sense of appalled admiration. A few moments of silence stretched between the two.

"What are you going to do?" Chip asked.

Mr. Cousins sighed. "I don't rightly know, son. I know what I *ought* to do, but I don't know what I'm *going* to do. For starters, since you know my name, why don't you tell me yours?" He looked at the teen and waited.

"Chip. My little brother's name is Mark," Chip said, nodding back behind him to the storage area where Mark was still sleeping.

Mr. Cousins leaned back against the cold, polished brick wall of the gym. He stayed quiet, thinking.

"Shall I assume you are or were a student here?" Mr. Cousins asked Chip.

"Yes. Still have a 4.0 GPA, too. But I had to quit track last year. Needed to work. Had to get a permit because I'm not 18 yet, but that wasn't too hard. I figured it out. I manage. But Mark..." Chip's forehead creased into a worried frown beneath long black bangs that needed trimming. "I just don't know what to do. He can't go back home. Our dad..."

Mr. Cousins watched him closely, and just nodded. "Let me guess, a mean drunk or an addict?"

"The former," Chip said, not elaborating.

"How bad is it?" Mr. Cousins asked him.

"He shot at Mark from out of our bedroom window when Mark ran late Monday night. He's got a .45 and doesn't mind using it when he's drunk. Mark told me he thinks Dad beat up his latest girlfriend and might have dropped her out cold in the living room; and then he was roving around the apartment looking for something else to pound. Mark took off for the woods. But the man is careful. Even when he's drunk, he doesn't leave anything for protective services to find. He strangled me until I passed out once. No marks. Nothing he does really registers when he's that loaded. Doesn't regret it later, either."

"Nope, that's not good," Mr. Cousins said, quietly, his voice floating into the empty space before them. After a long minute, he continued. "So, what do you want me to do? No promises…"

Chip looked up at him, surprised to see that Mr. Cousins was genuinely asking him his opinion. He didn't expect that level of respect. Taking a breath, Chip squared his shoulders, making the decision to lay it all out.

"I want to make sure Mark stays in school, and I need to as well. We need to stay together. Mark needs me to help him make sense of all this and come out wanting to make it. He's more anxious than I was at his age, and he stuffs his anger until it eats him up and then he gets depressed. I'm afraid he won't come back out of that hole if I'm not there to convince him we can get through this." Chip paused, letting a flood of his own memories of brief, unpleasant stints in foster care run through his mind, a surreal animation, black and red ink printed on broken glass. His jaw tightened. He was determined to keep them both out of that system. He swallowed, anger and hopelessness fighting for control, as he worked to make sure his voice would be even, his words clear and sober.

"The foster care system isn't going to work for us. They'll just send Mark back home and treat me as a delinquent runaway, which I guarantee I will be if they try to send me back there. So, it seems to me the best thing to do is for me to get a judge to declare me an adult somehow and get us a place to live and give me custody of Mark. Can you help me do all that?"

The tone of his closing question was not optimistic but also carried just a hint of challenge, expecting little, but hoping Mr. Cousins might get on board with his longshot of a plan. He didn't dare look at Mr. Cousins, so he stared off toward the basketball hoops in the shadows of the dark gym and wrapped his arms around his knees.

"You've clearly been thinking this through. That's a lot of responsibility for a boy your age. How old are you, anyway?" Mr. Cousins asked.

"Almost 17."

"With the maturity of a 30-year-old," Mr. Cousins responded, shaking his head again. "Chip, I'm going to tell you something, so you know I understand what you're dealing with. I was homeless at 13, a few years younger than you. I won't bore you with the mess my family was. But I got dropped into the foster care system as a teen, and it did not go well. I know it *can* go well, but that was not my experience. I get that you're in a real fix here, and you're scared. Do you have any relatives at all nearby?"

"No. I've been told I have an aunt up on the Redbud Reservation in South Dakota. But I've never met her. I think she and my dad don't get along. I know what my dad always said about her, but I don't know what to believe. I have no idea how to find her. I think we're Sioux, but I don't know how tribal stuff works. I don't think my dad cares about it. He never explained any of it. When I first ran away, I snuck onto a bus heading that way, up to South Dakota, but…it didn't go well. Some guy said he'd help me, and…well, he didn't," Chip said, his voice fading into an unpleasant memory.

Mr. Cousins looked at Chip sharply, trying to see if what he thought Chip was alluding to was accurate. Chip's face had turned into a well-kept mask. The old man closed his eyes with a wave of remembered pain and took a deep breath.

"I won't ask for details, but let's not try that again, okay, Chip?"

"Don't worry. Not in the plans," Chip said drily.

Mr. Cousins and Chip heard the soft sucking sound of the big door to the foyer slip open, and a dimly lit face appeared in the crack.

"Chip? Are you there?" It was Mark, whispering. He'd woken up and found Chip gone.

Chip twisted and spoke quietly back over his shoulder toward the door. "C'mere, buddy. We're busted, but it's okay. You didn't do anything wrong." He unfolded himself from where he'd been sitting cross-legged on the floor and went to the door to collect his brother.

"Mark, this is Mr. Cousins, our custodian. Mr. Cousins, meet Mark," Chip said gently, so as not to alarm Mark with a sense of either danger or disappointment.

Mr. Cousins put out his calloused hand for Mark to shake. "Good to meet you, Mark. Your brother and I have just been talking about your situation. Have a seat with us."

The three sat together quietly for a long moment before Mr. Cousins spoke again.

"Boys, I know I ought to report you and this situation to both the school principal and the police. But I'm not going to do that right away, God help me. I could lose my job over this, but…" Mr. Cousins' voice trailed off. "I need to think."

Both boys stared up at the old man, knowing their fate was in his hands. Mr. Cousins continued.

"The way I figure it, Chip here has been quietly trespassing in this building against all odds, in secret, for a year. And I haven't had a clue. Seems to me if you're willing to pretend this conversation never happened, I can keep not having a clue for another day or two if you're okay with it. Not for long, mind you, but long enough for me to find some safe people to talk to about what we might be able to do. I want to help you. I do. But I am out of my league. I need some help, and I know asking for it poses some dangers. And *not* asking for it poses different dangers, particularly for the two of you. It's a sad, sorry situation." Mr. Cousins stopped there.

"Who are you going to tell?" Mark's voice was so tiny it was heartbreaking. Chip looked soberly at Mr. Cousins, silently voicing the same question.

"I have a cousin. She's a social worker over in Carollton and I hope she'll be able to talk to me without blowing any whistles, since she doesn't work in our county. Okay? I'm going to go finish my rounds now, pretend I never saw the tape over that lock, and we'll talk again tomorrow night. God help me, this has got to be the most stupid thing I've done in my life, and that's a list that's hard to top."

Chip and Mark looked at each other, surprise and relief washing their faces in equal measure. Chip spoke up first. "Yes, sir, Mr. Cousins. Thank you. I'm super grateful you aren't going to call everyone down on us...at least not right away. Real grateful."

With that, Mr. Cousins waved them back through the door to the foyer, looked at his watch, and walked off across the gym.

***

Chip got Mark up early to leave the high school before anyone would see them. He bought two cups of oatmeal from the Starbucks about a mile away in the direction of Mark's school. The two boys ate quietly at a picnic table behind the adjacent restaurant that didn't open until noon. Chip walked Mark over to the elementary school at ten after seven, giving himself enough time to make it back to the high school for his eight o'clock math class.

The hours went by slowly, and Chip was preoccupied.

As kind as Mr. Cousins had been when he had discovered Chip and Mark, Chip feared the outcome of the man's consultation with his cousin. Mr. Cousins had promised to play dumb for 24 hours, and Chip felt every one of those hours drifting by on a sea of nauseous anxiety while he did nothing. He didn't know what he could do, but he hated feeling so helpless and scared for Mark.

At two thirty, Chip got out of his last class and headed over to Sparkle More Auto-Wash where he worked for three hours detailing cars. Then he ran back to meet Mark at the public library. It was the safest place Chip could think of for Mark to go after school, and he had told Mark to get his homework done if he had any.

Chip found Mark slumped over his crossed arms at the end of a study table, sound asleep with an open sketch book mashed against his cheek. The librarian had given Chip a raised eyebrow as he beelined for his brother, but she said nothing.

"Mark. Mark, it's me," Chip said, sliding into a chair beside his brother and gently nudging his arm. Mark scowled and looked up groggily, but didn't complain. "Come on. Let's find something to eat."

Chip shuffled Mark's few things into a pile, noticing the line drawings on his sketch pad.

"Mark, did you draw these? They're amazing!" Chip stared at the image of two flying dragons fighting in mid-air, talons extended and snarling. Mark nodded shyly and turned back a couple of pages, flipping the spiral-bound book sideways in front of his older brother.

"I really like how these turned out," Mark said.

Chip stared at an image of a turtle morphing into a fighting robot and facing off against a different winged dragon in front of a city skyscraper. He looked slowly from the page back to Mark.

"Dude. How'd you learn how to do this? They're killer!"

"Art teacher at school taught us about perspective. That really helped me get the three-dimensional part better. And she gave me a book about drawing. I had to sort of copy the dragons at first from gaming apps I found online in the computer lab, but now I make up my own." Mark was clearly proud. "But don't tell Dad. If we go back, I mean."

"I won't. And I'm still hoping that won't happen. We'll see if Mr. Cousins has any ideas when we talk to him tonight."

Chip ruffled Mark's hair and used his thumb to rub a pencil smudge off the boy's face. He handed Mark his geography book and let him finish packing his bag.

The two boys headed out of the library and down the street toward the edge of downtown.

"How about Chinese for dinner? I just got paid," Chip said. Mark nodded comfortably, like they'd been doing this for ages, not days.

Chip led them around the corner to a storefront with doors set back a few feet from the display windows. One door invited patrons in for Tarot readings, acupuncture, and herbal remedies. The other door was half-covered on the inside with a narrow, bright red blind that set off the name of the restaurant. Ching Mai's was one of Chip's favorite places to eat when he had some cash. Even though the family that ran it spoke little English, they were always nice to him.

Chip helped Mark figure out what he wanted to eat, and they ordered. When the food arrived, they dove in. After a while, Chip checked his watch. It was almost eight.

"We better get going," Chip said.

They packaged up their leftovers and Chip paid. Mark wandered toward the door and leaned against the wall, fidgeting with the worn gold fringe that hung from a wall tapestry of a mountain scene. Chip squeezed his shoulder when he got to the door, and the boys walked back down the street and turned toward the high school and their anticipated conversation with Mr. Cousins.

Chip was growing more nervous, and despite his efforts to be reassuring, Mark could tell. He stuck close to his big brother as they walked the last few blocks.

When they reached the back of the stands beside the football field and track, Chip stopped and pulled Mark into the shadows. He was used to waiting here until Mr. Cousins finished sweeping the wide cement landing outside of the double doors to the gym. Off to one side was the delivery dock, with its beat-up pedestrian door at ground level beside the dumpster. It was through that door that Chip had been entering the school after hours all year since Mr. Cousins left it open while he was working. Chip figured he'd catch up with Mr. Cousins while he was sweeping the landing.

But this evening, Mr. Cousins did not appear on his reliable schedule. Everything was quiet. Too quiet.

Mark was getting restless and looked up at Chip, frowning. "What's wrong? Why are we still waiting here?" Mark asked, wanting to get the meet-up over with and find out what would happen next.

"I don't know, Mark. Something's off. Mr. Cousins should have shown up already to sweep outside the doors up there."

"But he knows we're coming, right? Maybe he's just waiting for us in his office," Mark said.

"Yeah, you've got a point. I just don't like things being different. But I guess you're right. Come on." Chip placed his hand on his younger brother's back to signal that he was ready to go and led the way toward the back of the school.

There was only a sliver of moon in the sky, and passing clouds obscured even the tiny amount of light it offered. As the two got close to the loading dock, Chip stopped. He felt like a wild animal, sniffing for danger in the wind, straining his eyes to see what he might be missing, listening for voices or odd sounds. But there was nothing.

"Let's get this over with, Chip. Let's find Mr. Cousins." Mark gave Chip's arm a little tug.

Chip sighed, nodded, and walked toward the big dumpster and the narrow gray door beside it.

"Okay, let's see if the door is open like usual," Chip said as he reached for the door. He tugged on the handle. It didn't budge. The door was locked, and Chip couldn't see any lights on in the hall behind it.

"Should we knock?" Mark asked, tense and a bit confused.

"Um, I'm not sure," Chip replied, looking around. Then he stopped, staring at a spot just behind the dumpster. "Look over there, Mark. It's Mr. Cousins' push broom. He never leaves it outside," Chip whispered.

Chip walked carefully over to the broom and noticed that someone had propped it at an odd angle, the handle jammed between a rock and the bottom bracket of the dumpster. Sticking out from beneath the rock, Chip noticed a triangle of white paper. He leaned down and carefully tugged out an envelope, folded in half.

"What is it, Chip?" Mark asked.

"It's an envelope. I think there's a note inside. It has my name on the outside."

Mark came over to stand beside his brother as Chip tore open the envelope and pulled out a single piece of paper, also folded. He opened it and turned so the dim light of the buzzing security lamp above them hit the page. He read the message aloud to Mark.

"Boys. I am taking a few days off from work to complete some training. No one will be in the building at night, but the police will be making rounds like they usually do to check on it anytime I'm away. So be careful. Keep the doors locked up tight. Lights off. Stay safe. Talk soon. Mr. C."

Chip looked back in the envelope and realized there was a key in the bottom. He pulled it out and stepped over to the loading dock door.

It fit and turned smoothly.

***

Aloysius Cousins found the conference room just off the lobby of the county administration building at the end of 12th Ave. He double-checked the sign taped to the door to make sure he was in the right place. He felt nervous and decided there were too many reasons why to bother sorting it out. He knew he was doing what he wanted to do. He pulled the door open wide enough to step through.

"Welcome! Are you here for foster parent orientation?" The greeting came from a slender young woman with her chestnut curls pulled back in a challenged ponytail.

"Yes, I am," Aloysius responded. "Aloysius Cousins. But please, call me Al, everyone does."

The young woman smiled warmly and beckoned him over, presenting him with a tote bag bearing the county logo and a three-ring binder.

"My name is Caroline. Caroline Benniman. I'm a social worker with Foster and Adoptive Services here in the county. I'm so glad you're here."

Caroline handed Al a black marker to print his name on a sticky-backed name tag and said that first names were sufficient. Her attention turned to the next trainee coming through the door.

Al set his bag at the far end of one of the long tables, arranged like ribs along a central aisle. Then he helped himself to coffee from an enormous, battered metal urn at the back of the room and selected what promised to be a moist, oversized blueberry muffin from a tray next to the powdered creamer and sugar.

He returned to his seat, glancing around to take in the other participants. All couples, almost all White, with one Latino pair whispering to each other several tables back. Al was the only African American, the only single adult, and clearly the oldest person in the room by what he guessed was easily 20 years.

Al kept thinking about Chip and Mark, camped out in the high school. After weighing the risks to his job against their safety as functionally homeless youth, Al had decided to leave the older boy a key to the loading dock door. After learning that Chip had been secretly using the school as a motel all year, going to classes, and getting good grades while holding down part-time jobs under no adult supervision whatsoever, Al figured he could handle the responsibility of a key and some trust.

After consulting with his cousin, Al had spent one sleepless night making his decision and praying over it. The next morning, he had made a phone call and what he learned convinced him he was doing the right thing. Introductory training for prospective foster parents started that evening, and yes, there was still an available slot.

Al called in to the school and explained that he wanted to take four nights off. Since he hadn't asked for any time off in eight years, the assistant principal was more than happy to approve it, even on such short notice.

Al's next decision was whether to share his plan with Chip and Mark. He decided to keep it to himself, knowing that too many things would have to fall in place, and quickly, for his home to become a placement option.

But first things first. Al had to complete the training, fill out a mound of paperwork, receive a home study, and wait for the state to approve him as a foster parent.

"Okay, everyone, let's get started," Caroline called out, tucking a stray curl back behind one ear. She dug out a remote from beneath a pile of handouts and advanced her PowerPoint presentation to its introductory slide.

***

Al Cousins finished his training to become a foster parent, and the next day he filed a report of suspected child neglect with Mercer County authorities. His cousin Alice knew what to say in the report to trigger a prompt response. Reporting the presence and use of a gun, alcohol abuse, and the boys' report of previous violence including choking were all high on the list.

Al denied knowing the current whereabouts of the two boys but suggested that Mark's elementary school would have an address that might be a good place to find the father for a surprise visit.

He knew the odds were long that a judge would declare the father unfit based on just the boys' word; and if the boys were located, the courts were bound to seek family reunification depending on the parent's cooperation. But he had to try to get the system to work.

On Tuesday night, Mr. Cousins returned to work and left a note on the high-jump mats where he knew the boys slept. He avoided encountering them directly.

When Chip found the note, his heart started to hammer. Mark immediately came to Chip's side to see what had alarmed him.

"It's from Mr. Cousins," Chip whispered. "He's inviting us to dinner tomorrow, early, before his shift. He says we need to talk."

"Dinner? Where? What's he gonna do?" Mark's whispered voice was high and tight with fear.

"The Village Inn over on Patterson, not far from here, at four thirty," Chip said, forcing his voice toward calm. "I don't know what he has planned, Mark. But I don't think we have a choice but to trust him and do what he says. He knows we're here. I don't know why he let us keep staying here for this long while he was out. But it's not legal for him to not report us."

"Can't we just run, Chip? If we get far enough, no one will know who we are or where Dad lives. We can just make up new names!"

Chip wrapped his arm around Mark's shoulder and pulled him close. He seemed resigned, but firm, and looked Mark in the eyes. "I don't know why, but I trust Mr. Cousins. I think he really does understand. We just need to meet him tomorrow and see what he has to say."

Mark slumped down against the wall and dropped his head on his arms, crossed over his knees. He said nothing. And neither did Chip.

After a few minutes, Mark lifted his head and turned it toward Chip.

"Chip?"

"Yeah."

"Can we go rafting tomorrow instead of going to school?" Mark asked, sounding even younger than his nine years.

"Yeah, buddy, we can go rafting." Chip replied, tousling his brother's hair. "Let's get some sleep."

Early the next morning, before it got light outside, the two boys slipped out of the school and off into the cover of the woods along the athletic fields. They walked across town and spent the day rafting on the river and sitting on the big boulders near the bend where Chip stowed his raft. They got lunch at Maria's, then went back to poke around in the woods, avoiding being seen by anyone on the forest preserve trails.

Around four o'clock, they headed back toward town to meet Mr. Cousins at the Village Inn.

What they didn't know was that at eleven that morning, a social worker named Ophelia and two police officers had pounded on the door to their father's apartment. When no one answered, they used the landlord's passkey to gain entry. A half-torn eviction notice flapped on the door.

They had found a man alive but unconscious, reeking of alcohol, passed out on the sofa in the living room. They had also found blood smeared down one wall beneath a skull-sized dent in the paneling, a large broken mirror on the floor, and a kitchen so filthy the cockroaches didn't bother to run when Ophelia turned on the lights. It stank of rodents. Sure enough, there were bullet holes in the window frame of the boys' bedroom. Chilly air drafted in through the broken window, shards of glass scattered across the carpet in among Mark's clothes and toys.

The police had roused the man and asked him to produce I.D. before calling an ambulance to transport him to a crisis detox center. The social worker took photos to use as prompts for a little interrogative interview, later, when he sobered up. An evidence collection team arrived an hour later to deal with the bloody wall, the shell casings on the floor, and the bullets still embedded in the boys' bedroom wall and window frame.

The police officers were both fathers themselves. They didn't work overly hard to be gentle with the man as they helped load his slack form onto a gurney to go into the back of the ambulance.

Al Cousins arrived at the Village Inn at 4:20 p.m. and got a booth where he could keep an eye on the door. Alice was with him. At 4:40, they watched the front door to the restaurant swing open as Chip gave his little brother a gentle shove through. Chip looked grim with resolve, while Mark just looked terrified. Al's heart broke, even as he heard Alice whisper to him that it would be okay.

Chip saw Mr. Cousins and led Mark over to the table, making sure the nine-year-old scooched over against the window in the booth before he sat down. Chip didn't want Mark to bolt, and knew he was already thinking about it.

"Hello, boys," Mr. Cousins began. "This is Alice, my cousin. Alice, this is Chip and his younger brother, Mark."

"Pleased to meet you, Ms. Alice. Good to see you again, Mr. Cousins." Chip half rose and reached across the table to shake their hands. Alice smiled and nodded. Chip kneed Mark under the table and the boy looked up.

"Nice to meet you," Mark mumbled, then looked down at his lap again, the perfect image of misery folding in on itself.

Mr. Cousins plucked menus from the silver ring that held them in place over the collection of condiments and handed one to each of the boys. Chip took his, but Mark seemed to be trying his best to vanish into the floor and Mr. Cousins handed the second menu to Alice instead.

"Let's get us some food first, eh?" Mr. Cousins said congenially, trying to relax the boys a bit. It didn't work.

"Are you gonna call the cops on us?!" Mark blurted out, glaring first at Mr. Cousins, then at Alice.

"Mark!" Chip hissed, looking sharply down at his brother's face, frowning.

"It's okay, Chip. Mark has reason to be worried, I understand," Alice said. She glanced over at Al, seeking permission to proceed. He nodded, and Alice spoke directly to both boys, her tone quiet and gentle, but clear.

"The police aren't coming here. But they have paid a visit to your father. He's in a good bit more trouble than you are, and it is *not* your fault."

Alice waited for eye contact with both boys, but only got it from Chip. She reached across the table and placed two fingers beneath Mark's chin to raise it until he looked at her. "Mark? Look at me. That's better. Your father's drinking and the trouble he's in now are Not. Your. Fault. Hear me?"

Alice withdrew her hand but waited until Mark gave her an almost imperceptible nod. She sighed, knowing full well it would be months if not years before Mark got that message straight in both his head and his heart. Still, she had to try to deliver it. She looked back at Al before continuing.

"You can't keep living on your own like you have been. Al told me how you've been getting by, Chip, and I have to say, in all my years working with runaways, your ingenuity and focus on keeping your life on track is wildly impressive. And you, young man, have a big brother who cares about you a whole lot. That's obvious."

The boys sat silent and impassive, looking at her like mismatched lemurs on alert, Alice thought. When she had finished saying what she needed to say to start the conversation, she simply picked up her menu again and began reviewing her options for a late lunch. It was the boys' turn. Or Al's.

Finally, Chip spoke. "So, what *is* going to happen now?"

"That depends a bit on you. But I do have a proposition," Al said, looking from one pale young face to the other.

"What do you mean?" Chip asked.

Al looked over toward Alice and she nodded for him to go on. "I can't promise things will unfold as smoothly as I'd like, okay? But did you get my note last week about how I had to get some training?"

"Yes, we did," Chip said, evenly, and dug the key to the high school delivery dock door out of his pocket and slid it across the table to Mr. Cousins. "And thanks for that." Chip nodded at the key as Al picked it up.

"I knew I could trust you," Mr. Cousins said, nodding to Chip. "And I didn't want you sleeping in the woods. Anyway, that training. It was one of the requirements for me to become a foster parent. And Alice here helped expedite the rest of the process. There's at least a possibility that we can get you two placed with me. If you don't mind bunk beds, that is."

Al Cousins stopped, a bit tense himself, waiting for the boys to react. Alice remained quiet; her hands folded in her lap. The server arrived, setting glasses of water in front of each of them. Alice spoke to her softly and asked for a few more minutes before they placed their orders. The server nodded, slipping away without comment.

"You'd do that?" Chip's voice carried a strangled intensity as he stared across the table at Mr. Cousins in disbelief.

Al just nodded and took a deep breath as Chip's eyes welled up.

"I'd enjoy your company," Al said. "And I think I could help you get set up and independent when you and Mark are truly ready. But no rush."

"But...what about Dad? He'll lie! He always does! He'll say it's all our fault and he'll say he's been all worried and..."

Chip reached over and touched Mark's arm, shushing him. He had noticed a server looking their way in response to Mark's distress. Mark stopped talking but looked up at Chip, his forehead creased with worry.

"He is a really good liar," Chip said, supporting Mark's concern.

"Really good liars are our professional specialty, boys," Alice chimed in. "And from what my friend Ophelia told me a couple of hours ago—she's a social worker with CPS here in your county—the police who went to your father's apartment with her are more than happy to suggest alternative arrangements for your care. Your father wasn't even conscious when they arrived. I suspect you know all too well what that looks like." Alice paused, looking at Chip.

"Yeah. We do," Chip said, looking down at Mark protectively.

Al leaned forward, his elbows on the table, and looked from one boy to the other. "I'm going to go on in to work tonight, like nothing's happened. If you're willing to take a chance on us, Alice will take you two over to the office to talk to Ophelia in an hour. You'll need to tell her the truth—about everything. If all goes as planned, Alice will bring you home to my place and stay with you until I get home. I'm going to see about changing my work schedule. Hopefully, we can make it a permanent placement."

Al waited for some indication of willingness from the two young runaways.

Mark looked up at Chip for guidance about what to think. Chip looked back at Mark for a long moment, then spoke.

"Mark, buddy, this is as good a shot as we'll ever get. You okay with it?" Chip held Mark's gaze evenly, with total seriousness.

"Okay," Mark replied.

"Then order yourselves some supper and let's get on with it!" Mr. Cousins picked up his menu, plucked his readers out of his chest pocket, and propped them on his nose in one smooth motion. "I believe I'll start with a nice piece of cherry pie."

***

A year later, Ophelia, the boys' official county social worker, called for a case review with Al Cousins, the school social worker from Mark's elementary school, and the boys' therapist from the community mental health center. Over their visits, Ophelia had grown quite fond of Al as well as Mark and Chip. Ophelia listened carefully to Al's reflections about the first year of their lives as a new family. Looking in the rearview mirror over the last 12 months, Al felt enormous satisfaction. Ophelia put it in her mental record book as one of her top three cases where things had gone unexpectedly well.

Al had converted his wife's sewing room into a second bedroom, replete with bunk beds and two desks for schoolwork. The boys had settled in quickly and with no complaint. The brothers remained close, and Al had a hunch it had been their relationship with each other that had kept them whole.

Chip had done a lot of parenting with his younger brother, which Al had not encouraged, but watched with interest. It was obviously a longstanding pattern—Chip's protective instinct at work, coupled with an overly conscientious big-brother's role modeling. In one late night chat on the front porch not long after the boys arrived with their few personal possessions, Al had drawn more of their story out of Chip. It wasn't pretty. But what was truly remarkable was Chip's calm commitment to his own future and Mark's.

Chip's growing interest in forensic science was no surprise. As a senior in high school, he had earned a full-ride scholarship to an in-state college that was within commuting distance, majoring in criminology. The college allowed him to continue living at home with Mr. Cousins, allaying Chip's fears about leaving Mark too soon. Chip had never said it aloud, but the truth of his mother's disappearance was something he had a relentless desire to discover. His sense of justice was piercing. As was his pragmatism. He would make a good investigator.

In time, Mark relaxed about Chip being away at odd times, attending evening classes or picking up shifts at one of his two jobs. Al had made him drop one of the three he had when they'd met, in the interest of Chip's sleep and health. Chip created a calendar on their bedroom wall on which he wrote down when he had classes and work shifts at the car wash or the bakery so Mark could check and not worry about where he was. They scheduled time to do things together on weekends.

By the time Mark started fifth grade the following school year, the stability and safety Mr. Cousins provided had made an enormous difference. Mark had a couple of good friends at school he'd known since third grade, and all three of them were heading to the same junior high. His report cards reflected his improved adjustment and focus, and his art teacher, Ms. Beckham, was bending over backward to nurture his natural talents and give him useful experiences. She made him the illustrator for the school newsletter, teaching him how to convert his drawings to digital graphics. Mark was always working on a "project" after finishing his homework. Chip was relieved to see him so engaged and connected at school.

They were both on their way to building lives they could love, and Al Cousins could not have imagined that the last years of his working life would be so full of joy.

DANI'S WOLVES

Once upon a time, there was a little girl who lived in the forest of tall pines at the top of Great Bluff, above the ocean. When she was born, her parents thought she was perfect. She seemed unusually calm for a baby and though she rarely smiled, when she did, it was like the sun in the wide meadow that made the leaves of all the trees dance with delight.

All the older girls wanted to hold her and passed her around like a treasure. As she grew into an able toddler, they played with her, making up games where they could sit around the child in a circle and keep her safe as she explored. She brought each of them little gifts from the tiny stones and flowers she found as she crawled among them.

Even the boys seemed taken with her, and they rarely cared about babies. She seldom cried, and only laughed when the boys carried on pretending to be great hunters, roughhousing, and tossing the girl between them like a ball. They never let her fall.

Her parents named her Dancing Flower, and everyone called her Dani.

Dani grew quickly, and as soon as she could walk on her two feet, she was climbing trees and chasing the dogs that roamed the camp and belonged to everyone. Dani would disappear for hours at a time some days and tended to nap high in the trees. She had favorites where she could drape her slender, sun-darkened legs over two strong limbs that reached out in a convenient position, and sleep peacefully against the trunk. She didn't always come when she was called.

Once, Dani's mother found her in her favorite oak tree, asleep, with an enormous great horned owl perched beside her, one yellow eye opened protectively. Dani's mother told no one for fear they would think that Aman, the Dark Owl Spirit, had touched her or even taken her spirit away.

Meanwhile, a gathering of leaders of all the tribes in the known world was underway. Messages of concern had been sent from one to another, translated and verified, over the course of many moons. They all talked about changes that had been happening in the forest and along the shores. Things were growing unbalanced. Some of the coastal trees were dying in large numbers. The rains, when they came, weren't slow and steady but violent, lashing at the ground and making the sea rage. The fisher people had to range further and further to bring in a catch, and the gatherers were noticing the berries were smaller and not so sweet, sometimes even malformed with parasites and strange growths.

Each tribe had noticed something different, and not all at once. But when they brought their stories together, they knew it wasn't just their fears talking. And none of them knew what to do.

A day was set for a gathering to discuss the worrisome observations. The chiefs of every tribe, each with three of their most trusted counselors, made the trek to the gathering place near the Great Bluff.

They began praying together in their respective languages and ways and slowly came to believe that they needed a new way of seeing what was going on. And for that, they would need a young one. A child whose nature wasn't leading them to fit in, but instead to be different. To walk the margins rather than the center, and to listen to what the Great Spirit was saying rather than his or her elders.

When such a child was found, the boy or girl would be raised and tutored in such a way that they became familiar with all the tribes' ways and wisdom.

From their numbers, the chiefs selected a group of the wisest, oldest women and a few men with special medicine in their hearts. The group was named the "Ancianis," a term widely understood to mean an intertribal circle of elders.

The Ancianis began to look among all the children in all the tribes and clans for one who was different. Possibly difficult. Possibly strange. One with an old spirit and clear eyes who saw and spoke the truth, even when it was unwelcome.

When they heard about Dancing Flower, they agreed she was the one. Though she was young, they would bring her to live with them in their camp along the Great Bluff. There, they could watch both the sea as it stretched into the western sun and the forests reaching inland as far as anyone had ever travelled, and continue to learn together.

On Dani's sixth birthday, the elders of the clan came to her parents and told them that the Ancianis wished to take Dancing Flower to raise as their own.

The Ancianis made Dani's parting from her parents as gentle as possible, and everyone tried to be brave. The members of the circle welcomed Dani warmly and with great kindness, and they were amazed at how easily she adjusted. She seemed, in some ways, already one of them, comfortable in their company, and quick to learn enough of all their languages to make friends with each in turn.

The Ancianis slowly introduced Dani to the role for which they believed she was born. From each member of the circle, Dani heard the most important stories from each tribe. And she was told of the worrying changes each had observed that were making life more difficult. She was told what they most feared could happen if things got worse. Winter had not been bringing enough snow to the mountains, and the rivers and creeks were drying up without the renewal of the spring melt. The soil was cracked and dry, blowing to dust, and crops and gardens were failing. Certain insects were swarming in waves for months on end, from summer all the way into fall. They were destroying the flowering fruit trees and berry bushes, so there was no harvest at all for the gatherers. The populations of wild animals were changing in strange ways in the high country, with some, like the elk, disappearing completely; and others, like the bear, growing unusually in number. In the fall, with no berries or fruit to eat, bears were roaming the camps in search of food, and the great animals had taken and eaten several young children. The fisheries were silting in, with vast kills washing up on the dark sand beaches. The people were hungry, the hunters and fishers and gatherers and growers struggling more by the year to keep their villages in place, their families healthy.

The elders also shared what they hoped was possible with some sort of healing. She heard their creation stories, she learned their dances, she was present for births and coming-of-age ceremonies, and for the passing of old ones. She absorbed it all and came to understand that despite how young she was, they hoped she would see what they could not and know what they should do to reinstate the natural balance upon which all their lives depended.

Once a month, under the full moon, they would gather and sing. And at the end of the night, whenever the moon was at its peak in the sky, they would take Dani by the hand and seat her in the center of their circle. They would revisit what she had been taught over the preceding moon's days and give her a gift that commemorated her progress.

The gift was always the same. It was comprised of a loop of onyx beads and a loop of shell beads. The first two were long, and when placed over her head, they reached from one shoulder to the opposite knee and were fastened at each point to her tunic with deer leather ties, sealed with marrow wax. At the height of the next moon, two of the Ancianis fixed the next two strands of beads to her tunic, just below the first.

After four dozen moons, Dani had a cloak of shining black and luminescent blue-and-white beads. When she moved, the beads slid against one another and sounded simultaneously like the water at high tide playing in the stones on the shore and like the wind in the tall trees on the ridges that surrounded their camp.

Eventually, Dani completed the full round of lessons from all the tribes. She was 10 years old. Sometime in the next few years she would become a woman herself, and lose the youthful, new perspective upon which the elders had pinned their hopes for fresh insight.

They decided it was time for her to use all they had given her, don the now-heavy cloak of beads that carried the power of all they knew of both light and shadow worlds, and undertake her quest.

The circle had devised the shape of Dani's quest with elements from each of their coming-of-age rituals for both boys and girls. As they worked together, they discovered so many things in common across their rituals that the requirements for Dani's quest ended up far simpler than they had first expected.

The Ancianis agreed they would lead her to sit on the wide, flat, rocky outcrop they all knew as Raven's Ledge; it jutted out from the bluffs high above the sea. And there she would stay until she received the vision that would guide them all toward the healing work they needed to understand and do. She would take with her a single stem and blossom from the rare mirrapensa plant that grew only on the highest mountain in the region, above where the trees stopped growing. It had a wide, scarlet bloom with many petals that silvered with age, and a short, tough, wiry stem. Four of the tribes knew it well and understood that it was there to connect the highest peaks where they touched the sky to the very center of the earth, and anyone who carried it would have the benefit of its wisdom. A single blossom took three members of the circle many days to find.

When the flower-seekers returned with the single stem of mirrapensa, the moon was full. That night, they dressed Dani in her shawl of beads and gave her new moccasins, the tops of which one elder had decorated in a fine mosaic made with precious items from each tribe. In it were tiny pieces of eagle bone and owl feather, slivers from medicinal roots, tiny sunstones, and even the shiny pink scales of fish skin carefully dried in the sun and polished for the purpose. The moccasins were blessed to help carry her on her journey. The entire intertribal circle walked Dancing Flower to Raven's Ledge and quietly said goodbye.

Dani didn't know exactly what to do. Two days and two nights passed. She sat patiently, shifting only enough to keep her body from getting too uncomfortable. The cloak grew heavy on her shoulders, and she finally had to sleep. She held the flower carefully in her hands, worried that it had begun to wilt.

When she woke again, late in the night, her hands were cold and trembling. She sat up cross-legged, tucking her feet beneath her, and noticed that where she gripped the tough stem of the scarlet flower, it was turning white. She watched as she grew colder and colder and realized the entire flower she was holding had begun to freeze. Tiny shards of frost covered the stem and petals with starlit crystalline fur, and she gripped it tighter and tighter, afraid her hands and arms would tire and drop it, and that it would shatter on the stone beneath her.

She stayed completely still, clutching the frozen flower, for hours. In the darkness, the stars grew dim, and Dani began to feel muzzy-headed and anxious. She was hungry and thirsty, and the weight of the beaded cloak was becoming harder and harder to bear. She still didn't know what she was supposed to tell the circle, and she knew they were waiting for her back in the camp. Tears fell from her eyes, and she looked up into the sky and tried to empty her mind so that the Great Spirit could fill it with whatever she needed to know. Or until that same Great Spirit took mercy on her and came to take her away over the sea to the other side of life, where this burden would no longer be hers.

Then Dani heard the wailing howl of wolves coming from the deep forest behind her. She didn't move, but kept clutching the icy stem in her fists, her eyes focused on the deepest parts of the sky. She waited, and waited some more, and then heard the soft sound of the wolves' paws stepping off the silted dirt and onto the stone of the ledge.

She closed her eyes, knowing that the great black beasts could do with her whatever they pleased. She felt their warmth come near, and the shuffle of bodies as they gathered around her. She slowly opened her eyes and lowered her gaze to look at them, and saw that their eyes were soft amber, meeting hers. The animals stood well above her small shoulders, but they dropped their great heads in unison, all eight of them, and began to breathe on her hands and on the flower, panting softly.

Slowly, at the center of the circle of wolves, the brilliant scarlet flower thawed and expanded once again. Dani's small, pale hands began to warm and stopped trembling. She watched as eight leathery black noses snuffled closer, taking in the scent of the flower and the air around it, almost touching it and each other as they drew it in like a new language. Dani watched as the wolves withdrew, ever so slightly, and looked at each other as though they were simultaneously asking and answering a question.

Then the eight wolves leaned in and drove their foreheads underneath Dani's body, lifting her to their shoulders. They carried her back into the forest, straight along the trail that led back to the circle's camp. Dani relaxed into their slow, coordinated lope, and dozed, letting their bodies warm her and give her their strength.

And she knew that somehow, they would be the ones to tell the great circle of elders what they needed to know. She simply had to go with them and be willing to help translate.

HELEN THREDGOOD'S SURPRISE

Little escaped observation in the 1200 block of Henneker Street thanks to the location of Helen Thredgood's La-Z-Boy recliner. It sat in the corner of her living room, beneath an enormous arched reading lamp, and faced the street. Helen was at 1201 Henneker Street, in an enormous Victorian house on the corner lot.

The Minnesota mansion was gray with navy-blue shutters and a matching blue door. Helen's hair was an airy gray with a bluish gunmetal cast, and she was fond of wearing her mother's old navy cardigan with its large gray buttons. The pitched, angular woodwork over the two large front windows was an unsettling match to the shape of Helen's eyebrows, which gave her the appearance of either chronic surprise or appalled disbelief, depending on the tenor of your conversation with her. They say old married couples look and sound more alike as the decades unfold. Well, the same could be said for Helen and her house.

One damp November morning, Helen's knees were aching, and she decided she needed to set aside her crocheting and stretch her legs by collecting her mail from its box at the curb. As she rose and adjusted her cardigan, she peered down the street from her window and noticed an unfamiliar car slowly making its way down Henneker Street. The car's brake lights turned on each time it neared another house as though the driver was scrutinizing addresses.

"Lost or up to no good," Helen muttered to herself, stepping sideways to get closer to the window and peer discretely around her damask drapes.

She watched as the car stopped in front of number 1208, a yellow house belonging to a new family by the name of Ferrell. Helen had made no real attempt to meet the Ferrells since she had determined that neither Mr. nor Mrs. Ferrell had purchased the house from its previous occupant, John Stanger, when Mr. Stanger moved to Minneapolis. They were just renters. She religiously checked the real estate transaction listings in the newspaper, so she would know if new neighbors were likely to last.

An older gentleman stepped out of the sedan and patted the right pocket of his dark raincoat. He placed a fedora on his balding head and adjusted it. Helen watched as he walked around the front of his car, hopping over a puddle to reach the walkway that led to the front door. The man rang the doorbell and waited.

He didn't seem to be lost or up to obvious no good, which left unexplored options. Helen hurried to her own front door and made her way down the driveway to the street, keeping a carefully casual eye on the unfamiliar man waiting in front of the door at 1208.

What Helen saw next left her eyebrows arched higher than her two front windows. From his right pocket, the man withdrew what looked from a distance like a folded envelope made of shiny paper the color of ripe cantaloupe. But instead of tucking the envelope in the Ferrells' front door, as Helen expected him to do, he gave the envelope a sharp snap, opening it to its full size. Helen stared, holding her upper denture in place with her tongue, a habit she had when stressed. The envelope blew up to the size of a large balloon, then continued to expand within a bell-shaped frame, easily four feet tall. The entire apparatus appeared to be covered tightly in translucent ivory fabric. The man reached under its base and gave a tug at something Helen couldn't see, and an ornate metal tripod unfolded. He gave the tripod a spin, then set the entire contraption down in front of the Ferrells' door. Quickly, the man unlatched a small door in the side of the cage. He reached into his left pocket and withdrew something, which he then placed inside with a slight shake of his wrist.

After closing the door, the man bowed courteously toward the cage, strode quickly to his car, got in, started the engine, and drove away.

Helen couldn't contain herself. Tucking her mail beneath her arm, she walked diagonally across the street and straight up the walk toward the cage in front of the yellow door of 1208 Henneker Street. She had to know what was sitting on the Ferrells' front stoop.

When she was just three or four steps away, she heard a very loud flutter of wings from inside the cage and a single tufted red feather escaped and drifted to the ground. Why, she thought, it seems to be an enormous African parrot or some such…?

"Helen Thredgood, this is absolutely none of your business."

The stern admonishment emanated from the cage in a female voice with a British accent carried on a slightly Nordic rhythm. It was hard to place, but distinctive. Helen stopped in her tracks with a gasp. But she still couldn't clearly see what was inside the structure. So, she took two more quick steps, clutching her cardigan at her throat, and peered inside.

It was a glorious tall red bird with a bright yellow crest of feathers that brushed the top of the cage when the animal turned on its low perch. It had dark eyes rimmed with turquoise, and those eyes glared into Helen's.

The bird spoke again in the same warning tone. "I'm serious. Go home. Now. Or I'll have to turn you into a fussy gray pigeon with rheumy eyes that will live the rest of its days on the cupola of your aging gray house there on the corner. Now GO! Shoo!"

Helen fled back across the street to her house, slammed the door behind her, and whipped the curtains closed across her front windows for the first time in 45 years.

***

Gerard Ferrell had received word at two o'clock that the delivery to his home was complete. He worried about the bird being outdoors on this cool, misty day, not to mention visible to anyone passing by. So as soon as his last appointment at the watch repair shop was complete, he flipped the sign on the door from "Open" to "Closed" and headed for home.

His wife, Portia, would be tied up late at work due to having to supervise children waiting for their rides home from the after-school program. This normally wasn't in her duties as the elementary school's front-desk secretary, but the program's head teacher, Julia Fetterman, had called in sick and the whole program was being managed that afternoon by her young assistant, who desperately needed help. And that meant Gerard had no backup to care for the bird.

As soon as Gerard got home, he picked up the cage from the front stoop and brought it in. Speaking apologetically to its scarlet-feathered occupant, he removed the cage cover. He decided the cage belonged in the corner of the living room, which meant he had to move the sofa and both heavy end tables to make space beside their large, potted fiddle leaf fig. The fig, named Norbert, hated being moved at all and would announce its grave disappointment by drooping dramatically within an hour of detecting any change whatsoever in its location. Hence, the need to move all the furniture instead. When he finished, Gerard wiped his sweating forehead with the back of his hand and collapsed into an overstuffed club chair. He lifted his gaze to the bird, hoping she found the location acceptable. The tall bird was looking directly at him and settled her wings with a slight ripple through her shoulders.

"You and your wife may call me Edwina, but I'd prefer it if you would train your children to refer to me as Miss Sedgwick, both when addressing me directly and anytime they speak about me. I told my account representative to make sure this was understood before I arrived, but one never knows."

"Yes, yes, of course. Thomas will be very consistent about it, he's the diligent sort; but you may need to remind Jasmine a few times. She's still a bit flighty," Gerard said. Thomas was a seventh grader at Smithson Junior High School and Jasmine attended the same elementary school where her mother worked. Jasmine liked to be called Jazzy, though no one in her family had ever referred to her by any name other than Jasmine. Or Jasmine Elizabeth, if she was being difficult.

Edwina Sedgwick had been sent to serve as a tutor for Thomas. She had been chosen by a reliable source in Gerard's northern European network after Gerard described how Thomas was struggling to learn geometry, as well as his entry-level energy work in Frisian. Certain projects required a decent appreciation of geometry and physics, lest the forces involved begin to ricochet, interacting unpredictably and ending up where they ought not go. Whenever the family went back to the Netherlands, Thomas and Jasmine did fine switching to Dutch in everyday life, but Old-World Intentions were always expressed in the original "lost" language of Frisia, which wasn't written anywhere to begin with. Difficult for visual learners. Inaccuracy, even in dialect, could be problematic, or at the very least, ineffectual.

It helped his networking that Gerard was a well-known Time Keeper. In his Old-World circles, Gerard was known for having the unusual ability to keep track of people across time so that when they were assigned another round of earthly life, he could try to help make sure the souls were placed in the right location with the right people. It wasn't an exact science by any means. Everyone did their best. Even for those with solid Old-World abilities, communication with leadership on the other side of life wasn't perfect. Gerard hadn't sought the role of Time Keeper—no one did. He had fallen into it, more like encountering a family duty when you're an only child.

Sometimes the "right" assignments for a subsequent lifetime weren't easy ones. People thought it was all a happy affair, giving parents a child, but some of the matches were agonizing for either the parents or the child, and Gerard lost a great deal of sleep in the process. The final choices weren't up to him, of course, but sometimes none of the options he offered felt good. Those cases pained him for weeks.

Gerard's lighter duty was when young couples in love who had Old-World lineage wanted to meet with him to discuss their future children's future families. They came, hoping for a good array of potential matches in the area for their children, in the event the little tykes eventually wanted to marry.

He always started by orienting them to the ground rules. In the end, they would have little influence. Parents could give Gerard their input, but then they had to back off. He had so many variables to consider, and what they thought they wanted wasn't given all that much weight by the higher powers. Plus, modern life was what it was, and young people here were driven toward independence as though it would be their salvation. They had no idea what they were missing by having dashed some of the old customs, like matchmaking, to bits.

Gerard would cut that rant short when he caught himself lamenting reality and its limitations, including his own. He could try to help. He knew relationships went better when people had at least been friends in a former life and not mortal enemies. My, oh, my, he had stories to tell about some of the dreadful matches that had unfolded at the hands of inexperienced Time Keepers who mistook the intense energy of sworn enemies for enthusiastic romantic potential. It could be a thin line, but with a little diligence, one should be able to avoid setting up those proximity parameters again in another time.

Edwina was looking at the grandfather clock in the corner of the living room and cleared her throat to get Gerard's attention. He was staring vacantly off into space, lost in thought, which happened often when he got tired. His mind was working on two problems at once, which was never efficient. But he had a Time Keeping assignment with a deadline and he was also trying to figure out in advance how to manage Jasmine's jealousy when she found out that Miss Sedgwick was hired to help Thomas, not her. The bird's guttural "ahem" jolted Gerard back into the room, and he sat up and gave Edwina his full attention.

"When will the boy be home? I should like to get started immediately. No time to waste, or he'll fall even farther behind," she said.

"Yes, indeed, quite right. He should be here by five o'clock. He had hockey practice after school. I'll get snacks ready for both children. Thomas needs to be fed or he won't have a prayer of concentrating on your lessons."

Gerard stood quickly and went to the kitchen. He found some egg salad in the refrigerator, and a couple of apples he could slice and sprinkle with cinnamon for Jasmine. That would keep the girl happy until their mother arrived, and they could assemble dinner together.

A few minutes before five, Thomas came through the front door with Jasmine skipping along behind. Jasmine had stayed with her mother at the after-school program until Thomas came by on his way home to pick her up and walk her the rest of the way home.

"Hi, Dad," Thomas called from the front hall.

"What's to eat?" shouted Jasmine as she dropped her books and coat on the floor in the hallway and ran to the kitchen carrying a stuffed purple penguin Gerard didn't remember ever seeing before.

"Hello, son, how was hockey? Jasmine, go back and hang up your coat in the closet. Then you can have some cinnamon apples," Gerard said. Then he remembered Edwina. Trying to make eye contact with both children as they roamed the kitchen, he went on. "But first, you both need to meet our guest, er...tutor. She'll be with us for at least a few months. Manners, please."

Gerard watched gratefully as Thomas took Jasmine's hand and looked up for guidance.

"Is she here?" Thomas asked in a whisper. Gerard nodded. Thomas sighed with relief.

Gerard and Portia had told Thomas that they would get help when he came to them one evening after spending an hour in his room doing homework and then trying to hone his Old-World elementary energy skills. Mortified, Thomas had led them both back up the stairs and pushed open his bedroom door to reveal the smoking scar in the wallpaper next to his desk. He explained he had been trying to make a small stone bounce, but after the stone turned into a small streaking asteroid, he figured out that the word he had used in Frisian came out more like the word for "explode" than "bounce," and, well...that happened.

Thomas knew that his Frisian exam was coming up right before Christmas and he desperately did not want to embarrass himself in front of the other members of his class in the region. The Upper Midwest class was small, and everyone knew everyone. And their families.

Gerard walked his children into the living room and nodded toward the corner where Edwina was drawing herself up to her full, glorious scarlet height. With another slight shimmy that caused her gold crest feathers to fall perfectly in line, she lowered her eyes briefly in greeting, and raised them again when Gerard spoke to the children.

"Children, I would like to introduce Miss Sedgwick. She has come all the way from her last assignment in Amsterdam to help Thomas with his geometry and Frisian. Jasmine, if you are polite and respectful, she may be willing to answer questions about your classwork as well. But you mustn't intrude on her lessons with Thomas. And both of you, please remember that the only people who can converse with Miss Sedgwick are those in your own family. When your friends come to visit, she will appear to be a colorful pet parrot like those taken from the jungles of South America or deepest Africa. You mustn't correct their terribly mistaken beliefs. Understand?"

Thomas nodded, and let go of Jasmine's hand, which Gerard promptly grasped to keep the girl beside him. The boy then straightened his posture and walked quietly over to Edwina's cage.

"Miss Sedgwick, I am deeply grateful to you for the sacrifices you must have made to come all this way to help me. I need it. And I promise to work hard at my lessons. I have an exam coming up—"

"Yes, dear boy, I understand that your Frisian exam is just weeks—days, really—away. Shall we get started? Jasmine, dear, it is a pleasure to make your acquaintance. Now, if you both would leave Thomas with me for a bit, that would be helpful."

Edwina nodded curtly toward Jasmine and Gerard, dismissing them from the room with full authority. Jasmine was gawking and said not a word. Gerard tugged at her hand and led her away to the kitchen.

Edwina and Thomas set up a schedule of after-school geometry lessons and evening Frisian lessons in his room after supper. It was best that Jasmine did not see or overhear their Old-World Intentions work, as she would be far too tempted to try things on her own.

Jasmine had not yet been approved for preliminary assessment by the Regional Council for Old-World Arts and Apprenticeships. And her parents were still considering holding her back a year until she was behaviorally a bit more self-controlled. Jasmine might not even have Old-World vocational abilities and inclinations, except for understanding animals, which was on both sides of their lineage. Old-World vocations were concentrated in Gerard's lineage more than Portia's, though Portia had a grandmother back in Helsinki who had grown up in Russia and was also odd in all the right ways. Gerard and Portia half hoped Jasmine wouldn't have career gifts at all. They knew it could be a burden.

Meanwhile, life went on as usual beyond their front door on Henneker Street. It took a few days before Helen Thredgood opened her living room drapes again, but she decided it was irresponsible of her to simply fail to keep an eye on the neighborhood when she was the only one reliably home during the day. All the other adults were away working or too busy with their young children to pay any attention to what was going on outside their homes.

Besides, the funny business over at the Ferrells' warranted watching. Helen resumed her crocheting by the light of the big front windows, augmented, when necessary, by her high-wattage reading lamp. Minnesota days were short in late autumn.

For weeks, nothing was out of the ordinary. Mr. Ferrell left at the same time every day to go to his shop, and Mrs. Ferrell and the little girl left shortly after that for school. The boy walked himself past her house each day to the bus stop on the next block.

Helen noted that the blonde boy was unusually polite and well-mannered. Any time she was out on her front porch as he was walking to the bus stop, he would turn to face her, take off his hat if he was wearing one, bow quickly, and wish her a good day. His behavior was…courtly. Yes, that was it, courtly. Though still in possession of the round face and slightly pudgy form common to so many middle school boys before their bones took off in earnest toward manhood, he carried himself like a gentleman. A bit clumsily, given his age, but it was clearly inside him.

One morning, after one such exchange with the eldest Ferrell child, Helen left off watering her geraniums on the porch rail and walked inside, drawn most directly by a sudden thought of the family photographs hung on the wall along the stairs to her second floor. She pulled herself up along the railing to the first landing and stared at an old sepia photo she had been told was her great-grandmother and her eldest son, on her mother's side. It was the oldest photograph she had of family members in years past.

She peered at the image, which she knew was dated 1860 on the back. The boy was wearing a somber expression on his round face, which was held erect above a tight, white, high-collared shirt. He looked directly into the camera's lens, which made him appear to be looking directly at Helen. The boy was 12 or 13 and had been stuffed into a vested wool suit for whatever occasion warranted the portrait. He was blonde. And bore a remarkable resemblance to the Ferrell boy.

"Hmph," Helen said. "Curious." And with that, she walked gingerly back down the stairs to the kitchen and made herself a cup of tea.

A few weeks later, Thomas was coming home from school, walking past Helen Thredgood's house on the other side of the street, as usual. He was lost in thought, going back over the answers he'd given on his geography exam and worrying that he'd confused the location of countries around the Baltic Sea. That would be embarrassing, as it was the homeland of his forebears, and he would rather have messed things up around a different sea. The Black Sea would have been more forgivable.

It had snowed the night before, and while much had melted when the snow had turned to icy rain, Thomas noticed that Helen's front walk remained in shadow this time of year. It was still covered in six inches of heavy, wet snow. He frowned and thought of the elderly woman with concern. It would be slippery. That was dangerous for old ladies who never seemed to have stout boots or warm pants to wear in winter. Leaving it to turn to ice wouldn't do.

Thomas picked up his pace, his geography exam forgotten. He plunged into the side door of the garage and dropped his books on his father's workbench. Grabbing a snow shovel, he crossed the street and tromped back up to the corner lot to shovel Mrs. Thredgood's walk.

Half an hour later, he had the entire sidewalk shoveled down to the concrete, from the end of the 1200 block of Henneker Street, past her driveway and mailbox, and on to the beginning of the next lot, which had already been shoveled. He was mopping his brow and opening the front of his jacket to cool off when he heard Mrs. Thredgood's front door pop open and push against the snow that had collected on her front porch. Thomas looked up, nodded his head in greeting, and waved.

Helen was impressed.

"Young man, come over here," she called out. Thomas nodded again and slogged through the still-drifted snow of the walkway that led to her front porch, standing at the bottom of her stairs.

"Yes, ma'am?"

"You are kind to do my shoveling, and I am grateful. The man I usually hire has taken ill. Might I ask what your fee is?"

"Fee?" Thomas asked, confused.

"Yes, of course, the payment you expect for your services," she responded.

"Oh, no, ma'am. You don't have to pay me. I was just worried because your walk was still buried, and I didn't want you to slip and fall. I'm sorry it's taking me so long. The snow's heavy. I'll do your driveway, too, before I go home, and clear off your porch steps. Unless you don't want me to, of course." Thomas looked up at Mrs. Thredgood, concerned that he might have overstepped his bounds.

"No, no, that would be lovely. You really are a dear boy. What is your name, by the way? I know you're a Ferrell, but we've never formally met," Helen said.

"I'm Thomas. My sister is Jasmine. My dad and mom are Gerard and Portia Ferrell. And you're Mrs. Thredgood, right? I asked my dad a while ago," Thomas replied.

"Yes, that's correct. Mrs. Thredgood. Well, Thomas, I am delighted to meet you and grateful for your help. I have cinnamon oatmeal cookies in the oven that I need to take out. Would you like some when you're done?"

"Oh! That would be wonderful!" Thomas suddenly realized he was famished, having never made it inside for his usual after-school snack. Thomas finished shoveling and accepted a small paper sack containing three warm cinnamon oatmeal cookies from Helen Thredgood. He apologized that he couldn't stay to chat, because his tutor was waiting for him at home for his special lessons. He almost said "Frisian" lessons but swallowed the word after just getting out the "F." He didn't know Mrs. Thredgood well enough to get into all that.

It was the beginning of an acquaintance between Helen and Thomas that, much to her surprise, she enjoyed. Because Thomas was so, well, normal, and polite, Helen had fully convinced herself that the peculiar incident with the large red bird on the Ferrells' front stoop must have been an allergic reaction to something in that unusual organic tea she had purchased on a whim at the checkout counter of the florist's shop.

***

Late one February evening, Gerard and Portia sat at their kitchen table in quiet conversation. They had tucked Jasmine into bed and checked to make sure Thomas was finishing his homework without undue difficulty. They needed to talk. They were beginning to have an inkling about Thomas's unique gifts. Something had happened again today that was leading them to believe he might be a Messenger.

The gift normally manifested first among friends and family members where relationships were close, and at least mostly loving. And the early events were nothing earth-shattering. As they spoke, they identified another event, the first.

"Remember when we had Thomas with us downtown that Saturday, when Jasmine was at Emily's birthday party? Thomas kept reminding us that Jasmine's birthday was the next week, and that we should get her something special because turning five was a big deal. He was a fifth grader that year, so in his world, a big kid," Portia said. "Remember how protective he was of the little kids? How proud he was of being a crossing guard?"

"Yes, yes, I do remember that. He had that orange sash with the bib that he put on to stand at the corner opposite Mrs. Henley to make sure the kids all waited until there weren't any cars around," Gerard replied, nodding.

"We went into the pet supply store to get hay pellets for Thomas's guinea pig, and he was insistent that we should buy a special fishbowl for Jasmine that had pink coral painted on the sides. We ignored him because she had expressed absolutely no interest at all in fish. Then the next week the library lady came to her classroom and read that story—remember the one? *Freddy the Fish Goes to Town,* I think it was. And she became absolutely obsessed with getting a goldfish. She was relentless," Portia recalled.

"Yes, that's right, we ended up going back to the pet store and getting her the goldfish, and Thomas picked out the bowl. It was the one with the coral printed on the side, and she loved it. We still have that bowl somewhere, don't we? Or did I take it to the shop? There was something I needed it for..."

Gerard started to get that far-off look, and Portia knew she was about to lose him.

"It hardly matters, Gerard. The point is, he knew. Thomas knew Jasmine was going to become desperately interested in fish, and that she would love that bowl. Before she knew she cared a thing about fish. I think that was the first time, don't you?"

Gerard nodded, then leaned over to look at what Portia was trying to show him on her phone. It was a text that Thomas had sent to her. It just read, "I'm worried about the chicks."

Portia had seen it around noon while she was in the middle of answering calls to the school's switchboard and racked her brain to figure out what Thomas meant. She knew he wasn't supposed to be using his phone at school in the middle of the day unless it was an emergency, and this couldn't be an emergency, so she didn't respond beyond a quick "Okay, love you."

Shortly after lunchtime, a leak had developed in the ceiling of the school library beneath an area where the snow was backed up on the roof. She'd been asked to come and help move books out of the way of the dripping water. And she'd spotted a second leak that was directly over a little table with a heavy cardboard box and a heat lamp set low over incubating chicken eggs. It was there to spur interest among the children in a display of books about baby animals. Two of the chicks were just hatching. Portia had picked up the entire table with the incubation box and moved it safely to another spot by an outlet and plugged their heat lamp back in.

Then she whipped her phone out of her pocket and looked again at the text from Thomas.

When she got home from school, Portia had gone upstairs to Thomas's room and asked how he knew about the roof leaks at the elementary school. He'd just looked at her with a puzzled expression and said that he didn't know anything about a roof leak. Then he asked again if the chicks were okay. She explained what had happened and he just nodded and said, "Well, that's good then, they're safe," and went back to working on his history assignment.

Portia looked at Gerard across the table. Their eyes met and they smiled at each other.

"It suits him, doesn't it?" Gerard asked her. "Messengers are often such gentle souls, and he's always been kind-hearted, hasn't he?" He reached across the table and gave Portia's hand a squeeze. "I'm glad he isn't becoming a Time Keeper. It would be hard on him, you know?"

Portia nodded and smiled, a bit sadly. "Messengers don't always bring good news, though, do they? He'll have to get used to that, too, as he gets older."

Later that night, after they'd both crawled into bed, Gerard and Portia talked about who they knew back in the Netherlands who might be a good connection for Thomas. Someone who might know an older Messenger under whom Thomas could serve his apprenticeship. Gerard had yawned and gently settled his arm around Portia's shoulder, reminding her they still had a few years to sort it out.

Another few months passed and the steel grip of Minnesota's winter began to loosen. It was early April, and the days were longer, though still raw and chilly. Patches of grass were visible in the yard where the sun had melted the snow between the two big maples in front of the Ferrells' house. Portia stepped outside to stand in the sunshine one Saturday afternoon and noticed robins building a nest up high in one of them. It was cheering, even though the winter coats would not be put away for another month.

Portia was glad they lived on the north side of the street because the sun hit the front of the house and filled the living room with light through its south-facing windows; and the ice melted more quickly from the front stoop. Along the houses on the other side of the street, long stretches of sidewalk were still in shadow all day and could be treacherously slick. Their neighbors on the south side of Henneker Street were religious about clearing snow and spreading sand and salt to deal with it, and she was glad that Thomas had taken it upon himself to make sure Mrs. Thredgood's walks were cleared for her in a timely way.

Helen Thredgood was prim and reserved toward Gerard and Portia, but Portia thought that was just because she was one of the last old-timers on the block. It must be hard to have all your old friends and neighbors move away or die; and to have new people move in and change things all the time. She took a liking to Thomas, anyway.

Jasmine had told Portia once that the other kids her age were afraid of Mrs. Thredgood and thought she was mean. They used to dare each other to step on the edge of her well-kept lawn when they ran by in the summer, holding their breath in case there was something she put into the air that would turn them all to stone. At Halloween, they made up all kinds of stories about what Mrs. Thredgood put into the giant black iron cauldron they just knew she kept bubbling on her stove. They talked about the long, flowing purple robes she surely wore at night, and one girl said she thought they were covered in stars and strange shapes that shimmered under the moonlight.

Portia kept quiet, holding back her annoyance about the ideas left in children's minds from television and movies that made a mockery of Old-World powers and portrayed them as something malevolent. She understood Halloween as simply a popular tradition of fun. She'd call it all silliness, but it bothered her to see how it eroded Thomas's confidence and left him feeling self-conscious and peculiar. She knew the same could happen to Jasmine if she turned out to have any of the special ways. But Jasmine and her friends were too young to even try to explain how connected everything really was, or how the energies of life had powerful patterns of their own; and how all of that should be cherished and respected. Most people were just afraid of what they didn't understand, and Portia was more comfortable than most with mystery.

Portia sometimes wished they could speak more frankly of such things at church, but Gerard's Dutch Presbyterians preferred to keep their faith a bit more buttoned up and tidy than Portia's people. Both of Portia's parents came from the lake country northeast of Helsinki and were nominally Lutherans, like nearly everyone else she knew. But Portia always loved the small oil painting her father kept in his study of Ukko and Kuu, the old Finnish gods of the sky and moon.

The picture was a cause of disagreement with her more traditionally devout mother. Portia would ask her father about Ukko and Kuu and why he kept their picture there, and he would wave her off, just saying, "Well, one never knows anything for sure," or, "Life is more than we know, and the old ones had their ways, too." It was only as she got older that her father spoke about his personal gifts. When she told him that she could understand what the forest animals were saying to one another, he gave her a big hug and told her not to talk about it too much to her mother, as she might find it unsettling. When her ability only progressed, he quietly introduced her to some others in their region with similar gifts. That's how she had met Gerard. He was the son of one of her father's friends in Holland, and they had fallen in love at seventeen, never to part.

All of this had flown through Portia's head when Jasmine talked about what the children were saying about their elderly neighbor. What mattered in the moment was making sure Jasmine understood that poor Helen Thredgood was just an elderly widow with little else to do but keep track of everything going on in the neighborhood. Some older people just had a habit of managing change and the chaos of children through occasional expressions of smoldering dismay and generic disapproval. She sighed and told Jasmine to be nice to Mrs. Thredgood at every opportunity and know that she was a better person for choosing to do so.

Portia's philosophy was that you can't go wrong with kindness.

When Thomas came home from hockey practice late that Saturday afternoon, he was terribly agitated. She could tell from the moment he came through the front door.

"Thomas, what's wrong? Did something happen at practice?"

"No, Mom. But something is wrong with Mrs. Thredgood. I've felt it all afternoon. Would you come over to her house with me? I need to see if she's okay," Thomas said, his forehead furrowed deeply in worry.

Portia felt a surge of sympathy for Thomas in all his sensitivities. She wished she could reassure him and tell him to make himself a sandwich, but then again, maybe he knew something she didn't.

"Of course, son, let me get my coat," she said.

"Hurry, okay? I'll meet you out front. Is Dad coming home soon?"

"Your father is at the shop until four o'clock today, but it's three now, so soon. Why?"

"Never mind, just hurry!"

Portia threw on her parka and jammed her feet into her boots at the door and went out to join Thomas. They hurried up the street and crossed short of the corner, with Thomas making his way up her driveway ahead of his mother and ringing Helen's doorbell. Portia caught up to him on the porch and put her hand on his shoulder.

No one came to the door.

Thomas rang the doorbell again and peered through the narrow rectangular window beside the door, but had trouble seeing through the sheer white curtain that covered it. He looked around to his mother, concern deepening into an almost frantic anxiety.

"Mom, what should we do? She's always home," Thomas said.

"Thomas, we don't know that. She may have just gone to the store, or perhaps she's off visiting family," Portia said, trying to reassure him. But she had already absorbed some of Thomas's certainty that all was not well.

"Mom." Thomas said it as though he were the 45-year-old in this exchange, telling Portia she was being ridiculous.

"Okay, I'm sorry. You need to trust your instincts. Does Mrs. Thredgood have a back door?"

"Yeah, it's off the kitchen," Thomas replied. He took off running around the side of the house, into the shadows beneath the tall pines that stood between Helen's house and the neighbor's. Portia followed, placing her booted feet into the holes in the crusty snow Thomas had left as he headed toward the back of the house. She heard him call out.

"Mrs. Thredgood! Mrs. Thredgood, are you there?"

Portia caught up to Thomas again, seeing him peering through the small panes of the back door into what must have been her kitchen. Then she heard him let out a breathy, frightened squeal before he grabbed hold of the doorknob, pulling it fiercely.

"Mom! Call 911!"

Helen Thredgood was sprawled on the floor of her kitchen in her gray slacks and her cardigan, her house slippers askew. She had been there for several hours, having slipped on a little puddle of water that her housecleaner had left on the polished hardwood that morning. She was able to move her arm to wave a hand, indicating she most definitely wanted them to come in.

Thomas met the fire department ambulance at the curb and led the EMS workers to the back door where Portia had remained, talking to Helen through the door. Thomas burst into the kitchen the moment the men had broken one of the windowpanes to unlock the door and he slid to the floor beside Helen to pick up her hand and squeeze it.

"It's all right, Mrs. Thredgood, I'm here now. I knew you needed help, and we're all here to help you now. It's going to be okay," Thomas said in a rush.

"Thank you so much, Thomas; you are a faithful friend and a gentleman, as well," Helen said, before promptly passing out from the pain. She had broken a hip and sprained both her wrist and shoulder, trying to stop her fall.

Portia called Gerard and told him she was going to the hospital with Thomas to stay with Helen Thredgood, who had taken a bad fall. Gerard agreed to come by the hospital as soon as he could leave, and would pick up Jasmine at her friend's house, which was on the other side of town.

When Gerard reached the main entrance to Fairview Hospital and began to follow the signs to the emergency department, he noticed a familiar woozy feeling and saw a thready bluish light appear around the heads of roughly every fifth person he passed. These were people, he knew from experience, who weren't on their first trip through life. Older souls were often drawn to healthcare professions, where matters of life and death were a bit more matter of fact. Gerard shook it off and kept walking as quickly as he could. Portia had sounded distressed, and he knew Thomas would be as well.

Usually, when Gerard wasn't in the mood to entertain communications related to his work as Time Keeper, he could shut it off until a more convenient time. It was a bit like sending a message from your boss to voice mail on your day off, and mentally telling yourself you'll call her back as soon as you can get free.

But as he rounded a corner and headed past the entrance to the hospital cafeteria, he saw more than just the usual pale-blue light. He saw people doubled, both here and now in their lab coats and carrying their clipboards, and with their shadowed former selves, still half attached. Gerard could see what they looked like when they were last here. Some people were the opposite gender, some wore top hats and tails, there were a few nurses in bloodied, war-time smocks who had clearly done this same work before. Gerard had to step aside for a burly orderly pushing a gurney whose shimmering past self was equally burly but wearing a thick Norse fur coat and boots, carrying some sort of bludgeon, trying to keep people out of the way.

This hadn't happened in a while, and Gerard was unsettled. He stepped out of the hallway into an alcove where he saw the entrance to a men's room. No one was inside, much to Gerard's relief. Staring into the mirror, he took a deep breath to compose himself. Though he had come to the hospital to comfort his wife and son, and his elderly neighbor, some other duty awaited. He splashed some water on his face, dried it, and combed his fingers through his hair. Turning away from the mirror, he breathed deeply again, squaring his shoulders. He knew he just needed to stay calm, and somehow, he could sort out what was his to attend to and what was not.

Gerard stepped back into the hallway and proceeded to the emergency room, stopping at the nurses' station to find out where Helen Thredgood had been taken. She was sedated in Bay 6, with her two friends. Gerard crossed the room to where he saw the curtain pulled across the wide sliding door marked "6." Helen Thredgood was lying flat in the small bed, her head resting on a thin pillow, an IV hooked up and dripping into her arm, and some other monitor blinking behind her bed. A heavy white cotton blanket was pulled up beneath her chin. Thomas sat beside the bed, holding her hand where it rested on top of the blanket. Portia was sitting in an uncomfortable chair in the corner beside a set of shelves and drawers. She stood up and came to him when he peeked around the curtain. She wanted to fill Gerard in on what was happening, but not in front of Thomas. She joined him just outside, closing the curtain behind her.

"She's stable. But she's broken her hip and is going to need surgery to pin it back together somehow. They're just waiting for an operating room to open. Gerard, Thomas knew…"

"I figured as much, just from what you told me on the phone. We're going to need to get him into an apprenticeship sooner than I'd thought, aren't we?" Gerard said.

"Yes, I think so, but for right now…Gerard, I don't have either of the gifts you both do, but there's something different about the connection Thomas has with Helen. It's as though they're related. He loves her. And she seems so comforted by his presence. Do you think…?" Portia's voice drifted off as she watched Gerard just nod.

"I do. I've been seeing people with their former selves all through the hospital. So, this must be the reason," he said. "Thomas and Helen were both here before."

Gerard looked vaguely off across the bustling emergency department, not really seeing the doctors and technicians and the movements of people from one place to the next. Portia gazed into his face and took hold of his hands.

"Are you ready to find out?" she asked.

"I suppose so. It won't really change anything here and now, but this could sure get interesting." Gerard gave Portia a quick hug and softly pushed the curtain aside.

Gerard could see his 13-year-old son, Thomas, still wearing his ski jacket and hockey team T-shirt, his hair mussed, looking into Helen's face with concern. He could also see a young man wearing a white cotton shirt with a stand-up collar and a black vest, a loosened black bow tie dangling down from his neck. Gerard placed the attire as typical of about 1840, and the boy was the same age Thomas was now. Both had round faces, blonde hair, and a stocky build.

Helen's most recent past self was also in view. Gerard saw an older woman who had lived in the early and middle nineteenth century. The frilly, high collar and hairstyle, the brooch, the black cloth of her dress was all suggestive of the period.

"Hello, son," Gerard said.

Thomas looked up. "Oh, hey, Dad. Thanks for coming. Mrs. Thredgood is hurt. She fell," Thomas said, looking back down into Helen's sleeping face.

"I know. I'm proud of you."

Portia was standing against the wall, watching Gerard and Thomas. Gerard didn't say anything more, just let the impressions made by the parallel lives before him gently resolve into a better understanding. It didn't take long. Gerard was looking at a grandmother and her grandson, from a different time. He smiled. It made perfect sense now. He looked up at Portia and nodded. He would explain in a few minutes.

Almost immediately, the curtain behind them swished back and an orderly let them know they were ready to take Mrs. Thredgood to surgery. Portia, Thomas, and Gerard could wait in the waiting room, or leave a number where they could be reached when she was out and in recovery. As soon as the orderly had wheeled Helen out of the bay, Thomas looked up at his parents with tears in his eyes.

"I'm not leaving," he said.

"We know," they chorused.

"It's okay, son," Gerard said. "We know how much you care about Mrs. Thredgood. Your mom will wait with you, and I'll go home and get your sister. We'll check in. She's going to be fine, Thomas, you'll see. It's not an uncommon injury, and she has a very sturdy temperament."

"Do you think so, really?" Thomas said, wiping the sleeve of his jacket across his face.

"I do. I wouldn't say so if I wasn't quite confident. We'll make sure she recovers well, too. Don't worry," Gerard told him. "Now, let's go to the waiting room and get you two settled."

On the way down the hall to the emergency room waiting area, Gerard leaned over to Portia and whispered what he knew. In a previous lifetime, Thomas had been Helen's grandson. Portia closed her eyes for a moment, letting the news sink in, her step hesitating. Then she continued walking forward, holding Gerard's hand, and looking at the back of Thomas's head, just in front of them.

The hours passed and Gerard was right. Helen came through surgery like a champion and was clear-headed and firm with everyone regarding her recovery process. A niece, Ann, from St. Paul was found, and the Ferrells connected with her and offered their home and support in whatever might be needed. Helen was discharged from the hospital in four days and was home from her stay in the rehabilitation facility in a month. Ann took family leave from her job and planned to stay with Helen for three more months while she regained her strength.

Thomas stayed close to Ann and Mrs. Thredgood throughout her healing and recovery process. As soon as they had the date when she would be released to go home, he was insistent that they plan a celebration. Ann agreed.

Ann and Portia planned a lovely dinner for the day after Helen came home, allowing her time to adjust to her temporary first-floor bedroom in the drawing room of the old Victorian house. With Helen's permission, Ann brought out the silver and polished it, then set the table with the lovely pale-gray porcelain dinnerware ringed with blue flowers that had been in the Thredgood family for several generations. Crystal glasses were set at each place, and linen napkins were pulled from the drawers where they had been folded away for many, many years. Portia brought over some lovely pale-blue candles, since it seemed blue was one of Helen's favorite colors.

At seven sharp, Gerard, Thomas, and Jasmine arrived. Thomas was carrying an enormous bouquet of iris and baby's breath wrapped in silver paper and Ann scooped them up, giving Thomas a big hug and telling him to come with her to the kitchen to find a vase.

Portia met Gerard and Jasmine in the foyer and took their sweaters and jackets to hang in the closet. Gerard looked around, taking in the beautiful old home for the first time. He had never been inside. The floors were original and polished to a shine. A long mirror hung along one wall of the hallway, with gold sconces on either side. The wallpaper was a soft ivory with a pale gray-and-blue floral pattern that looked both vintage and timeless. It truly was a lovely home. Gerard glanced up the stairs that led from the foyer to the second floor, admiring the dark wooden banister. Family portraits were hung along the wall, heading up to the landing.

Gerard's eyes stopped to stare when he caught sight of the sepia photograph framed on the landing, facing directly down the flight of stairs to the first floor. It was Thomas, looking at him with somber eyes, wearing a nineteenth-century woolen suit and standing beside an older woman who looked remarkably like a much, much older version of Helen. The boy in the photograph even had the same tightness around his eyes that Thomas got when he was stressed, or uncomfortable. Gerard felt electricity run from the veins in his neck into his throat and down his arms, leaving his hands trembling slightly.

"Portia?" Gerard called out, hoarsely.

"What is it, Gerard," she responded from down the hall somewhere.

"Would you please come here for a moment?"

Portia caught the strain in Gerard's voice and came back down the hall immediately, sending Jasmine into the kitchen to join Ann and Thomas. "What is it, honey?"

"Look," Gerard said, pointing up the stairs to the portrait.

"Oh, my…" Portia whispered. "You were right. We're… related, somehow."

Portia looked back up at Gerard. "Should we tell her?"

"Let's just show her, shall we?"

Gerard climbed the flight of stairs and gently took the framed photo from the wall, turning it around to examine the back. In faded cursive handwriting, he saw the date and two names: Maia Heikkinen, Jouko Heikkinen. They were Finnish.

Portia and Gerard walked slowly down the hall to the drawing room, which was the first door on the right, just past the kitchen.

"Mrs. Thredgood? May we come in?" Portia tapped on the doorframe and called into the room quietly.

"Of course, please come in," came Helen's voice.

Portia stepped into the room, followed by Gerard, carrying the framed photograph. A slender gray cat folded itself around the corner of Helen's armchair and looked up at Portia intently. In the back of her head, Portia heard it greet her with interest. "Well, hello there," the cat said in Frisian. Portia was a bit startled, but recovered, giving the cat a polite nod of recognition.

"We have something to tell you," Gerard said quietly to Helen. "I think you'll be pleased. It's something about Thomas, and, I think, you."

Portia and Gerard sat beside each other on the loveseat that had been moved opposite the armchair in the drawing room, on the other side of the temporary hospital bed. Helen was dressed and sitting in the armchair, waiting for dinner, her walker to the side. Gerard asked her a few questions about the people in the photograph, learning that Helen wasn't sure exactly who they were, but thought that the woman was her great-grandmother. And the boy, a son from that generation. They explained that the name Heikkinen was in the Ferrell family tree as well, just two generations back, in Finland, north of Helsinki.

"We think we may be distantly related," Portia said. "Or at least, you are to me and Thomas."

Helen stared at the photograph, then back at Portia and Gerard.

"You know, I thought I noticed a resemblance to the boy, your boy, months ago. That day he first shoveled my sidewalk, I came inside and went upstairs for something, and the photograph caught my attention. I remember thinking it was uncanny," Helen said.

Then she just smiled. Really smiled. For the first time that Gerard and Portia could remember.

Helen cleared her throat softly, then called out, "Thomas? Thomas, dear, would you come here, please? We have something to share with you."

Portia looked into Helen's eyes intently for a moment, then decided. "Helen, I have one more question for you," Portia said, quietly. "I hope it doesn't offend you."

"Yes, what is it?"

"Have you, at any point in your life, perhaps not since you were a very young girl…thought you might understand what animals were saying to one another, or to you?"

A hundred fleeting emotions seemed to cross Helen Thredgood's face in a whirl as she took in a sharp breath. She remembered a scene from her childhood, walking across a stone bridge over a wide brook, on a visit to a distant relative overseas who lived in a cottage in the woods. Her parents were inside. She was bored and tired and tossing leaves into the water and watching them tumble down the current. Then she spotted a pair of ducks, swimming slow circles around each other in a calm eddy near the bank below the bridge. She had heard them softly chatting. About the weather. And the challenges of finding proper nest-building supplies. Then her mother had called her inside. Helen's sense of time collapsed, and she remembered sneaking up the Ferrells' walk to look inside that peculiar cage that had been delivered to their front stoop. And that enormous, red bird. Scolding her.

Helen looked back at Portia, who was still watching her face, gently but intently.

"Why, yes…yes, I have," Helen said, her face relaxing into the loveliest expression of surprise and delight. She looked over at Gerard, who was also smiling at her, a look of tender-hearted kindness filling his eyes.

"Well, then. It seems we *are* family!" Portia placed one hand over her heart, beaming.

"Ah, there you are, Thomas, come here," Helen said, holding out her arms to the young man to give him a hug.

JONATHAN'S UKULELE

Jonathan's destiny as a musician would forever be tied to a butcher shop in Queens. One Saturday afternoon in his sixth year of life, Jonathan's mother Caroline had a lengthy list of weekend errands to run, and an equally short sum of patience left for her youngest child. Jonathan's siblings had already disappeared from the apartment for the day, and Caroline couldn't find a cousin to watch him. That meant she had to drag him along, kicking and screaming, to the butcher shop for some lamb.

Jonathan hated the butcher shop. He'd been there once before when he was four and had suffered nightmares for weeks. He was convinced that it was only a matter of time before the police hauled Mr. Kastellanos off in handcuffs, finally discovering he was the serial killer that starred in all of Jonathan's older brother Michael's bedtime stories. One look at the giant legs and loins hanging from enormous silver hooks toward the back of the shop and Jonathan's eyes had grown large as fried eggs. When he was told that the material into which fresh sausage was being pressed was intestine, Jonathan had tried to run out of the store and back into the street where it was safe.

But the second trip had changed his life. Mr. Kastellanos' butcher shop was two stops away on the subway, and a short bus ride north from the Steinway Street Station. Caroline had kept a bone-crunching grip on Jonathan's small hand as they squeezed into the crowded train that afternoon, and when they stepped off a few minutes later, the most amazing sound filled the heavy, dank air. Someone was busking along the wall on the way to the stairwell. Jonathan all but dropped to the ground, dead weight on his mother's arm, trying to make her slow down so he could take it all in.

The man behind the music had curly dark hair and the heavy shadow of a two-day beard. He looked just like Jonathan's uncles on weekends, except more serious. His sad eyes were focused on the cement somewhere in front of him, concentrating on making the music that poured from his mandolin. The sound was enchanting, echoing through the train tunnel and filling the space with a soulful Greek folk song in a minor key. Some travelers slowed as they paced by, nodding, or briefly holding a hand to their hearts. A few tossed coins into his open case. Jonathan made his mother stop so he could listen, his whole body rocking slightly, entirely transfixed.

Eventually, Caroline decided they really needed to move along, but tossed a quarter into the man's case at Jonathan's insistence. Jonathan never forgot that experience.

Caroline's brothers, Matteo and Hector, were both musically inclined. Matteo played bouzouki and Hector the aulos, and they could do everything from traditional folk music to Maroon 5 covers. For years they had been playing Saturday afternoons at their father's bar, Kosta's Taverna, just for fun. When Matteo learned about Jonathan's obsession with the busker at the Steinway Street Station, he started to put the word out.

Not long after, one of Matteo's high school friends named Theo called to say he scored a little ukulele from the Queens equivalent of a garage sale. Theo's next-door neighbor, Harry, had died suddenly, and the old man's daughters were hauling all his stuff in trash bags down five flights of stairs to the dumpsters behind the building. When Theo poked his head into Harry's apartment and spotted the case against the wall, he asked the women if he could have it. A grunt and an eye roll constituted assent.

Now, a ukulele isn't a Greek instrument, per se, but it was small enough for a boy pushing the age of seven to handle. And transitioning to bouzouki or any of the family's other stringed instruments wouldn't be difficult. Matteo began to teach Jonathan how to play the ukulele, and the little boy took to it with even more passion than he had for airplanes and dinosaurs. And every time his mother mentioned that she needed to go to the butcher shop, Jonathan begged to go along. Caroline knew how much he hated the butcher shop. Which was how she also knew that Jonathan really, really wanted to hear the mandolin man again. And about every third trip, the mandolin man would be there, strumming his heart out into the vacuous space, ignoring the smell of stale urine and damp cement, and replacing it all with beautiful music.

Jonathan practiced and practiced his ukulele. And within a year, he was good enough to play with his uncles. They had a three-man band now, and while Caroline refused to let her brothers take Jonathan with them to play down at Kosta's on Saturdays, she let them perform for family events. Jonathan loved every minute of it. He had no fear of performing in front of people, and his dramatic flair as an entertainer kept everyone laughing. But it wasn't enough.

Starting on his eighth birthday, Jonathan began badgering his mother. Jonathan wanted to play the subway. To him, it was the big time. His family wasn't wealthy, so the biggest public venue he had ever experienced was lit with garish overhead fluorescence that cast deep shadows into every corner. It was grimy and damp, but to Jonathan, the walls of square, white tile lined with gray grout and oversized film posters was the setting of miracles. The subway was Jonathan's Broadway.

Caroline's answer was always, "Maybe when you're older." Then Jonathan's negotiation skills improved. He started asking her for a date, a time when "older" would be old enough. Every day he was older, he told her, every week's worth of eternity, he was older. "When I say you're old enough is old enough," she said. He was frustrated, but not daunted. He talked to Uncle Hector. Then he talked to Uncle Matteo. He leaned on them, hard, to pressure their sister into doing the right thing. He chided them, asked them if they were afraid of their baby sister, told them he'd leave the band if they didn't talk to her.

So, one Sunday morning, Hector and Matteo went to mass at St. Joseph's and made sure they sat in the pew directly behind Caroline and her family. After the last note on the organ died, they waited until Jonathan headed off with a buddy's family for lunch at their house and Caroline's husband, Tony, was jawing in the center aisle with Father Frank. They eased out of their pew, following Caroline, and cornered her against the wall next to the confessionals. She knew trouble with those two when she saw it, and she tucked her purse under one arm and planted her free hand on her hip, fixing them with one eyebrow raised over her best baby-sister's glare.

They knew the look. And they asked her to hear them out.

They said that for Jonathan's ninth birthday they wanted to let him play down in the subway. But they said they would go with him, and she could, too. They'd make sure it was safe and find a clean spot with good lighting. They'd never be more than 10 feet away. Eventually, she gave in, after fixing them each with a stare that let them know they'd die before she granted them another favor like this.

For Jonathan's ninth birthday, Hector and Matteo brought home a heavy glass olive jar from the bar and taped a label on the inside that said "TIPS." They wrapped it in a huge box with white paper covered in gold stars. After the entire family had finished eating dinner that evening, and Jonathan had blown out all nine candles on his cake, and opened his other birthday presents, they brought out the big white box.

As he opened the box, Jonathan wondered why his dark-haired uncles looked like they were scheming. It made him wonder if something would jump out at him. Or if it was a box of those horrible sausages from the butcher shop as a joke. But when he pulled out the glass jar and read the label, his face changed from wary confusion to hope. And when he saw the subway tokens in the bottom of the jar, he looked up at the two men like they had just given him the keys to a Ferrari. They were both grinning. Jonathan looked over at his mother, his mouth gaping.

"Yes, son, you can go play the subway. *With* your uncles. Both of them. And I'm coming, too."

Jonathan leapt up from the table and ran to his mother, throwing his scrawny arms around her neck. Then he ran to both his uncles and kissed them and hugged them in turn as they slapped his back in congratulations. And Jonathan immediately extracted a date and time from them all as to when they would make it happen.

The next Sunday, Hector and Matteo came over to Caroline and Tony's apartment for lunch. They stuffed themselves on chicken souvlaki and dolmades. Caroline made a fresh pot of strong coffee, and they all had a cup while they waited for Jonathan to change. A few minutes later, Jonathan reappeared in his best jeans and a white dress shirt, a red-and-blue polka-dot bowtie clipped into the collar. This was his stage outfit. He even had a stage name: Leo Andino. He thought it sounded manly and memorable. He had even borrowed his grandmother's ancient silver label maker and carefully pressed out a little black plastic strip with LEO ANDINO in white letters and stuck it onto the outside of his ukulele case.

When Jonathan's father saw the case, he lowered his head to peer over his glasses and look more closely. He frowned, then looked from Caroline to Matteo to Hector and back to Jonathan.

"What the hell is wrong with Jonathan Theodoropoulos? It's your family name; half of Athens is related to you," Tony said, his hands raised to the ceiling, palms up. Jonathan winced. Hector and Matteo stepped in, clapping their hands on Tony's shoulders and leaning in toward his ears on both sides. They spoke to him in Greek, reassuring him it was just for playing the subway, and safer for the boy to use a fake name when performing, anyway.

Tony muttered, shook them off, and wandered toward the kitchen, snagging another piece of lemon bougatsa next to the melting ice cream on the table. Jonathan looked at his mom and uncles, who just shrugged in unison and motioned toward the door.

Caroline took the ice cream to the kitchen to put back in the freezer and they heard her say something to Tony. "Good luck, already," Tony shouted through the doorway of the kitchen without reappearing, and Caroline emerged, nodding. She went to the door, grabbed her jacket, and followed her brothers out the door with Jonathan in tow.

Jonathan was ready. He'd been working up his 15-minute set for months, hoping this day would come.

Together, the four of them walked down the street to the subway station. They huddled together in a happy knot as Jonathan led the way, one step ahead, to the platform. To make it official, they had to take the train two stops, to Steinway Street, and find just the right location that wouldn't compete with mandolin man's spot but be just as good. Even better. They ended up going to the other side of the platform, as though they were coming home already.

True to their word, Hector and Matteo scoped it all out, checking stairwells and dark corners for anyone who might cause a problem. Hector set up the little folding stool he had found in the storage closet in the basement of his apartment building. He placed it directly beneath one of the brighter overhead lights, about 30 feet away from the bottom of the stairway that led up to the street. Then Caroline, Hector, and Matteo faded discreetly away to watch from behind a concrete bench by one of the subway kiosks.

Jonathan set his case at his feet, pulled out his ukulele, hauled his olive jar to one side of the case, and rotated it carefully so those walking by could see the word "TIPS." He took a deep breath, glanced surreptitiously at his uncles where they were leaning against the kiosk like they were just waiting for the next train, and began his first solo performance as Leo Andino, ukulele maestro.

But it was not his last performance.

Leaning against a column in the shadows on the far side of the train tracks was a tall man in dark clothing holding a mandolin case. He'd been there since the little family had trundled down the stairs into the subway and started setting Jonathan up. He had a little smile that quirked the corner of his mouth. He recognized the boy. And he noticed that the first song the boy played was the same song he opened with every time he came down to the subway to play his mandolin. The boy had been listening. And he had talent.

The man with the mandolin was normally a cellist with the New York City Ballet Orchestra. His name was Nicholas Diakos. For fun, he also gave private lessons to promising young musicians who found their way to the newly re-established Folklore Center, down in the heart of Greenwich Village.

Nicholas had arrived in New York City from East Macedonia, Greece, with his parents, two uncles, an aunt, and a raft of cousins when he was just five years old. They brought their music with them, hoping to leave abject poverty behind. It had taken quite a while. But he had grown up surrounded by music and song and the joy of performing for others. He had learned to play every instrument in sight. And had won a full scholarship at the Manhattan School of Music, graduating from their classical program in strings and harp. His career quickly soared.

But he never forgot where he came from. He never forgot his first teachers—the unruly, fun-loving, hardworking array of music-loving Greek siblings, cousins, uncles, and aunts, all assimilating to various degrees in the United States of America.

Nicholas watched Jonathan run through his set three times, grinning from ear to ear at the sound of each coin pinging into his olive jar from passersby who appreciated the boy's earnest efforts. His second and third set were even better than his first because the boy relaxed, and his confidence grew as he heard his own music echoing back to him off the sound system of the subway walls. Nicholas felt his heart taking him right back to his boyhood.

When the boy finished, Nicholas watched the two middle-aged men and the woman wrap him up in huge hugs, giving him celebratory slaps on his small back and high-fives as though he'd just won over all of Carnegie Hall. He noticed that one of the men had glasses held together with tape at the nose, and the boy's jacket was neatly patched at the elbow. He suspected they were not financially wealthy, but the love and joy he could see were both palpable and familiar. He smiled again, and, fading back into the shadows, headed back up to street level.

Three weeks later, Nicholas had a Sunday afternoon free and felt like playing the subway, where he could be anonymous and play simply for pleasure—his own and others'. He collected his mandolin, which was still the instrument he loved the most, and took the train up to Steinway Street. As he jogged down the stairs to the train tracks, he heard the bright sound of someone playing a ukulele. He wondered immediately if it was the boy.

Nicholas slowed his pace and followed the sound. He was right. It was the youngster he had heard play a few weeks earlier. He looked around at the stream of people flowing by and noticed, again, two sturdy men with black, curly hair leaning against a post, trying to be invisible. But they were watching the boy, grinning the entire time, periodically glancing around protectively. A father and an uncle, or a family friend. This time, the boy's mother wasn't with them.

When the boy began his second piece, he sang the lyrics while playing. His voice was clear, strong, high, and so far, without a hint of cracking. He was a natural entertainer. He sang the words as though telling a story, his voice and expression playful, full of heart, mischievous or flirtatious in turn, as the story evolved through the verses. Nicholas thought to himself that the boy was going to have a bevy of girls vying for his attention as he got older.

Nicholas hung back, waiting for Jonathan to finish. As the last chord settled and his family members moved forward to help him pack up, Nicholas stepped into the circle of light around them. Jonathan was standing with his ukulele held loosely at his side and looked up, a bit startled. Understanding the role the older men had, Nicholas shook each of their hands first, introducing himself. He didn't expect any of them to recognize him by face or name. They would never have had the money to buy tickets to the ballet, even if they were inclined.

But Jonathan recognized him. His small mouth opened, and his eyes went wide. He reached up to shake Nicholas' hand, following his Uncle Hector's cues. As the oldest, Hector spoke to introduce Jonathan.

"Nicholas, this is our nephew, Jonathan Theodoropoulos. Jonathan, this is Nicholas Diakos. He plays mandolin and cello. He wants to say hi. It's okay, you can talk to him." Hector motioned between the tall man and Jonathan.

"I know you," Jonathan said. "You're the mandolin man who plays on the other side of the tracks. Usually on Saturdays. You're amazing. You're why I wanted to play. I've been coming here with my mom for ages when she goes to the butcher shop up the street and I always, always look for you." Jonathan's words were rushed, his eyes bright with awe. He was finally getting to meet his hero.

"Good to meet you, Jonathan. So—Leo is your stage name?" Nicholas pointed at the name stuck on the side of Jonathan's ukulele case. Jonathan looked embarrassed in the presence of a real performer.

"No, I mean, yeah, I guess. It's just made up, though. I thought it sounded cooler than my real name," Jonathan replied.

"You should be proud of your real name. It's a strong Greek name. Andino is a good one, too, but be proud of your heritage. Theodoropoulos—do you know what it means? In Greek?"

"Yeah, my dad said it means 'gift of God,' right?" A shy smile crept across Jonathan's face.

"That's right. And I'm sure that's how he feels about you. Your mom, too," Nicholas replied. Hector and Matteo smiled at Nicholas appreciatively.

"So, Jonathan, what I really came over here to say is that you're good; you're really good. Both your instrumentals and vocals. I'm impressed. Have you been performing for a while now? Because you have terrific stage presence, too." Jonathan's eyes grew wide and he stood up straighter. He grinned up at his uncles with pride, then turned back to Nicholas, adjusting the clip on his bow tie.

"Yeah…I mean yes, sir, thank you, sir. I've been playing for a while. My uncles taught me, and we have a band together. My Mom only lets me play for family so far. But we're hoping to get some bigger gigs soon," Jonathan said, standing up a little taller. He suddenly remembered he was the front man for the band and needed to play the part. "We can handle more, for sure. When my whole family gets together, they make a pretty big audience all on their own, so we're cool playing for bigger groups and bigger…venues. Uncle Hector and Uncle Matteo have been playing at my grandpa's bar in Queens for years. It's called Kosta's. There are tons of people there on Saturdays." Jonathan nodded assertively, squaring his small shoulders and looking Nicholas in the eye like Matteo and Hector had taught him.

Matteo and Hector both started to laugh and squelched it behind their fists. Hector faked a cough. Jonathan was such a little mover and shaker.

"Sweet, man, that's cool," Nicholas said, nodding encouragingly. "Here's the thing, Jonathan. I'm kind of a performer, too, in a little orchestra uptown. With my cello. And I love playing traditional stuff, too, like what you've heard me play down here. I give lessons. And I know some people at one of the music schools in the city. If you want to, and your family says it's okay, I might be able to get you a deal at the music school. Seriously, Jonathan, you're really that good. You're as good as any kid I've ever worked with." Jonathan whirled around to face his uncles, his mouth opening and closing like a fish out of water, beaming with stunned excitement.

Nicholas looked at Matteo and Hector and quietly said, "I mean it." Then Nicholas pulled out his wallet and fished out three business cards, handing one to Hector, Matteo, and Jonathan. They looked down at the cards and saw the logo for the New York City Ballet, with "Orchestra" beneath in italics. Nicholas' name appeared below, with a phone number and Twitter handle. Matteo and Hector looked at each other in disbelief for just a moment, then turned and shook Nicholas' hand again, thanking him for his kindness.

When they got back to Caroline and Tony's apartment, Tony had gone to the store. Matteo and Hector sent Jonathan to his room to change clothes and grabbed Caroline to tell her about their meeting with Nicholas.

"Caroline, you really should call this guy Nicholas. He was serious. He thinks Jonathan is good enough to go to a music school," Hector said.

Matteo chimed in, "He talked like there might be financial aid available. Who knows? You don't know if you don't call, right?"

Caroline closed her eyes, then looked to the ceiling of their small apartment as though God were there, above the fan rotating slowly in the lingering heat that had leached out from the kitchen into the dining room.

"Guys. Don't get his hopes up, okay? We can barely pay for the supplies to keep him in public school. I can't imagine..." Caroline shook her head, thinking about how many days there were untill the end of the month when Tony would get paid again and she'd take another check from her catering business. It was always tight the last week, even if they never talked about it.

Jonathan reappeared and pulled up a chair next to his uncles, across from his mom. He looked at Hector, then Matteo, then his mom, trying to read the room.

"Have you told her?" Jonathan asked his uncles.

"Yes, we have, Jonathan. But she and your dad will have to talk, and it'll be up to them to decide if talking to Mr. Diakos is the right thing to do," Hector said, trying hard not to let his feelings show.

Jonathan looked at his mom, hopefully. But she was looking down at the table, her face tight and closed. The odds of going to music school looked no better than the odds of playing at his grandpa's bar on Saturdays with his uncles. He pushed his chair back and spoke across the table.

"It's okay, Mom. I know we don't have a ton of money. It's expensive. Don't worry about it," Jonathan said, as evenly as he could manage. "Thanks for letting me play the subway. Thanks, Uncle Hector, Uncle Matteo, for going with me today. I had fun."

With that, Jonathan excused himself and headed back to his room, saying he had homework. His shoulders slumped as soon as he left the dining room. Matteo let his head drop to the table with a thunk. Seeing Jonathan so dejected after the high of meeting his "Mandolin Man" killed him. Hector pushed back his chair and clapped his brother on the back. "C'mon, Mattie," he said, "time to go."

The two brothers gave their sister a hug and let themselves out. But Matteo had slid one of Nicholas Diakos' business cards under Caroline's purse on the end of the table. He couldn't help himself.

Caroline got herself a cup of coffee and sat down again at the table. She slowly slid the card toward her. She decided to pray about it. Maybe if she let the question alone for a few days, the right path would become clear.

She was used to letting difficult issues float around the apartment for a while after she'd lit a candle or two, inviting generations of Greek mothers to help her think, no one pressing her for an answer. Over the next week, she kept seeing her grandmother's shrugs and nods in her imagination, the kind of shrugs that said, "Why not? What can it hurt to talk to the man?"

Caroline called Nicholas Diakos one day while Jonathan was at school.

Jonathan started lessons. Diakos quietly offered Tony and Caroline the pride-preserving rate of $2.00 a session, knowing they wouldn't accept free lessons. Diakos took a lot of joy in Jonathan's joy and in the process of helping the boy build his talents. The lessons prepared him well to be accepted to music school after junior high.

The family grew close to Nicholas over time and got to know some of the other musicians in the ballet orchestra. When Jonathan turned 16, his mother finally let him play with his uncles down at the family's bar in Queens.

Before Jonathan could graduate from New York City's Manhattan School of Music, he had to do a senior performance. All of Nicholas' friends from the orchestra and the Folklore Center pitched in to buy tickets for everyone in Jonathan's family who wanted to come. The Theodoropoulos clan filled three rows, from one side of the stage to the other. Their friends and patrons from Kosta's Taverna filled four more.

Nicholas Diakos performed that night as an honored guest of the school, just before Jonathan took the stage. He responded with warmth and humility to the standing ovation he received from the crowd.

Jonathan sang and played beautifully. It was a piece he composed himself that featured three different traditional Greek instruments rotated into refrains. When he finished and took his bow, the front half of the audience leapt to their feet, cheering. The applause rapidly became laced with noises more commonly found at football games. Jonathan had to step off stage to ask Nicholas how to handle his family after the third ovation filled the theater with raucous stomping and whistles for a solid five minutes.

Nicholas laughed and said, "Take the microphone and invite them all out for a drink. I'll meet everyone at Kosta's. And I'll buy."

FINDING GRACE

Chris

Chris Tomlinson stood in the doorway to her own office, looking around one last time. The morning light reflected brightly off the modern glass and brushed nickel of her desk, and the pale birchwood shelf units gleamed.

She had left an abstract oil painting on the one wall that wasn't glass, knowing she would have no need of it where she was headed. It suited this Michigan Avenue high-rise address, with its slashes of bright yellow, thick orange rectangles, and contrasting grays. It was sized to fit the space. She wondered if the next occupant of the office would even notice the subtle dappling of lavender in the gray that had been what drew her to the piece originally. Who knows, she thought to herself, they might replace it with one of those dreadful meeting space white boards.

With that repellant thought, Chris turned away. She had worn her favorite summer power suit, a cream-colored skirt and jacket with a subtle herringbone weave to the fabric. She was wearing three-inch spike heels that matched the suit and had a creamy gray leather clutch resting in one hand.

She had already turned in her security clearance card and key, and she knew her IT director would have dutifully wiped her thumbprint file from the entry reader that limited access to their secured files and the server room. It was time to bid her CEO adieu and leave.

Chris exchanged proper expressions of mutual gratitude with Mr. William

Shaheen. On her way out, she snagged a hanger from the guest closet and went down five floors to where her first office at the company had been located. Security was far more lax on this floor. She stepped through the door to the office suite and grinned at Sally Abrams, who had been in that spot behind the worn reception desk for at least 20 years. They were good friends now.

Sally smiled back, a little sadness in her eyes, and came around to give Chris a big hug. "Girl, I can't believe you're leaving all this joy and delight for the wild West of your crazy forebears," Sally said, her smooth alto reflecting both sharp intellect and proud Chicago Black Southside dialect.

"I am going to miss you something fierce, Mizz Sally Abrams," Chris said with great affection. "The joy and delights, not so much. The paycheck, probably, but life is cheaper where you can hunt for dinner."

Clucking amused disapproval, Sally stepped back toward the wall where Chris had stowed a giant, well-worn backpack on its sturdy aluminum frame. Grunting dramatically as she hefted it, Sally brought it over to Chris, who was already reaching for it.

"I certainly hope the means for securing your hunted dinner are *not* inside this filthy thing," Sally said, stepping back and fixing Chris with a stern gaze.

Chris smiled. "Don't worry. All that is safely stowed in my truck. One more thing, Sally." Chris dropped her voice to a more conspiratorial level. "If you know any good women who are champing at the bit for a big promotion, send them to the last stall in the ladies' room in about 10 minutes."

Chris winked and waggled the hanger in her free hand. Sally rolled her eyes and looked at the ceiling, muttering an invocation for divine guidance.

"You take care, okay? Seriously. I want to see you again in one piece, not absent an arm donated to some mountain beast out there," Sally chided, returning to her seat behind the desk. "And yes, Laura Federici is about due for a big raise and would look really nice in that little size 10. Leave the shoes, too, if you're serious."

"It's a deal," Chris said, lifting the pack to her shoulder. "You take care, too, Sally. You know you mean the world to me."

The two women exchanged their traditional air kiss and Chris headed for the bathroom in the hallway to change.

She emerged in jeans, a purple polo shirt of indeterminate brand, and light hiking boots. She took the elevator to the lobby and called out a greeting to the startled security guard who had never seen her looking like anything other than a CEO-to-be.

"So long, James Marcus! Keep everybody safe!"

Chris shoved open the big glass doors to the street and checked the windshield of her Ford F250, incongruously parked in front of the high-rise office building, its stock trailer taking up two more spaces in what was normally a taxi queue. No ticket, she thought. Excellent. James Marcus had done her one last favor in fending off Chicago's finest before they issued her a hefty fine for her very illegal parking.

She heaved the backpack up into the passenger seat and jogged around to the driver's side. She started the engine and grinned when she heard its satisfying diesel roar. It was time to leave the Windy City behind and head West.

Becca

At least 30 shiny yellow-and-black striped wasps crawled over each other, adjusting their translucent wings as their fellows moved in and out of the same four-inch gap between the worn boards of the deck. They were a little sluggish in the late September chill. So was Becca MacLeod, kicked back in her favorite chair, absently watching the insects.

Normally, Becca would be swiftly preparing their demise, riffling through cans and bottles of various lubricants and poisons in the garage, snatching up the tools to take out those boards and be rid of the obviously growing nest. But this morning, all ambition had left her. She just sat, rocking slightly, her hands wrapped in the flannel tails of an ex-boyfriend's shirt. It was a nice shirt, even if he'd turned out to be an ass. She'd silently kept it right where he'd abandoned it in the coat closet, slight but satisfying compensation for those last few months of misery before she'd given him the boot.

Becca sighed, briefly recognizing her own state of immobility, and wondered if she'd ever figure out what to do next. It had been three months since she'd settled the last of her mother's estate. She had sold the house and placed her mother's antique furniture in the hands of a dealer to sell and arrange for the proceeds to be donated to the hospice that had kept both Becca and her mother sane and fairly calm those last long weeks. She was profoundly grateful to them. Besides, Queen Anne wasn't exactly her thing. She smiled to herself, looking fondly at the vaguely chair-shaped tree stump she'd axed and crudely planed. It routinely welcomed her denim-clad rear end when she was ready to take a break in the shade from projects around her little acreage in the mountains. Her retreat. Home. A place where she could breathe and forget about work for a bit.

Work, which now did not exist. She sighed again. She suffered a work ethic that was in her bones like a recessive gene for plague. But two weeks ago, she had decided she no longer wanted to be the over-achieving, boss-pleasing superstar of the public defender's office. She had spent 10 grueling years enmeshed in the worst of what human beings could do to one another. It wasn't any one thing that had pushed her over the edge. She had just woken up one Tuesday morning and realized she was profoundly tired. So she quit her job, with no effort to create next steps.

She reached for her rapidly cooling mug of coffee, looking off into the blue-gray folds of the Sleeping Elk Mountains.

The heavy rattle of a pickup truck hitting the washboard section of dirt road on the switchback below her place roused Becca from her musing. She stood, craning her neck to see around the big stand of juniper and oak that obscured her view of the road. It was an unfamiliar truck towing a trailer, and it turned off onto the road leading up into the national forest, the driver expertly handling the deep ruts that served as fair warning about the quality of the path forward.

In a few weeks, Becca would know the truck as well as she knew those that belonged to her other neighbors. It was Chris Tomlinson's Ford F250, heading to her new home in Colorado for the first time.

Chris

Chris was getting acclimated to her new home. The rental sat perched on the back of a ridge where no one would come unless given directions by her, or by the dead owner's son, Mark. Mark lived in Baltimore, a continent away, and just wanted it sold. A local property manager and real estate agent named Don Harlow now looked after the rundown cabin. Mark had been desperately hoping to get some income out of the place before it sold. Don had told him he'd list it, but due to its condition and location, Don was clear it would not rent or sell anytime soon.

Don was clear it would not rent or sell anytime soon.

Harlow was stunned when the property popped with an online inquiry. He sure didn't market it widely, since it wasn't much more than a hunter's cabin designed primarily for shelter. Getting there involved five miles of rutted dirt switchbacks, the last half of which didn't get plowed in winter. And though Mark had paid him handsomely to clean the place out, fix the plumbing and fill the propane tank, it was still barely habitable.

Chris Tomlinson had called from a downtown Chicago area code. She wanted someplace quiet where no one would bother her; and she didn't care about amenities. He'd laughed, telling her if she wanted to set up a distillery in a dry county, this was the kind of place where success might be born. She hadn't laughed, and said she'd take it for three months, maybe longer, sight unseen.

Don sent Chris the lease over email and told her to stop by the office to pick up the key when she got to town. Don added that she should just call the sheriff's office if anything strange happened out there that she didn't know how to handle. The sheriff was the only one left in the county who knew the cabin was there. Don was thinking about nosy black bears, more than anything else, and knew the guys down at the county sheriff's office would be amused but kind in their response if she rang them up, frightened out of her wits. He'd warned her, he thought, shaking his head.

But Chris knew more about what she was getting into than her Chicago skyline address suggested. She had quickly sold her Lake Shore Drive con-dominium at a ridiculous profit. It would be enough, she figured, for five years, if she was careful. She knew how to live frugally and off land just like the property she was renting. Her crazy prepper father had raised her to homestead competently in the steep rolling hills and basalt cliffs that formed the glacial beginnings of the Never Summer Range in Wyoming. She would never thank him for those bizarre and isolated years, but yes, she could get by quite well.

That became apparent to Don Harlow when Chris pulled up to get the key. He'd been expecting a convertible Volvo but saw her climb out of a Ford 4x4 with a horse trailer. She had a topo map in hand, not a GPS app or Gucci bag. Through the trailer windows he spotted a rack of heavy-duty snow tires, two large and obviously well-used toolboxes, and if he wasn't mistaken, a gun locker. Strapped securely to the far side of the trailer was a big pull-behind sled typically used with snow machines. When she caught him eyeing the array, she just said, a little irritably, "I imagine winter comes early at that elevation." He nodded, glancing away self-consciously, but never dropping his always-friendly smile. It was September, and he had figured when he'd accepted the lease that she wouldn't last the three months, scurrying back to the city when the first big snow fell in October. Now, he shifted the odds of her completing that initial lease to 50-50.

Chris hadn't found need or cause to return to town until a mid-October morning when she set up the ramp to her trailer and rolled her big snowmobile down onto the first few inches of snow. She knew she needed to check the mechanics and make sure it was running smoothly now, before the weather got more unpredictable. And, sure enough, cleaning the plug points required a wire brush she didn't have.

She headed to town in search of the local hardware store with a concise list of additional essentials written after a complete assessment of the cabin and its contents, or the lack thereof. The sky was producing a sleety mix up on the mountain, and as she wove her way down the dirt roads, the precipi-tation turned to steady, misty rain. She was glad she'd stowed her long black slicker in the space behind the front seat. She pulled it out as she parked in front of the hardware store, then stepped out of her truck.

Her attention went immediately to a child's squeal coming from the store's front entrance. A wiry man with long, stringy hair stood in the doorway. He was red in the face, the muscles in his neck and shoulders wound tight and angry. His big left hand dug into the child's shoulder while he backed through the opening, clenching a bag full of his purchases in his other hand. The child's eyes looked around wildly, and she yelped again as the man shoved her outside after she had grabbed the big door handle, trying to pull it toward herself.

The man looked up and caught Chris staring at him in disbelief at his roughness—the girl couldn't have been more than 12 or 13. She was bony and small, with long, partially braided blonde hair falling over the collar of a jacket that might have once been a pretty, pale blue.

Chris slammed her truck door, feeling protective fury well up within her, and glared at the man. She quickly stepped toward the two, trying to establish eye contact with the girl.

"Hi, sweetheart, what's your name?" Chris asked quietly as she stooped over to get to eye level with the girl. "I like your blue jacket. It brings out the blue in your eyes!" The girl looked panicked for a moment, then her eyes turned to the ground and sideways up to the man who had hold of her.

"Move it, chicken-legs." The man shoved the little girl away from the threshold and into the gravel parking lot. Chris stood, slack-jawed, gazing after the pair, and her heart lurched in her chest as the little girl looked back over her shoulder directly into Chris's eyes. The man pushed her into the back seat of an older model sedan, got into the driver's seat, and pulled out of the parking spot. Chris heard the dull thunk of door locks dropping into place.

Behind her, Chris felt someone else step out of the hardware store and join her on the paved apron, staring after the sedan as it turned south on the two-lane highway. It was a tall woman with an athletic build, short-cropped chestnut-brown hair, wearing a heavy canvas Carhartt jacket and ancient hiking boots.

"Don't suppose you got the plate," she said, her voice sober.

"Nope. Wish I had," Chris replied.

The woman pulled her eyes back off the highway and turned to Chris. "Hi. I'm Becca." Becca shoved her hand toward Chris, inviting a shake. Chris took it, nodding her head comfortably in greeting. Hardware stores were friendly, uncomplicated places.

"Chris Tomlinson. I live up the mountain past the Circle K Ranch. And you're right. That, whatever it was, was not good."

They both turned and walked back into the hardware store. Chris found what she needed for the snowmobile repair and headed back home.

Chris

Three days later, Chris had to come down the mountain again, and she was irritable about it. She kept finding things wrong at the cabin and had no patience left with Don Harlow, who ostensibly was responsible for repairs. First off, he was slow to respond. Second, he was clearly trying to put as little money or time into the place as possible. She had already made numerous proper repairs to what had obviously been cheap fixes.

Chris understood the lack of attention to the property as a business proposition. It was a long way from town, up a set of looping Forest Service roads that got really sketchy in places and weren't well-marked. The cabin had a wood stove that doubled as cooktop, the well was shallow and barely fed the plumbing to the kitchen, which must have been a 1940s luxury added to please a tired ranch wife. The bathroom was an outhouse which, thankfully, was still in one piece. The hole beneath it was plenty deep to serve. There were smoky kerosene lamps in brackets on the walls that Chris thought the original rancher might have installed early in the previous century. She had already bought solar-chargeable battery-operated LED lanterns to replace them.

When Chris took it upon herself to fix things up to her own satisfaction, she saved receipts and hoped to get a month free for her trouble at some point. Today's trek to town was to pick up a grooved joint and some pipe dope to repair the sink plumbing. She had just discovered the pipe was leaking due to a previous application of duct tape believed by someone to be sufficient. She had fumed about it for an hour and practically ripped apart the shed behind the cabin in hopes of finding the right hardware, but no luck.

It took over an hour to get to town, and she was hungry. She walked into the Sunflower Café and nodded to the sole server, responding with a thumbs up when the woman lifted a coffee pot toward her as a question. Chris took a table in the back by one of the two big plate-glass windows that looked out onto Main Street and plucked a menu from behind the napkin holder.

Movement on the sidewalk caught Chris's attention. It was the tall woman she had met at the hardware store last week, heading toward the café. Chris remembered her name: Becca something. She focused her attention back on the menu, but heard the front door swing open suddenly in a gust of wind and slam against a big pot of geraniums that sat on the front stoop.

"Oh, dang it! Sorry, Angie," Becca's voice called out from the entry.

"No worries, Becca. I've been asking Stan to fix that door since spring. It's not your fault," Angie, the server, said to her with a grin from behind the counter. "What can I get you?"

"Besides coffee, what are my chances your ham and mushroom quiche survived the breakfast rush? I know it's a longshot, but I'm starving," Becca said, hopefully.

Angie nodded and called out as she turned back into the kitchen. "Your lucky day, darlin'!"

Becca looked around the café and spotted Chris, giving her a smile and wave. "Hey there, mind if I join you?"

Chris nodded. She was glad to see Becca. She could use a friend, despite her affinity for solitude.

"It's Chris, right?" Becca asked as she slid onto the worn brown bench opposite Chris.

"Yes, that's right. And you're Becca?" Chris responded.

"So, what have you been up to lately? Settling in okay?" Becca opened with friendly chit-chat, and Chris was grateful. It had been a while since she had talked to anyone, and she wasn't sure she remembered how to do casual conversation. Becca proved to be down to earth—friendly, but not intrusive, and easy to talk to. She also knew everyone in town.

After a few minutes, Chris asked the question she'd wanted to ask since seeing Becca walk into the café. "So, anyone have more info on that little girl or the guy who was manhandling her?"

Becca's expression went sober. "Not really. I asked around and a couple other people had seen them in town. No one noticed much except that the girl didn't look very well cared-for, and the guy was pretty gruff and unfriendly," Becca explained. "It's still bugging me."

"Me, too," Chris replied. "Before I left Chicago, I worked in marketing. One of my accounts was a New York City Police Department project to elevate the visibility of kids who had disappeared, particularly young girls. I learned a lot, none of it good. I don't suppose your local police department keeps track of that kind of thing out here, do they?"

"Yeah, they do. One of my cousins is a deputy sheriff with the county. We talked a while back about how this part of Western Colorado is a kind of throughway for human trafficking. Between Denver and Salt Lake. There are a lot of places to hide someone out here in these mountains, and west of here, it turns into canyon country fast. Lots of wild, isolated territory where bad actors can get away with doing their thing. My cousin and Angie are good friends—they've known each other since high school. Just a second..."

Becca turned in her seat, throwing one arm back along the top of the booth. She looked around the empty café and called out.

"Hey, Angie! I got a question for you," Becca hollered, just loud enough to get Angie's attention at the far end of the counter where she was fussing with receipts.

"Need more coffee?" Angie asked.

"I will, but not yet. This is about something else. Got a sec?" Becca cocked her head to the side, indicating her hope that Angie could join them. Angie walked down the length of the counter and over to their corner table.

"What's up?" Angie asked.

"Remember that little girl and the scruffy guy who was hauling her around town last week? Several folks noticed them and thought something was strange," Becca said.

"Yes, I do. He pulled in here for about five minutes, left the girl locked in the backseat of the car. Asked for a couple turkey sandwiches to go," Angie said.

"Any chance you know if Dustin is still circulating those photo sheets of missing kids they're trying to find? It might be worth looking through them," Becca said. Angie nodded once and disappeared back into the kitchen. She returned a minute later with a three-ring binder, the cover bearing the insignia of the Butte County Sheriff's Office. She walked back to the table and dropped it in front of Becca.

"If you think any of those kids are your girl, I can guarantee Dustin will want to know. Of all the nasty human business he deals with, this stuff just drives him up the wall," Angie said. "Give me another minute and your quiche will be done. You decided what you'd like?" Angie asked Chris.

"Something quick. How about a couple scrambled eggs and some wheat toast?"

"You got it." Angie gave Chris a smile and turned back to the kitchen while Becca pushed the binder into the middle of the table where they could both look at the photos.

"What do you remember most about the girl?" Becca asked Chris.

"Dirty, light-blue rain jacket. Blonde hair in braids that hadn't been done right for a while. White or Hispanic, 80 pounds, four- to five-feet tall. Jeans. Hard for me to tell how old she was. I haven't been around kids for a long time."

"I've got a million nieces and nephews," Becca said. "I'd put her at about twelve. Or a scrawny thirteen. I remember her eyes. They were big blue eyes with long lashes. She looked so scared. And kind of a button nose. I think if she'd been fed and cleaned up, she would have been pretty. She was wearing white sneakers, I think, with ankle socks that had red polka-dot cuffs. Filthy, but cute," she added.

Becca had flipped past several photos of boys, older girls, girls about the right age, but wrong race or ethnicity. She paused as she flipped the next photo over and stared. Chris leaned in and pulled the book toward her for a better look, then slowly looked up at Becca. Becca was still staring at the photo.

"Holy shit. I think it's her," Becca said.

Chris just nodded slowly. "Want to give your cousin Dustin a call? See if he has time to chat?"

Chris

Chris opened the passenger door to her pickup to collect a pair of worn leather work gloves from where they had fallen off the seat. She was 25 miles from home, at a machine shop whose head mechanic said he knew how to repair an old generator she had found in the barn behind the cabin. It could come in handy mid-winter. She anticipated the power going out during storms, and it would take a lineman a long time to get to her.

When she went to close the door, she stopped, still as a mannequin.

A middle-aged man with greasy, shoulder-length brown hair held back by a bandana was stepping out of his car on the other side of the lot. The man was familiar in a way that unsettled her, and as he made his way to the shop door, she realized why. It was the broken nose and the hard, dark eyes she remembered from when he was hauling the struggling little girl out of the hardware store over a month ago.

The man entered the shop and Chris listened to the fading sound of the bells hung from the door handle to alert the guys in the garage that they had a customer. She strolled around the back of her truck and opened the gate, pretending she had something stowed in the bed. She was trying to decide what to do.

Chris pulled out her phone and scrolled through her few contacts to find Becca's number.

Chris dialed, her heart thumping. She listened, the face of the phone smashed into her ear, while it rang once, twice, three times. Chris swore to herself, dreading the sound of Becca's voice mail message. Becca answered on the fourth ring.

"Hey, Chris, whazzup?" Becca answered cheerfully. "Ya caught me out at the woodpile."

"Becca, you're not gonna believe this. But I just bumped into that guy who had the little girl we were so worried about at the hardware store last month."

"What? Are you sure?" Becca's voice focused instantly.

"Yeah, I'm real sure. Same old car, same black, beady eyes. I still don't like him."

"Is the girl with him? Where are you?"

"No, I don't see our little munchkin. I don't want to go peering into the back seat and draw attention, but I'll see if I can get the plate. I'm over at Tony's Machine Shop in Gandy. Know where it is?"

"Yeah, I do. On 135 past the grocery store, right?"

"That's it. Do you want to call your cousin Dustin the deputy? Like, maybe right now?" Chris reached under the tonneau cover, mindlessly shifting objects around. "Shit, he's coming back out. Becca, I'm gonna follow him. Call Dustin, okay?"

"Chris, no! That's dangerous—"

"Becca, this jackass has a little girl who belongs somewhere else, I can feel it in my bones. Call me back after you get hold of Dustin. We can stay on the phone then and I can let you know where he's going. Or something. I'll be careful."

Chris disconnected the phone and shoved it into her hip pocket, slammed the gate up on her truck and got into the driver's seat, careful not to look toward the blue car or the man climbing into it. She backed out of her parking spot and pulled along behind the sedan as its brake lights popped on, the engine starting.

"Gotcha," Chris whispered to herself. "KJR 1437, KJR 1437, KJR 1437..." She rolled on by and parked under a tree, grabbing a pencil stub she kept stashed in a cup holder. Pretending to reach for something on the floor, Chris scribbled the plate number on a receipt and waited for the man in the blue sedan to drive around her. She watched him turn right on Route 135, away from town. She forced herself to count to five before turning in the same direction to follow him.

Chris told herself not to be stupid and to keep her distance as she tailed the guy north on the winding two-lane hardtop. The road would soon be curling up switchbacks into the Redlands Canyon, and cell service would drop around the backside of every hairpin turn. The patches of private land, with their ranch entrances and outbuildings, would be replaced by wild public lands and the irregular border of the national forest. Soon there would be no one around. But she had to try to figure out what this guy was up to.

She tried to hang back, but each time she spotted the dark-blue sedan ahead of her, she felt more obvious. The county road they were on would run out of pavement in just a few miles, turning into a forest road with a four-digit number she couldn't recall. She knew it got steep, rough, and petered out at a shallow lake that turned to mud in late summer. Not exactly a tourist destination. She had been up there once, looking for a fishing spot.

Neither Becca nor Dustin had called. She glanced down at her watch, and 20 minutes had passed. She knew she should let it go and head back to town. But she couldn't get the missing girl named Grace out of her mind's eye. The terror. The silent pleading. The fierce dislike for the man who was shoving her into the backseat of the sedan. And that man was the driver of the car she was tailing. She was sure.

Chris reached the end of the pavement and turned around. But the dust filtering through the afternoon sunlight from behind the car ahead was taunting her. The forest road didn't go that far. It ended at the lakebed. In a car like that, without four-wheel drive, the guy couldn't go far.

Her heart was pounding, and she felt cold and a little lightheaded. She had to decide. She looked at her phone again. No texts. No missed calls. And no bars.

Chris swore under her breath and slammed her right hand onto the steering wheel. Becca knew which way she had headed. There weren't any turnoffs. The cavalry was on its way. She'd just go as far as the lake and have a look around. Like she meant to do some birding or check on the water depth.

It sounded lame even in her imagination, but it was a plan of sorts. Chris thrust her truck into gear, flipped on the four-wheel drive, and headed up the forest road.

The ruts got deeper, the road base of heavier rocks more exposed, jutting sideways or creating washed-out ledges. Her truck could handle it, but she really had to concentrate on maneuvering forward. She wondered how the sedan, with its low clearance, could have pulled it off.

Slowly, the trees closed in on either side of the narrow track, and she cringed as broken branches scraped along the sides of her truck. Had she missed a pullout, or camping area where the car might have exited? She didn't think so, but maybe...

Chris rounded a corner and listened to her engine growl in low gear as she pushed it up a short, steep incline and felt one wheel give as a rock shifted beneath her truck. She slammed the differential on and crawled up and over the lip of the rise. A small glade of grass and late-season wildflowers came into view on her right, and the track she had been following ended in a muddy wallow about 100 feet back from the edge of the dried-up lakebed.

She stopped, looking around for evidence of the car or its driver, but saw nothing. Chris put the truck in park and rolled down her driver's side window, listening for anything revealing. She killed her engine.

It was quiet. Too quiet. As Chris opened the driver's side door and stepped out of her truck, her ears strained to hear anything beyond her own breathing. There should have been birds. The sound of chipmunks or wrens scrabbling in the leaf litter. Something. But all she could hear was the wind in the aspens behind her.

Moving around the front of her truck, her eyes scanning the far side of the lake, Chris took a few steps into the grass and up a bit of a slope to where the ground looked less muddy. She started to take a deep breath to calm her nerves when she heard the quick swish of slick fabric just behind her.

Rain jacket. Navy. Zipper. That was all that registered before she felt the blunt crack of something smash into her temple and saw the pretty blue petals of delicate-stemmed wild flax blossoms approaching her face. Then everything went black.

Becca

Deputy Sheriff Dustin Anderson was way past his tolerances for necessary political duty in his boss's absence. But he remained standing behind and to the left of the fourth speaker approaching the podium. Fifth would be the governor, at last, the heart of an agenda celebrating passage of legislation introduced by their state representative that would translate into more funding to fight drug trafficking in rural Colorado.

Those were issues that were important to Dustin, but he'd been standing there in his dress uniform, representing the sheriff, for an hour and a half of talking heads. His phone had been buzzing on his belt the whole time, and he just kept wondering how many hours of overtime were in those unchecked texts and calls. Plus, he really had to pee.

Thirty minutes later, he watched as the congressman and governor clasped hands and grinned widely while the cameras flashed in the dimming late-afternoon light. This final photo opportunity spelled impending freedom. Dustin waited for the first of the local glad handers to get their bits of recognition from the two visiting celebrities. Then he approached them both to offer the sheriff's congratulations and gratitude for their work. As soon as both men were absorbed in conversation, Dustin left, stopping in the first restroom he could find before heading out to his patrol car.

The cooling late-afternoon air was beyond refreshing as he shoved open the side exit from the county administration building. He took a deep breath to clear the cobwebs from his brain and unclipped his phone, thumbing in his security code to open it. At least two dozen text messages. More than he'd expected.

He opened the messaging app and scanned the sources, frowning. Half were from his cousin, Becca. The rest from a variety of sheriff's office and community contacts. What was Becca trying to reach him about with a dozen messages?

Dustin started reading from the top, since the last eight were just urgent requests for him to respond. They started almost an hour ago. He stopped cold in the middle of the parking lot, 50 feet from his vehicle, as he read the series with substance.

Dustin, Chris saw the guy we think has the girl we told you about from your notebook of missing kids–Grace Martinez. Call me.

Dustin, Chris just texted that she's following the guy! He's in a beat-up, dark-blue sedan. Going east on 135 toward the canyon, starting from Tony's machine shop west of the grocery store over in Gandy. Can you come? Or send someone?

Dude, I'm getting nervous–it's been 20 minutes. I haven't heard from Chris. She may have lost signal up in the canyon. Can you help?

"Shit," Dustin muttered, breaking into a run to close the distance to his car. He threw open the door and climbed in, thumbing a fast reply to Becca.

Becca–just got your message. I'm 40 minutes from Tony's. I'm calling dispatch to see about backup. Meet me there? Call me.

Dustin knew it was close to the end of shift and the other deputies still on duty were distributed all over the county. Odds of backup were slim, given that he couldn't tell dispatch there was a fire, a highway pileup, or gunshots. They were down two patrol positions, so the bar was high for calling someone else out of the field.

"Shit," he said again before flipping the radio on to tell dispatch what he was doing. He hit the switch that illuminated the light bar on top of the car and sped out of the parking lot, mentally mapping the fastest route to Gandy.

His heart sunk as he thought of Becca's friend Chris, driving alone up into Redlands Canyon, tailing someone who could be truly dangerous. Dustin had only met Chris once, but she seemed level-headed, practical, capable of taking care of herself. She had a good 4WD truck, he remembered, and lived on her own way up the mountain in the boonies. She had survival skills and smarts. But he also remembered the simmering, restrained intensity he'd sensed beneath her even-handed questions about Grace and the kind of people who kidnapped kids her age and kept them. Or sold them. She felt exactly like he did about it.

The three of them had talked about the known details around Grace Martinez's disappearance. The family members close to her. The last sighting of the little girl, now three months past.

Chris got it. Dustin could tell that her brief encounter with Grace had seared into her memory, and a chance to help find her would be compelling.

Yet Chris was an untrained civilian, not law enforcement. Dustin wondered if she carried a weapon and had any skill with it. Part of him hoped not. Often, civilians with weapons ended up having them used against them by a less-inhibited criminal.

Dustin glanced at his watch. It had been at least 90 minutes since Becca had tried to reach him. If Chris hadn't called Becca or returned to town, that wasn't good. She would have run out of paved road 60 minutes ago, and even at a crawl, she would have run out of dirt forest road 30 to 45 minutes ago. What had happened?

Dustin's cell phone rang.

"Deputy Anderson," Dustin answered, his voice brusque and focused.

"Dustin, it's Becca. Where are you now?"

"About 30 minutes out. You?" Dustin asked his cousin.

"I'll be there before you are. Should I head on up 135? You could catch up with me!" Becca's suggestion made Dustin's heart lurch. He'd already been reviewing possible scenarios for what had happened to Chris, ranging from a blown tire on the optimistic side to body recovery on the other end.

"NO!" Dustin heard his voice echo in the cab and winced. He pulled his commanding tone back toward civility. He and Becca had been close since they were toddlers. "Becca, I know you're worried, and so am I; but you've got to wait for me, okay?"

"I could stop and wait where the forest road starts if I don't find her before that. Dustin, she just had trouble with her truck. That's possible, right?"

Dustin closed his eyes against the fearful hope in Becca's voice. Chris didn't strike him as the kind of woman who would need AAA to fix a flat or a fluid leak.

"Possible, Becca. She's probably fine. But just...don't. Wait for me at Tony's, okay? I've got lights on and I'll be there soon."

Becca agreed, but obviously didn't want to. Her own memory of the wiry man with the ropy muscles and clenched jaw, swinging Grace into the backseat like a resistant sack of potatoes, was swimming in front of her eyes. She focused on the road, switching her headlights on as the sun dropped below tree line, driving as fast as the familiar curves in the road allowed.

She wanted to be blasting up that forest road to the lake in the worst way, looking for Chris before the last of the daylight escaped.

Chris

Chris's brain first registered a dimly lit room, and the outlines of fuzzy, gray cabinets and a countertop. She thought she was in a dentist's chair, the anesthesia wearing off too soon, instruments and half a fist in her mouth, causing her to gag. A face swam into focus, and she saw it was the new vet in town, whose acquaintance she had made while selecting avocados from a bin at the grocery store. He was good-looking, in a serious, studious way, but why was he doing dentistry? A shadowy image of her mom appeared, leaning against the doorframe at the back of the exam room, partially obscured by the dental hygienist.

That made no sense. Chris remembered her mom had died five years ago. She shook her head, trying to wake up from the dream. Her head throbbed sharply, in rhythm with her pulse, and she groaned.

Chris tried to orient herself. Her head hurt. She had what felt like a wad of cotton cloth jammed into her mouth and something tied around her face. Only vague light sifted through the fabric. Pain speared her left shoulder, but when she tried to shift her position, she realized her arms were tied behind her back. Something narrow and hard bound her wrists and bit into her skin without much give.

The pain from trying to move woke her up, completely. She remembered walking away from her truck, clambering up a grassy rise speckled with blue wildflowers to get a better view down to the muddy, dried-up lakebed. The car she'd been following should not have just disappeared. Then she had heard the soft noise of quick movement behind her and had turned. She remembered a man cocking his arm back, and the smell of alcohol on his breath as she'd tried to duck.

Chris focused on breathing slowly through her nose and then through her mouth, around the gag. It wasn't easy. Her sinuses were congested. Her priority was to lose the gag, somehow.

She turned her head and lifted her chin, trying to get a sense for what kind of surface her body was leaning against. She wriggled into a sitting position against the rough wall behind her. It smelled damp, earthy, with a mineral edge when she turned her face to the wall. A cave or a...

Her heart sunk as the word "hole" morphed to the concept of "grave." Then a fierce resolve gathered in her chest like a fist on fire. *No.* She would *not* be stuck here wherever here was.

Chris turned her entire body sideways and jammed her chin and jaw against the rock behind her, scraping it up and down to shift the blindfold. It moved, a bit. She dropped her head and shoulders lower to make a longer arc and succeeded in getting the cloth down below her left ear. Three more times she ignored the pain of abrasion against the exposed skin of her temple and cheekbones and got the blindfold past both ears, away from her mouth and down below her chin. She jammed her tongue against the back side of the wad of cloth in her mouth and ejected it, gasping deeply with relief. Air. Air was good.

Chris leaned back against the rock wall and breathed, slowly, to let the adrenaline surge fade a bit. She needed to think.

She started with a methodical assessment of her body. She was cold. Her head was throbbing, and she could taste the residue of blood in her mouth. The tightness in the skin on her face was from an abrasion and drying blood, but that wasn't serious. Her left shoulder hurt in a powerful way, and both shoulders—her arms and chest muscles were strained from having her arms pulled backward and wrists bound together behind her. Her right hand was numb. She didn't think she was otherwise injured. That was good. Her legs were not bound. That was good.

Next, she took stock of the space around her. It was dark in the cave, but a bit of light seeped into the space from somewhere above her. She thought she could make out a solid ledge near the ceiling that partially obscured what looked like a rough grate made of brushy tree limbs over an opening. Unfortunately, she estimated it was at least 15 feet above her.

She could just barely make out the sound of wind rustling the leaves on the limbs laid across the opening. She breathed deeply, sniffing at the chilly, close air. There was something in the slight waft of outside air that drifted down to her. An edge, bitter and ashy. Campfire smoke, doused some time ago, leaving a residue from hot stones and charred wood.

That meant there was something recognizable as human presence near the opening of the cave. Something that might lead a searcher to pause, look around. Someone could find her, Chris thought, and she knew her friend Becca would come looking. A tendril of hope brushed to life inside her.

Or it was a hidden place in the woods where her captor had taken up residence and would return. Fear swirled at the bottom of her stomach again. She was thirsty. The need for water shot another rush of adrenalin from her brain to her heart.

"Don't. Panic." The words came out of Chris's mouth in a croaking admonishment to herself.

Becca

Becca pulled into the parking lot for Tony's Machine Shop and wheeled around so she could depart as quickly as possible. It was killing her to wait for her cousin Dustin. She wanted to be heading up the canyon after Chris. She had received the text from Chris two hours ago. It had taken forever for Dustin to get back to her. Becca had expected progress reports from Chris. None had come.

Becca had her driver's side window down, despite the chill in the air, listening for a vehicle approaching over the sough of wind in the spruce trees that lined the parking lot. She checked her watch for the zillionth time. Two whole minutes had crept by. She could hear the faint high-pitched whine of a power tool coming from inside Tony's shop. Nothing more.

It was nearing five o'clock and thick clouds from a brewing storm were approaching from the west. The late afternoon sun lit the clouds from behind. The wind picked up, and a small flock of little gray and brown birds flushed up out of the brush, their quick movement startling Becca. She could feel her own pulse rise in her chest and neck.

That was it. She couldn't take waiting any longer. She thumbed a quick text to Dustin with the time and told him just to head west on 135 and catch up to her.

In 20 minutes, Becca reached the muddy pullout where the pavement ended, and Forest Road 1265 began. She got out of her Jeep Cherokee to look for tire tracks. There were fresh ones, wide enough to be from Chris's pickup truck. It looked like she had backed in and stopped, before turning right to head up the dirt track.

Becca stood still beside her Jeep, weighing her options. She guessed she had gained 3,000 feet in elevation, and the cloud deck was low. She watched feathery trails of mist reaching into the conifers. It was becoming a freezing drizzle.

She thought of Chris and wondered if she had a coat in her truck and rain gear. Probably. But who knew where she was, or if she'd caught up to the guy in the blue car. What would she do if she had caught up to him? What if she'd found Grace, the little girl?

Becca folded her arms around herself and paced out into the road, peering back down the last curve. She walked in a circle, listening for the sound of Dustin's patrol car. She paced back over to her Jeep and reached into the back seat to grab her old denim jacket and a scarf. It was getting chilly, and she started the engine and flipped on the heater even though she left the window down to keep listening. If Dustin didn't get there in the next five minutes, Becca decided she would drop her old SUV into 4WD and start up the dirt road before it got too muddy.

Becca watched the digital numbers flip on her watch. At three minutes gone, she heard the soft whoosh of wheels on pavement and a vehicle braking onto the loose stone at the edge. Her heart leapt with relief, knowing that Dustin would know what to do, and she wouldn't be heading up the dirt road alone in search of her friend.

But it wasn't a county sheriff's patrol car pulling up across the front end of her Jeep. It was an old blue sedan with the engine running, and the driver walking briskly over to her door, a hefty-looking .45 caliber handgun held in both hands and trained on her head.

Dustin

Dustin added sirens to the light bar on his police cruiser when he saw the text from his cousin, Becca. He also added a colorful back-country array of curse words that included the phrase "peanut butter-brained SQUIRREL" in reference to his favorite cousin. He was furious that she had gone ahead of him, looking for Chris. He was scared. And his angst about the whole situation notched up several levels.

It launched to a level just short of nuclear red when he rounded the final long curve of pavement on Route 135 before the road ran out and turned to dirt. Ahead of him, he saw Becca's old red Jeep Cherokee parked in the turnaround with the driver's door standing open, no Becca in sight. He pulled over and parked his vehicle 20 feet back from the muddy turnaround. He called dispatch with his position, scanning the area carefully. Dustin reiterated his fervent desire for backup.

Dustin noticed a couple of canvas tote bags flopped out onto the ground next to the Jeep, and a green plastic water bottle rolled partway beneath the car. It didn't take much in the way of detective skills to suspect Becca had left her SUV in a hurry, distracted, if not against her will.

Dustin got out of his cruiser, looking up the sloping hillside thick with conifers and oak brush. He walked slowly toward Becca's vehicle, unsnapping the holster for his service weapon without pulling it from his belt.

"Sweet Jesus," he whispered to himself.

There in the mud beside the SUV were neat imprints of hiking boots, he guessed a woman's size eight, the pattern on the sole visible in the damp, silty soil. She'd gotten out of her Jeep, stood, turned around, then stepped back.

That wasn't what ratcheted Dustin's heart rate. It was the mess of her footprints that mixed with some larger ones a few feet away, and the skippy double trail of dragging heel marks leading away from the muddy turnaround.

Dustin pressed the button in his shoulder mic to radio dispatch again. "Dispatch, Anderson here again out on 135 at the forest road. Need backup pronto and get a detective from State out here ASAP. Possible abduction of an adult female."

He hadn't even thought about Chris while his mind processed what was immediately in front of him, his usual police response a bit jacked up by his personal concern for his cousin. Then he looked up the muddy dirt forest road and saw the fresh overlapping ruts of multiple vehicles. He clicked the mic button again.

"Darla? I'm not sure what we've got going here but better make that possible abduction of *two* females," he said tersely.

Grace

The sounds that came through the earthen walls of the fruit cellar were always muffled and distant. But after three months of straining to hear even the faintest cues from beyond the locked door that separated her from the rest of the world, 12-year-old Grace Martinez thought she had decoded some of those sounds.

She knew the thump and scrape of his footsteps on the wooden stairs that led down into the basement from the door off the kitchen. She knew the sound of the old furnace kicking on and off in the mechanical room on the other side of one wall. And the jolt and hum of the garage door above folding open when he would come home from wherever he went.

And she knew particularly well the rattle and metallic twist of the doorknob as he unlocked it. Then she would watch the wedge of light widen as the door to the cool cellar separated from its frame. The man would enter to toss her food or escort her to the bathroom. Her eyes would narrow against the punishing light, and she would scoot back against the wall, the hairs on her skin rising with the cold knot that tightened with resolve in her stomach. Her fear of him had turned to acid hatred. She never knew what he would do, say, or demand. He would never answer her questions about going home, about her parents and her sister. She had stopped asking.

But Grace Martinez had not stopped thinking. She was still determined to escape from this man, from this place, and get help.

Tonight, she heard the jolt and mechanical hum of the garage door opening, and then closing, but then something different. There was a vent opening in the ceiling of the cellar that she had figured out was near the door into the kitchen from the garage. She could sometimes discern more about what he had been doing by listening to the sounds that drifted down through the vent. For example, she could tell if he had come home from the store with food by the number of trips he made back and forth from the old blue car into the house.

This time, after the garage door closed, she heard one car door open and slam shut, then another. And then the trunk open, but not shut again. And she heard what sounded like a struggle, banging and a thump against the wall of the garage. Then a woman's voice talking to him, low but stressed, with short, tight questions she couldn't make out, but he didn't answer. She heard him yell at her, tell her to shut up.

Grace could tell that the woman did not want to be here. It sounded a whole lot like when the man had first brought Grace to the house after grabbing her on her way home after school. But she thought the woman was a grownup. Or at least a teenager. She wondered what he was going to do with her.

She hoped the man would bring the woman down to the fruit cellar to stay with her. Together they could figure out how to get out and past him. But maybe the man would take her out to the cave in the woods near the campground.

That's where the man had put Grace at first. It was a deep hole with rock and dirt walls. The only way in or out was a rope ladder he would throw down after pulling the cover off the opening to the cave. It was at the end of a narrow trail that led away from the overgrown backyard of the house, behind a stinking garbage pile. That's all she remembered from when he led her from the cave to the house, blindfolded and tripping on roots and branches in the forest. She could just barely peek down through the bottom of the blindfold, but she would never forget the smell of the rotten garbage pile just before getting to the house.

Grace stood in the dim light of the cellar and took three steps toward the door from the thin cot she slept on. She knelt on the cool dirt floor and pressed her ear to the keyhole beneath the knob. Above her, she heard a kitchen chair being pulled away from the table, then another knocked over. The man barked something, mean and short, and the woman shouted something back.

Then Grace heard the door to the basement stairs open. Next, it was something heavy crashing against the wall and the gasp and grunting and thumps of a person falling and hitting stairs. The man followed, swearing at the woman, telling her to get up.

Grace dove back to her cot and scrunched up in a ball as the man jammed the long, old-fashioned key into the lock, opening the door. She stared, breathing hard in the dark, as the man shoved the woman through the door and hit her in the head with the butt of a gun. The woman crumpled to the floor and the man kicked at her until her unconscious body was far enough inside that he could shove the door closed again.

Grace stayed quiet and listened to the clatter and snick of the lock turning in the door. The light disappeared once again. She wondered if the woman curled in a heap just a few feet away was dead.

Becca

Becca wasn't dead. She determined that fact when she half-consciously moaned but the vibration caused by that brief utterance made her head throb. She let herself drift back down into the well of unknowing before an annoying accusation from her brain halted her journey.

"You know better than to drink tequila."

Becca then felt the need to respond, to defend herself from her inner accuser. "I wasn't doing shots last night. There wasn't any Jell-O!" This peculiar line of mental logic made her start to giggle. But that hurt more.

Time to wake up.

Becca opened her eyes, trying to figure out where she was. It was dark, and cool. She shifted to extract her arm from where it had folded awkwardly beneath her body and felt the gritty surface of packed, dry dirt beneath her. She reached up and adjusted her glasses, which were half off her face but remarkably intact. She rolled over to try to sit up slowly and the smell of old urine hit her sinuses. Her stomach rolled.

"Eww," she muttered to herself.

"I know. It stinks in here. You'll get used to it."

Becca startled at the sound of the reedy young voice coming from the darkness a few feet away.

"Who are you?" Becca demanded, her body's adrenal system unsure if it should be throwing fight, flight, or relief into her muscles.

"Chill," came the slightly annoyed, whispered response. "And be quiet. I'm only twelve, I'm not your biggest problem. The bad guy lives upstairs, not in here. But there's a vent. He can hear. Sometimes."

"Grace?"

Becca was fully awake now and had reconstructed the day's drama and its unfortunate conclusion in a rapid, animated series of images. Tony's Machine Shop parking lot. Leaving to look for Chris. Parking at the pullout. Looking up to see a car blocking her in. Wiry, angry dude getting out, striding toward her, pointing a big freaking handgun at her head.

He was stronger than she thought he'd be. She ended up in the trunk.

And here she was.

"Yep. That's me. Grace Martinez. Wish it weren't," the sassy little girl responded to Becca's question.

"We were looking for you! My friend Chris and I saw you last month with that guy when he was dragging you out of the hardware store. Chris saw his car today and tried to follow…"

"Yeah. I remember you. At least, I think it's you. Can't really see your face too well," Grace pointed out the obvious, her dry humor showing through. "Glad you're alive. What's your name?"

"Oh. I'm Becca. Sorry."

"Thanks for trying to find me."

Silence fell between them. Becca heard the click and deep thrum of the furnace kicking on from the other side of the wall near where Grace was sitting.

After a few minutes, Becca spoke quietly again. "So, I'm assuming we're locked in here."

"Yeah," Grace replied. "It's one of those old-timey locks with a long metal key. He keeps it on him. I tried fussing around at the lock inside the keyhole with the end of a fork, but it didn't work."

"There's not much light in here," Becca said, inanely. She felt ridiculous immediately after the words escaped. Grace sighed.

"So. You want the rundown on what I've figured out?" Grace asked.

"Yes, catch me up. You've been stuck in here for what, three months? Jesus, Grace. We have to get out of here."

"Yes, we do. He's getting crazier." Grace sounded like she had way more life experience than was possible given her age.

"Do you know who he is?"

"Not his name. He worked at the gas station where my mom took her car for repairs. Decided he was in love with her and started coming around our apartment building in town. But Mom clocked him for crazy and told him to buzz off. He didn't. I asked her what his name was and she just said 'nobody' and told me to stay away from him. Like I hadn't already figured that out."

"Grace, what happened? How did he get you?"

"I was walking home after school and he pulled his crappy car right up on the sidewalk in front of me, out of nowhere. I was thinking about my math test. He came out, barreled around the front of his car, and tried to grab me. I ran, but he's quick and I had a lot of stuff in my backpack from school and he snagged it, with me still attached. That was that. I pitched a fit and tried to crawl over out of the backseat to scratch his face and make him crash, but he hit me hard and when I woke up, my nose was bloody, and I was in this cave in the woods with the opening way above me. I was so mad."

Grace fell quiet again. Becca didn't know what to say.

"Grace, I am so sorry this happened to you," Becca said, gently. "Some men are such jerks."

"Mmph. This one's a total dick." Becca almost laughed. Grace might be twelve, but she told it straight and did not mince words.

"So sometimes he takes you out, but mostly you're trapped in here?" Becca prompted, again, gently.

Grace sighed again, then started in. "He comes down once a day, sometimes twice, you can hear the door at the top of the stairs open. He turns on the basement light, comes down, unlocks this cellar, and tosses a bag of food in. He'll take me upstairs to the bathroom sometimes so I can wash up. I got him to bring a pot with a lid so I can use it when I have to go and he's not around. Sorry, it's disgusting."

"Don't worry about it, Grace. Good solution under the circumstances," Becca said. "What else?"

"The vent above you lets a tiny bit of light in when the kitchen lights are on or it's sunny outside and the light comes in the kitchen window. And sound. You can kinda keep track of him by what filters down from there. You can hear the garage door open and close, and his car coming or leaving. And where he's walking if he's in the kitchen or near it. The floor creaks."

"Has he hurt you? Physically, I mean?" Becca asked.

"Not since that first day. Not really. He gets rough with me if I don't do what he says. And lately, he's more impatient and shoves me around more. He keeps blathering about how he knows my mom really wants him, how we're gonna be a family someday. Like he's up for some Father of the Year award." Grace's voice trailed off for a moment. "I'm worried about her. My mom. She's got to be losing her mind."

"I know she is, Grace. She went to the police, that's how I figured out who you were. From the pictures of missing kids. My cousin is a county sheriff's deputy who looks for missing kids." Becca tried to sound reassuring. "He's looking for you."

"Are they close? To here, I mean?" Grace sounded hopeful but restrained.

"Probably. Dustin was on his way to meet me so we could look for my friend who was following the guy who took you. Us, I mean. She spotted him in Gandy and called me."

"Is that in Utah? We live just over the state line on the Utah side," Grace said.

"Colorado. But close to Utah. An hour's drive. But where we are now? I think it's near the national forest, outside of Gandy." Becca was mentally reconstructing what she'd felt and heard through the trunk of the car, after the guy had started driving. It felt like forever, but she didn't think it had been more than half an hour until he pulled into the garage.

"Do you think Dustin will keep looking for you? Us?" Grace asked.

Becca didn't respond right away. She had just remembered something she had done after ending up in the trunk.

"I am absolutely sure of it, Grace. And so will my friend, Chris, unless he's got her, too. Which he might. Before I got there. To the bottom of the forest road, I mean..." Becca's voice trailed off, distracted by her memory.

"You lost me there, Becca," Grace nudged.

"Sorry. I was just remembering something I tried. To help people find us, maybe."

"What did you do?"

"My niece. I was going to bring her this big plastic bag of gold glitter for a poster she was doing for a school project about the sun. I stuffed it in the pocket of the jacket I put on right before Mr. Jackass turned up and forced me into his trunk. I started trickling it out of a crack that I could just barely reach, near the taillight of the car. Trying to make a trail. If they see it, that is...It was windy, a storm was coming in, but still...it's something."

Becca remembered starting to spill the glitter when the road was bumpy but before it started to drop in and out of deeper ruts, throwing her from side to side. He must have been driving up the forest road. Then the car swung sharply left and her head hit the trunk lid. Then there was a lot of brush scraping the bottom and sides of the car. It took her a while to squirm back so she could reach the taillight crack and empty the rest of the glitter out of the bag. She remembered smelling pine, like from crushed branches, and then the rank stench of garbage when the car had lurched over a mound of some sort before coming to a stop.

"Grace, is there a garbage heap near this house?"

"Yeah, it's back behind the house near where the brush and trees get thick. It's gross. There's a path behind it that leads through the woods to the cave where he put me. At first, I mean, the night he grabbed me on my way home. The cave is near a campground. Or at least a campfire circle. I saw it before he lowered me into the hole."

"Okay. So, there's a path that leads right here from somewhere public. That's good. Not smart, but good for us. And anyone looking for us," Becca whispered, thoughtfully. She paused, and her heart turned to little Grace, so strong, so determined.

"You are one tough kid, Grace. We're going to get out of here," Becca told her.

Chris

Chris had passed the night alternating between sitting, standing, and walking in circles doing shoulder rolls to try to keep the circulation going to her arms and hands, still pinned behind her with what she thought was a plastic zip tie. It had bitten through her skin, and at this point, the pain in her wrists was more difficult to ignore than the pain in her head.

It was morning and Chris had just awakened after falling into an exhausted sleep, curled sideways sitting up and leaning against a small cleft near the floor of the cave. Even the faint light sifting down along the cave walls was comforting. Chris thought it must be a bright day up there, beyond the grid of tree limbs and leafy branches that covered the opening far above her. She could hear birds. Up there was normal. She wanted normal.

She stood, awkwardly, and began again to explore her options. The walls of the cave were mostly smooth, planed dirt. But there were a few places where uneven edges of dark rock were exposed. None were in convenient locations to use for climbing.

She had to get her hands free. Just a foot or so off the ground, mostly buried in the wall, she noticed a six-inch wedge of hard black rock. If she could expose an edge of that, it might be something she could use to try scraping through the plastic around her wrists.

Chris looked around and noticed another low cleft in the wall toward the back of the cave. In the dim light, she knelt again to get a closer look. It smelled awful. A sharp, animal scent made her think of a packrat midden she'd cleared out of an old shed last month. It had been full of hoarded bits of all sorts of things—small pieces of wood, scraps of chewed leather, twigs and dried grass, and the stench of rodent urine and feces.

But this had been a stash of a different kind. She saw some odd items toward the rear of the cleft, not entirely visible, and steeled her nerves to shift her body around to use the toe of her booted foot to nudge it out.

An aluminum pie plate came first, and she recoiled, realizing it contained what looked like dried feces, not animal. She closed her eyes and swallowed, hard, determined not to vomit as she realized she was not the first occupant of this hidden hole in the ground. She wondered if she had found one of the former residences of the missing girl, Grace Martinez. They shared a captor. It made sense.

Breathing slowly through her mouth, Chris stretched one leg out again and probed the space for any other objects. She needed something sharp. Her foot found another lump, but it was soft, like fabric. After toeing it a few more times, she hooked the back and dragged it out from under the ledge of rock.

It was a small, blue knapsack, the zipper broken, and one of the shoulder straps torn away. Chris's heart sank. In the dim light, she could see the outline of a stack of school books and a spiral notebook.

Grace had been in here.

Dustin

By noon, less than 24 hours after Chris and Becca disappeared, offers of help had maxed out Dustin's voice mail. Volunteers had inundated the sheriff's office with calls, asking to help search. No one in the sheriff's office had leaked a word to the press, such as it was in Western Colorado, but the regional grapevine was in flames. With the additional assets of social media and technology, relationships were taking care of important notifications just as they had since the 1850s.

Becca's family had been in the area for longer than the town had been incorporated. Her dad ran the local hardware store, and her aunt owned Farm and Ranch Supply. Becca's relatives alone constituted a solid quarter of the population. They were ready to tear down the woods to hunt for her, and if the sheriff didn't organize it, some poor hiker from out of town was likely to get thrown into a headlock on the trail for the sheer fact that he wasn't a known party.

Chris was a newcomer but well-liked and respected, ever since word got out about her encounters with Don Harlow, who had made the mistake of underestimating her. That had led in turn to a series of now-hilarious humiliations rapidly becoming part of town lore.

Don had enjoyed a week of telling tales down at the café about his "city-girl" client, prognosticating about the number of trips he'd likely have to make before winter, delivering nail polish and explaining the difference between a German Shepherd and a coyote. His reckoning began when he swerved off the road while going to her off-the-grid rented cabin and got his shiny, clean SUV stuck in the muddy ditch. Chris had appeared, unbeckoned, an hour later, with a chainsaw, two lengths of tow strap, several pieces of 2x4 to jam under the wheels, a battery-operated jack just in case, and two shovels. He had the good graces to tell that story down at the café, too.

The sheriff had organized a search, and the first 50 people were gathering at the county building by two o'clock for instructions.

Because Dustin knew the disappearance of the two women was related to missing Grace Martinez, the sheriff told him to go back to headquarters and call the Utah State Police and the FBI. Both had a role in inter-state crime.

The FBI phone operator received and transferred Dustin's call immediately to the investigator assigned to the Martinez case, who answered before Dustin even heard a ring.

"Martin, FBI," the woman's authoritative voice filled Dustin's ear.

"Agent Martin, this is Deputy Sheriff Dustin Anderson, over in Butte County. We think we have a lead on Grace Martinez. But your case just got messier," Dustin said.

"They usually do, Deputy. Spill it."

Dustin brought the FBI agent up to speed on the possible sightings of Grace's captor, and Grace, and about the involvement of Dustin's cousin and her friend Chris. When he got to the part about finding both women's abandoned vehicles, Joyce Martin swore softly into the phone. She listened carefully, not interrupting, until Dustin finished.

"Thanks, Deputy. I appreciate your transparency about all this. So let me add a little color from the Utah side of things. This all started when Grace's mother, Cora, received a rambling love letter from a man whose name she didn't even know. She finally figured out he was one of the mechanics who had worked on her car back in early July. The guy's name is Ronald Mathews. Goes by Ronnie. She hadn't spoken to him except when she was paying her bill on her way out, but she thinks he got her phone number and address from the shop's customer database. He was mooning around off and on for almost two months, despite her efforts to shoo him away. Ronnie wouldn't quit calling and loitering by her apartment building. She finally complained to the shop owner, which got him fired on September 8th. A few days later, Grace didn't come home from school. Yesterday, the mother got another letter, which gave us more to go on. What you've told me about the events of the last couple of days fits right in."

The most recent letter from Ronald Mathews, while not entirely coherent, included an invitation for Cora to join him and Grace in a new life as a happy family in Colorado. He said he had a nice house with a big yard, and Grace loved it there. It was postmarked out of Grand Junction, near the Utah border.

Joyce Martin peppered Dustin with a series of short, insightful questions, probing the story he had told her. Even though Dustin's responses were variations of "I don't know," he appreciated her obvious experience. She urged Dustin to do everything he could to keep the volunteer search parties away from the immediate environs of Becca's abandoned SUV, Chris's truck, and the forest road leading up to the lake where Dustin and another deputy had already searched.

Dustin hung up and dutifully called his sheriff to convey Agent Martin's guidance about how to corral the searchers and put them to work without trampling evidence or putting them in danger. Sheriff Copeland was well-accustomed to directing volunteers without compromising a crime scene but would be glad to know that Joyce Martin was on the same page with protocol.

Dustin booted up his laptop and started pulling up county maps that showed the location of every structure within 20 miles of Gandy, right down to the outhouses behind remote hunting cabins. He already knew where most of them were but didn't want to overlook anything.

Becca

In the fruit cellar where she and Grace had spent the night, Becca was kneeling in front of the wooden shelves that lined one wall. Grace was balanced on her back. Grace had already felt her way along all the empty lower shelves, looking for anything that might help her get out. But she couldn't reach the top two shelves on her own. Until now.

They had started at one end of the shelves and methodically worked their way over toward the middle. Grace felt along the surface of each shelf, then climbed off Becca's back so Becca could crawl another foot or two to the right. Grace would climb back up and start again.

"Got something," Grace whispered, and hopped off Becca's back, clipping the side of her head with one sneakered foot.

"Ow!" Becca lurched, clutching the side of her skull with one hand. It was the same side that had taken the hit that had rendered her unconscious.

"Sorry," Grace murmured. "But look!" She was all business, and Becca sat back against the wall and took a deep breath while the pain subsided.

"What did you find?" Becca asked.

Wordlessly, Grace reached out and located Becca's hand, placing the six-inch long metal rod in it. Becca quickly recognized it as the business end of an old screwdriver, absent the convenience of a handle. She explored the tip with her fingers.

"Grace, this is gold, it's a Phillip's."

"Who's he?" Grace asked.

"No, it's a type of screwdriver, with a star-shaped point." Becca was already crawling over to the door, feeling her way around the knob and the plate beneath it where the keyhole was.

"What are you going to do?" Grace asked, urgently.

"With any luck, I am going to disassemble the lock. I used to help my dad with projects. He owned the hardware store in town. He's also the only locksmith in miles," she explained.

Dustin

Agent Joyce Martin left Salt Lake City at one in the morning after a nap, downing a Red Bull she picked up from the 24-hour Maverik convenience store just short of the interstate. She had a reputation for driving like a banshee, but she knew her usual Utah highway speed would be impossible on Southwestern Colorado's back roads, and she had to meet Deputy Anderson at dawn.

In the wee hours of the morning, as she reached Colorado's higher elevations, a light snow sparkled in her headlights, swirling in the crosswinds. She felt grim, thinking about how much harder that could make finding evidence deposited by the kidnapper and his victims the previous afternoon. Things went well for criminals more often than anyone in law enforcement wanted the public to know.

She passed Tony's Machine Shop, its windows and work bays still dark. She continued up 135, slowing as necessary for the tightening curves and switchbacks leading up the canyon toward her destination.

The clouds were thinning and tinged a salmon pink. The snow had left a dusting on the ground and in all the tall spruce and fir trees, but she figured it would melt in the next couple of hours if the skies cleared.

Rounding a long curve, Joyce spotted Dustin standing outside his patrol vehicle in a broad turnout, leaning against the hood. He was drinking coffee from a lidded paper cup. The red Jeep Cherokee belonging to his cousin, Becca, one of the missing women, was in the shadows behind him, the doors now closed.

Joyce slowed her government car to a stop. Dustin reached back toward his windshield and held out a second still-steaming cup in greeting. He waited while she grabbed gloves and got out of her car.

"Good morning, Agent Martin. Deputy Dustin Anderson. Hope you don't mind it black," he said with a tight smile.

"Perfect. Thank you. Snow isn't going to help much, is it," Joyce said, getting right to business.

"It'll make new activity in the area easier to spot, but no, anything we missed yesterday will be harder to find. I've got a list of buildings in the vicinity that our suspect might be crazy enough to call 'a nice house in the country.' Getting to each one ASAP is my priority at this point. What's yours?"

Dustin was edgy and swallowing the irritability that covered the fear he felt for Becca and Chris. All the tracks they'd found yesterday, including tire tracks, had petered out to nothing in the fading light last evening. He had spoken to Joyce hours ago while she drove over from Utah, briefing her on everything they'd done.

Now, the two law enforcement officers walked the area around Becca's red Jeep Cherokee, and he explained in more detail how they had processed the scene.

"Like I said last night, we found two sets of tire marks that looked fresh headed up toward the lake, but the road is rocky and well-used. One set matches Chris's truck and the other was narrower, consistent with a regular passenger vehicle. The truck tracks followed and covered the car tracks in places. Chris's truck is still up there. The car seems to have disappeared. There are two rough roads that lead away from the lake up to camp sites, but there was no sign of the car, or anyone using the camps, in either place. We're guessing the car came back down the forest road and it's just so rocky and rutted, it was hard to determine the direction of travel." Dustin's voice dropped at the end as he shook his head, frustration apparent.

Joyce nodded, peering up the forest road in the growing light. "So, our suspect could have taken both women to a single location, or separate ones. And one or both could be up off the lake somewhere, or anywhere off 135 between here and town."

"Right," Dustin said, grimly acknowledging just how vague that sounded, and how little help it was. "But the letter Grace's Mom got suggested the guy had her with him in some sort of house. That's the best we've got to go on. Let me take you up to the lake, and then I'll show you the map I've got with the locations of structures in the area that might qualify."

Dustin motioned to Joyce to get into his SUV and she hurried around to the passenger side, slid equipment and a clipboard out of the way, and buckled in, carefully preserving her coffee.

Up where the road ended, Dustin showed her Chris's truck, walked her around the area for about 15 minutes, and they drove back down. Nothing had jumped out at Joyce anywhere in the area. It was cold, quiet, and felt empty.

"Now what?" Dustin asked as he parked back at the turnout, turning to face Joyce. She was staring out of his windshield, thinking, holding the coffee cup against her knee.

"Are there any side roads or trailheads that leave 135 anywhere within a few miles of here? I didn't notice any on my way in, but you'd know." Joyce turned to look at Dustin, waiting for his response.

"No side roads, that's for sure. And the hillsides are steep where they meet the road. No official trailheads associated with the national forest land. There are a couple of places where folks park along the ditch and head up on snow machines in deep winter, but I doubt a passenger vehicle could get up in there," Dustin responded, mentally covering the distance.

"Our suspect doesn't seem to have much regard for the underside of his vehicle," Joyce said wryly, nodding back toward the rough forest road they'd just traversed. "Let's just take a quick look at those sled trails and then I want to see that map of yours."

Dustin nodded and pulled out of the turnout, heading back along 135. He slowed after about a mile, peering up at the brush above the ditch.

"First one is along in here somewhere…" he said. "The ground flattens out a bit just above the ditch, over a little ridge—"

"Stop. Right there. What's that?" Joyce was rolling down her window and leaning out, pointing up at something about four feet above the ditch.

Dustin pulled over and stopped the vehicle, peering through the windshield toward where Joyce was pointing.

"Get out," Joyce ordered as she opened her door and started clambering across the ditch. He turned off the engine and followed.

The morning sun was hitting the tops of the thick shrubs between two trees. Dustin noticed broken branches close to the ground that he hadn't seen before, but Joyce was pointing higher, into the top of a rangy serviceberry bush. He saw the glistening moisture on the leaves where the dusting of light snow had melted. Joyce had stopped, just above him, still pointing. His eyes followed.

A highly unnatural spill of bright gold glitter sparkled where it had caught along the central vein of half a dozen reddish brown leaves in the shrub.

"How did *that* get there?" Dustin asked, his brows pinched together in a frown. He looked up at Joyce, who was staring up the hillside to their left. She reached over and grabbed a fistful of his coat sleeve, hauling him closer and pointing again, her entire right arm aimed up hill on an angle.

"Look."

Dustin caught his balance and peered out along the line of Joyce's extended arm.

"Holy shit." He saw what Joyce saw. The snow had settled lightly in two parallel tracks heading away from above the rocky ditch through a scrabble of short undergrowth, invisible from the road. And in a rough line, a splotchy trail of bright gold glitter highlighted the right wheel track, up through a diagonal break in the trees.

"Any of your erstwhile houses up that way?" Joyce asked, one eyebrow raised, grinning.

Chris

Chris decided that circumstances justified her abuse of Grace Martinez's math book.

Her hands still secured painfully behind her back, she needed something with an edge that she could manipulate and hold with her booted feet. She flopped over onto her left side and used her right foot to scrape the thick textbook over to a spot beneath a wedge of hard, black stone jutting from the cave wall near the floor. If she could trap the book between her feet, she thought she could use it to dig enough dirt away from the side of the rock to expose its edge. And that cold, hard-edged rock might be just abrasive enough to gradually cut through the plastic tie on her wrists.

Chris tipped the book on its side and grasped it between her feet, wriggling it into position so the corner of the book was pointing above her boots. She propped herself half up, wincing as she let her weight fall back onto her left elbow and wiggled her butt over into position in front of the rock. Bending her legs at the knees, she banged the corner of the book into the dirt at the lower edge of the rock and watched as some of the silty grit gave way. She took a breath, tightened her stomach muscles for balance, and stabbed again at the same place. Knowing that the stiff corner of the book would be too battered to use more than a few more times, she aimed carefully with each kick. More dirt, and a couple of tight, pebbly clods fell away from the edge as Chris let herself fall back onto her side, breathing hard and feeling cold sweat trickle down her temples and dampen her armpits. She kicked the book out of the way and used her boot heel to jab more bluntly around the rock, four, five more times.

She stared at the stone in the dim light, memorizing its position before turning around to position her bound wrists beneath the sharpest edge. She began the agonizing process of scraping at the binding.

She was exhausted. The pain in the bones of her wrists and the joints of her elbows and shoulders ached and shot into her back and neck with the tiny movements she made against the sharp edge of rock behind her.

But she knew her life depended on getting her hands free. She needed water. She had to be able to climb. She couldn't count on rescue.

One more scrape. One more tug. One more lift, one more shove down over the tie.

The hours lay suspended around her in the damp air, going nowhere, as she lost herself in the effort to produce the grating sound of steady abrasion behind her back. The work was punctuated only by her own involuntary grunts as she stubbornly pushed the pain into the back of her mind, over and over.

Dustin

"We need a warrant. Let me call the sheriff to see who's on the bench this morning," Dustin said, circling a tiny square on the printout of a map and handing it to Joyce Martin while he reached for his phone.

"What's this?" Joyce asked.

"That's the property that just bounced up to our number one hidey-hole for Ronnie, the rat-bastard we both want to nail. Hang on a sec." Dustin tossed his phone onto the dash (no signal) and keyed open his radio.

"Dispatch, Deputy Anderson here, out on 135. We've got a lead on a location for our suspect. Can you put me through to the sheriff, please?"

Dustin didn't have to wait for more than the count of five before he had the sheriff on a recorded, but not broadcast, line. He filled his boss in on what Agent Martin had helped them find. And got what he wanted without asking. He turned back to Joyce.

"Sheriff Copeland is getting us the warrant. He's going to Judge Abram's house to get it signed since the court's not in session until nine o'clock. She'll be home with her kids, getting them out the door to school. He wants us to wait for him. He wants to go up there with us as backup. In case we get lucky."

Dustin didn't wait for a response from Joyce but bumped his patrol car off the shoulder of the road and accelerated back onto 135, heading toward Gandy.

"Where are we going? I thought your sheriff was meeting us here. Time is precious on something like this." Joyce's tone turned pedantic for the first time.

"And don't I know it. I got a family member missing out here, remember?" Dustin's annoyance showed and he didn't even turn his head to acknowledge what Joyce had said.

"Sorry. That was a stupid thing to say. What are you thinking?"

"That snowmobile track runs out along the base of Crown Mountain and then cuts back up into the national forest. It crosses another forest road, 1262, not more than a half mile in, and that road is in good enough shape for a passenger vehicle. At least one you didn't care about beating up." Dustin paused as he maneuvered a little too fast around a curve.

"Okay, and..." Joyce nudged.

"Forest Road 1262 leads back up the hill toward the other side of the lake I just showed you where Chris's truck is parked. It doesn't go all the way, though. It peters out by a remote campsite that was closed off by the forest service. It's too close to a couple of vents off an abandoned coal seam that's been smoldering for decades. Mortenson Mining left pits all over that area when they abandoned coal mine exploration. The Forest Service gated the area, but the pits are dangerous—just deep enough for some kid screwing around out there to fall into. Too many risks to encourage people to camp and hike in the area."

"And what did you just circle on this map?" Joyce flicked the map she was holding toward Dustin.

"That property," Dustin nodded toward the map, "is a cabin built around

1930. An old man named Martin Davis owned it last, but he died five years ago. His son comes out here from Missouri once or twice a year to check on it, since he hasn't decided if he wants to sell it or not. It's just sitting there, furnished, with a well and a wood stove and electrical service. Move-in ready, as they say," he said, drily.

"How far is it from here?" Joyce asked.

"Not far as the crow flies, but the actual access road is on the other side of Crown Mountain. The property is long and narrow and butts up against the national forest right along Forest Road 1262. Not far at all from that old campsite, if you know the area."

"You're right, we need backup," Joyce said, her voice grim but intensely focused.

Dustin hit a straight stretch of road and called dispatch again to tell Sheriff Copeland where to meet them on Forest Road 1262.

The two law officers dropped into their respective silences as Dustin drove. When they hit the edge of town, Joyce unclipped her phone from her belt.

"Oh, good. Four bars again. Civilization," Joyce muttered. "What's the actual address on that property, Deputy?"

"Number 24 Picket Spring Road. Random number. There's nothing else out there so Picket Spring is a long dirt driveway that runs along the creek. It's a marked right turn off Crown Mountain Road, though. Why?"

"Google Earth is my friend when I want to see where we're going. Sorry, I'm a control freak."

Becca

"Wait!" Grace hissed as Becca felt around the facing of the doorknob in the dark, hunting for the screws that held it in place.

"What? What's wrong?" Becca whispered back, confused.

"Listen. I heard the garage door," Grace said, moving to the vent to listen more closely. "He's coming back into the house. We can't let him know we think we have a way out."

Becca sat back on her heels, holding the screwdriver shaft they had found, and listened. She heard what Grace did. The rough mechanical clatter of a garage door rising. A car engine's roar, and then silence. The garage door closing again. He was back.

"What was that?" Becca had heard a click, then the sound of wood scraping on some other surface.

"That's the door at the top of the stairs to the basement. He's coming down," Grace explained, her voice tight. "He may just be bringing food."

"Do we make a run for it? Knock him over and bolt?" Becca hadn't thought this through.

"He carries a gun, remember? Bad odds."

It was too late for more problem solving. Becca crawled away from the door, reaching for Grace, and positioning herself between the door and the little girl, one hand on Grace's leg for orientation in the darkness.

The next thing they heard was the scrabbling sound of the metal key going into the door lock and turning. Becca's heart was pounding but a sudden blast of fury overcame her fear and she got up, wanting to be prepared to fight. The knob turned and a wedge of blinding light spread into the cellar along with the greasy scent of fried fast food.

Becca raised one arm to block the light, hoping to see the man's face, but he stepped quickly into the small room and grabbed her by the hair, yanking her forward. Becca's head twisted sideways, and she saw the dark glint of light on the barrel of his handgun. She tried to knock it away with her left hand, but the man was quick and strong, hauling her into his body and stepping backward through the door. Becca shifted her weight onto her left foot, drew her right leg back, and rammed her knee up toward the man's groin as hard and fast as she could.

"BITCH!" The man grunted and fell backward, out of the doorway, rolling sideways and clutching his crotch. He let go of Becca's head, but he didn't let go of the gun. Becca scrabbled backward, trying to regain her balance as the man rose to his knees snarling incoherently and fixing a black glare into her eyes.

He smacked the door closed in front of him, the bottom of the door catching Becca's fingers. She yelped and fell back into the cellar on her knees, clutching her hand to her belly and wincing. Becca and Grace could both hear the man swearing as he turned the lock again, slamming the upper part of the door with his fist and kicking it.

"Fine! Die in there! Starve!" They heard the soft *thwap* of the paper bag thrown against the outside of the door, and some of the contents spill. But then they heard his angry footsteps pound back up the stairs. And the sound of scraping wood just before the door at the top of the stairs banged closed.

Neither Grace nor Becca spoke for a full minute, sitting close to each other, breathing hard from the adrenaline blast they each had to settle.

"Nice crotch shot," Grace said with genuine admiration. But Becca could hear the tremor in the girl's voice, just under the bravado.

Becca was still catching her breath. And thinking. After another minute, she spoke. "Grace?"

"In attendance," Grace replied, as though her teacher was calling roll. Becca grinned in the dark.

"We gotta get out of here. The man upstairs is not pleased with me."

"Yeah. I agree. On both points. But how do we get past him?"

Becca sighed and was quiet again for a few moments. She scooted around so she was facing Grace in the darkness, her big knees touching Grace's smaller ones. "What do you know about the layout of the house?" Becca asked.

"I've only seen part of it. He's taken me out of here a few times when someone was coming to the house. Like a repair guy. He had to have the septic fixed once—I heard him talking on his phone, pretending to be a property manager or something, giving directions. He'd drive around with me in the backseat until the house was empty again."

"Okay, what did you see?"

"The top of the basement stairway opens into a little hallway off the kitchen. The door to the garage is off the kitchen. There's a bathroom with a sink and toilet in the hallway. He lets me use it sometimes. The other direction is a little living room, and I could see a front door with curtains in a little window in the door. It was right at the bottom of the stairs that go up to the second floor. I haven't ever been up there, but that's probably where his bedroom is. I don't know. I heard a TV on up there. It isn't a very big house." Grace's voice trailed off.

"That helps. A lot," Becca said reassuringly. "Is there another door or some kind of outside entrance to the basement?"

"I don't know. He's always just taken me up the stairs. But there is something on the other side of the stairs. Through another door that's usually pulled over. I couldn't see in, and it was dark."

"Okay. There's the garage exit, a front door, and not sure about another way out from the basement. And windows, on both the main floor and second floor, right?"

"Yeah, there's a window that opens in the kitchen, over the sink. But I don't know about the living room. Never been in there. It's not like we sit and stream Disney Channel together," Grace said, dry wit back in place.

Becca spurted a laugh and grinned into the darkness, shaking her head. "You crack me up, Gracie."

"That's what my mom calls me. Gracie." Grace's voice was suddenly soft, and strained.

Becca's heart broke, hearing the pain held back behind Grace's brave demeanor. "Hang in here with me, honey. I'm hatching a plan."

Gracie swiped at her eyes and took a deep breath. "Do say more."

"Let me work my magic on this door lock first. Then…how about we find a door that's somewhere Jackass isn't?"

"I like it. Simple. Low-tech. Not sure about the odds, though, Becca. He's in the house, and it's not exactly a sprawling mansion."

"Yeah, I know. But there are two of us and one of him. And you're small and quicker than I am. I'm betting at least one of us can escape and get help."

Becca crawled back over to the door, pulled out the screwdriver, and started the job of taking it apart again. She spoke very quietly to Grace over her shoulder.

"Plan A is finding an exit to the outside from the basement. These old places sometimes have a funky, wide, slanted door and a few steps that made it easy to deliver coal or wood to a furnace under the house. Plan B is to get to the top of the basement stairs and listen really carefully to try to hear where he might be. You said you heard a TV up on the second floor. If we're lucky, he'll be holed up there with a beer and a ballgame or something, and we can slide on out of the kitchen to the garage. Plan C is, well…innovation in the moment. Based on data we don't have right now."

Grace didn't respond but listened to the small sounds of screwdriver on metal, and Becca jostling the doorknob occasionally.

"Okay, I've got the facing off. If I can figure out how to remove the knob, or jimmy the locking mechanism, or…" Becca's voice drifted off in concentration. Then Grace heard a light clatter of metal pieces sliding against each other and a little thud as something hit the dirt floor by the door.

"Voila! Daddy's girl, now and forever," Becca declared softly. She pushed the door gently and it swung open in front of the cellar, the basement appearing beyond in the soft light of a small, ground-level window up near the ceiling. "C'mon, Grace. Commence Plan A."

"Bring the screwdriver, Becca," Grace said quietly. Becca already had it jammed in the hip pocket of her jeans and patted it to show Grace.

Grace got to her feet and followed on Becca's heels, pointing toward the bottom of the stairs. They got there and paused, listening, but heard nothing from the floor above. Becca reached over and gave the door to the other side of the basement a light push and poked her head through. There was a narrow window near the ceiling over a decrepit-looking washing machine, and she could see the frame of a door on the other side of the room. But it was boarded over.

Grace's head poked through under Becca's elbow and Becca pointed to what had once been the door.

"No joy. Plan B," Becca whispered to the top of Grace's head, which nodded once.

The two crept carefully up the stairs to the door they knew opened into the hallway beside the kitchen. On the top stair, they stopped, listening.

"Can you hear anything?" Becca wasn't sure Grace could even hear her. But Grace stepped up to cup one hand against Becca's ear.

"TV is on. From upstairs."

Becca nodded and reached up to take hold of the old, round metal door-knob. There was no landing or railing at the top of the stairs. Becca thought briefly and irrationally about what it would take to bring the stairwell up to code. She shook her head to focus again and leaned down so her mouth was against Grace's temple.

"You ready?"

Grace nodded. Becca nodded. Becca took a deep breath, twisted the knob slowly until the latch gave with a snick, and slowly pushed open the door just a crack. She waited, listening again. No movement. No noise. She pushed the door open the rest of the way and motioned Grace to squeeze past and go ahead of her. Becca followed, silently, and could hear the prattle and cheers from something on the TV coming through the floor above them.

Grace turned quickly and hustled through the kitchen with Becca right behind her. In four steps, they were at the door leading to the garage. Grace twisted the small button lock on the cheap inner door and opened it, stepping down one stair and into the musty garage. She squeezed along the side of the beat-up blue sedan, making room for Becca to follow. Becca cleared the door and closed it silently behind her. They were out.

Becca looked up at the wide garage door, checking the rack and looking on the wall to see if it was operated electronically or manually. There was a wall button next to the door they'd just come through, lit faintly by an LED bulb. Grace turned to go back up the step and reached for the button, but Becca grabbed her hand to stop her.

Grace looked up at Becca, her eyes seeping fear and confusion. Becca pointed to the old motor mounted from a sagging metal bracket on the ceiling of the garage.

"It's crap. And noisy enough that we could hear it all the way down in the cellar. He'd hear it for sure," Becca whispered. "C'mon."

Becca took hold of Grace's hand and led her quickly around to the back of the car, squeezing through the narrow space between the bumper and the garage door.

"Get down," Becca said, indicating Grace should kneel on the floor, out of sight at the back of the vehicle. Becca slipped around to the drivers' side and peered in the window around the steering column, hoping to see keys dangling helpfully from the ignition. No such luck. She crept back to Grace's side and knelt beside her.

"Grace, there's a manual pull cord I can reach, hanging down above the hood of the car. When I pull it, the locking mechanism will release, and we'll be able to lift the door enough to roll out under it. But the release will be loud. He might hear it, so we're going to have to move fast, understand?"

Grace nodded, and Becca watched her start to work her small hands under the decayed rubber of the insulation strip at the bottom of the garage door. Smart girl, Becca thought, as she slipped back around the side of the car and reached for the pull cord. She took a deep breath, grabbed it, and pulled firmly, trying not to jerk it. She felt it give, with a heavy thunk and a metallic rattle coming from the locking mechanism. No way that wasn't audible inside the house.

Becca dove back to the garage door and crammed her own hands under the small gap that Grace had already made, then squatted and pulled up on the heavy panels. Grace scooted under and Becca lifted the door a bit further until it held about two feet up from the ground. She rolled out and got onto her knees, frantically gesturing for Grace to run for the trees. But Grace was bending over at the edge of the driveway next to the door, picking up a rock.

"Grace, *run!*"

"No, give me the screwdriver!"

"What are you doing??"

"Just give it," Grace hissed, reaching toward Becca's hip pocket. Becca grabbed the long Phillips from her pocket and handed it to Grace as she got to her feet, looking around to get her bearings.

It was a bright, sunny day, cold and clear. She looked down to see Grace rolling like a tiny log back under the gap beneath the garage door, gripping the rock in one hand and the screwdriver in the other. In less than the count of two, Becca heard a hard rap of rock hitting metal, followed by the hiss of air escaping a tire. She saw the bottoms of Grace's sneakers flip and roll about four feet to the left, and the same sound started coming from the other back tire. Grace had just disabled the car.

Becca leaned over to pull Grace out by her ankles, and the little girl squeaked but emerged, grinning like a little demon.

"Let's get outta here!" Grace said and started running. Becca was unfolding herself upright when she heard the door slam against the wall inside the garage and a string of expletives as the man's big fist hit the automatic garage door opener—to no avail.

"He's coming, Grace! Faster!!"

Becca's feet slipped on the gravel, and she caught herself with one hand and regained her footing to start running. She heard a deep, guttural howl right behind her as the man hauled open the garage door the rest of the way.

She didn't look back. Grace was already 20 yards ahead of her, long blonde braids flying back and forth over her narrow shoulders.

"You BITCH! I'm gonna kill you! Grace, get back here right now!"

Becca looked over her shoulder, saw the crazed, dark look in the man's eyes, and wanted nothing more than to keep running as hard and fast as she could. But Grace...Becca knew she needed to buy Grace more time.

Becca whirled around and watched as the man closed the distance in three long strides, his right arm cocking back like he meant to take a hard punch at her head. She flashed back into a memory of playing backyard football with her three brothers and tucked her head slightly to her left, lunging forward and planting her right shoulder into his solar plexus.

Her face scraped down across something metal on the side of his belt, but the loud whoofing grunt she heard, with all the air leaving the man's lungs, was immensely satisfying. She fell hard, half on top of his chest, and rolled to the left, trying to get her legs under her.

But he was fast. Out of the corner of Becca's eye, she saw him clasp both hands together, raising them above her back, and felt the impact of his body weight slamming into her kidneys. She dropped hard, feeling the gravel of the driveway grind into her cheekbone. It hurt.

A second later, she saw his booted foot lashing toward her ribs, and she curled sideways to try to absorb the blow. In the same movement, she reached up and grabbed his other leg with both arms and yanked as hard as she could. As he lost balance and dropped with a yelp, she stood up, reared back, and kicked his startled-looking face as hard as she could.

Then Becca ran, as fast as she ever had, fueled by adrenaline and terror, knowing that the sharp object her face had encountered on the man's belt was his gun. Grace had already disappeared ahead of her, around a curve in the narrow dirt lane that led away from the house.

Becca didn't know whether the man on the ground behind her was still conscious or not. She didn't look back. She leapt the ditch and stumbled between the trees, smashing through a snare of shrubs and tearing her shirt in the brambles. She kept running into the forest, vaguely keeping the dirt lane to her right, wanting objects between her and the man behind her, if he was following or about to start shooting.

She had no idea where she was, but she knew the guy behind her couldn't chase them both simultaneously. She decided getting lost in the woods was preferable to being out on the open lane. Bizarrely, a line from a novel she'd recently read, set in the twisted lanes and canals of Venice, popped into her head: "Getting lost is the only place worth going to."

She kept running.

Dustin

Dustin Anderson and Agent Joyce Martin both had a grim confidence that they were going to find something at the small, remote house they were approaching. Dustin's boss, Butte County Sheriff Jim Copeland, was following them, light bar flashing blue and red against the light snow covering the hills.

What they weren't expecting, when they turned off Crown Mountain Road and onto the mile-plus dirt lane that led down to the house, was to see a 12-year-old girl charging up the road to greet them.

"Jesus, Dustin, it's her! It's Grace! Pull over!" Joyce was half out of the passenger side of the police vehicle before he rolled to a stop.

Joyce ran up the road to meet Grace, her own maternal instincts swimming over her FBI agent identity.

"Grace, honey, I'm an FBI agent, are you okay?"

"You better be carrying, lady," Grace panted, looking over her shoulder back down the road. "And my friend Becca should be right behind me, but she's not, 'cuz she stopped to kick the living shit outta the asshole who took us."

Dustin was jogging up to join Joyce and Grace, looking past them up the road and scanning the surrounding woods.

"Grace. I'm Deputy Anderson. The sheriff is right behind us…"

"You need to get back in your car and get down this road, mister, and find Becca. The guy has a gun and he's mean, and I don't know if he's got her again or not." Grace was glaring at them impatiently and pointing back at Dustin's SUV. The sheriff was pulling up behind them.

"Joyce, get back in and take my car back to the main road with Grace," Dustin said, tossing her his keys and waving the sheriff forward.

Dustin jogged back and leaned in the sheriff's driver's side window to tell him what was happening. Grace watched the sheriff nod, and Dustin ran around the beefy SUV and got into the passenger seat as the sheriff pulled forward to head on down the road.

Joyce understood jurisdictional authority. She had Grace. They had a missing woman and an armed felon to deal with, both of whom were county business.

Sheriff Copeland drove forward slowly, scanning the forest margin along both sides of the road. If Becca had managed to get away from her captor, she would be somewhere between them and the house.

"The missing woman is your cousin, right, Anderson?"

"Yes, sir. Her name is Becca MacLeod. About 5'8", lean, athletic build, short brown hair, glasses, my age, 32, 33. She's tough, but she's got a heart of gold. We need to find her."

The sheriff slowed to a stop and pointed off to his right.

"Over there, I thought I saw movement," he said, quietly.

Dustin opened his door slowly, scanning the woods in both directions, and planted one black booted foot on the ground. He called out, his voice low and forceful.

"Sheriff's Office! Make yourself known! Move slowly, hands in the air!"

"Dustin?" The voice, a breathless alto, was coming from a stand of aspen.

"Becca! Is that you?"

"Be careful, Dustin, I think he's on foot behind me, back up toward the house somewhere. And armed," Becca said, stepping out from behind a huge aspen tree.

"Stay there, Becca! I'm coming to you. We'll come back to the vehicle together." Dustin's heart lurched when he saw Becca's face, scraped, bleeding, a huge black-and-green bruise spreading across her cheek from her right eye. He ran to her in a crouch, his service weapon drawn but pointed toward the ground, and knelt in front of her.

"Jesus, Becca, are you okay?"

"Fine, given the givens. Have you found Grace?"

"She met us, running like a little Olympian up the road. She sent us to find you before we could even get her in a vehicle." He smiled. "She's a spunky kid."

"She really is. You have no idea. The guy…"

Becca squatted back down low behind the tree, leaning against it, wincing. Dustin peered into her face, concerned, trying to check her pupils. He scanned the woods again, quickly.

"Becca, can you walk?"

"Yeah, I'm fine." Becca stood, looking back toward the road, frowning. "I don't know where he is, though. He was down when I got away from him. I thought he was out, but he was still squirming. A little." She looked back at Dustin and saw the quirk of a smile.

"We'll find him. Come on, let's get you back with Grace in my car."

Dustin holstered his weapon when he saw Sheriff Copeland behind the open door of his vehicle, weapon drawn, scanning the area, and giving them cover. Dustin placed one big hand on Becca's back and nudged her toward the road.

Dustin tucked Becca into the back seat of Sheriff Copeland's vehicle as he made introductions and climbed into the passenger seat beside Sheriff Copeland. The Sheriff turned the car around and sped back toward the turnoff where they knew Agent Martin had taken Dustin's vehicle while Dustin radioed for EMS support and provided coordinates.

After dropping Becca off with Agent Martin and Grace, Sheriff Copeland and Dustin took off back down the dirt road, hunting for their suspect.

They were 95 percent sure they were about to find Ronnie Mathews. They now knew the man had a history of second-degree assault, robbery, child endangerment and a list of more petty crimes dating back to his teens. He'd been out of prison for six months after serving 10 years.

Sheriff Copeland slowed as he came around a curve where tree branches hung over the road from a steep slope on the right. The house was less than 1,000 feet ahead of them, but they still couldn't see it.

"There," Dustin said, pointing to a sprawled male figure lying off to the side of the driveway, one arm folded beneath him awkwardly, the other extended off to his side, loosely clutching a .45 caliber handgun. He wasn't moving.

"Well, we've got him on weapons possession at least. If he's still alive," Dustin muttered.

"You want to take him?"

"My pleasure, sir." Dustin stepped out of the car, weapon drawn, and called out the series of warnings and commands that embodied protocol. He saw the man's lower leg move and heard him moan, but he didn't get up. Dustin had him cuffed in under 30 seconds. The right side of Ronnie's face was shredded and bloody and he wasn't entirely coherent, other than spitting a few curse words through his teeth.

Sheriff Copeland had joined Dustin. Both men looked up in surprise at the sound of a vehicle approaching. It was Joyce, driving Dustin's County SUV, slowing to a stop some distance back on the road while she assessed the situation. After a brief pause, Joyce pulled forward. Dustin frowned as she rolled down her window to look at Ronnie, sitting cross-legged on the ground, tipping slightly to one side, head lolling against his chest, one eye socket looking not right.

"Nice work, Becca," Joyce said over her shoulder into the back seat where Grace and Becca were buckled.

"What's going on, Agent Martin? EMS out of Gandy are on their way," Sheriff Copeland said quietly, none too pleased that she had left the main road where EMS would be looking for her and the two victims.

"These two say they're okay. Your suspect will go to the head of the line since Becca left him in worse shape. And Grace here thinks she may know where Becca's friend Chris is."

Grace's head popped up to the small opening in the thick acrylic shield between the back and front seats of Dustin's police vehicle.

"Lemme out of the car. The child locks are on back here," Grace demanded, loudly, one palm plastered to the barrier.

Joyce used the controls to roll down the back windows and Dustin stepped over to Grace's side. She was looking past him to stare at the pitiful heap that was Ronnie Mathews.

"Yeah, that's him, in case you needed an official ID," Grace said. "He's a real jerk. Don't let him loose."

Dustin grinned. "Yes, ma'am. Now what do you know about Chris?"

"Not sure. But when he"—Grace jutted her chin toward her captor—"first brought me here, he took me out of his car and put me down in this rocky pit, like a cave, but deep. I couldn't get out. It was nasty. He left me there awhile." Grace's voice dropped, the memory obviously filling her head.

"Do you know where it was?" Dustin had knelt to look at Grace eye to eye, speaking softly and respectfully.

Grace responded, her voice sober but calm. "Not exactly. But I think I can get us close if you drive. We'll need four-wheel-drive. It's off in the woods. And Becca's coming with us. Chris is her friend." Grace said it definitively, no negotiation offered to the armed, uniformed, six-foot, 200-pound officer in front of her.

Dustin looked past Grace to Becca, one eyebrow raised in question.

"Yeah, Dustin, I want to come. I've got a headache but I'm okay. Concussion protocol can wait. We need to find Chris."

Dustin sighed, pushed off the car door and walked over to the sheriff. He spoke to his senior officer quietly, out of hearing from the three women in his car. The sheriff nodded and gestured to Joyce to join him.

Dustin walked back to his own vehicle and thanked Joyce for taking guard duty with Sheriff Copeland. He folded himself into the drivers' seat as Grace sat up again, her mouth pressed to the barrier behind his head.

"Hey! I need to see so I can tell you where to go, okay?! Let me out!"

Dustin looked up in his rear-view mirror to see a fierce pre-teen glaring at him, and without a word, he clicked open the rear door locks. Grace scrambled out of the car, gave one disgusted look toward Ronnie Mathews, and reached up to yank open the front passenger-side door.

She climbed in and looked around, wide-eyed, at all the gear and extra switches and controls on Dustin's dash.

"Cool!" Grace said, eyes bright.

"Seatbelt, Grace," Dustin ordered, with just a hint of amusement.

He looked into his rearview mirror again to see Becca grinning.

"Where to?" Dustin asked, looking over to Grace as she finished clicking her seatbelt in place.

"Behind the house. Look for a trash dump."

Chris

Chris was slumped against the wall of the pit, exhausted. She was dehydrated, hungry, sleep-deprived, and in pain. After hours of agonizing effort, she had freed her bound wrists, the result of freakish persistence at the wedge of rock she had exposed to serve as an abrasive surface against the plastic zip tie handcuffs. But her wrists were shredded down to bone.

She knew that despair led to death. But the fleeting thoughts equating death with relief begged to be entertained. She mentally slapped them away, dropping back into a numb daze, too tired to think, much less move.

She had hoped that when she had the free use of arms and hands, she could find a way to climb out of the hole. Her injuries had severely sapped her energy, though, as had the dehydration. She could barely lift her arms, much less use them to climb a nearly vertical wall of earth.

She knew it was day, probably mid-day, by the angle of the shafts of light that reached partway down the cave walls through the leafy grid that covered the opening to the cave. She looked at the rope lashing that held the branches together and knew the opening was invisible to anyone casually walking by.

Chris forced herself to concentrate on her own breathing, the internal resonance of her heartbeat, and reminded herself that staying alive was the key at this point.

Minutes later—or hours, she didn't really know—a faint, unnatural humming vibration reached her through the rock or the air. She thought she was hallucinating bees. Or a distant jet passing over. But the vibration steadily consolidated into sound. A sporadic, mechanical, definitely man-made sort of sound. Chris managed to get to her feet, palms flattened against the wall of the cave, straining to hear.

Grace had led Dustin out the back of the property, over a stinking heap of dumped and rotting garbage that both she and Becca recognized. Ronnie had brought them both to the house over this obscure, rough path through the woods.

The SUV that Dustin was driving had a wide wheelbase, and he was grinding his way through dense brush and over the ends of fallen trees. He ignored the screech of broken branches etching long scratches in the vehicle's paint job. He just didn't want to end up stuck.

After a mile or so of maneuvering through the woods, Dustin bumped up onto a cleared track. He stopped and reached past Grace to flip open the glove box and pull out the map he'd made of the area. He thought he knew where they were.

"Hey, Becca," Dustin spoke over his shoulder into the back seat.

"Yeah?"

"Remember that old coal mining area up in the middle of the national forest? The one near the far campground that the feds shut down for safety reasons?"

Becca retrieved a 20-year-old memory, the fragments of which held images of deep woods, the fear and thrill of getting lost or attacked by wild animals, and the adventure of 13-year-olds looking for the caves that might hold hidden treasure. "We used to sneak out there as kids, right? From the lake?"

"Yeah, that's right. There are exploration pits out there in a zone the Forest Service closed off ages ago. But 'closed off' is a relative term. That's why they shut down that campsite. Didn't want anyone stumbling into them."

"Dustin, I bet you're right! I bet that's where he took Grace and maybe where he has Chris! Can you find it? From wherever we are?"

Becca was excited. The description Grace had given them of the cave-like pit matched what both Dustin and Becca remembered from their childhoods.

Dustin looked at the map, angling it to catch the light coming in through his windshield. He had it memorized but wasn't sure of their orientation coming out of the woods from the house.

"I think the guy turned left off this road and straight through the woods to the house," Grace said, leaning over to peer at the map Dustin was holding, even though she really couldn't make sense of the squiggly lines and tiny squares and other symbols.

"That's good, Grace. That makes sense if I'm reading this right. We'd need to turn right here to connect to the other forest road that goes near where we need to be. Want to hold this for me?" Dustin looked down at Grace, grateful for the little girl's resilience and determination to help. Most kids would just be crying for safety and wanting to go home.

"Okay. Let's find Chris." Dustin spoke into the windshield as he leaned forward, deciding where to aim the vehicle as he turned onto the rutted surface.

After about two miles, they came to a rough intersection with another forest road, no better than the one they had been on, but marked by a small metal sign stamped with the road number Dustin was hoping to see for confirmation. He turned left, heading up the mountainside. In his mind, he was on the road that would come out on the far side of the open meadowland near the dry lakebed where Chris had abandoned her truck. The closed campground and mining site were about a mile short of that opening.

"Found it," Dustin said, determined satisfaction in his voice. He pulled up next to the bar of a closed metal gate decorated with warning signs prohibiting entry. The paint was scraped and faded to dull silver with only a few hints of forest-service green remaining.

Dustin, Grace, and Becca climbed out of the car, and Grace migrated quickly to Becca's side. The two females looked to Dustin as he scanned the area on the other side of the gate.

"A little way beyond this gate we should find old campsites that haven't been used in forever. If I remember right, the area with the exploration pits lies about a half mile into the woods, straight back from where the camp toilets used to be."

Becca ducked under the arm of the gate. "That's what I remember, too, Dustin," Becca said. "We used a path that led away from the back of the toilets."

Dustin looked at Grace as she followed eagerly on Becca's heels, not even giving him a glance. He was about to tell her to wait in the car, then decided it was futile. He called forward to them both. "Hey—we're going to have to be careful walking out there past the campground. It was closed off for a reason. Some of those pits and caves have collapsed and I don't want any of us falling in."

"Okay, Dad," Becca said with a smile, reaching back to grab Dustin's hand and give it a squeeze. "We'll stick together."

Dustin gave her a wry smile in return. "Thank you for humoring a protective male."

The three hustled up the path and had no trouble finding the wide, overgrown circle of weedy campsites. At the far end, they found the cement pad where the outhouses had once stood, the twin septic pits filled in long ago.

"I think it was this way," Becca said, pointing straight back and a bit to the right of where they were standing beside the crumbling square of cement.

Dustin nodded and plunged into the overgrown brush, holding back the thicker branches so they wouldn't snap into Grace's and Becca's faces. After 10 minutes, they started yelling Chris's name. Dustin directed Becca and Grace to split off about 50 feet to his left so they could cover more ground as they looked for the mining pits.

Fifteen minutes later, Becca reached out and grabbed Grace's shoulder. "Did you hear something?"

Grace looked up like she was sniffing the air, listening. They heard Dustin off to their right, still bellowing Chris's name.

"Dustin, quiet! I heard something," Becca called out. "Come this way!"

Dustin picked his way over and Becca shouted for Chris again. They stood together in silence, listening to the soft sounds of the breeze in the trees. A raven flew overhead, and the air was so still they could all hear its wingbeats.

"Over here!" The faint cry drifted toward them from somewhere off to their left. Becca and Dustin looked at each other, eyes wide, and Dustin nodded and took off in that direction.

Becca began crashing through the brush behind Dustin. "Chris! We're here, where are you, yell again!"

She heard Chris's voice again, though it was difficult to tell what direction it was coming from, exactly. Grace was quickly picking her way over the ground in a slightly different direction.

"Guys! Over here! I remember that busted-off tree!" Grace was pointing at a huge lightning-blasted Douglas fir, its top half skewered into the ground in a heap of thick branches. Dustin and Becca followed Grace toward the fallen tree. "I know we're close," Grace said.

"Chris! Where are you!" Becca shouted again, her voice echoing back off the hillside.

"Here! I'm down here!"

Dustin lunged to his left about 10 feet and went down on his knee, grabbing at something on the ground and heaving it up over his shoulder. It was a leafy platform of crisscrossed branches. He dropped to the ground and peered over the edge of the hole. Fifteen feet below, he saw a pair of exhausted eyes looking up at him over a very tired but happy smile.

"Judging from the tan uniform, you must be Dustin," Chris said, her voice weak but incredibly relieved.

Becca dove to the ground next to Dustin and looked down at Chris. "Chris! Oh, God, we found you!"

"Hey, Becca. Thanks for bringing the cavalry."

Grace called out from behind the two adults. "Um, I could use some help over here..."

Becca and Dustin turned in unison to see Grace trying to fish something loose from the crude platform that Dustin had hauled off the pit opening. Dustin rose to his feet to help.

"It's like a rope ladder. It's tied into these two big, heavy branches in the middle. You have to slide the cover partway back over the hole, but it's what he used to climb in and out," Grace explained.

Dustin and Grace untangled the rope and stretched it out on the ground. Dustin checked the knots and made sure it looked like it would hold together. Becca didn't want to leave the cave opening and just kept talking to Chris, explaining what they were doing.

Dustin returned to the edge of the cave, Grace plopping down beside him. "Hi," Grace said to Chris, grinning. "I'm Grace. It sucks down there, I know. We're gonna get you out."

Grace leapt back up, turned, and started tugging on the edge of the platform. Dustin stood up and quietly asked her to step back while he crouched at one side of the grid, locked his ham-like hands around the main branch, and dead-lifted it up and half over the opening. Grace grabbed the end of the rope ladder and with Becca's help, started feeding it down the wall of the pit.

Chris watched the end of the ladder snake toward where she was standing. She reached up to grab the bottom and winced against the pain she now felt acutely from her damaged wrists. The cuts were deep and raw. With the addition of light, she could see ligament moving over bone in her right wrist. If she looked, which she had been avoiding doing. She flopped back against the wall, cradling her right wrist in her less-damaged left hand.

"I'm not sure I can climb this thing without help," Chris called out, pain and frustration in her voice. Escape was so close.

Dustin quickly realized she was hurt.

"Chris, tell me what your injuries are," he asked.

Chris explained that her legs were okay, but her wrists were hamburger and her left shoulder hurt like hell.

"Do you think you can wrap your arms around Becca for balance while standing on each rung of this ladder, going slowly up, one at a time, until I can reach your upper body to haul you out?" Dustin's voice was worried but hopeful.

"Let's give it a try. God knows I'm motivated," Chris replied.

Dustin had Grace sit on the outer edge of the platform as additional counterweight while he sent Becca down the ladder to help get Chris in position. Chris wrapped her arms around Becca's neck and jammed her feet onto the lowest rung of the ladder. Becca hauled her friend up, one step at a time, Chris using the last of her energy just to hold on to Becca and use her legs to push up from each rung of the ladder.

At the top, Chris let go of Becca and wrapped her arms through the last rung of the ladder above her and hung there, panting. Becca clambered out of the hole and looked back down, catching sight of Chris's bloody wrists and forearms in the sunlight for the first time.

"Oh, Chris, your wrists!"

Dustin grimaced and then extended his upper body out over the opening, reached down, locked his hands under Chris's armpits, and pulled her up, his neck and shoulder muscles bunching beneath his shirt. Becca leaned down and grabbed Chris's shirt and then the waistband of her jeans and hauled backward as hard as she could. Chris got her foot onto the top rung of the ladder and shoved her weight upward to help clear the edge.

The three of them collapsed in a relieved heap on the ground. Grace looked on with a big smile.

"Let's get you three back to town," Dustin said. "I want all three of you checked out at the clinic, and Chris, those wrists are going to need some serious patching up."

"Got any water in your car, Dustin? I'm down a couple quarts," Chris said.

"Yeah, I do."

"I'll go get it," Grace offered eagerly, and took off running in the direction of the campground.

Dustin looked after her, shaking his head, and let her go, signaling Becca to help him get Chris to her feet.

Dustin and Becca half-carried Chris back to the campground and got her settled on a big flat rock.

"I think I've got something in my vehicle I can use to vandalize federal property," Dustin said. "I'm gonna open that gate and drive down here to get you. Stay put."

Dustin started jogging back out of the campground as Grace came running back past him, two small water bottles clutched in her hands. He nodded to her and kept going.

Fifteen minutes later, Dustin reappeared, driving his SUV toward them, bouncing over the rough ground. He got Chris settled in the back seat with Becca, who helped get a seatbelt fastened around Chris's body and then placed her hand reassuringly on Chris's thigh.

Grace climbed in front with Dustin, and he waited while the little girl jammed her seatbelt into place and nodded permission for him to go. With a deep sigh, Dustin put the SUV in low gear and headed back out toward civilization.

"Grace, Sheriff Copeland called your mom. She knows you're okay and she's driving over from Utah right now. Agent Martin is going to meet her at the border and lead her down to our office in Cortez, so she doesn't have to drive all the way up here. We'll get you two back together there," Dustin explained.

"Can I call her?" Grace asked.

"Absolutely. We'll have cell signal again in a few minutes and you can use my phone," he replied.

"Tell you what," Chris said from the back seat. "As soon as they get me bandaged up and moderately rehydrated, I'm buying us dinner. *All* of us. Including your mom, Grace. I want to meet her."

No one argued. They were all starving. Chris turned to Becca.

"What's the best place in Cortez?"

"Hands down, The Three Swordsmen. You wouldn't think a British pub would fly in Southwestern Colorado, but they've got awesome burgers, and fish 'n chips to die for. They've adapted—killer burritos, too."

Chris let her head drop back against the seat, eyes closed and moaning with anticipated delight.

"Drive faster, Cousin," Becca quipped, "this woman is having olfactory hallucinations."

AUNT CATHERINE'S FIREHOUSE

After Kate Perrin graduated from Cal Poly's architecture and design school, she came home to her parents' turquoise split-level outside of Sacramento for a visit. She dropped her duffel just inside the door, looked down to her right, and found her mom and dad ensconced on their respective ends of the tan sectional sofa. It took up half the traditional sunken living room, which a designer friend said they could make look bigger by hanging a large mirror on the walnut-toned paneling.

Kate checked her appearance in the mirror. She still looked exhausted from finals, and she tucked an escaped strand of brunette hair behind her ear.

"Hey, Katy-girl, how's it feel to be a full-fledged architect?" Her dad looked up from his *Sacramento Bee*, from which he was carefully setting aside pages with coupons for later clipping.

"I'm good, Dad, glad it's over. Hey, Mom."

Her mom looked over her cheaters with a smile, keeping her hands attached to either side of a pale wood embroidery frame. Kate peered at the center of the tightly stretched linen fabric, out of which an exceptionally colorful rooster appeared to be sprouting.

"This one's gonna be the bomb, honey. Wait 'til you see it. You'll be wanting a matched pair for your new apartment." Her mom nodded happily and plucked a length of scarlet thread from the jumble beside her on the sofa.

Embroidery was Annie Perrin's newest hobby, part of a long quest to "keep the old domestic arts alive."

"I'm sure, Mom. Except I'm more into mid-century modern than rustic farmhouse these days," Kate said, taking three quick steps across the living room floor and giving her mom a peck on the cheek. She backed around the worn ottoman and plopped down next to her dad on the side of the sofa that was not occupied by his disassembled newspaper.

"So," she said, peering up into her dad's face.

"So, what?" he replied, the beginning of their old banter.

"Sooooooo, how's Aunt Catherine?" Kate had picked a topic sure to elicit a roll of the eyes and a good story. Her dad's twin sister, her namesake, was as close to a second mom as Kate had, but "maternal" was hardly the first adjective that would come to mind when meeting the flamboyant 67-year-old.

Her father's response began with the predicted eye roll.

"She's in the middle of building a potting shed in her backyard. Remember where she built that crazy tower sculpture out of bicycle parts? She must have plundered several hundred garage sales for that one."

"Of course I remember! Eighth wonder of the world," Kate nodded, grinning.

"Well, she took it apart, which was no small feat given that she'd welded it all in so many places it would withstand an earthquake."

Kate waited, knowing there was more to come.

"She left the footings and decided to repurpose the 15x15 cement pad to build that shed for her potting operation."

Randall Perrin laid his paper in his lap and stared into space for a long second. "Thing is, Katy..." He sounded unexpectedly sober, his voice trailing off.

"What is it, Dad?" Kate heard genuine concern in her father's voice.

"She's made up her mind to build that shed in homage to Firehouse 6, that old decrepit fire station a few blocks away that just got torn down. She fought the city's decision to demolish it, you know. Tried to get it named a historic landmark, but she was a committee of one. Well, two. Her friend Doris is always along for the ride."

Randall gave Kate a wry smile.

"She could probably use your professional help, Katy-girl. She's built scaffolding to make it a three-story structure with a hole down the center for a fire pole instead of stairs. Says she's signed up for pole-dancing classes to build up her upper body strength so she can use it."

"*What?* Has she at least hired someone to do the structural on it?!" Kate pulled back from where she had snuggled into her dad's shoulder, alarm on her face.

"Not that I'm aware of."

Kate was on her feet in a flash, scooping up her purse and car keys from the floor in front of the front door where she'd dropped them minutes before.

"Jesus," she muttered, swinging her bag over her shoulder. She sprinted to her old Corolla and yanked open the door.

Twenty minutes later, she pulled up in front of her aunt's house at the back of a cul-de-sac bounded by a thin strip of trees and neglected brush. A failing irrigation canal provided a bit of water for the weedy trees but served primarily as an occasional habitat for mosquito breeding. Aunt Catherine referred to the area beatifically as "The Wilds."

"Aunt Catherine? You home?" Kate shouted through the open front door, peering through the screen. She didn't get a response. A second later, she heard the high-pitched whine of an electric saw starting up behind the house.

"Holy Mary…" she stated, half curse, half invocation, as she jumped off the front stoop and picked her way through the patches of vegetable garden that comprised the front yard. She headed toward the gate in the wood fence, which was only three feet tall and surrounded the back and side yard. Catherine had built the fence so she could let her giant pet tortoise, Lucy, out to roam safely. It wouldn't contain a Pekinese, which was yet more evidence that her aunt was not one to care about resale value.

"Hey, Lucy," Kate said in greeting to the tortoise who appeared to be hiding behind a raft of rangy rosebushes. The tortoise extended her head when Kate hopped the fence but retracted it quickly. Kate leaned down to pat Lucy's heavy shell.

"I know, I'm worried, too, Lucy."

"Aunt Catherine!" Kate called, as she did a quick appraisal of the shed's framing, which was already two stories tall. Catherine had closed in the bottom floor but for a tall arched opening hacked out with a Sawzall. Kate flashed back in memory to the huge arched front door of the old fire station.

Kate walked through the shed entrance and looked up. There she saw the lower half of her beloved aunt's body, heavy calves braced against the steps of an old wood ladder. The ladder disappeared into a round opening in the ceiling of the first floor. Aunt Catherine had her signature Hawaiian floral "work skirt" hitched up and pinned by her knees against one of the steps on the ladder. Kate waited for a pause in the loud sawing before shouting her aunt's name again.

"Katy?? What on earth are you doing here?" Aunt Catherine's fuzzy gray head appeared under one arm as she looked down through the big round opening.

"I was told by your twin brother that you were possibly engaged in another life-endangering activity and thought I'd come by to see for myself," Kate replied.

"Pphhllp." The older woman made a familiar dismissive noise with her lips that was one of numerous odd verbal expressions she shared with Kate's dad. Kate understood its meaning.

"No, really, Aunt Catherine. Come on down for a sec and let's talk. I might be able to help." Kate tried to keep the pleading in her tone masked with some level of new-professional confidence.

Kate heard a long sigh filter down through the opening, followed by the clunk of the saw being set down. She watched her aunt remove a pair of old black stereo headphones that served as Catherine's version of hearing protection during tasks involving power tools and small engines lacking mufflers. OSHA would not have approved.

Aunt Catherine lumbered down the ladder after giving the second floor a satisfied scan, illuminated as it was by virtue of being entirely open to the sky. Catherine was approaching building construction as she did life, one step at a time, not bothering to look too far ahead.

Kate reached out to grab one of her aunt's hands once the older woman had both feet planted on the ground. Her skirt swung around her knees in a swirl of blue and magenta hibiscus.

Kate tugged her aunt toward the screened porch that jutted into the backyard off the kitchen. "C'mon. Let's make some tea. Time for a break."

The porch contained an industrial-sized washer and dryer on one end that Catherine had scored cheap at a dry cleaner's bankruptcy sale. The other end held a cute little ironwork table and matching French bistro chairs that looked straight out of New Orleans' French quarter. Catherine had painted them bright red. After stepping through the screened door to the porch, Kate leaned over and flipped down the bunched-up corner of the rug under the bistro chairs.

"Tripping hazard," Kate said, looking back over her shoulder to her aunt, who was coming up the porch steps behind her. She registered the eye roll she got in response, which was identical to her father's.

"Kate, dear, tripping is the least of the hazards I'm planning."

"Yes. I can see that," Kate replied, gesturing vaguely toward the miniature firehouse replica rising in the backyard. "We need to talk. You're scaring Lucy."

Catherine sighed again and followed Kate into the kitchen. She sat down at her own little two-top while Kate bustled around making tea preparations and checking the cookie jar for the accompanying sustenance. It was full, as usual.

"So, tell me more about your inspiration for this project, Aunt Catherine," Kate asked gently. "Dad told me you were building a potting shed. It's on the ambitious side for baby tomatoes."

"It's a multi-purpose space. The potting shed part will take up the first floor, of course. I'm not hauling sacks of dirt and fertilizer up the pole. Well, it will take up part of the first-floor space, in back, behind the curtain. Might need to expand it out the back, now that I think about it..."

"So, the first level will have two functions?" Kate asked carefully.

"The front door will be a perfect replica of the old firehouse entrance. I took a ton of pictures on my phone at various times of day before they tore it down so I could get the proportions right and match the color of the stain for it. When you come in, the front room will be a compact museum space with tons of pictures of the old firehouse, inside and out; and enough room for me to host soirees. And do educational talks about the importance of historic preservation and the ignorance of the current band of capitalist thieves known as the city council, of course. That's the whole point. Bastards. This town needs a gathering place for the opposition."

"Did Chief Rollins put you up to this?" Kate asked, frowning.

"He did not."

"But he knows about it, doesn't he," Kate said, not framing it as a question.

"Well, in a manner of speaking..."

"Aunt Catherine." Kate tried to use the same call-to-task tone her dad did when speaking to his twin.

"John Rollins was devastated when he found out that they planned to tear down the old station to put the new one up on the same city property. He'd worked out of that firehouse for years before becoming Chief, as did his father and his grandfather. His grandfather died on a run out of that firehouse trying to save the ladies of the night who worked hard in a bordello in the West End that caught fire when some careless customer dropped a lit cigarette on a mattress. That building was part of this town's history, not just his own. Broke my heart to see how torn up he was after the vote. He barely made it out of the council meeting with his game face still on. Someone's got to make it right for him, or at least try."

"I see," Kate said.

Catherine nodded, point made, rationale complete. Kate let Catherine's final statement float in the air for a long moment, giving it its due before proceeding.

"Did you get a permit for the structure?"

"Permit? What do I need a permit for? It's on my land, I can do what I want in my own damn backyard," Catherine said.

Kate stared at her aunt, mute, as the list of potential fines and public complaints scrolled through her brain like film credits. She struggled to form words.

"Aunt Catherine, that's not quite how it works. You have to submit plans and the plans have to meet building codes and get approved before you can break ground on something like this."

"Oh, pshaw. It's just a potting shed," Catherine harrumphed.

"A three-story potting shed with a hole through all three floors for a pole, and a public education center that will likely need lights, heat, plumbing, and non-profit status!"

"No plumbing. Folks can use the house for that."

Kate set down her mug of chamomile tea, picked her phone up off the table, and started typing something furiously with both thumbs, staring at the screen.

"What are you doing, Kate?"

"I'm looking up Chief Rollins's number."

"You are not going to call him, Katie, this is a surprise! For his birthday!"

"The alternative is the building inspector," Kate said, not even looking up. "Or maybe 911, about an hour after I let you climb back up in that thing."

"Why on earth are you so upset about this?"

"Aunt Catherine, it's *dangerous*. And I love you, but I don't think you know what you're doing, and I'm worried. If you fall and break a hip and die in the hospital of pneumonia, there will be no one left on earth who can make fluorescent green pistachio pudding cake with goth-black chocolate frosting for my birthday. And that is entirely unacceptable."

"I am not going to break a hip. My osteopath said I have strong bones, and he should know."

"Aunt Catherine, your bone density is not the point. Seriously," Kate exhaled, putting her phone to her ear as it rang the non-emergency number for the fire department.

"Oh, all right, we can talk about this, but put down that phone this second!"

Kate eyed her aunt severely, still letting the phone ring in her ear.

"I mean it!"

As Catherine pushed back her chair and started to come around the kitchen table, Kate hit the disconnect button surreptitiously, but spoke into the phone as though the receptionist had answered.

"Yes, hi, I'd like to talk to Chief Rollins about a relative who wants to build a three-story threat to life and limb in her backyard in homage to the old fire station. I need to find out if he thinks that's a problem."

Catherine caught on that Kate was faking it and sat back down, smiling at her niece's pluck, despite her annoyance at the interference.

The two women looked at each other for a long moment, each taking a sip of tea, listening to the old German cuckoo clock tick from the wall over the table. Kate glanced up and saw that it was about to strike the hour and smiled to herself. Two seconds later, she heard the whir of the little internal mechanisms start, and the tiny door above the number 12 popped open.

"Cuckoo, cuckoo, cuckoo," sang the little bobbing bird, twelve times. Kate pointed silently up at the clock. Catherine closed her eyes, shook her head, and waited for the bird to disappear back inside the clock. She looked over at her niece until she was sure she was truly paying attention.

"I really want to do this, Kate, and I will find a way. I always do, once I set my mind to something, and you know that," Catherine said.

Kate regarded her aunt, reading her face. She was quiet and determined, and there was something more fueling her passion. Kate let her impressions sift around for a moment before saying anything more. Then she decided to ask. "How long ago did Chief Rollins's wife die, Aunt Catherine?"

Catherine met Kate's gaze. The young woman was quick. "Four years and five months. I think he's finally starting to recover."

Kate nodded. "You really care about him, don't you?"

"I've known that man since we were in grade school. He needs to retire, but he's afraid to. John told me he thinks he'd be bored silly if he quit the department, but last week he admitted that big old house is just too quiet. He misses his wife, and he gets restless."

"And when did you have this conversation with him?"

"Last Saturday. At dinner. Here."

Kate smiled. "Did you make him your pork roast with the tart cherry sauce?"

"I did," Catherine said, finally smiling back at Kate. "And he lit up like he'd never seen food before, just like I'd hoped."

"You're in love!"

"Well, I'm not sure I'd call it that, but I am seriously fond of the man. I want to make him feel better. He's lost a lot, and he's trying to figure out how to gracefully lose a successful career on top of it. The least I can do is something to let him know I understand how much that firehouse meant to him."

"Okay, Aunt Catherine. I get it now. But you simply must let me help you."

Catherine raised an eyebrow and nodded, then held up a finger, silently telling Kate to wait a moment. She reached across the table to a little blue pottery bowl, its ceramic finish swirled with white and gold. The bowl held a jumbled pile of little white cards about a quarter inch wide and two inches long. On each one was a cartoon angel and a single word in bright blue italic script. They were Catherine's source of spiritual direction for unsettled moments. She dug her fingers into the pile of cards, mixing them around until she felt her fingers settle around one as she stared at the wall, not cheating by looking. She plucked up the card and set it on the table between them.

"Openness," Kate read aloud. "See?"

Catherine nodded. "So, what's your idea. I'm listening."

Kate took a deep breath and told her about her friends from school who were either aspiring architects or new in practice and all talented, ambitious, artistic people. She wanted to pull together a team to work with Catherine and design a potting shed to put all other potting sheds to shame. And she wanted to do it so that it would have a beautiful space on the first level to showcase the photographs and memorabilia from the firehouse. It would be big enough for a small group to gather comfortably, and it would have heat, and light, and plumbing, and permits. If she really wanted a fire pole going up to a second floor for fun, they could make that happen. She wasn't going to do a third floor. That's where she drew the line. The image of her aging aunt flinging herself down the fire pole from the third floor, howling with delight as she plunged to ground level, simply terrified her too much.

"Can we keep it a secret from John?" Catherine asked when Kate finished.

"If you talk him into eating out for a couple of months, yes. We'll be making a mess in the backyard for at least that long," Kate replied.

"And you'll make the fire pole sturdy?"

"Of course," Kate replied, looking a little confused.

"I have secondary interests in that fire pole," Catherine said, grinning wickedly.

"Oh, good GOD," Kate muttered.

Five months of long summer evenings and sacrificed weekends later, Kate was running backward from the curb in front of her Aunt Catherine's house, gesturing wildly to help her friend, Adam, back a truck load of clean fill dirt into the driveway and on back through the gate into the backyard. The firehouse cum pottery shed was built, and this late Saturday morning delivery from the landscaping firm Adam worked for was the last installment for the project. They were down to constructing the patio and putting the final touches on the garden area in front of the firehouse.

Following closely behind Adam's truck was a beat-up Subaru with its hatch open, the tops of two trees poking out and dangling strips of red fabric as a warning to other drivers. Catherine had asked for red trees to match the firehouse theme, so Kate had picked out an "October Glory" Maple and an Oklahoma Redbud. The footwells of every seat but the driver's were filled with potted perennials, waiting to be planted. Kate's friend Veronica had made the run to the garden center, timed to arrive the same time Adam would.

Kate waved and jumped up and down, clapping her hands, when she saw Veronica turn into the driveway. Aunt Catherine was out back, dropping the gate on Adam's truck, her favorite shovel in her free hand. She had been involved at every step along the way and had happily made adopted nieces and nephews out of every one of the pals that Kate had talked into being part of the firehouse project. She always had a crockpot full of soup on the kitchen counter on low, a loaf of fresh bread and a plate of cookies ready to feed them whenever any of them expressed the slightest need for fuel.

The four of them made quick work of emptying the soil into the garden areas, laying the patio stone, and settling the trees and plants into the holes that Catherine had already dug and labelled for each plant. By the time the October afternoon light was fading, the project was done. Catherine brought them each a glass of iced tea, and they leaned against the back wall of the house in the shade to admire their work, chatting amiably.

Catherine pushed a long, sweaty strand of gray hair back out of her face and tucked it up into the bun on top of her head. She was wearing muddy denim coveralls over a peasant blouse with a pattern comprised of large magenta peonies. The drawstring neck had come loose hours ago, exposing the straps of her purple sports bra. She looked knackered, but happy, and Kate stepped over to give her a congratulatory hug.

"We did it, Aunt Catherine. We pulled it off!" Kate said, nodding to her grinning friends.

They enjoyed a few quiet moments just savoring the extraordinary two-story structure. The front was dominated by a shining replica of the old arched fire house entrance, its heavy dark oak wood replete with sculpted fire axe blades that served as door handles. The windows on either side of the huge front door were smaller versions of the towering stained-glass windows from the fire house. Catherine had spent a chunk of her retirement savings to commission those replicas. Saint Florian, patron of fire fighters, overlooked the front garden from the window to the left of the door; on the right, the window held a large brass-colored circle in which a fire helmet bearing the logo of the Sacramento Fire Department hovered over a lion wielding a fire hose. Just inside the front door, visitors would find neat displays of memorabilia in cases and on shelves all along the walls, with a central seating area in front of the battered wood lectern salvaged from the briefing room where generations of fire chiefs had delivered remarks to the public or awarded medals and commendations.

At the back of the first level room was Catherine's gleaming brass fire pole, sourced from a condemned fire house in Boston. It was the fast way down from the second-floor loft, which contained a cozy reading nook in front of large windows looking out into the trees along the side of Catherine's back yard, and a cupboard stocked with good hard liquor and glassware. Through the door at the back of the meeting room was the private space in the structure, which was indeed where Catherine stored her gardening equipment and had the potting table of her dreams. In a nod to practicality, Catherine had also let Kate build a set of narrow stairs with a hand rail to reach the second level. It was on the potting shed side of the door, out of sight of guests coming to the old fire station museum space.

Kate leaned toward her aunt and gave her shoulder a nudge. "So, when are you going to bring Chief Rollins over to see it?"

"Oh, good heavens, child, I haven't thought that far ahead. Though he has started to wonder why I haven't been letting him come over for dinner. I've been going to his place for pizza and a movie on weekends since we got this going. Or coming by the firehouse to see him, just to keep fuel in the rumor mill," she said, giving Kate a wink.

Just then, the sound of a diesel pickup truck drifted around to the back of the house from the street out front. Catherine cocked her head to one side to listen as she heard the engine shut off. The heavy door slammed closed a moment later.

Kate watched as her aunt slowly leaned forward away from the wall, looking alarmed, and reached out to grab Kate's arm. "Katy, go see who it is. That sounds like John's truck!"

"What? Aunt Catherine, what do you want me to do if it's him?"

"*Stall* him!"

"How?"

Catherine was already half-way through the screened porch at the back of the house. "I don't know, be creative!"

Kate grabbed Adam and Veronica and took off running around the side of the house. Sure enough, John Rollins was walking up the front sidewalk to Catherine's door, looking exceptionally dashing in his black dress uniform. He was carrying an enormous bouquet of bright yellow roses interspersed with baby's breath and purple sweet pea. He stopped in surprise as the three sweaty young people came dashing toward him.

"Hi! Chief Rollins! Fancy meeting you here!" Kate called out.

"Yes, how wonderful to meet you! I've always wanted to meet an actual, um, fire person!" Veronica chimed in.

Adam slowed to a forced stroll behind Veronica. "Chief Rollins! How are you? I always wanted to tell you my uncle is a firefighter in Spokane. Great guy. Got promoted recently. Do you know anyone from that agency? About the same size as Sacramento's department, I think. What a coincidence!"

Kate was panting from the sprint. "Oh, um, I'm Kate, Catherine's niece. And these are my friends, Adam and Veronica. We were just, uh, helping Catherine with some gardening out in her back yard. Total mess back there. Still have a truck parked sideways and big holes everywhere."

"Yeah, *big* holes. And rock. Piles of rock. Total hazard, no one should go back there. You'd for sure get your uniform all dirty," Veronica gushed.

"Okay, well, no problem," Chief Rollins said slowly, examining each of their faces in turn as though they might need medication. "I was just hoping to catch Catherine at home. Do you know if she's in?"

They all turned in unison as the front door opened behind them. Catherine poked her head out. She had reassembled her blouse and re-wound the bun on top of her head but was otherwise still just as dirty and sweaty and rumpled as were Kate, Adam, and Veronica. "It's all right, kids. Hello, John, what a lovely surprise to see you," Catherine said, clearly having regained her composure with a quick trip to the bathroom. "We've been working in the backyard all day."

"I can see that," John said, his eyes crinkling in amusement. "You look... amazing, as always."

Catherine locked eyes onto the beautiful floral arrangement the handsome older gentleman was holding as he walked the rest of the way up to the front door. "I wanted to surprise you. It's been a year to the day since you tricked me into meeting you for dinner the first time. Best thing to happen to me in years, Catherine. Happy sort-of-anniversary." John leaned around the half-open door to give Catherine a kiss on the cheek.

"Oh! They're gorgeous, thank you," Catherine murmured, reaching up to cradle his face with one hand and leaning in to kiss him properly on the lips. When she pulled away, she was beaming.

Kate, Veronica and Adam smiled broadly from their position in the middle of the front yard. Kate grabbed Veronica's hand and clutched it to her chest. "Gawd, they're adorable," she whispered.

Catherine opened the front door the rest of the way and joined Chief Rollins on the front stoop, taking his hand. She called out to the trio of young adults, a quiet smile on her face. "Meet us around back, you three. I think we have a little surprise for the fire chief, too, don't we?"

Catherine winked at them and pushed the man into the house, turning to follow him. In a stage-whispered falsetto they all could hear, Catherine called out over her shoulder, "Best time for fun is always now, kids, always now!"

MYSTERY ON LITTLE DUCK ISLAND

A pair of old green mud boots belonging to Angus Kingery flopped over on the dock next to the last boat slip. It was his preferred parking spot. The wading boots were his way of lifting a leg over it so the other residents of Little Duck Island would leave the slip for his use.

Odds of that were good, since there were only two other families with homes on the island and they were part-timers. Still, Angus reckoned consistent messaging was in order. The Kingery clan had been on Little Duck since around 1740. Everyone arriving after that he considered a newcomer, not to be counted on to have the sense God gave chickens.

It was late afternoon on a Thursday in September, and the shadows from the tall pines on the western shore angled across the water. Angus was out fishing Pickerel Cove. To be more precise, he was sitting in his Lund 1650, watching someone he didn't know in an aluminum boat with maybe a 40-hp outboard engine putter around the outer end of the cove. From what Angus could see, the boat had a solo operator with a ponytail through the back of a gray baseball cap and what looked like a cooler trapped between her knees.

As Angus watched, the woman in the little skiff cut her engine and let herself drift while she dug around in the cooler and pulled out something small that caught the sunlight in a way that suggested it was glass or metal. After holding it up so the late afternoon sun hit it, she appeared to twist off a lid, lean over the side, and scoop up water. Angus watched as she placed it back in the cooler and repeated the action two more times.

Hmph, he thought. Must be some biologist up from the university taking samples of something or other. Long way from home, though. He shook his head and tended his line, reeling it in enough to spin out toward another still spot in the shallows.

He heard the motor on the other boat roar to life and expected the sound to recede as quickly as it had appeared. To his dismay, the other boater was coming right toward him. Angus muttered and cussed and pulled in his line. Fish weren't about to surface after all this commotion. He set down his rod in the bottom of his boat and looked up, watching the woman approach.

She killed the motor about 40 feet away and drifted toward him.

"Afternoon, sir, sorry to disturb you," the woman called out. "I'm Susan Snow, I work for Maine Inland Fisheries. I was hoping to ask you a couple of questions."

She waited for Angus to respond, which he did, at least to his way of thinking. He pushed his hat back and raised an eyebrow, nodding once. And waited. It took a long moment for Susan to recognize this as conversation. She went on.

"We've been picking up traces of some toxins in the water around here. If you live nearby, could you tell me if there's been any unusual activity on shore, here, or up to the north a bit?"

Angus frowned. That sounded bad. His part of Maine was far enough north that "unusual activity" was limited to events like sighting a moose with triplets.

"No, ma'am, can't say that I have. My family's lived on Little Duck for a long time, and I keep track of things. But not much new has happened in these waters since FDR was president and decided to pay a visit to Frenchman's Bay."

Angus didn't elaborate. Susan waited. The old man had said all he had to say, so she nodded, got his name, thanked him for his time, and apologized again for the intrusion. She hit the ignition on her outboard and swung her boat around, heading back toward open water.

The next day, after what should have been dinner time, Susan Snow was slouched in front of her desk at the Maine Inland Fisheries' lab in Bangor. The desk was a cheap metal thing scrounged from the state's excess furniture stash and cut down to fit beneath the one small window in the cramped space. She was thinking. And staring absently up into the dark sky outside, watching lightning prance across the clouds like wild white horses.

Twenty-four hours earlier, Susan had banged open the door to the lab with the cooler she had brought back from her trip down to shore. She dumped the rest of her gear just inside the vestibule and walked straight to her favorite microscope. Something strange was happening in the waters near Little Duck Island. They had received a call from a lobsterman who had seen gulls flopping in the water like they were ill. Susan had gone to check it out.

After examining the samples and running some tests, Susan determined that the water had unusual levels of cadmium and some odd proteins in it she had never seen before. There wasn't an abnormal level of the algae or other microorganisms present that are associated with various shellfish toxicities. But the structure of the proteins was troubling her. They had close similarities to saxitoxin, a potent neurotoxin that causes paralytic poisoning in humans and other animals. The shellfish eat algae containing the toxins but aren't bothered by it. The meat tastes and smells fine. But just a few grams can be lethal when other animals consume those shellfish. If the proteins she was seeing caused similar effects, it could be a nasty situation. But where was this material coming from?

If the pollutants had an industrial source, she would have expected to find those in less remote areas of the Maine coast, closer to manufacturing or lumber operations, and to transit. It took forever to get to Little Duck, by land or water, and there was only one small town anywhere nearby. She shook her head and decided to stop for the day, hoping that sleep would shake something loose in her brain and give her a new line of inquiry.

She was shuffling her printouts together to file when the lab phone rang behind her. Startled, she grabbed for it, knocking over her long-abandoned coffee mug. She cradled the phone against her shoulder and threw a stack of paper towels on the coffee spill to contain it.

"Marine Science, Snow here," she said, glancing at the clock. Her department administrative assistant had left three hours ago.

"This is University Main, and I've got an old man on the line who is incredibly determined to find you. Says his name is Angus Kingery. Can I put him through?"

"Sure, I guess," Susan responded, her mind racing to figure out why the name sounded familiar. Then it hit her. The fisherman she'd met yesterday afternoon in the quiet cove near Little Duck Island had said his name was Angus.

"Hello, Mr. Kingery? I don't know how you found me, but this is Susan Snow. How can I help you?"

"You were right. Something strange is going on up here and I'm not too happy about it. I got two gulls wandered up from the shore into my backyard, toddling around like they're drunk. And when I went down to the beach by my dock with a flashlight, we got little birds dead—looks like plovers and sandpipers. What the Sam Hill is in my ocean?!"

Susan's grip on the handset tightened, her own sense of alarm escalating rapidly.

"I don't know, Mr. Kingery, but I'll be back up there at first light. And don't touch those dead birds, okay? If you can find disposable gloves, put them on and then stick a few of the birds in a plastic bag and keep them cold for me, okay? And just to be safe, don't eat any shellfish."

Susan heard Angus acknowledge her request with an irritated "Okay," muttering as he hung up.

Well before dawn the next morning, Susan drove a state fisheries truck hauling a trailer and her boat back down to the coast. She also had a sleep-deprived colleague with her from the Environmental Protection branch of the Department of Natural Resources. They met Angus and relieved him of his bag of dead birds and took more water samples and scoops of mud containing local crustaceans. They packed it all away in coolers. Susan told Angus she didn't think the toxins she was finding were from shellfish, but they needed the lab to rule all that out. She handed him one of her business cards.

Angus thought to himself that he could have told her that and saved her and her overeducated friend a long drive and a boat ride. He'd lived through more algae and other marine "bug blooms," as he called them, than he could count. Not once had those unpleasant but natural events made gulls and terns stagger around like they'd stayed for last call at the Dinghy, his favorite local bar and bait shop.

After Susan left, Angus pulled on his rubber wellies and headed down to the dock. He decided he might as well tool around the bay a bit on his own and see if he could spot anything that might provide a clue to what was polluting the water.

The sun was high and there was a light chop in the water. It was a beautiful day. Angus took his time, following the familiar shoreline around Little Duck Island. Then he headed north toward the long peninsula that separated his cove from the much larger Frenchman's Bay. Nothing seemed amiss. He knew how the tides and usual flows of the sea curled around in the open water, bringing storm-broken driftwood and other flotsam down his way. If some bad actors were putting toxins into the water anywhere along the southern shore of that peninsula, it would eventually drift down toward Little Duck.

Angus angled his boat in toward the base of the peninsula. He planned to go in and out of the small coves, checking the estuaries where snowmelt flowed down from the woods in streams or over the bluffs in waterfalls each spring. About halfway down the peninsula, his eye caught a reflection off something shiny that didn't match the muddy greens and browns and grays of the Maine coast. He turned and slowed as he approached the shallows.

"What in the world…" Angus spoke aloud to himself.

A low plastic fence had been dug into the mud right about where high tide would just cover it. It was about 100-feet wide. The sides came out from the beach into the shallows until they disappeared beneath the water. Red plastic poles stuck up where Angus guessed the fence had corners. There were monitors of some sort mounted on heavier metal stakes driven into the ground beneath the water at regular intervals. Angus could just make out yellow signs on another set of stakes up on the beach that he thought read "KEEP OUT."

Angus cut his engine and looked around. This was a remote section of the coastline, and he thought it was toward the far end of a state marine reserve. But it could be private land. He noted his coordinates. He wanted to be able to identify the location again when he called Rich Staunton, the local fish and game warden. Whatever it was, Angus wanted to know if Rich knew about it.

He tipped his hat back and peered up the steep bluff that rose from the beach. There was a rocky cut at the top, and he suddenly realized where he was. About a quarter mile back into the woods was an old stone bridge that took Route 108 over a wide creek that poured down every spring to the beach below. There was a rocky foot trail that led from that bridge all the way to the bluff and then meandered back and forth in steep, muddy switchbacks down to the water. Angus and his pal Jimmy Noonan used to skid down that trail on their butts when they were teenagers, after "borrowing" Jimmy's dad's old pickup to drive up the coast when they skipped school.

Who else could possibly know about this area and choose it for some crazy experiment?

Angus shook his head, fired up the motor on his boat, and headed for home. He needed to talk to Rich Staunton, pronto.

***

Rich Staunton was rudely awakened early in the morning on the last day of his precious vacation. His brain had latched on to the distant sound of his cell phone vibrating from the bottom of the empty porcelain cookie jar on his kitchen counter. He had unceremoniously dropped it there six days ago, hoping to not think about work for a week.

Stumbling to the kitchen in his favorite ratty flannel boxers, he plucked out the phone, scowling at the general administration number lit up on its face. The call was coming from his employer, the Maine Department of Inland Fisheries and Wildlife.

"Staunton. I'm on vacation," he said flatly.

"I know, Rich, but I need you to get downtown ASAP. I want you with me when I return the call I just got told to make."

"Dan, you better motivate me with a little more information. No one's made me coffee and brought me breakfast in bed today."

Rich had a good relationship with Dan Routhier, the Director of the Regional Office of Fisheries and Wildlife. But OFW gave the warden service some of the lamest assignments imaginable, and Rich did not want to drive to Bangor on his last day off for an upside-down ATV in a creek.

He heard a sigh and a long pause on the other end of the line.

"Rich. It's the FBI. And Homeland Security. In a room. Together, which never happens. In Augusta. From D.C. Is that enough to get you to put pants on, for Chrissakes?"

There was a brief silence on both ends of the line.

"I'll be there in 30. Make coffee, Dan." Rich disconnected and went back to his bedroom to find clothes.

He got to Bangor District HQ in 25 minutes, pausing long enough to pour the week-old contents of a water bottle over his head in the parking lot and madly finger-comb his tousled hair. Rich had suddenly realized this could be a video conference. He dried his head with a garage rag he found in the back seat of his Jeep and tossed it back on the floor.

The conference call originated from a secure line in an office building in Northwest D.C. At the end of it, Dan and Rich sat together in shock, pens still held above their respective notepads.

"So, let me recap this situation," Rich said slowly. "An angry former industrial scientist recruited from some city in Russia I can't pronounce got fired from his job with a chemical company out of Boston and decided to go rogue with his research. On a toxin that can only be grown in living shellfish fed jacked-up algae and kept either in an expensive industrial lab or in their native habitat—which would most likely be somewhere along our freakin' million-mile coastline."

"Yep, that's what I heard," Dan said with his signature nihilistic cheer. "With the added feature that his desired end-product is a neurotoxin deadlier to humans than any of our known and highly poisonous saxitoxins. Potentially quite profitable. If you're tight with enemies of the United States."

"And I'm supposed to get right on it as the nearest member of law enforcement responsible for the natural resource in question, am I right?"

"Well, given the level of request, I might be able to go up the bureaucratic food chain and draft someone from over in fisheries to help you out," Dan deadpanned.

Rich just stared at his boss and didn't blink.

"Dan. Seriously."

Dan sighed and changed his tone. "Right. This is nuts. We've got a grand total of 125 wardens to cover over 35,000 square miles of land and 3,500 miles of coastline. At my last count, about a quarter of those positions were open and stuck that way due to the state's hiring freeze." He looked up at Rich and tapped his pen on his notepad.

"Let me make some calls. It's time for specialty teams to come through for us for a change."

Rich just nodded. He knew that, under the sarcasm, Dan was as effective in working the system as anyone he'd ever worked for. And they did need help. And a plan.

Rich went back to his rarely visited desk. It sat in the corner of the "Bunker Room," a converted conference room jammed with well-worn desks and phone lines. Since it was Sunday, no one else was there. Rich leaned back in his chair and propped his legs up on an overturned waste basket to think.

If this ill-mannered scientist really was using the Maine coast as his personal lab, it would no doubt be somewhere remote. They could rule out the bays and harbors with a lot of activity. So, generously, that left about 2,000 miles of rocky coastline full of islands and coves and a billion tiny inlets to hide in.

Rich's phone vibrated in his pocket. He pulled it out, looking at the number to decide if he could let it go to voice mail. It was old Angus Kingery, a fisherman from the northern coast who came from a long line of old Mainers, which he was happy to tell you again, anytime you tried to tell him something you considered news.

Rich wasn't ready to play friendly cop to Angus's curmudgeonly concerns today. It was Sunday. And he was still technically on vacation. He put the call to voice mail and stood to get more coffee.

Before Rich could walk back down the hall from the kitchen, his phone buzzed again. Angus. The man clearly had a bee in his bonnet about something. Might as well get it over with and let the man talk.

"Hey, Angus. How's things up Little Duck way?"

"'Bout time you picked up, Rich. My taxes pay your salary, remember?" Angus barked.

Rich rolled his eyes. The exchange was a familiar one. "Indeed, they do, boss. How can I help you on this fine Sunday morning?" Rich kept walking back to the Bunker, carefully keeping his coffee from spilling while he held the phone to his ear.

Then he stopped.

"Hold up, Angus, say that again? You cut out a little."

"I said I was looking around the waterfront south of Frenchman's Bay, upstream from Little Duck, and came across something that doesn't look right. You state people running some kinda research project down from the bluff by the 108 bridge?"

"Angus, no, we are not. Hang on a sec and let me get something to write with. And then tell me *exactly* what you saw. And where."

Angus described what he had found and how to get to the spot from the road above. And he read off Susan Snow's contact information from the card she had left with him Saturday morning. Angus had been dealing with state officials for long enough to know that even when two people worked for the same state agency, if they were in different departments or units or even next door to each other in the same hallway, communication didn't reliably happen. Angus wanted to make sure that whatever information Susan was gleaning from her samples and his dead plovers was in Rich's hands. He knew Rich was smart enough to add things up. Angus had been interacting with Rich Staunton since his warden's uniform was fresh out of the bag 15 years ago. He wasn't sure yet about Susan Snow.

Two and a half hours later, Rich was parked on the side of the road next to the stone bridge where Angus had directed him. He was talking to Dan Routhier and asking that Dan contact Susan Snow about what she'd found from the samples she'd taken. As it turned out, Dan had already called fisheries to ask for some staff back-up, and Dan's counterpart in that department had already tagged Susan Snow to work the case with Rich.

Dan told Rich what Susan had passed up her chain of command about the saxitoxin-mimic proteins in the water samples. She had nothing conclusive yet from the dead birds or the soil and crustacean samples.

Rich took that all in and mulled it over. Then, given the travel times involved, he asked Dan to send a couple of guys in a boat with dive gear and serious waterproof hazmat suits. He provided his GPS coordinates. Someone would need some serious nerve as well as the equipment to go in the water safely. He didn't know if Susan Snow had that kind of mettle or if she was just a nature-loving lab rat.

Right about then, Angus Kingery pulled up in his old blue pickup truck and parked right behind Rich on the side of the road. Rich unpacked his camera and pulled some plastic evidence bags and paper envelopes out of the console in his truck. He was glad the old man was there. This whole situation was sketchy, and he didn't know if it was related to the briefing with the feds that Dan had hauled him into that morning. It could just be some weird water or soils testing a new landowner was doing. He was proceeding, as usual, in his "plan for the worst, hope for the best" mode.

Rich heard the old hinges on Angus's truck door moan and turned to watch the old man approach. He was a bit gimpy and was holding his left hand against his lower back.

"Glad you could find time in your busy social calendar to come on up here, Rich," Angus said with a wink. He was a curmudgeon, but not a total jackass. He liked Rich. This was the teasing he did with his own sons.

"Always eager to respond to the concerns of a good citizen, Angus. How the hell you doing, anyway? That back bothering you again?"

Angus just shrugged. Without saying anything to each other about the unsettling situation down below them on the water, they were keeping their voices low. They both knew something wasn't right about it.

Angus pointed Rich into the woods at the beginning of the old foot trail and told him to follow it until it looked like it was going to plunge off the bluff. Angus warned him to be careful, because that was where the river turned into a waterfall each spring and the ground was loose and undercut in spots. Then Rich was supposed to poke around in the brush about 20 feet to his right until he found a path that would zig-zag down to the beach along the muddy switchbacks.

It took Rich a good half hour to carefully pick his way along the narrow trail, looking for any sign that someone else had been using it. He found enough along the way that he felt his senses sharpen, as they always did when he was working an active scene solo. Which was most of the time.

He noted broken branches and fresh boot prints against smashed wet ferns pressed into the mud. At the heel of one boot print he found a red plastic cap that looked like it screwed onto some small vial. Rich photographed the boot prints and bagged the plastic cap as potential evidence, marking the location with a numbered stake. The boot prints suggested he might have unwelcome company, and he took the time to stop and listen, scanning the forest around him every few minutes.

When Rich got to the bluff, he found some brush that had been ripped up and tossed aside. It exposed the edge and probably made the trail back up easier to locate from the waterfront and the beach. He stopped and crouched down on one knee, listening for any sound that wasn't natural. There was a light wind in the pines above and behind him, and the sound of waves rolling softly over the small rocks on the beach below. He picked up the smell of the tide pools in the breeze coming off the water, but nothing else.

Rich stood and began making his way down the slick, muddy trail. He found black metal stakes driven into the ground beside the trail at the steep parts, convenient hand holds where the return trip uphill would be difficult. Again, he photographed, but didn't touch, each stake. He hoped a fingerprint technician could pull something later.

At the final switchback, he stopped again, carefully peering around a spindly pine snag jutting out into thin air from the sandy soil about 15 feet up from the beach. No one was there, or at least no one was visible. But he spotted three dark-green camouflaged game cameras set up to monitor the approach to the fenced-off area. Rich thought he recognized the make and model. Not expensive. And the range of the cameras wasn't long.

Though he had turned off the sound on his cell phone, he felt it vibrate in his pocket. He stepped back up the trail, putting the trunk of a big spruce between him and anyone who might be watching from below. He pulled out his phone and saw a brief text from Dan.

"Do not approach scene. Wait for backup."

Well, you're a little late, Dan, he thought to himself. He was already at the scene. But okay, someone knew something he didn't. Rich debated with himself. He was already down the trail. But being shot at didn't appeal. Normally, the command to wait for backup meant that was a possibility.

Rich pulled out a small pair of field binoculars from his jacket pocket. He scanned the waterfront below, being careful to remain protected by the tree trunk as cover. He couldn't see much. The layout was exactly as Angus had described. He didn't recognize the equipment or metering devices that were mounted on the heavier poles.

Rich adjusted the focal point on the binoculars as he peered at the signage around the vinyl netting that comprised the fence line going out into the water. One sign was facing toward him enough that he could make out the words "DANGER" and "KEEP OUT." But beneath those words in English was another line in smaller font. He didn't know what it meant, but the letters were from the Cyrillic alphabet. Serbian. Bulgarian. Russian. Not too many people in that part of Maine were so multi-lingual that they would special order signs in English and any of those languages. French, maybe. But this? Rich ratcheted up his internal caution flag and decided to bail out.

Rich pocketed the binoculars and sent Dan a text to let him know he was okay and headed back to his truck to wait.

Going up the trail took longer. The mud was slick, and Rich face-planted twice, swearing softly. He'd almost lost his keys out of his pants pocket. He was glad this wasn't being filmed for officer training. Being a game warden wasn't like being a cop in the movies.

When he got back up to the top of the bluff and through the brush back to the road, he found Angus leaning against the closed gate of his truck, a rifle cradled comfortably in his arms across his belly.

"It isn't moose season, Angus," Rich called out, knowing full well Angus was just watching his 'six.'

"Just covering your baby game warden's pink behind, Rich," Angus replied.

"I appreciate it," Rich said, more seriously. "Something is going on down there that is probably way above my pay grade, but I can't tell you everything I know. I want you to be careful, okay?"

Angus fixed him with a stare, one eyebrow back up. "I'm too old not to be careful, Rich. What else can you tell me?"

Rich thought about it for the count of two.

"Let's just say that federal agencies normally concerned with parts of the world on the far side of Europe are suddenly trying to learn the difference between New Hampshire and Maine on the map, okay?"

Angus's other eyebrow went up.

"And this has something to do with Susan Snow's water tests and my drunk birds over on Little Duck?"

"'Fraid so, Angus," Rich said as he brushed the mud off his hands on his pants and unlocked his truck doors. "At least we have reason to believe it might."

Rich heard the radio in his truck crackle to life. He slid into the driver's seat, pulling the door behind him as he picked up the radio. It was Angie Murray, a seasoned dispatcher who had been on the job since Rich started as a warden in Maine.

"I'm here, Angie, what's up?"

"Rich, boss says you need to get out of there. Go home," Angie said, using more familiar language than the usual coded dispatch commands.

"What? Why? He pulled me back off the scene, and now he wants me to leave the area. There's definitely something going on that needs investigation, he knows that, right?"

"He is aware. Big dogs are on it. Federal dogs. It's okay, you can bail," Angie said.

"Copy that, Angie. I'm packing up," Rich replied, getting more alarmed by the second.

Rich hung up his radio and stared out the windshield for a long moment. Then he looked over at Angus. Angus needed to clear the hell out, too. Whatever was brewing, it was big, and the agencies on the phone this morning had way more resources than he did. Meaning more resources than books of laws and regulations and a ticket pad with his hand attached to a pen. Rich stepped back out of his truck.

"Angus, we need to clear out of here," Rich said flatly.

"And do nothing about that mess down on shore?"

"That's right. *We* are going to do nothing about that mess down on shore, Angus."

Rich watched as the color in Angus's neck passed rosy into apple red. It crept into the old man's face while he struggled not to say anything.

"These are my waters. I live here. I feed myself out of this ocean, and it's being poisoned by some ratbag who thinks he can play with his chemistry set and use the natural environment as a free lab. That isn't right, and you know it. This is *personal*, Rich, and you oughta know that!"

"Angus…"

"Don't 'Angus' me, Rich, I'm not going to let that pus-filled toxic waste dump just keep leaking into the water!"

"Listen to me, old man, I don't like it either, not one bit. But I've been told federal agents are on it, even though we don't exactly see them sitting on the horizon line with bazookas mounted on the rails of a Coast Guard cutter. I wish that were the case, and I know you do, too. But I've got to trust my command," Rich responded, trying to keep his voice calm hoping to transmit that calm to Angus Kingery.

"Maybe you do…" Angus huffed, as he swung around, emptying the ammunition from his rifle before securing it in the gun vault in the back of his truck. He slammed the lid down for emphasis and slammed the gate up immediately after. Wordlessly, Angus yanked open the door and climbed into the driver's seat, started the engine, and drove away. Rich was still standing next to his fender.

Well, at least he's out of here and safe, Rich thought to himself, though he felt bad about having to leave Angus knowing even less than he did about who was responding to the situation and what they planned to do. He had little to share, even if he could.

Rich took one last look around, listening to the wind in the trees and the occasional sound of surf drifting over the bluff. It just didn't feel like anyone else was here. Maybe they'd gone to ground, whoever they were. He finished tucking away the evidence he'd collected and recorded, and drove back down Route 108, retracing his steps home to Bangor. He'd at least get home in time to watch Sunday Night Football.

***

Susan Snow was walking through her small living room early Monday morning, a piece of wheat toast in one hand and coffee in the other. She was angling toward the sofa where she'd left her phone, hoping to scan headlines before leaving for work. The phone started to vibrate while it played Dolly Parton's hit song, "9 to 5." It was the office calling. Weird.

She set down her coffee and answered, frowning. "Susan here."

"Susan, it's Gary." The head of her lab at Maine Inland Fisheries sounded grim. "Pack an overnight bag before you come into work. We've got to get you down to Bar Harbor as soon as possible. I'll have a state car ready for you."

"What's going on, Gary? The sun's barely up and we've already got a crisis?"

"We do," he said. "Just get into the office. I'm on my way now. I'll tell you what I know as soon as you get here."

Gary Barnes was normally a confident, light-hearted guy. He took the work seriously, but not himself, and one of the things Susan loved about him was he knew that very few things were worth getting worked up about. He was a good supervisor, a solid scientist, and Susan respected him. It was troubling to hear him sound so full of urgency.

Susan left her toast on top of a magazine on her coffee table and went to pack. Then she went to the kitchen, poured the rest of her coffee into a travel mug, and headed into the lab.

Gary was hanging up the phone on his desk when Susan stepped into his office, her coat still on. "Fill me in," she said.

"You know those weird samples you were working on from up near Little Duck Island on Friday?"

"Yeah, the ones with the saxitoxin look-alike proteins and nothing else I recognized," Susan replied.

"Right, those. Fish and Game called me. You met Dan Routhier?"

"No, I don't think I have."

"He's a good guy, a good friend, actually. Runs the regional office for the warden service out of Bangor. Doesn't overreact too much. Turns out he got a call over the weekend that turned into a conference with guys from Homeland Security and the FBI. We've got a really bad actor cooking up what could be a functional chemical weapon and using a blind cove in Frenchman's Bay as his lab," Gary said.

Susan just stared at him, her jaw going slack.

"Yeah, I know, I thought Dan was pranking me at first, but no, it's dead serious. It's a disenfranchised scientist who was employed by that chemical company, Clean Harbor. They were developing a new marine herbicide that would be effective in cold northern waters and had a chemist on the project from Russia. The Russian dude had worked on similar projects in the Arctic, north of Siberia. But they caught him making little knock-off compounds that were super dangerous, without approval, and they fired him."

"Are you serious?" Susan could tell Gary wasn't joking, but her mind was still catching up with the information. Gary just nodded and took a deep breath.

"Susan, the stuff he's making? It's synergistically more powerful than what causes Toxic Shellfish Poisoning, and it can be concentrated in tidal crustaceans that are unaffected by it, just like with saxitoxin. The Clean Harbor people were freaking out, and they're not exactly huge friends of the environment," Gary said.

"So, does anyone know where exactly he's operating?"

"Maybe. Dan sent one of his officers down to an area of interest that a citizen called in about. Some old guy who lives on Little Duck Island was

222 | BEDTIME STORIES FOR GROWN UPS

nosing around in his boat after you left the coast on Saturday. Did you talk to someone like that, too?"

"I know who you're talking about. He was out on the water when I was collecting samples last week. His name is Angus something. He got hold of me later by phone and said the same thing we'd been hearing from the other people who called us. He'd found dead shorebirds by his dock, and had seen some gulls the evening before, walking like they were suffering from neurotoxicity of some sort. That's why I went all the way back down there to Little Duck on Saturday morning."

"Well, your friend Angus isn't one to let a bad situation fester, I guess. Dan told me his officer knows the guy, and his family has been on Little Duck for generations. Has a strong attachment to the area and it bothered him that you didn't know what you were finding or where it was coming from. He went out on his own—and found an area along the shore fenced off with plastic netting just beyond the tide zone, warning signs all around and some equipment mounted on poles he didn't recognize. That's when he called the warden he knew best, a guy named Rich Staunton. Rich talked to Dan. They agreed he needed to head down there and check it out, given what the feds had told them on their conference call."

"And?"

"Staunton was on scene investigating when Dan got another call. The scientist-gone-bad is working with the Russian government and they want to fund him to keep going, producing a small supply of the compound as a chemical weapon. They've sent in protection for the scientist and his in-situ lab here in Maine. The situation is escalating, fast."

"And what on earth do we have to do with all this now?" Susan was envisioning black helicopters and Navy SEALs in dive suits and night-vision goggles. "I'm not sure I want to be in this movie, Gary," Susan said.

"I know. But they need one of our scientists to get up there with a team of feds from D.C. and the Coast Guard. By the time the game warden responded, the feds had already sent a Coast Guard chopper over the area, and they saw exactly what Angus had described. Dan pulled his officer, Rich, out of there as soon as he could reach him. Now they're sending in a high-end hazmat team of chemical weapons specialists and marine scientists from Clean Harbor to pull everything out of the water. They're going in with military cover because they don't know for sure what the Russians have in place yet. It's crazy. This is *Maine*, for god's sake," Gary said, getting up and pacing.

"Ummm, can we go back to the part where you said, 'They need one of our scientists,' please? Is this why you had me put an extra T-shirt and underwear in a bag this morning? Tell me you're not thinking what I'm afraid you're thinking."

Gary stopped meandering around his office and turned to face her.

"Susan, they need our best. You're our best. Once they clear the area, they need someone to start sampling the water and the beachfront soils—and keep doing it for a while—to make sure they got it all. Shutting this guy down could just be the beginning of the intervention. And that falls back on our shop. Public and environmental safety for the citizens of Maine—that's on us."

"Jesus, Gary."

Susan walked over to the one chair Gary had in his office for guests and plopped down, running a hand through her long, blonde hair. She was thinking, hard, about what she'd need to have to do this kind of testing in the field. After a minute, she looked up. Gary was just standing in the middle of his office, looking at her, watching her process the information.

"You know what?" Susan said to him. "This really, really sucks."

Gary sat down at his desk and booted up his computer. He asked her what she was going to need and started an expedited requisition. Then he made phone calls to have every item on her list pulled off shelves, located in other departments, sent over by messenger, whatever it took to get it to his office within an hour.

Susan went to her lab and reviewed every one of the analyses she'd done the previous Friday. She pulled up coastal maps on her desktop computer, downloaded several to her field laptop, and put two on her phone for easy reference. Then she called her brother in Boston for the hell of it, just because it felt good to hear his voice. Breezily, she told him about a new special assignment in Bar Harbor that was going to be messy. Susan wanted to tell him how much she loved him, but then he'd get worried and start asking questions she couldn't answer. When he got concerned and started to probe, she cut the call short. She didn't call him at work very often and that alone had been enough for him to suspect something strange might be going on.

Gary poked his head through the door an hour and a half later and said everything she wanted was ready to go. Susan grabbed a cart and started loading it with coolers, portable equipment of various kinds, sampling supplies, and last, but not least, snacks. When she went past his office with the loaded cart, Gary hopped up from behind his desk and followed her outside to the car to help her load everything.

"Okay, Susan. They'll be waiting for you at the Coast Guard sub-station in Southwest Harbor. You know where it is?" Gary was holding open the driver's door for her.

"Yeah, it's been a while, but I've been there before. It's a left off 102, just past the hardware store, right?"

Gary nodded. "That's the one. There are a couple little restaurants right around in there if you need to grab some food. Just keep receipts. This trip is *so* on me…"

Susan laughed and climbed in behind the wheel, setting her water bottle into the cup holder.

"And Susan?" Gary looked at her closely.

"Yeah, boss," Susan said, a little preoccupied already.

"You're good. The best I have. Remember that. There's no way I could ever replace you," Gary said somberly.

"Gary…don't scare me like that." Susan met his stare, her face flaring with nervous annoyance.

"No, I mean, the state hiring freeze. There's really no way I could replace you," he said, letting his face break out in a huge grin.

"Asshole," Susan replied, smiling at him, and pulling the car door closed in front of his face. She waved goodbye and headed out of the parking lot.

Two and a half hours later, Susan pulled into the Coast Guard station at the bottom of Somes Sound out on Mount Desert Island. Taking nothing with her but her water bottle, phone, and wallet, she locked the state vehicle and headed inside to introduce herself.

A receptionist led her into a small conference room, where several other people waited. Among them was the Coast Guard district commander out of Boston, which shouldn't have surprised her, but did. He introduced himself as Bob Samuels. Dan Routhier, from the warden's service up in Bangor was there, as well as the chief of police from a town she'd never heard of but was the closest thing to local law enforcement in the area nearest the Russian's little experiment in growing chemical weapons.

Commander Samuels spoke first.

"Alright, we're all here. 'We' are the clean-up crew. As we speak, an intervention is starting that will take out the low-tech chemical weapons factory up on Frenchman's Bay. With any luck, that will go smoothly and the Russian operatives we've heard about but never laid eyes on will either be clumsy or not show up at all. Federal and local law enforcement are all over the place up there, along with Dan's local warden, hoping to snag anyone involved who may try to run. They are hoping to catch Andrei Drozdov on site. He's the scientist Clean Harbor fired and who we think has been developing the poisons. We're not sure that's his real name. It could be code—it means 'blackbird' in Russian. The people on scene control the timeframe for all this. It could be a few hours."

Samuels took a long drink from a paper coffee cup and began to lay out the steps they would take to secure the area and keep it free of public intrusion from either land or water. Then they would let Susan in to establish baseline data for monitoring environmental safety. Most of the hard, ongoing work would fall to Susan. For now, they waited.

Back on Little Duck Island, Angus Kingery was restless. He hadn't slept much the night before and had been up twice to stare out the window in his kitchen or sit outside on the porch in the cold air, hoping to settle his mind.

But it wouldn't settle. He kept seeing the dead plovers on the beach, the gulls landing and losing their balance in his backyard, the red-legged guillemot he'd spotted, tipping over and rolling off the rocks on its back at the edge of the shoreline down by his dock. It was awful. Whatever was coming down on the currents to Little Duck Island had come from that netted-off area with the "KEEP OUT" signs where he'd led Rich Staunton. And where no one was doing a damn thing, as far as he knew.

Angus spent the morning in his workshop, refinishing the small bench where he dropped his things just inside the mudroom off the kitchen. It was something that needed to be done, and he needed a project to occupy his mind. He got the first new layer of stain applied and then cleaned his brush at the big utility sink in the corner. After placing the brush over a tray to dry, he stood back, staring at the wall.

Every minute, more of whatever toxin was being generated up the coast was drifting down around his beloved island. Angus couldn't bear knowing that and doing nothing.

Exactly what he was going to do wasn't clear, but something in the water was poisonous. That much he knew. He pulled his newest waders off the peg on the wall and checked his mud boots and gaiters for any breaks in the seams or little slices in the rubber. Then he remembered the vinyl fencing and the odd-looking meters on poles, and he wondered what else might be under the surface of the water. Angus grabbed long rubber gloves and tools that might come in handy if there was something that needed to be taken apart.

He stacked everything in his wheelbarrow and headed down to the dock. After he'd transferred the load into his boat, he looked out across the water for a long moment, ducked his head, said a prayer, and headed back up to the house. A .45 caliber handgun and a rifle were the final additions to his boatload of personal problem-solving resources.

It was a little after one in the afternoon when he started the outboard motor, backed out of the slip, and headed for the top of Frenchman's Bay.

***

Andrei Drozdov had rented a house on Spruce Point for a month. He'd told the owners little about why he needed to be in such a remote part of the Maine coast for so long but mentioned that he was authoring a novel and needed privacy. They were happy to have a single booking, and he prepaid the full amount. It was the perfect location for Andrei, since it wasn't in any town, there was only one other house on the lane that wandered into the woods off Route 108. It was walking distance to the path he'd found that led to the small beach where the conditions were perfect for what he needed to do. He'd made a shortcut to the trailhead so he could carry what he needed in a backpack, unseen.

Today, he needed to go down to the water and check the meters to make sure the water temperature, salinity, and clarity were still optimal for the tiny shellfish that were silently meeting his needs. All they had to do was keep eating and growing for another three days and he would be able to pull a few gallons of mud from the shallows, separate the tiny creatures from the silt and water, process their flesh, and concentrate the toxin he had discovered. Once transferred and sealed into small, thick glass vials, the compound could be transported easily for use by his contacts in Russia.

A small back bedroom in the rental house served as his lab. All he'd had to do was remove a child-size bed and shove it into the end of the hallway. There was only one window in the room, and it faced into the woods. He had covered it with aluminum foil, just in case.

He loaded his sampling supplies and waterproof laptop into his backpack. He rolled up a fully rubberized hazmat suit and pressed it in over the top of the computer. He slung the backpack over his shoulders and headed for the trail through the woods to the bluff overlooking the beach. Two of his Russian colleagues would be there, somewhere, at the time he told them he would arrive to tend to his business. He would have cover. He knew he wouldn't see them, but they would be there.

Unbeknownst to Drozdov, Rich Staunton had given final directions to special agents on the ground, and on the water with the Coast Guard, to make sure they could find the location of Drozdov's experimental site as well as good cover. The many nooks and crannies of Maine's jagged, rocky coastline and dense forests worked in their favor. You could be 20 feet from someone in those woods and remain unacquainted for as long as you wanted to.

Rich himself was staying out of the way, as instructed. He was in his personal pickup truck rather than a marked game warden vehicle. He was driving down a narrow dirt road that led to a small, rocky beach where locals sometimes backed down to the water and put in a fishing boat or kayak at high tide on nice weekends. He planned to park there and wait. It was only about a mile and a half away from the action, in a little cove that sat deep in the protection of a larger bay. A narrow, densely forested peninsula of land sat between him and where Andrei Drozdov was doing his dirty work. If anything crazy happened, Rich would hear it, but he couldn't watch what was happening directly. That bugged him, but at this point, the rules weren't his to make.

He looked at his watch. The feds would be closing in soon to secure the area, hopefully without incident. Then they would unleash their specialists to disassemble Drozdov's equipment and do their best to sterilize the water and sub-surface soils that had become the source for the toxic flow into the ocean.

Rich heard a helicopter slowly moving closer. It was coming north from the air strip on Mt. Desert Island. It would stay offshore, capable of monitoring activity along the waterline, and conducting technical rescue if needed. Getting that chopper in place was the last step before someone called go-time.

Rich slowed to a stop before the lane dipped sharply toward the water. He expected the little beach to be empty in the middle of a workweek. It wasn't.

Bobbing just off the beach on a rope in water that was only three- to four-feet deep was an old red-and-white fishing boat that he recognized as belonging to Angus Kingery. The engine had been tipped up out of the water to avoid hitting ground close to shore. The only thing he could see in the boat was a beat-up cooler and a folded set of heavy-duty waders. And a gun case.

Rich swore quietly. The old man just couldn't leave it alone. But where had he gone? They had identified every residence and business within three miles and quietly locked everything down. Angus was supposed to be home on Little Duck Island.

Rich ran back to his truck and grabbed his cellphone. He called Dan Routhier, who he knew was sitting in a room in Southwest Harbor with the district commander for the Coast Guard.

"Rich, what is it, everything okay up there?" Dan's voice was urgent. He knew it was go-time, too.

"Dan, I just found Angus Kingery's boat at a locals' mud ramp only a mile or so from the site. He's not in it. But the case for a deer rifle is, and I'm betting that case is empty. I don't know where Angus is, but I'd bet good money he didn't think anybody was taking this seriously and decided to do something about it. I'm afraid he might be right in the middle of the action," Rich said. "What do you want me to do?"

Before Dan could get a word out to respond, Rich heard automatic weapons fire.

***

Angus had tied his boat up at the little mud beach that was just around the peninsula from the experiment he'd reported to Rich Staunton. He figured he knew his way around the woods and coastline better than anyone who hadn't grown up there, friend or foe. About half the peninsula was a marine coastal reserve and the rest was privately owned but not occupied except for a couple of rustic cabins used for hunting and fishing by locals and their families. There was a network of trails that extended up and down the peninsula and out above the bay. Angus knew it wouldn't be much of a hike to where he could get an unobstructed view of that fenced-off area in the water.

Angus had his .45 in a leather holster on his belt, and his rifle held in both hands in front of him. He had a pair of compact field glasses pocketed in his vest. He'd left the rest of his gear in his boat, for now. Once he knew no one was around and he could get down on that beach to see what he was dealing with, he'd go back and motor over with his tools and waders.

He walked quietly through the woods, ducking under overhanging branches and stopping every 20 paces or so to listen. The main trail he was looking for went right up the middle of the peninsula, then forked, with the smaller path leading to the edge of the bluff. Angus found the trail, and the fork, just as he remembered it. As he approached the overlook to the bay at the top of the bluff, he stepped around a large granite boulder and heard the throbbing beat of a helicopter's rotor in the distance. It was coming closer.

Angus didn't want to be seen. He bent low, staying behind the brushy beach rose and brambles that thrived in the loose soil where the land dropped off to the water's edge. The last time he'd been up there hunting, he had found a neat opening in the brush further down the bluff with a long view out to sea. That spot, if he recalled it correctly, would be less than 200 yards from the fenced area down in the water. After a bit of poking around, Angus found the break, knelt down, and started to pull out his binoculars.

Movement caught his eye. A slender, dark-haired man in a long-sleeved maroon shirt carrying an oversized backpack was part sliding, part hopping down the last section of trail Angus had sent Rich Staunton down just the day before. Angus swung the field glasses up to get a closer look at what the man was doing.

That's when Angus heard and saw the chopper come around the bottom of the bay into view. It was a Coast Guard helicopter flying slowly into position along the waterfront. The man in the backpack froze, right at the bottom of the trail, 20 paces away from the warning signs and orange fencing. He scrambled backward, obviously alarmed. A moment later, Angus heard gunfire. He spun on one knee and lifted his field glasses again, this time in the direction of the source of the rapid series of shots. It was an automatic weapon. The shots were coming from a spot below him, and a little further down the coastline toward the entrance to the bay.

Angus spotted the shooter. Wearing dark green-and-black camo from head to toe, a man was holding an assault rifle no civilian ought to be carrying. Angus thought to himself that he never would have been able to see the guy if he hadn't moved, he blended in so perfectly with the big black rocks and dark-green algae of the tide pools. The guy was shooting at the chopper, and Angus heard a round ping off the helicopter's landing gear. The pilot immediately pulled up and veered away from the beach. Angus reached out with his left hand and pulled his own rifle closer to his boots. Rich Staunton had been right. Something was going down, and federal agencies were involved.

Angus looked back toward the guy in the maroon shirt and saw him drop the pack and start scrambling back up the trail. Two men appeared out of the woods beside the trail, one above the man and one beside, and quickly subdued him. They had weapons drawn but didn't need to use them. They looked to be wearing full protective tactical gear, their torsos heavy with body armor, their heads in black helmets. One tactical officer put the slender man in handcuffs. The other started making his way down the beach, keeping boulders and upended driftwood logs between himself and the shooter in camo further down the waterfront. He was carrying a rifle and looked fully prepared to use it.

Angus knew he was in the middle of a massive operation. His heart was pounding, and he could feel the electricity of adrenaline in his chest and shoulders. But he couldn't move. He had no idea who or what else was in the woods around him.

That's when Angus saw another man in green-and-black camo edge out from behind a tree up on the bluff. Angus figured the guy with the backpack was the one running the experiment in the water. That meant the guys in tactical black were ours. The men in the green-and-black camo were on the wrong side.

Angus looked up at the guy on the bluff. He, too, had an automatic rifle and was swinging it around to take aim at the officer down on the beach, currently hunkered down behind a boulder, getting closer to the shooter who had fired on the helicopter.

Angus Kingery was a good shot. He pulled his rifle off the ground, flipped off the safety, the stock against his shoulder, aimed, and squeezed the trigger. A breath later, the short, stocky man in green-and-black camo tumbled down from the top of the bluff and landed, writhing, in the shallow water below. Angus had hit him in the shoulder, right where he intended.

The loud report of Angus's rifle shot distracted the other man in camo, who stood up from his crouch and turned to look up toward where Angus was positioned on the bluff. He wasn't expecting a challenge from up there. When he turned and leaned out from the rock, the officer on the beach took his shot. The second man in green camo collapsed awkwardly across the rocks in the shallows. He didn't move.

It was over. The officer on the beach had control of the injured man Angus had shot, and Angus could see him turn his head toward a radio on his shoulder. Angus could only hear a few words drift up over the sound of the surf. The officer stood and signaled to the pilot of the Coast Guard helicopter, who responded by retreating toward the open ocean and then south out of view.

Angus didn't know it, but the helicopter pilot had already contacted the Coast Guard station in Southwest Harbor. He let the waiting team there know it was time to bring Susan Snow and her equipment up to the scene in a fast boat.

Angus knew he needed to make himself known to the authorities. Explain himself. And not get shot in the process. He secured his rifle and set it down on the ground. Then he stood, slowly, and pulled his bandana from his pocket and shook it open. It was red, white, and blue with a bald eagle on one side. He tossed it into the air when he felt a gust of wind come up and watched it float out and down toward the beach. He saw the man in tactical gear catch sight of it, and then look up the bluff toward where Angus was now standing, his arms in the air, waving.

Angus found another trail that led back into the woods and then down a ravine to the beach. He picked his way along it, using shrubs and tree limbs as handholds on the steep sloping sections. It took close to an hour. He was old, and slow, and his knees hurt. But he made it down, and then clambered awkwardly over the wet rocks and pooled water back toward the buzz of action around the fenced-off zone. He was looking for the officer who was nearly shot in the back by the camouflaged bad actor up on the bluff.

There were people in hooded white suits on the sand; and others moving into the water, covered from head to toe in a bulky neon-green rubber material with red hash marks down the arms and legs. He thought he saw the officer he was looking for in a knot of agents on the other side of the fenced area.

Coming out onto the beach from the bluff trail was someone Angus recognized. Rich Staunton was staring directly at Angus, shaking his head.

"Angus Kingery?" A deep voice right behind Angus made him jump and stumble as he tried to turn around. It was one of the guys in black tactical gear, the letters DOG and a gold trident in an insignia on his chest.

"Yeah, that's me," Angus said, looking up at the man.

"James O'Connor, Coast Guard Deployable Operations. I'm not sure if I have to arrest you for assault with a deadly weapon or see about getting you a Congressional Gold Medal," the man said. "At the moment, I'm just damn glad you're a good shot." He stuck out his hand, still wrapped in black leather, and Angus took it firmly in his own. James O'Connor thanked Angus for saving his life.

"I'm glad you're okay. Is that piece of pond scum I shot in the shoulder whining about it too much?" Angus jerked his head toward the man on the ground who had fallen from the bluff.

Officer O'Connor laughed, tossing his head back. "Well, I'm not sure, but I think the Russian I heard coming out of his mouth wasn't appropriate for polite company. My buddy over there didn't work too hard at being gentle when he hauled him to his feet," he said.

"Hmph," Angus muttered.

"Mind if I wander over there and find out if they're finally going to clean up that scum going into my ocean? You can arrest me later," Angus said, turning away to head over to talk to Rich.

Over his shoulder, Angus called back in O'Connor's direction. "My family's been on Little Duck Island for 200 years, you won't have any trouble finding me."

RABBIT VALLEY WATER

On a 100-degree day in the middle of July, Billy Carnes was slowly driving his pickup down the wrong side of the dirt road that led to Nate Cramer's old ranch. He was leaning out of his window and craning his neck to see down into the ditch. Water was low again, but still flowing. Barely.

As ditch captain, he worked for the Rabbit Valley Water Users Association, known locally as the Ditch Association. It functioned a bit like a homeowners' association but focused on the application of water rights tied to each parcel of land in the area, water conservation strategies, and maintenance of the common irrigation infrastructure. That included keeping the ditches maintained and clear of debris.

As Billy crested the low hill right before what used to be the Cramer's farmhouse, he let out a low whistle and reached over to the passenger seat to ruffle the fur on his dog's neck.

"Well, I'll be darned, Hap," Billy mused, talking unselfconsciously to the long-haired black-and-white unemployed herding dog who was always beside him on his ditch runs. "Someone's been by to pretty up the place."

Nate Cramer had died last year, and his wife, Betty, the year before. The small ranch, with its old barn and farmhouse, had been left to rot while the estate got settled by Nate's only son, Terry. Terry was doing his best, but the probate process had taken a long time, and Terry was busy with his job in New York City. It had gone on the market without fanfare and without improvements.

Out of respect for the Cramer family and the fact that they'd ranched that little homestead since the early 1800s, Billy swung by occasionally to check on the place, making sure the doors were still there and the windows intact. What he now knew was that someone shared his concern that the much-loved ranch kept its dignity.

In a 20-foot-long rectangle below the front porch was Betty's beloved rose garden. Over the years, she had planted and tended the prettiest combination of red, pale-yellow, and pink roses anywhere in the county. Each year, she fended off the voles, plucked off bugs, fertilized, pruned, watered, and mulched those bushes so that every summer, they exploded again with color, roses spilling up and over the porch rail.

Since Betty had died, the rose garden had languished into rangy delinquency. The first summer, everyone figured Nate just couldn't bring himself to work on it. It was the one place he had left under Betty's care without even bickering about her approach, and Nate was never short of opinions about anything. Then Nate had passed on as well, and the whole sad place had become overgrown. Even the house looked abandoned, as though its soul had floated up and away from the chimney. The white paint had peeled, the worn steps were sagging, and weeds were filling the spaces between the stones in the walkway that led around to the side door. Betty's roses had collapsed on one another in a tangle, the bed covered with tufts of rangy grass and bindweed twisting up the stems.

Billy pulled his truck onto the shoulder of the road, just short of where the driveway headed up to the house. He was built like a fireplug, standing about five feet six inches in his boots, barrel-chest over a little paunch and bowed legs. He slid out of the driver's seat and walked around his pickup truck to let his dog loose from the passenger's side.

"C'mon, Happy, let's go check this out," Billy said to the dog, who leapt out of the truck, tongue lolling, tail wagging, and looking as cheery as his name suggested he should.

Billy walked up toward the house and stood in front of the rose garden, shaking his head and smiling.

"This has to be Mary's doing," Billy said aloud to no one.

Mary was Adam Donovan's wife. She, too, loved to garden and had been close to Betty for decades. Adam owned a good-sized ranch on the other side of town and Mary and Adam had a way of quietly looking after people. That had been true for years, well before Adam had been elected county sheriff.

The rose garden was cleaned up and staked, the weeds gone, the beds watered and mulched. Billy noticed little colored pellets turned up in the mulch that he recognized as slow-acting plant fertilizer. The roses weren't as plentiful as they had been in the past, but there were some of every color blooming brightly and much more a focal point now that the dross was gone.

Billy walked up to the porch to take a closer look at Betty's window boxes. One to a window, they had been cleared of cobwebs, whitewashed, and planted with bright-red geraniums. There was no note on the door, but a new, thick coir doormat had been put in place. It had a little border of singing meadowlark silhouettes and the word *Welcome* in italics across the middle.

"Mary, you do have a way..." Billy said quietly, and turned to look for Hap, whistling. "C'mon, boy, let's go," he said as the dog came trotting around from the back of the house.

The two walked back to Billy's pickup truck, Hap nosing in front to jump into the driver's seat. Billy shooed him over to the other side as he grabbed the wheel to pull himself the rest of the way up. He started the truck and pulled onto the road, headed for the Tractor Supply to get another 50-pound bag of dog food.

When Billy ran his windshield wipers to clear the road dirt, he saw a plume of dust in the distance, getting closer. As the vehicle approached, Billy pulled over again, curious, about 200 feet from Nate's driveway. To his surprise, a big old Chevy Silverado came crawling by, looking for the turn, hauling a stock trailer that looked packed to the roof, full of boxes and household belongings. The driver made a slow turn into the driveway, the trailer dipping dangerously into the overgrown culvert next to the drive.

Billy heard an unfettered string of expletives erupt from the driver's side of the cab and decided it might not be the best time to introduce himself to the folks he guessed must be the new owners of the homestead. He paused long enough to make sure the driver navigated the rest of the turn okay, then pulled back onto the road and went on his way.

The irritated driver of the Silverado pulled up facing the barn door, with the end of the stock trailer in the general vicinity of the front door to the house. He turned off the engine and opened the door. From the other side of the cab, a petite, middle-aged, dark-haired woman stepped out, and a gangly teenaged boy unfolded himself from the bench seat behind the two adults up front.

"Well, here we are," the man declared, walking around the front of the truck, waving the heat from the engine compartment away when it hit him in a blast. "Whaddaya think, Annie? You like it, Pete? Check out the barn!"

The woman named Annie took a few steps toward the front porch, shielding her eyes from the sun. Pete slowly joined his mom, saying nothing. Annie and Pete stared at the house. The paint was peeling, the white topcoat curling away in spots to reveal gray undercoat in patches across the siding. One rail at the side of the porch was broken and leaned out into the arms of what might have been a forsythia bush. The grass in the front yard had been cut recently, but the rest of the property was completely overgrown, with huge flowering bull thistle and yellow sweet clover in four-foot clumps across the front of the barn door. The small door to the side of the barn had a cracked window, repaired with short lengths of dirty gray duct tape, partially obscured by cobwebs that drifted in the breeze.

Annie looked up as her husband walked over to her and clamped a hand on her shoulder, grinning broadly and looking at her expectantly.

"Well, Stu…" Annie seemed to be reaching for something to say as she looked around at the neglected buildings. Her eyes settled on the rose garden. "This rose garden sure is lovely."

"And look at those pretty flowers in the window boxes! Someone's been looking after this place real nice, can't you tell, Annie? This is going to be *great*," Stu proclaimed, striding briskly toward the front door.

"They are pretty," Annie replied, her voice trailing off as she spoke to Stu's back. She looked back at Pete and extended her right arm toward him.

"C'mon, honey," she said quietly, nodding to Pete and making eye contact, one eyebrow raised in a way that said *No, son, you're not crazy. This place is a disaster.*

Pete looked up to make sure his father's back was still turned and returned his mother's gaze, mouthing, "HELP ME," eyes held wide in mock terror. Annie smiled and motioned him to her side as they followed Stu up to the front door.

The newest members of the Springdale ranching community had arrived.

***

Stu Chesterton and his family worked steadily for several days, unpacking and getting the farmhouse habitable. Stu was eager to move on to getting the ranching part of the property ready for business. He had some years of experience with farm and ranch work, having had a job as a hand on a dairy farm back near their home in Missouri. He relied on his years as a truck driver for the skills he needed to get the neglected farm machinery on the property cleaned up and operating. But it was an uphill battle. Stu was not good at asking for help.

By late July, Stu and his son, Pete, had the barn cleaned out, the doors and windows fixed, and one tractor running. The pasture was still a mess, but the breaks in the fence line had been repaired, sometimes with pieces of plywood and chicken wire, but they were at least continuous. Stu decided it was time to buy some cattle.

The next cattle auction was down in Lifton Springs, about 100 miles from Springdale. Stu had never been to a stock auction before, but he was cocky about it when Annie asked him how it worked. Annie had gone with Stu to an estate auction once, trying to get furniture cheap, and he told her it was the same process. He had experience with Holsteins, but not beef cattle, and it was beef cattle he was aiming to buy. After reading up on breeds and deciding how much money he had to spend, Stu figured he just needed to get a start on building a herd and see how it went.

Stu dragged Pete with him early in the morning of the first day of the auction, hauling their stock trailer behind the big Chevy pickup. He quickly realized that the Angus and Charolaise were extremely costly and decided to wait to dive into the bidding until the last day of the auction. He came home with two Red Angus, a Hereford, and an underweight Texas Longhorn he was told just needed some fattening up.

Truth was, Stu did not know what he was doing. He let the animals loose in the pasture, and after three months, none of them were gaining weight the way he had hoped. The two Red Angus had taken to just hanging out in one corner of the pasture, their heads hung, looking listless and snotty. Annie finally talked Stu into calling a local large animal vet just to check on them.

When Doc Nurmeier came out to the ranch, he took one look at the cattle and started peppering Stu with questions about a whole host of things he hadn't done. Vaccinations, feed supplements, the list went on. Doc was respectful and understanding, but let Stu and Annie know that the two Angus might not make it as the pneumonia they were suffering from was advanced. Within a week, the animals were in obvious agony, and both had to be put down. Annie did not speak to Stu for two days. She was angry that his stubborn neglect had caused such needless suffering.

There were similar tough lessons learned with the four milk goats, the two horses, and the flock of chickens they had purchased. Pete had liked the idea of a chicken coop and had grown fond of the birds when they were just chicks, so had taught himself a lot about their care. He had fought with his father to get them the right feed, a heater for the coop in advance of chilly weather, and a fenced run to make sure they became good layers. It took time, but the hens did start laying eggs. It was one of the brighter spots in the family's new life in the country.

Pete and Annie had also sought out the organic grower who stocked the Farmer's Market tables in town every Saturday. Kevin and Carla Peterson were incredibly gracious and eagerly volunteered to give them guidance on establishing a productive organic garden for their family. With starts from their own greenhouses that were well enough along to produce in late summer and fall, Kevin coached Pete through the process of constructing hills and rows for the different vegetables, a lattice for the climbing beans, and a patch off the end for planting sweet corn next year. The Chestertons didn't have the money to put in irrigation, but Carla loaned them an extra hose long enough to reach the garden from the side of the house.

By the middle of August, the Chesterton family had settled into a routine. They had found the grocery and feed store, Tractor Supply, the Valley Bank, and the post office. Annie got Pete registered to start his junior year at the high school and had taken him over to the clinic in Rushton for his physical. The family didn't go to church on Sundays, but nonetheless, most of Springdale had met either Annie or Stu and had tried to be welcoming. But no one had managed to truly become acquainted.

Stu had earned a reputation for being irascible and demanding. He waved off well-meaning advice, and despite personal invitations from his nearest neighbors, Stu had skipped the semi-annual Ditch Association meeting. Had he attended, he could have learned a whole lot more about the region's water supply and irrigation system and built relationships with the other property owners. That would have been smart. Water supply could make or break agricultural operations in the arid West, and Stu just stubbornly tried to make do with what came. And he acted as though he had no obligations to the other water users in the area. He refused to pay his monthly association fees.

Eventually, the necessities of community life would catch up to them.

***

Billy Carnes was knee deep in mud and only half visible, bent over in the ditch, tearing out bunches of thick grass and weeds. He was trying to free up the lift mechanism of the headgate at the top of the irrigation line that ran through part of Stu's property. The ditch had become so overgrown he couldn't even find the metal bracket that held what was jammed.

Billy twisted his head over his shoulder to wipe the sweat from his eyes on his T-shirt without taking off his gloves. He almost had the weeds and litter cleared away enough to start the job. He paused long enough to pluck a tick off his chest and fling it into the grass above the ditch. He enjoyed the work of being ditch captain. He hated ticks.

He had put this bit of ditch maintenance off for a couple of weeks for a whole list of reasons, but the truth was, he really did not want to run into Stu. Billy suspected Stu did not understand the irrigation system that everyone outside the Springdale town limits depended on. And Billy did not want to be in the position of having to provide the man a tutorial. He hoped that in tackling this project late in the morning on a weekday, Stu would be busy somewhere else on his property and wouldn't turn up out by the ditch road.

Then Billy heard a pickup truck rolling along the gravel toward him, and when he lifted his head to see who it was, he recognized the big Silverado as Stu Chesterton's.

"My lucky day," Billy muttered. He told himself that he needed to get acquainted with the man eventually. Even though Stu's property came with very junior water rights, the ditches and headgate needed the same level of maintenance as everyone else's section of the system. Billy chided himself for avoiding the man for so long.

Stu Chesterton pulled over to the side of the road close to where Billy was working and left the engine on his pickup running. Black clouds of diesel exhaust drifted down across the ditch from the truck's rear end. Billy coughed as he stood up, preparing to climb out of the ditch to greet the rancher.

"Hullo there! I'm Billy Carnes, your ditch captain. How you doin' this morn—"

"I don't care who you are, you're on my property messing with my equipment!" Stu shouted at Billy, crossing his arms over his chest and standing with his feet planted wide as an ox on the shoulder of the road, directly above Billy's head. He was scowling.

"Well, now, let me tell you what I'm doing. It's actually my job," Billy said evenly, hoping to appease the man.

"The hell it is! I don't remember signing a contract with you or any other ditch company, and if we don't have a contract, you aren't workin' for me!" Stu proclaimed. "You owe me an explanation before I call the sheriff and have you arrested for trespassing!"

Stu had no idea how amusing his belligerent threat was. The county sheriff was one of Billy's best friends and the chairman of the Rabbit Valley Water Users Association, which employed Billy to do exactly what he was doing. Adam Donovan and Billy had known each other for decades. But Billy just clambered up the rest of the way out of the ditch to stand next to

Stu and try to explain how the association and its management worked. He was nervous. He wasn't that good with words, and even less good when someone was already mad at him.

"Now, just relax. Believe me, there's no need to bother Adam. Let's start this conversation over," Billy said, forcing a friendly tone, trying to change the sour start to the exchange. "I'm Billy Carnes, and I take it you're Stu Chesterton, the fella who bought Nathan's place earlier in the year." Billy looked up to meet Stu's eyes and offered a handshake in greeting. It was ignored.

Billy raised both his hands in front of his chest apologetically and slowly stepped back another pace, hoping that putting a bit more distance between him and the irrationally angry rancher would calm the man down. He waited until Stu registered the gesture.

"Can I please tell you what I'm doing?" Billy asked.

"Make it quick, I don't have time for this nonsense," Stu responded.

"Well, I'll make it quick. As ditch captain, it's my job to maintain the ditches and the headgates on the whole regional irrigation system. I work for everyone, the whole Ditch Association. This is routine—"

"I did not give my permission for anyone to work on my equipment! Now get back in your truck and get off my land!" Stu barked, jabbing his arm and pointing toward Billy's truck where it was parked on the grassy crossover above the nearest culvert.

"All right, if that's how you're gonna be…" Billy hated arguments of any kind, and Stu was being completely unreasonable. He needed to get that headgate working, but it wasn't going to be today. And someone else was going to have to explain how the system worked to Stu. Billy would talk with Adam about that later. Maybe at next month's Ditch Association meeting.

Billy wouldn't see Stuart Chesterton for another month. In late September, Stu decided he needed to cut what little hay was growing in the pasture along with all the weeds and bale it up for winter feed. He had found an old baler behind the barn and Stu had managed to get it hooked up to the tractor. He made two or three passes across the field before the thing broke down. He repaired it as best he could and got going again, but just as he was making the turn along the fence closest to the main road, he'd accidentally dropped one end of the baler down into the ditch and it caught, hard, jerking the hitch out of alignment on the back of the tractor and breaking the safety chain.

At just that moment, Billy Carnes was driving by on his way to another ranch. Billy saw the partial wreck with the baler and pulled over to see if he could lend a hand. He and Stu had not gotten off to a good start, but Billy wasn't one to hold a grudge, particularly when someone was clearly in trouble. Billy told Hap to stay in the truck and hustled across the road. Stu was swearing as he kicked the side of the tractor in frustration.

"Stu, you okay? I saw you took a rough turn back there," Billy called out as he hopped across the ditch and levered his short body over the fence to check on Stu.

"What?" Stu glanced up. "Oh, it's you." He picked his hat off the ground where he had thrown it. "Damn baler Cramer left us is in shit-shape. Caught on a rock back there and just about went sideways and took the tractor with it."

Billy knew full well that was not what had happened. Stu had made the turn too late and dropped the end of the baler right into the ditch. But he knew better than to say anything to the hotheaded man.

"Bad luck, Stu, I'm sorry." Billy came around the back of the tractor to survey the damage. It was ugly.

"Well, that hitch sure looks messed up, but the rest of the assembly looks all right to me. Could be worse," Billy said, trying for optimism, then walked on back to the baler. "You've lost some tines off the right side of the baler, but those can likely be straightened out and welded."

Stu came around next to Billy and looked blankly at the machine. "Well, I do have a welding torch," Stu said glumly.

Billy looked at him and tried not to react. It was not an easy repair. "Well, the bigger problem is going to be the damage to the tractor hitch, I'm afraid," Billy said, returning to the back of the old John Deere. "Nothing for it but to get it down to Jason's."

"Who the hell is Jason?" Stu growled, reacting badly because they really didn't have the money for major repairs.

Billy ignored his tone. "Jason Toffer. He's the best, and only, ag mechanic in the area. He's kept most of our equipment running for more years than they deserved. I'm sure he can help you out. Tractor's still fine to drive, but you'll need a trailer for the baler if you want him to look at it, too," Billy offered.

"Don't have a trailer that size. Gonna have to come up with something else," Stu said dismissively.

"Stu, don't take this the wrong way, but none of us has everything we need. It takes a while to build up a business like a ranching operation, and equipment's expensive. We all understand. I can get a trailer down here for you. I know of two in the area that can handle a baler this size. If you want me to."

Billy added that last qualifier to make sure Stu didn't feel pressed. But he also knew that Stu didn't have a choice if he wanted the rest of his hay baled. He would either need to get his baler and tractor fixed up or hire someone else to handle his hay.

Stu was not happy, but he truly didn't know what else to do.

"Yeah, okay. Guess I don't have much choice." Stu looked and sounded miserable.

Billy started to give the man an encouraging slap on the shoulder, but stopped himself. Instead, he told Stu to hold on and jogged back to his truck for his phone and a scrap of paper and pen. Billy wrote down Jason Toffer's number, then asked Stu for his phone number so that someone with a free machine trailer could call him and arrange a time to pick up the baler. Stu reluctantly agreed.

When Billy got back in his truck and started back down the road, Stu waved to him. Billy decided that was satisfactory progress in and of itself.

The following Sunday, Billy Carnes and his wife, Janine, got to chatting with Jason Toffer at the coffee hour after church. Jason asked Billy if he knew Stu Chesterton. Billy nodded carefully. Jason shook his head. Stu had taken up a good hour of Jason's time ranting and raving about John Deere's irresponsible manufacturing, and how much of an ass the prior owner of the ranch was to have failed to keep the machinery in better shape. Jason wryly suggested he thought death was a decent excuse to allow routine maintenance to slide, but didn't say anything more. The two men chuckled about all the things they hadn't said to Stu Chesterton.

Janine quietly reminded the two men that everyone learns what they learn when the time comes to learn it. Stu was probably just having trouble being new at something. Billy and Jason looked at each other, restraining themselves from further comment, given the fact that they had just listened to a sermon on grace and patience.

Two weeks into November, temperatures plummeted, and autumn disappeared abruptly into winter. Winter held on well into April. It was months of hard cold, and not enough snow, which did not bode well for Springdale's water supply. When the aspen greened up and the songbirds returned, hopes rose, but freshening rain was rare. Everyone braced for another year of drought. They'd had two bad ones already.

Stu had not responded to communication from the Ditch Association and had not bothered to attend the annual meeting back in November. Everyone else went, given it was when the budget for the following year was presented by the board of directors and ratified by the membership. That, in turn, set everyone's dues for the year. The fact that Stu Chesterton had not been paying his dues was part of the discussion, since everyone's contribution to revenue mattered.

Stu's neighbors shared their concerns that he still might not know how the system worked. They had educated others who had moved in from elsewhere in the country, not knowing enough about water rights and irrigation systems. With junior rights like Stu had, they all knew he couldn't count on much in the way of water supply, particularly in a drought year. They were aggravated, but worried for the family as well.

A year into his attempt to make a go of ranching outside of Springdale, Stu's financial troubles had mounted. He hadn't realized just how much a cattle operation cost, and he kept making costly mistakes that could have been avoided. The worse things got for him, the hotter his temper grew. And the longer the list became of people and circumstances he blamed for his sorrows.

Stu had figured out enough about his junior water rights, and the implications, to complain about it regularly down at the Old Goat Tavern with some friends he had made over the winter. The whole group was related by blood or predilection to Steve Carter, an octogenarian whose continued health defied science.

Carter had sold off most of his land, but still acted like he owned 10,000 acres. And everyone within earshot was told directly that his need to sell was purely the government's fault, at every level. He was a paranoid old coot, but so confident in his ranting opinions and conspiracy theories that he'd accumulated a ragtag band of followers who were more than eager to pull up a chair at the Old Goat and buy another round of whatever Carter was drinking. Stu Chesterton had joined their ranks.

High on Stu's list of causes for his own ill fortune was Adam Donovan. He had learned that Adam was one of the more successful ranchers in the area. Stu didn't know that the ranch had been in the Donovan family for four generations. Donovan Street crossed Main in the middle of town and was named after Adam's great-grandfather. Adam had also served the county as sheriff for 12 years, elected the first time by a good margin, and serving ever since through unopposed elections.

Adam's wife, Mary, had indeed been the one to spruce up the rose garden and porch window boxes of the Cramer residence to make the place look welcoming right before the Chesterton family arrived. It was typical of both Mary and Adam. They were generous, caring, understated people who loved Springdale, and loved the rural life for which they were so grateful.

The fact that Stu had placed Adam in his personal doghouse and wasn't afraid to be vocal about it said more to members of the community than anything else Stu had said or done. Even Steve Carter and his cronies were reticent to jump on Stu's bandwagon about the Donovan family. They knew Stu and his junior water rights weren't Adam's fault, but they nodded anyway and bought Stu another beer to keep him company as he grumbled.

It was the height of summer again. Adam Donovan stood in the blazing

August sun, staring down the irrigation ditch for his northernmost hayfield. The water was low, and even though he held the senior rights and could place a call on the river until he got what he needed for his crop, he knew that would place his neighbors in a world of hurt. The summer monsoonal rains hadn't come, just as everyone had feared.

He was waiting for Billy Carnes to show up so they could talk. Billy knew every landowner and where they stood in the chain of seniority for water rights. Those with the most junior rights only got water once those with more senior rights got theirs. Those laws went back to the Gold Rush days in Colorado.

The system seemed fair, especially to those who owned or inherited more senior rights. Too many folks who bought land and moved here from out of state had no clue about the arcane system and its governance. They saw a river and a ditch across their property and figured if they needed more water, they just opened their headgate. They could not be more wrong.

Adam had been the one to go with Billy on more than one occasion when a new owner needed an education on Colorado water rights and Billy was afraid to be the solo bearer of unwelcome news. Adam had a kindly way of managing those situations, and people in the area were grateful for his diplomacy. It was no small part of why he had been elected county sheriff.

Billy pulled up in his pickup and hopped out as the dust cloud from the gravel road drifted off. He hitched up his jeans as he made his way down the grassy bank to where Adam was standing.

"You think we're gonna see rain this month?" Billy called out to Adam as he plucked his co-op ballcap off his balding head to swat at the deer flies.

"Billy, if I knew that, I'd hold a position a whole lot higher than sheriff." Adam grinned as he stuck his hand out to shake Billy's. "How are you doin'? Janine feeling any better?"

Billy's wife had been suffering lately from debilitating headaches, and their doctor hadn't yet figured out what was wrong. She hated even thinking about making the long trip to Denver to see specialists and kept trying to convince Billy it was nothing.

"I don't know, Adam. She keeps saying those headaches are easing up, but I've known that woman for 27 years and been married to her for 24. I think she's hurtin' bad and too darn stubborn to admit it." Billy shook his head and sighed. Adam frowned, concerned.

"Do you want me to send Mary down to have a chat with her? You know Mary, she'd be more than happy to make the drive to Denver with her for company if you can't get away. They could stay with our daughter in Lakewood to keep expenses down, no problem."

"Oh, I know she would. And I appreciate the offer more 'n you know. But I think my gal will have to get a bit closer to desperate before we get a 'yes' out of her for something like seeing specialists." Billy swatted at another fly. He wanted to change the subject.

"So, you need to put a call on the river yet?" he said it with a carefully neutral tone, knowing full well Adam had the right to proceed.

"Well, Billy, that's what I wanted to chat with you about."

The two men stood there along the ditch for an hour while Adam asked Billy for information about each of the landowners and the condition of their fields and crops, their animals, and how the water level was looking further down the network. Adam wouldn't act until after he called a meeting with the Ditch Association to talk with folks directly. When he did, he wanted to offer a proposal that would recognize the seniority principle but not leave anyone bankrupt with a dead crop and weakened stock.

After Adam had asked all his questions and Billy had figured out what he was planning, the two stood together quietly for a moment. Adam spoke first.

"So. Who do I need to worry about?"

Billy coughed out a stunted laugh. He knew what Adam was getting at. Adam was clearly already worried about his neighbors' well-being and their ability to get through the drought. That wasn't it.

"Adam, there's a reason you keep getting elected," Billy said as he grinned at his friend, who was careful not to respond beyond allowing a smile to crinkle the corners of his blue eyes. Billy went on.

"It's Stu Chesterton you need to worry about. He was already losing money on his cattle operation because he kept putting off vet care and was overbreeding his heifers. At least that's what I heard. Won't take advice from anyone and he doesn't have much experience. So, he's been blustering all over town, blaming everyone from the bank to the Dalai Lama for his troubles. Janine heard from a friend of hers at church that he might have lost his marbles. Stormed out of the bank last week cussing a blue streak and threatening to come back with his shotgun." Billy shook his head and absently kicked at a rock with the toe of his boot, then looked up to examine a growing set of cumulus clouds building in the west.

Adam waited. He could tell that Billy was debating whether to say more.

"The thing is Adam…" Billy went quiet. But he swallowed once and continued. "Well, Stu's been running with some of those crazy conspiracy theorists who just hate everything, especially government. My buddy Charlie heard Stu and a couple other guys down at the Old Goat last weekend carrying on about the sheriff's office and how you all could put in martial law, confiscate their guns, take their land and their rights. Stu was just fixated on telling his pals to watch how water is handled. Kept saying over and over that takin' away folks' water rights was the first sign that martial law was coming. And he talked about you, personally, Adam. And he was all worked up and sounding downright paranoid, about hoppin' out of his own drawers. I mean, granted, they'd all had more than a few beers, but…"

Billy stopped and looked down the road. At nothing. Then he looked down at his feet and back up at Adam.

"Adam, you're a good man. We all know it. And there's more than one of us who's worried Stu might just crack here one of these days soon. Be careful. He's hotheaded."

Adam nodded once, his jaw tight. He took a breath and looked over at his old friend with a crooked smile. He reached over to give Billy's shoulder a quick reassuring squeeze with one hand, then let it drop.

"Well, Billy, I wish I could reassure our fine citizens down at the Goat that with 1,300 square miles to cover and two deputies to do it, I'm not going to rush into declaring martial law across the county." Both men chuckled. Adam continued, but his tone sobered. "I could always count on you to give me the truth, even if it wouldn't exactly make my day. I appreciate that, my friend."

Adam pushed his old tan Stetson back further on his head and squinted up toward the sun.

"We'd both best get out of this heat before the vultures start circling. Do you want to come up to the house for a glass of iced tea? I'm sure Mary would love to see you."

Billy knew Adam had work to do, and he needed to get back to clearing out some tree limbs and trash that were threatening to clog one of the gates down on Bill Peterson's property.

"Naw, but thanks, Adam. I'd best get back to Bill's place and finish that cleanup. Sure good to see you, though." Billy began to clamber up the ditch bank to his truck. He turned back toward Adam as he pulled open the driver's side door with a creak of metal on a hinge, in need of oil.

"Adam? You watch yourself now, okay?"

"I shall, Billy, don't worry. Give my best to Janine."

And with that, Adam Donovan began to walk back along the hay field toward his barn. He had a lot more to think about than just irrigation.

Over the next couple of months, Adam Donovan met with every member of the Ditch Association to talk about their needs and how they were all dealing with the now three-year drought. Billy's information and the property owners' input had helped develop a plan for intensified water conservation efforts and some closely choreographed water releases designed to get each user water at the time they most needed it, with more withheld at other times to meet others' needs. It wasn't perfect, and those with more senior water rights were making more sacrifices than they legally had to.

Adam met with the board of directors in October for a final run-through of the agenda and plan, reviewing the budget and fee structure for the coming year. Some of what they had agreed to do included costly expansion of the small reservoir that had been constructed 50 years ago. Fees were going to go up, and the budget they approved reflected that.

Due to Adam's personal meetings, no one was surprised about the budget, and he got the expected vocal objection from the same two members who reliably opposed anything the association did that cost money. Adam was confident they would be outvoted and hadn't lost any sleep over it.

Then Adam asked for an executive session with the board. The tape recorder the secretary used to double-check notes was turned off. He needed to talk with the group about Stuart Chesterton.

While the recorder had still been running, they all agreed to the facts related to the unpaid bills Stu had run up and discussed the policy for non-payment that now had to be invoked. They agreed on the necessary action, which was to put a lien on his property requiring payment of back dues before the place could be sold.

What Adam needed to talk about did not need to be recorded in the minutes.

"Folks," Adam started, "I want to talk with you about how we might get Stu more engaged and less hostile about participation in the association. We all know it's in his best interests, but he doesn't see that yet. And he's about to be hit with a lien on his property that's going to upset him even more." Adam paused to ensure the group of directors were with him.

"We've all known fellows like Stu before. They get in over their heads, they're embarrassed, and so they don't ask for advice. Then they make more mistakes and things just spiral until they're down at the bank begging for mercy while their families suffer. They do not always emerge chastened and ready to learn. The more stubborn and angry they get, the more respect they lose in the community, and the more they tend to blame everyone but themselves. Stu Chesterton is heading down that road," Adam said quietly.

"Adam, Stu Chesterton's got himself locked in a spin down where that road ends already, from what I hear. And I'm afraid Annie is suffering the consequences. Plus, he's started drinking too much," said Jason Toffer. Besides being deeply familiar with Stu's unpaid bills for equipment repairs, Jason's uncle owned the Old Goat.

"And Pete's not doing so well in school. He just seems exhausted and out of it, and he misses a lot of days with his excuses just saying his dad needed him to work. At least that's what I've heard from one of his teachers." That tidbit came from Joan Weller, whose next-door neighbor was a teacher at the high school.

"Okay, okay." Adam put his palms out in front of him, gesturing for restraint. "We're not here to gossip, and it seems we're all aware of the family's challenges. I want to suggest something, and I'm going to need your help."

Adam spent the next 40 minutes talking about the psychology of providing help to a man like Stu who is fearful and feels like a failure, and is even more fearful of being humiliated by others who find out what he thinks they don't already know about the mess he's in.

Adam said he was going to do what he could to make sure Stu attended the November annual meeting. He predicted that at some point, Stu would start getting hostile and make demands he had no right to make, given his water rights. Adam predicted he would be a real pain in the ass, might even start yelling at people and throwing things. He had seen it happen before. Adam wanted the board to prepare themselves for this, and to stay calm.

The group had no trouble imagining this scenario, which is why they were all secretly hoping Stu wouldn't show, even though they knew that wasn't constructive in the long run. The association needed his dues to make budget, and they did not wish his family ill.

Adam recited a list of each of the problems the Chesterton family ranching operation had. It included large and small animal care, poor soil and resulting low yield in his pasture, a garden that was planted with vegetables that needed more water than they were getting, buildings with too much maintenance postponed, a house in need of some new siding and a paint job, and fruit trees out back of the house that Adam wasn't sure they even knew were fruit trees—apricot, peach, and apple. He said he was sure Stu needed equipment he didn't have, too, but there was no way he would be able to buy anything more if his ranch wasn't more productive and efficient.

The people gathered looked around at each other, nodding once again. That was a good list, and it reflected things they'd experienced directly with Stu or heard about.

Adam went on and asked for ideas about how the community could help in a way that Stu and Annie experienced not as charity, but as a way they could "give back" or help others. He talked about how to approach this without making Stu feel he was a failure, or ill-informed, and instead to build him up, work on his confidence, point out his successes wherever they could be found.

"I know this sounds like a big effort for a guy who doesn't appreciate the community he's part of and seems to shirk responsibility right and left. But I've wracked my brain and worn out the knees of my jeans praying about this, and I just can't think of anything else to try but bringing him around with kindness," Adam concluded. "Are you all willing to give it a try?"

Everyone agreed, and most even seemed tickled to give it a whirl, just to see if it was possible. They identified individuals in the community who might be best suited to participate, who had the skills or the relationships to engineer part of the community intervention. They divvied up the outreach calls and visits, based on who knew whom. All the contacts were to be made by the end of the week before the annual meeting, the second Saturday morning in November.

Saturday, November 9th arrived. Adam, his wife Mary, Billy and Janine Carnes, Carla Peterson and Jason Toffer arrived early to set up the chairs and tables in the basement meeting room of the First Presbyterian Church. The back door of the room led straight out into the church parking lot, and Pastor Jon Windermere strolled in half an hour before the meeting was to start, in dusty coveralls and boots with a sweatshirt pulled over his head for warmth. He'd been out in his own barn since dawn, moving bales around to make room for another goat pen.

"I see someone came up with a key to the place," Jon said, taking off his hat and scratching his head.

"Pastor Jon, any one of us could stand in the middle of City Market's parking lot and yell, 'Anyone got a key to First Presby?' and you know 10 people would pull one out of their pocket," Mary said, amused.

Jon grinned and shook his head in feigned displeasure. "Guess we ought to budget to have those locks replaced every hundred years or so, eh?" Everyone in the room laughed good-naturedly.

Janine emerged from the church kitchen with a huge urn of coffee and set it on a table, crawling underneath to plug it in so it would stay warm. Mary started bringing out plates of cookies and a big bowl of fresh fruit. Plates and bowls, cups and napkins and plastic forks appeared next, and Janine came around the corner again with a large jug of lemonade.

Billy came in from the parking lot with copies of the agenda, handouts, the sign-in sheet, and the tape recorder he had stashed in the back of his truck, and Janine got all that set up at the front table.

They were all ready, and members began to trickle in around ten. By ten thirty, most everyone was there, and Adam opened the meeting. Stu had not yet showed up.

They were about halfway through the agenda, and things were going smoothly, with only the usual squabbles and commentary. That's when the back door swung open, slamming against the inside wall, and everyone turned in their seats to see Stu standing there, fuming.

Adam spoke up quickly. "Well, good morning, Stu, glad you could make it! Come on in and have a seat. We'll get you caught up," he said, full of warmth and welcome.

"I will *not* sit down. This here meeting was scheduled without my knowledge, and you have no right to be making decisions without me!" Stu's words were a bit slurred, and he was clinging to the door frame, wobbling halfway over the threshold.

"Now, Stu, you got the same invitation we all did," said Jason, from the front table. He was vice president of the board and felt obligated to defend Adam.

"The HELL I did!" Stu shouted the words as he reached back behind him and grabbed something, then whirled back around, taking a step into the room. He was holding his shotgun.

Pastor Jon was seated in the back row, nearest the door, and stood up quickly, knocking over his own chair. He took two steps toward Stu and held his hands up in front of his chest, palms out.

"Stu, calm down, please," Jon said, his voice low and soothing.

"This association is an EMBARRASSMENT," Stu pronounced, at the top of his lungs, his hat shifting sideways on his head. He grabbed it and shook it for emphasis. "NOBODY can farm if they don't get water and YOU people are hoarding all the water!! I GOT RIGHTS! You all got NO RESPECT for an individual's RIGHTS!"

Stu had shoved Jon out of the way and was stalking unsteadily forward. Jon regained his balance and stepped alongside Stu. "Stu, we want to make sure you get your concerns heard, okay? Come have a seat with me right up front and we'll get your worries discussed right away, okay? I can see you're mad as hell, and that means we need to listen to what you have to say." Jon tried to keep from sounding as scared as he was.

Adam had come around the front of the head table to greet Stu, his hand over his heart, ignoring the shotgun. "Pastor Jon is right, Stu, we want to hear what's on your mind. Especially since it's the first time you've been able to make a meeting. I know how tough it is to make time when you've got a ranch to run," Adam said, respectfully.

Stu looked up, glaring at Adam.

"YOU. You're Donovan, aren't you! YOU'RE the one who makes the rules that are putting my ranch out of business!" Stu had switched his shotgun over into his left hand, his right moving toward the business end of the stock.

"First thing, Stu, is that I'm the pastor of this church, and we have a rule that we've all got to leave our guns out in our trucks." Jon stepped forward again, slipping around in front of Stu as two other men stood and began to move toward where Stu was standing in the middle of the aisle between the seats. "Let me just set it back by the door for you."

Jon leaned in and put out his hands, asking Stu to give him his shotgun. Mary Donovan appeared at his side, a plate of cookies and a cup of coffee in hand.

"Here, Stu, I made these myself. And the coffee's fresh. Come on and sit down up front with me. Pastor Jon will take care of your gun."

Mary's voice was so sweet and maternal, Stu looked at her with complete confusion on his face. He handed Jon the shotgun so he could take the plate of cookies.

"C'mon, Stu, I'll bring your coffee up front with me. There's plenty of room." Mary just started marching in front of Stu, waving him forward like she fully expected him to follow. Her gesture was the same one she used with the gaggle of children she led to Sunday school each week from where they'd gather in front of the altar for the children's sermon Pastor Jon offered.

Unbelievably, Stu followed. He sat down awkwardly beside Mary on a folding chair and ate one of her cookies. He looked like he was trying to remember what he had been saying.

Jon came up front and sat on his other side, after setting Stu's shotgun by the back door, guarded by another member of the church who had recently returned from a tour of duty in Afghanistan. In his inebriated state, Stu would not be retrieving that shotgun anytime soon.

Everyone settled back in their seats, looking wary, but relieved. Adam returned to the podium and picked up the agenda. He looked around the room, making eye contact with each of the people he and the other board members had met with over the preceding couple of weeks, planning their intervention.

"I think we're ready to jump ahead to member discussion. The reports from the working committees are in your folders and we've sent them by email as well. I think we have at least a couple of you who have some real concerns, and we all need to hear those and figure out how to address them.

Stu, I'd like to start with what's on your mind," Adam said, with his most earnest and respectful tone.

With the diplomacy skills of a United Nations Ambassador, Adam Donovan got Stu to say what he was upset about. It was a litany of challenges related to junior water rights; and the fact that he didn't know when he bought the ranch that those rights were a set of cards comprising a permanently challenging deal.

With a nod from Adam, two of the other owners with junior rights offered their sympathy and understanding, avoiding adding fuel to Stu's sense of unfairness.

Adam then probed until Stu was able to list, one by one, the problems he was facing without the water he needed, and how those problems layered one on top of the other. Adam held back discussion until Stu had talked himself out. Then he glanced over to Jason Toffer with a tiny nod.

"Hey, Stu, glad you came today," Jason said. "You know, I've been thinking. Ever since you had that bad luck with the rock your bailer hit, and I saw just how old your tractor is, I've been worried that the engine in that thing might not last much longer."

"It's a piece of crap, and it's all I got," Stu said, defensively.

"I know, Stu, and that's where I was wondering if you might be willing to help me out. I teach equipment mechanics down at the high school and I've got a couple of young guys who have completely rebuilt a John Deere tractor engine. That engine runs so sweet I've thought about taking it home myself. But what they really need is the chance to learn how to install one. With supervision, of course. I was wondering if you might let us come and take out that 100-year-old engine on your tractor and put in the rebuilt one. We wouldn't charge you anything because the kids need the practice. But I can guarantee that engine they've built is as good as any you'd buy down at the dealer. Would you think about it? No pressure, of course."

Jason stopped and watched Stu's face. He was thinking it over. Trying to decide if this was charity in disguise. He couldn't sense it in the way Jason had talked about it.

"Well, yeah, I guess I could do that," Stu finally said.

"Great, Stu, that's really generous of you! I'll give you a call next week and find a time to come out that won't be too inconvenient." Jason nodded and looked back to Adam.

It was just the example that Adam wanted, and exactly the response he'd prayed for from Stu.

"Hey, Stu, now that I've heard some of what you're dealing with out there on your place, I've got an idea, too," This came from Doc Nurmeier, who was sitting in the back of the room. Stu twisted around in his seat to see who was talking.

"Remember me, Stu? I'm a vet here in town. Do you still have goats and chickens as well as those cattle you bought last year?" Doc waited.

"Well, yeah. Chickens are doing good now. Pete's taken to 'em. Got two horses, too. And the goats. Annie keeps thinking they'll produce milk if we breed them, and she can make something of it. Why?" Stu asked cautiously.

"Here's the thing. I've got a new intern coming on board soon. She's smart as a whip, but green, straight out of vet school up at CSU. And she's hoping to work in a mixed practice, some large animal work, some dogs and cats. I need to give her some experience, have her go on some runs with me. Would you be willing to have us come out and give your animals a once-over, just so I can orient her to the prevention side of things? The mix of animals you have would be a perfect learning opportunity. We'd bring the meds and vitamins and such, to repay you for your time and trouble. You don't have to answer right away but give it some thought. She's starting next week."

Doc stood up and walked over to Stu, handing him a card with his number on it, then nodded to him and whispered, "We'd sure be grateful," and returned to his seat.

That was enough. Adam didn't want to overwhelm Stu or offer so much that he got suspicious. But he knew he could count on Jason and Doc Nurmeier to role model the approach for the others who were lined up to reach out to Stu, one a week, with similar ideas for how Stu could help them out in one way or another.

Doug Pearson had just taken down an old barn and hadn't decided what he was going to do to get rid of the wood, which was still in fine shape. He was wondering if Stu could use it to make repairs to their barn.

Jenna Wilson and her oldest boy were starting up a residential and commercial painting business and needed to get a couple of jobs done with photographs to put on their website, to start building a reputation. She called Stu and wondered if they could do his farmhouse before winter and told him the hardware store was having a big sale on paint.

One by one, smooth as could be, Stu and Annie finally got more deeply acquainted with other members of the community. As they worked, and talked, each neighbor shared their own stories of struggle, and how they got along. Those who also had the burden of junior water rights told him what they'd done to maximize conservation and choose things to plant that could do well in the arid soil.

Best of all, Carla and Kevin Peterson, the local organic farmers with a big set of greenhouses as well as outdoor production fields, gave Pete Chesterton a part-time job. They needed help with the greenhouse work over the winter, making repairs to the buildings and doing maintenance on the equipment and tools. Then they would need help with late-winter indoor planting, getting seed-starts going.

Pete seemed to thrive, and learned a lot that he then took home, talking to his mother about how to put their garden plots to bed over the winter with fall fertilizers applied to soak in with the snow. He told her how they needed to care for their perennials and make sure they got enough water by shoveling extra snow on them. He and Annie put together a new plan for spring planting based on what he was learning.

The Chesterton ranch was looking much, much better by the time the following spring rolled around. Stu was beginning to recognize how much better off they were now that they were more a part of the community. He had finally learned enough about Colorado water law and how the association worked to meet the needs of members that he no longer carried his most cherished hostilities wherever he went. He even stopped meeting up with Steve Carter and his cronies down at the Old Goat Tavern every week. But the family's finances were still not even close to healthy. Stu and Annie had to have some serious discussions.

***

The house phone rang as Carla Peterson was clearing dishes from the family dinner table. Kevin was filling the sink. They had a deal. Whoever cooked didn't have to clean up. It was Kevin's turn to wash dishes.

"I got this, Carla, why don't you grab the phone." Kevin nodded toward the old landline, attached to an even more ancient answering machine. It was dependable. Cell service out on their place was sketchy. Carla set down the dishes she was stacking and stepped over to pick up the phone.

"This is Carla," she said cheerfully, then waited. She heard a man clearing his throat on the other end, followed by a slight pause.

"Oh, um, hey there, Carla. Stu Chesterton here." Carla's eyebrow went up and she looked over her shoulder at Kevin, mouthing "Stu?!"

Kevin turned off the running water to listen in. Stu had become more civil of late, since Pete had started working for them. Annie and Carla had become good friends.

"Well, hey there, Stu! How are you doing? Good to hear from you!" Carla gushed, over-compensating for her surprise.

"Oh, I'm doing fine. Hope I'm not interrupting your supper. Didn't want to call too late." Stu sounded oddly self-conscious for a man whose normal interactions were bluster first, listen later. Usually much later.

"Good to hear that, Stu. And no, you aren't interrupting anything. We were just clearing the table. What can we do for you? Is anything wrong with Pete?"

"Oh, no, Pete is fine, Annie is fine. We're just making some family decisions and I was hoping to talk to Kevin for a few minutes about something. If he has time. It's about his organic farming operation."

In truth, Carla owned the farm, and she and Kevin managed every aspect of it together. But she knew it wasn't the time to discuss misogyny with Stu.

"Sure, Stu, let me get him. He's right here. I'm sure he'd be more than happy to chat." Carla covered the receiver with her palm and whispered to Kevin. "Says he's making some family decisions and wants to talk with you about our farm." Carla shrugged, handing the phone over to Kevin while he dried his hands.

Kevin took the phone from her and walked around the table to lean against the doorframe between their tiny kitchen and the front hallway.

"Hi, Stu, what's up?"

"Kevin, thanks for taking my call." Stu cleared his throat again and took a deep breath before continuing.

"Kevin, I want to tell you how grateful we are, me and Annie, for taking Pete on and giving him a job. It seems to have done wonders for his attitude. At school and at home." Stu still sounded uneasy. Kevin could tell that he was working up to talking about something else.

"Stu, I am happy to hear that. Pete has been a terrific employee for us. He works hard, doesn't complain about the work or the heat, and he's always personable with our customers. We couldn't be happier with him." Kevin wanted to lay it on a little thicker than necessary. Pete had indeed flourished since he started spending 20 hours a week on the farm, but he also knew that Stu had given him a tough time for breathing air, for years, at least according to Pete. Kevin wanted Stu to hear another perspective on Pete's character.

Kevin continued. "Is there a problem, Stu? Is Pete having trouble keeping up with his schoolwork with the extra hours he's taken on over here?"

"No, no, nothing like that. He's doing all right." Stu hesitated, and his voice dropped like he was looking out a window, collecting his thoughts.

"I'm glad, Stu. We wouldn't want to be a distraction for Pete. Is there something else on your mind?"

"Well, actually, yes, there is, Kevin. I've been thinking about this a lot, ever since you and Jason Toffer gave me so much help over here, getting my machinery and animals and buildings back in decent shape. The others, too, but you two are real stand-up guys and taught me a lot. I know I wasn't always as open-minded as I should have been, and Annie says I'm more stubborn than two mules set to walk in opposite directions. But I mean…"

Stu was rambling, but Kevin could tell he was getting closer to saying what was on his mind.

"Stu, it's okay. We all know how rough it can be when you're trying to expand your business and you find out you've been handed a set of bad cards. You've done well for yourself down there. We're all happy to lend a hand on occasion. You really didn't need all that much, you had things heading in the right direction from the start."

Kevin cringed a little internally as he spoke. That last part was solidly in the category of fibbing. He and everyone else in Springdale knew Stu's ranch and farming efforts were a complete disaster before they'd figured out how to help him. Truth was, Stu had been so difficult, some of them had done it more to keep Annie and Pete from starving than to help Stu. But they had also learned that Stu's blustering was a big, boisterous cover for his lack of confidence. The man hated to be wrong and hated even more to feel others thought him a fool. They had all found a way to help him fix up his mess of a business while providing the kind of encouragement they would give a boy learning to ride a bike who was self-conscious about being a novice.

"Well, you're being kind. I appreciate it. More than you know, Kevin."

Stu's tone was uncharacteristically genuine, even humble. Kevin started to wonder if Stu was about to tell him he had inoperable cancer. He waited for Stu to continue.

"Here's the thing, Kevin. Annie and me, we've been taking stock of our situation over here. We're sure better off than when we got here, and the place is looking sharp overall. But the land, what with the water rights as they are, it really can't support a cattle operation. Even if we were the best darn ranchers on the planet, with all the capital we ever needed, it would still be an uphill battle."

Stu stopped again. Kevin heard him take another deep breath on the other end of the phone.

"Annie and me, we've decided to sell the place and head back to St. Louis. Annie misses her family back in Missouri something fierce, and I know I can get work back there with the trucking company, no problem. They're still hiring long-haulers."

"Wow, Stu, I'm sorry to hear that. Are you sure about this? You've put so much into that place. That's a tough decision." Kevin's concern was genuine. He couldn't imagine how painful it must be to have to wrestle with those realities. But he thought Stu was right. Cattle take a lot of money and a lot of resource out of the land to make a profit. Stu's property wasn't big enough, and he'd need even more equipment to run a larger operation.

"Here's the thing, Kevin. Annie—well, me, too…we want to do something to pay you and this community back for being so good to us. I know I didn't exactly come in here making friends. I'm sorry about some of what I said to the sheriff and some of the rest of you to this day. I was an idiot." There was real pain and regret in Stu's voice. Kevin was almost stunned.

"Don't worry about all that now, Stu, it was just words," Kevin reassured him.

"Kevin, you and Carla have a great operation. Pete says that you could really use more land to expand production. You don't have a retail presence in the area, and that could help you expand your markets. I should have talked to you first, but I wanted to see if what I was thinking could even be a possibility before I raised it with you. I talked to the bank, our loan officer. I asked him if he thought the bank would support you if you wanted to buy our farm and add it to yours. Annie and me, we're willing to put the money we make from the stock sale and the equipment sales into converting the house into whatever you'd need it to be. Pete has all kinds of ideas, but we'd leave it up to you to say what you might want. We need to sell the place for enough to get started again back in Missouri, but we don't need to make a killing on it. So. That's what we want you to think about."

Stu had managed to get it out. He had nothing more to say.

Kevin could barely find words. "Stu. That's…that's an incredible offer. And you're right, Carla and I have been talking all year about being in the margin where we need more production acreage to support the growth in demand we're enjoying. And to have a local farm store in addition to shipping out to the groceries and restaurants could help us go in a completely new direction."

Kevin stopped speaking and was staring off into middle distance, somewhere in the air three feet above the kitchen table. Carla had been watching. She stepped into his field of vision and waved her hand in front of his face, as though she was checking for consciousness. Kevin snapped back to the present. He mouthed, "This is *incredible*," to Carla, and watched as her eyes opened wide with question.

"It's okay if you and Carla aren't interested. I just needed to put it out there for you to consider," Stu said, reading negativity from the shocked silence on the other end of the phone.

"No, *no*! Stu, believe me, this is an interesting and generous offer. I just need some time to talk with Carla about it. How long—I mean, when do you need an answer from us?"

"Oh, okay, I'm real glad you'll think about it, at least. We'd feel good if we could make this work for you. And there's one more thing, Kevin. You'll be wanting to talk to Carla about this, too, I'm sure." Stu's tone was vaguely amused and a little apologetic.

"Yes, what else?" Kevin asked.

"Well, the boy—Pete, that is—he made me promise to ask you one more thing." Stu paused. "We have no right to even ask you to think about this, and I can't believe I'm even flapping my jaw…"

"It's okay, Stu, just put it out there, what are you thinking?" Kevin urged him on.

"He wants to finish his senior year here in Springdale, and he's already applied to the college over in Durango. He wants to get a degree in agriculture, in horticulture. He wants to go into organic farming. And he wants to know if he can stay in the house here and keep working with you instead of coming back with us to Missouri. He'll be 18 in a month, so legally, I suppose he can do what he wants, but me and Annie, we don't want to put you out."

Kevin grinned. "Stu, I can answer that now. I know how Carla and I both feel about Pete. If you and Annie are comfortable with him being on his own, we'd be happy to be his backup parents here in Colorado. And we'd absolutely love for him to keep working for us. If his interest in farming lasts the way you're saying it might, I can see us hiring him full-time when we expand. For real. But yes, let me talk to Carla about that, too." He reached out to pull Carla over toward him, his arm around her shoulder.

"Alright, then. You two talk. I'll want to put the place on the market next month, but if you decide you want to buy it, we can talk through the details, and I won't even approach Ranch Realty. We'll just get the deal done right with a lawyer and call it good." Stu sounded happy. "You just give me a call when you're ready to make a decision, one way or another. And no hard feelings at all if you decide the time's not right. Have a good evening."

Kevin hung up the phone and wrapped his arms around Carla. After kissing the top of her head, he pulled back to look her in the eyes, smiling like someone just told him Santa is real.

"Honey, we've got some things to talk about." Kevin pulled her over to the table and shoved the dirty dishes out of the way so they both could sit down next to each other. The kitchen table was where they had all important conversations about home, family, or business.

"Let me have it," Carla told him, her own face softening with the look she always gave him when he had another big idea. It was part skepticism, part curiosity. His ideas were often just outside of her comfort zone, but spot on. And Stu's call obviously had gone in an unusual direction. "I can tell this is gonna be good."

***

Once their decision was made, Stu and Annie agreed that everything seemed to fall in place as smooth as the frozen custard down at Nicky's Diner. With a little help, that is, like everything else that went well in Springdale.

Kevin, Stu, and Marnie Carroll—who owned the hardware store in town with her partner, Beth—all teamed up to renovate the old farmhouse. The first floor was now a market with two big display rooms, a corner with refrigerated goods, a back area for storing inventory and prepping deliveries, and a smaller kitchen with a half-bath for staff and customers off to one side. The upstairs was Pete's space, with a bedroom, study, den, and bathroom. He used the kitchen downstairs whenever he had the urge to cook.

Pete graduated with a degree in horticulture, including a minor in marketing, and used the opportunity presented by his senior thesis requirement to build a business plan for the Peterson's retail operation. He had so many ideas that Kevin and Carla let him take over the role of promoting the business, including giving it a bright new logo and name: Western Sun Organics. Pete dove in with so much energy and enthusiasm that the business grew quickly. After he convinced the managers of all 10 City Market locations in Western Colorado and Eastern Utah to carry Western Sun, Kevin and Carla had the revenue to bring Pete on full-time.

Carla and Pete's mom, Annie, made a pact before the move that they would speak at least once a week to make sure the arrangement with Pete was working and to problem-solve as needed. So, every Sunday afternoon at four, they were on the phone. They'd chat for an hour, just catching up, and then Annie and Pete would talk. As expected, Stu started driving trucks again for a living, and any time he could get a run that would take him through Southwestern Colorado, he'd plan to visit.

Pete never left Springdale. The disaster that was his parent's attempt at a small farm and ranch was the miracle that shaped his life. He loved living there. He met a young woman and married, they had two daughters, and as they grew up, he became increasingly entwined in the community. When Kevin and Carla were ready to retire, well into their 70s, Pete bought the entire farm and business.

When he passed away, 70 years after arriving, Pete had become one of the most beloved members of the Springdale community and had more than once been asked to run for office as the region's state representative. He had declined, mainly because he didn't want to have to be in Denver that much. First Presbyterian Church hosted his funeral, even though Pete attended his wife's church, Springdale United Methodist. First Presby had the larger sanctuary, and they knew everyone in town would want to come.

Two weeks later, the town council passed a resolution. Maple Street would become Chesterton Street, one block east of Donovan, which crossed Main in the center of town.

NATHAN'S DILEMMA

Nathan Riley had a new problem, and it was a real puzzler. There was this girl. Woman, really. She was his age, 25 or 26, and her name was Shannon O'Dell. She was a post-doc in biology in the lab down the hall from where he was working.

Yesterday, Shannon O'Dell had done a guest lecture for the class Nathan was teaching on sustainable agricultural practices. It was about her research on pollinator recovery in the Netherlands. There, the government required growers to plant mixed native wildflowers in wide strips along farm fields and highways to help restore beneficial insect populations. Shannon's presentation was brilliant. And her passion for the subject matched his. He wanted desperately to tell her all about his work on pheromone-based inter-species communication. He'd already published a series of articles about the relationships that develop across whole communities of living things, all because of the organic chemistry of interacting biological compounds wafting between species. But she had to leave right after she wrapped up the Q&A to get to a department meeting. He was in the botany department, and they didn't go to the same staff meetings.

Nathan couldn't stop thinking about Shannon. This hadn't happened to him in a long time. He still remembered the moment during his first year in high school when Cindy Cho invited him over to her house after school to see the new microscope her dad brought home from work. But he had screwed that up, because he thought she really cared about the microscope and it turned out she just wanted him to pay attention to her, which he had not done as soon as he realized what that microscope could do and got into it with Mr. Cho.

That painful memory made Nathan even more determined to make better decisions. The problem was, most of what he knew about courtship came from the insect world, and his close observations of how the six-legged creatures interacted with plants and each other. It wasn't encouraging. He was staring off into space at his desk, counting the number of insect species he knew in which the females ate the males after copulation. Nathan always thought this behavior would disincentivize the males involved, leading to a serious evolutionary disadvantage for the entire species. But it didn't seem to work that way. He started musing about why.

Then he realized he was getting distracted. He thought of his mother, who was an ardent feminist, and knew what she would say about female insects that put their males on their post-coital menu: that some species are better at fighting patriarchy than others. Thinking of her made Nathan smile, and it helped him switch gears.

It was the end of the day, and already dark outside, and he needed a different kind of inspiration about Shannon. He shoved back from his desk, jammed his laptop into his messenger bag, and headed out of the building across campus. He needed to figure out what might be an attractive proposition to Shannon that would involve a little time spent with him where they could get to know each other. He thought they should both get away from work to make that happen, so he narrowed his options to a place off-campus.

That put him on tenuous ground for generating ideas, since he didn't leave campus much. He knew that was lame and could lead someone to think he was an irretrievable nerd. But he wasn't, not really. His interests were simply different from those of most men. And didn't tend to involve other people.

He was an early morning runner, which was more or less solitary. And he loved to borrow a car and go hiking and exploring in the state parks and forest preserves there in southern Illinois. He loved to read. And he was fascinated with art forms that capitalized on negative space to achieve their impression. Photography and digital art, woodcuts and relief printing, ikebana. All rely on the art of attending to what isn't present, and what absence allows in the observer's mind. It was fascinating to him. But he knew it was an odd set of interests. He had no idea what Shannon O'Dell liked.

He caught the campus line bus and got off a block away from an outdoor marketplace right on the edge of the central city arts and theater district. He couldn't afford to take Shannon to any of those mainstream venues, but he had heard that the marketplace was kind of cool.

First, he had to adjust himself to the environment. It was busy. Noisy. Crowded. Two of the business establishments in front of him had neon signs in the windows in assorted colors, one flashing rapidly. Someone jostled him and he stumbled, catching himself against the rough brick wall behind him. A child shrieked off to his left. He cringed and felt anxiety pulse in his chest. He wanted to run, but he took a deep breath and stood up straight.

For most people, Nathan reflected, this was fun. He had been thinking he needed to invent a fun experience to share with Shannon, and suddenly realized that he was using indices of fun that were relevant to people he didn't really want to spend time with. What was the point of that? Momentary confusion overwhelmed him. What was he doing down here?

He started walking toward the marketplace, because that was what he had told himself he would do before he left campus. He needed to get his mind back on track.

The entrance to the market was a short tunnel formed by an overhead construction of blue-and-white striped canvas stretched over an aluminum frame. The market center was a tall, hexagonal atrium over a circle of food vendors. Off the atrium were six tented hallways labelled "A Lane" through "F Lane." In the ceiling of the atrium were broad chevron-shaped windows of sky blue and pearl white, framed by fluorescent lights that flashed slowly on and off in sequence, pointing down toward each of the hallways.

Nathan hustled through the intense light of the atrium and dove into the first of the hallways where the booths began. There, everything changed. It was quieter. The garish light of the atrium was gone. The ceilings were lower, and all sound was softened by artful textile pieces hung on the walls between each vendor's set-up. Conversation was muted. Each booth had delicate white or pale-blue lights strung along the sides and top of their spaces.

Each display was tasteful and not overcrowded. Most had holiday greenery strung up as well, and the subtle scent of pine found him as he wandered. It was pleasant. The space felt like a comfortable village lane of shops. He could focus again. He slowed down and noticed more.

It was a fascinating place. He looked at the little stacks of business cards that most had in front of their booths, and all were local. He saw African beadwork, bonsai, sculpture entirely created from found materials, a few thrift stores with a peculiar assortment of things like teapots and cowboy boots. And one booth had homemade jam and honey in tiny jars.

He stopped and politely greeted the woman who worked at the honey booth. She smiled at him and told him where her bees were from. The bees were local. She had two kinds of honey, because one of her large hives was in an apple orchard and the honey those bees made tasted different from the honey made by bees who frequented the open fields and gardens in the area. She complemented Nathan on his familiarity with pollinators and their important contributions.

And that's when he knew. This is where he would bring Shannon. It would be right. Exactly right. Especially if all six lanes of vendors were as interesting as this one. They could buy a little something to eat from one of the restaurant vendors in the atrium, or from one of the booths that sold baked goods or cheeses. And then they could find a quiet spot to sit and eat and talk.

He needed to scope out options for that part, too. If it was cold, he would take her out of the marketplace over to the tea shop on Fairmont that was never as crowded and noisy as Starbucks. If it was a nice evening to be outdoors, there was a little pocket park next to a bank across from the entrance to the art museum that had benches beneath the trees and old-style iron streetlamps.

He was excited. He couldn't wait to talk to Shannon now that he had a plan. But first, he needed flowers. At the far end of the lane, beyond the honey booth, he spotted a display of racks of fresh flowers, all arranged like a little French flower shop. Cut flowers were in bunches, in galvanized tin buckets. As he came closer, he saw small potted plants on shelves above the cut flowers. He scanned the plant labels and the prices. Nathan was puzzled and slightly annoyed. The pricing made no sense to him. Heliopsis were showy but easy to grow, so why were they more expensive than, say, lobelia or heuchera, which were delicate and required more care?

He tapped his toe on the floor, concentrating. A living plant, or cut flowers? She wouldn't want him to give her something that had been killed for human pleasure. He focused on the flowering potted plants. Purples and blues? Yellows? Pink and white? Not pink, too girly. Shannon was strong, smart, confident, kind.

He chose a potted calibrachoa, common name million bells, with its beautiful dome of tiny yellow-and-orange blooms that spilled exuberantly down the sides of the pot. It was cheerful. And generous. And easy. If she liked him, the calibrachoa would stay in her office on her desk by the window and bloom for at least another month. That would be good.

Nathan paid for the plant, and the shop keeper nestled it in a box with some paper to keep it stable for the bus ride home. She sensed it was something special to him because his eyes were so bright, and he thanked her at least 12 times.

He ducked out the back of the marketplace, avoiding a return to the flashy atrium, and walked quickly to the bus stop. He was glad the bus wasn't too crowded, and he got a window seat where he could stare out into the darkness and think. He didn't want to lose his nerve.

Nathan stepped off the bus and slung his messenger bag over his shoulder so he could balance the potted plant in his hands as he walked back across campus. As he approached the big front doors to the natural sciences building, he looked up to the third floor, where Shannon's office was, and his heart quickened. The light was on. He took the elevator up to avoid the possibility of tripping on the stairs and dropping Shannon's plant. Walking down the silent hall, he was conscious of the squeak his running shoes made with each step. He stopped just short of the door to Shannon's lab and took a deep breath.

Nathan knocked on the door, even though that suddenly struck him as a weird thing to do, since it wasn't her house, it was a lab, and 20 people worked in there at all hours. He balanced the plant in his left hand and pulled open the door with his right. Shannon was at her desk along the wall, staring at her computer, which had three windows open. One of them was a reference manual he recognized that displayed the most common pollinators associated with flowering native plants of the Midwest. She looked up when she heard the door open. No one else was in the lab.

Nathan strode quickly toward Shannon. "Hi. I brought you something. To say thanks for the great lecture you gave to my class." His foot caught on a table leg, but he caught himself. Don't screw up, he thought, slow down. Be nice. See how she reacts.

Shannon looked up at him, and at the million bells, and back to his face. She smiled. Big time.

"Nathan, they're beautiful! My favorite colors, too. Thank you!" Shannon rose from her chair to greet him.

"Good, I was hoping you would like them. They'll do well in this light," he said.

"Yes, they will," she replied as she accepted the plant and set it on the corner of her desk nearest the window on her side of the lab. She turned back to face him, still smiling, entirely at ease with herself.

"Umm, I was wondering…would you like to go out with me this weekend? There's a marketplace downtown that's fun to poke around in, and it's not too noisy even though downtown is crazy, and not too far is a teashop I like, and there's a park in the other direction if you'd rather?"

"Yes. Yes, Nathan, I would love to go out with you. You're a sweetheart. I was going to ask you, but I hadn't worked up the nerve," Shannon said gently, saving him from his panic, which had obviously been growing with every word that tumbled out of his mouth.

"Good. Oh, *good*," Nathan said, not even trying to hide his relief. "That's *awesome*. I'm so glad! Thank you!"

"For what, Nathan? You just brought *me* flowers! How about Saturday? Maybe late afternoon, so we have some time to wander around before we hunt for dinner?"

"That sounds perfect. Should I meet you here or pick you up—wherever you live?"

Shannon smiled again and turned to her desk. She picked up one of her university business cards and wrote her personal cell and address on the back.

"I live two blocks off campus in the old Green Street apartments. Third floor, entrance at the back of the courtyard. I don't have a car. Meet me there. We can figure out how to get downtown then."

Nathan took Shannon's card, scrutinized it, and looked back up at her as he slipped it into the outer pocket on his messenger bag. He suddenly felt awkward and self-conscious. He hadn't thought ahead about what to do next. He was staring at her, still clutching the canvas bag, the strap dangling off his shoulder.

She laughed, tipping her head back so her long blonde hair cascaded away from her face. Then she leaned forward quickly and kissed him on the cheek and gave his shoulder a light shove.

"Go. I'll see you Saturday. It'll be fun," she said.

Nathan grinned again, turned, and walked out of her lab. As soon as he heard the click of the door shutting behind him, he raised his messenger bag over his head and did a little dance in a circle, silently whooping toward the ceiling. A pen and his chapstick fell out of his bag and skittered in opposite directions. He leaned over to grab them, and his campus ID swung around on its lanyard and looped over one ear. He swatted it back in place, stood up, and took another breath.

Nathan headed home, a happy man.

Saturday turned out to be a glorious autumn day, with clear skies and cool temperatures, the sunshine dappling the ground through bright gold and scarlet maple trees along the streets near campus. Nathan met Shannon at 4:00 and they took the bus downtown, chatting comfortably. The time passed quickly. They were enjoying one another even more than they each had hoped.

Before they left the marketplace, Nathan told Shannon he wanted her to meet one of the vendors, down A Lane, about halfway. He explained about the honey lady he had met when he was scoping out the marketplace. Shannon agreed. She sounded like an interesting person.

Nathan's good luck held. The honey lady was there at her booth, just finishing a conversation with another customer. She remembered Nathan, and their conversation about his research on how creatures communicate within ecosystems. He introduced Shannon, and Shannon took the initiative to ask the honey lady's name, since Nathan had neglected that little bit of social grace. It was Anna. Anna Gandert. Her parents had come to Illinois from Hungary. Now, her whole family ran a small organic farm and Anna was trying to increase their income without major investments in additional equipment or infrastructure. She had built the bee hives herself.

Shannon got a dreamy look in her eyes. "Anna, where exactly is your family's farm located?"

"It's about 15 miles out of town on the divided highway that runs up toward Hudson," Anna replied. "Why?"

"Well, I've been looking for a zone where I could talk either city or county officials into letting me establish some long swaths of perennial plantings that are particularly attractive to pollinators for my research. The median along that highway would be perfect. And there are easements along the frontage roads. I wonder if the property owners would allow you to install more hives. We could plan the location of different plant species so you would end up with distinctive honey products with their own subtle flavors. Wouldn't that be fun? A little science-enabled entrepreneurship."

Anna had been stacking jars of honey as they talked, and was now standing stock still, a jar in each hand, staring at Shannon. "Are you serious? That sounds fabulous!"

Nathan was grinning, looking back and forth from Anna to Shannon. "I just knew you two needed to meet," he said. "And there are some things we could do with the sequencing of the plantings to make it easier for the bees to communicate with each other to find their favorites. I might get a paper out of this, and all the better if you and your family profit from it, Anna!"

Shannon just nodded and started digging around in her handbag. She pulled out a pen and one of her business cards. "Anna, do you have a piece of paper?"

Anna whirled around and reached into a box in the corner of her booth, pulling out a blank invoice form. "Will this work?"

Shannon moved a few things out of the way on the table and started sketching a stretch of the highway, showing the median, the frontage road and several of the small country lanes that intersected with it. She jotted the names of several plant species in sections of the median, and placed asterisks where she thought hives might be optimally placed. When she finished, she spun it around for Nathan and Anna to see.

"There. See? I really think this could work, Anna. Nathan, would you sequence these any differently?"

"Just a little," Nathan said quietly, tapping an index finger against his lower lip and reaching out for Shannon's pen. "Switch these… and put this one at the end. It would put a bit more distance between the species with the most distinctive scent traits and make it more likely the bees would choose hives nearby and make honey that customers could really tell had unique flavors."

Anna looked at the paper, absently running her fingers along her long blonde braid, which she had pulled forward over her shoulder. "I would love to do this. Absolutely love to. What would we need to do to get the money for the work?"

A wicked grin crossed Shannon's face. "Anna, I have contacts through the ag school with seed and fertilizer and pesticide companies that desperately need better public relations. Let me see what I can do. Give me a couple weeks. Meanwhile, work up a budget for, oh, I dunno, quadrupling your honey operation. Don't forget to include bottling, labeling and distribution costs."

Anna's jaw went slack. "How would you use that information? Your research funders wouldn't care about the end product, would they?"

"Yes, they will. Maybe not the labelling and retail aspect, but the bottling could be part of measuring production volume. Tracking that variable would let us estimate the profitability of the practice. Which I expect will far outpace the cost of inputs, just like in the Netherlands." Shannon reached out toward Anna, inviting her to shake hands on the deal.

Nathan agreed with Shannon. The concept had scientific merit and measuring the profitability of the attendant honey operation could make the case to local governments to invest in expanding the practice. Shannon let go of Anna's hand and reached over to wrap her arm around Nathan's shoulder, pulling him into a hug.

"How are your design skills, Nathan? Your lecture slides are gorgeous, so I'm guessing you have more hidden talents. Want to design a fundraising campaign for corporate sponsorships? Maybe a new line of Anna's honeys? A website? Opportunities for volunteers to get involved tending plantings and picking up roadside litter?"

Nathan nodded shyly. His artistic talents did indeed extend to the digital realm, he just hadn't had reason to play with it. And what made him even happier was that he now knew there were going to be lots of opportunities for him and Shannon to spend more time together, working on a project they were both excited about. He had hope. This was going so much better than it had with Cindy Cho.

"Hey, guys, what do you think of the name of our new honey line?" Anna had written something on the back of the sheet of paper Shannon had used to sketch the plot plan. She turned it to face Shannon and Nathan.

"Cool! Sha-Na-Anna-Gans Bees! I love it!" Nathan said. "It's our names, and shenanigans!

HENRY'S FRONT PORCH

Fran Solcati stood in the shower with her eyes closed and her head leaning against the wall for a full 20 minutes, letting the jet pummel first one shoulder, then the other. Her right shoulder had been good until a rugby injury led to surgery, from which recovery had been slow and never complete. Her left shoulder was permanently damaged by absorbing a bullet discharged from a gun held by a 19-year-old seaman who intended to end his life.

The young man chose to take that action when he was in port in Norfolk, but had not planned on an encounter with the indomitable force of a newly retired female commander leaving a restaurant after a couple of beers down on the fishing pier. It would be many years before Fran's sense of responsibility for everything within eyesight and earshot faded even slightly. Fran made sure the young man lost possession of his firearm in that moment of distress over a two-timing girlfriend and got help, but she had ended up going with him to the emergency department for treatment that night. He got an on-call clinical social worker. She got a surgeon.

She had learned that gratitude was a survival skill as important as any other. She had left the Navy at the end of a particularly trying tour that had nothing to do with the messy maritime security mission she had completed flawlessly. It had everything to do with vicious misogyny. She had plenty of experience handling the latter without losing perspective and focus on the job at hand, but she finally recognized that she was tired of it. It doubled the trouble presented by the actual enemy; and that was annoying. Even so, she missed military leadership tremendously. In retirement, she had done every-thing she had told her crew to do when they left the service. Find something to believe in, do work you can be proud of, find some other people to love, monitor your vices, and don't dwell on the bullshit.

She was back in North Carolina, close to the coastal community where she grew up. Fran had bought a small two-bedroom house with a big yard near the river which flooded every so often, bringing in the herons and an occasional cormorant to roost on the rocks over her koi pond. The koi pond had become a never-ending project. The most recent addition was an elaborate raised netting over the water that defended the fish from both birds and raccoons. Indoors, she had a dog and three cats who had wandered into her yard and never left, her partner, Caroline; and often one of several young veterans she had taken under her wing during her years in the Navy. Periodically, one of them came looking for her after they'd gotten out of the service and found themselves lost without even the stars for navigation.

For the boys, as she called them, she had only a few rules. Clean up after yourself, no noise after ten o'clock, find something you can get paid to do at least 10 hours a week, and if you go out and party on Saturday night, you still get your ass out of bed Sunday morning and come with us to church.

Fran had built up a small engraving business out of her workshop, which was formerly a three-car garage. She also worked part time for fun as the property manager of a retirement community nearby that comprised three aging buildings and the landscaping around each. There wasn't much she couldn't repair or rebuild, including anything with an engine. She wasn't crazy about gardening, but since several of the older folks were, she organized them into teams for weeding or pruning, depending on their ability to bend down or kneel to reach the weeds.

Fran and Caroline went to the church around the corner, which turned out to be a little Presbyterian establishment with a female pastor named Sue, who had a good sense of humor and low tolerance for anyone discouraging new members of any persuasion. Fran and Caroline had been welcomed to St. Mark's with a couple of sharp pastoral glares promptly taking care of anticipated prejudices. Caroline came from a devoutly religious family and had studied her theology with the same seriousness she had applied to becoming a mathematician and professor at the university in nearby Greenville. Fran had grown up poor in a family with too many kids to feed and an absence of sobriety among the adults involved. As a result of being the oldest sibling, she had a more practical approach to practicing her faith. You fed the hungry, then fixed the toilet, pronto.

The first Sunday Fran had joined Caroline for the Sunday service, she'd headed for the ladies' room downstairs immediately after the final chord faded in the recessional hymn. On the way, Fran automatically started making a mental list of needed repairs. The next Saturday, Pastor Sue handed over a key to the church and Fran proceeded to repair the dripping faucet in the bathroom sink and patch a leak in the roof, along with the related water damage on the ceiling in the entry vestibule that everyone had been looking at for 20 years. Because it was bugging her, she made an extra trip to the hardware store late in the afternoon and replaced and glazed a cracked ground-level windowpane downstairs in Fellowship Hall.

It was while she was schlepping tools and supplies back and forth from her truck into the church basement that Saturday that Fran had met Mr. Henry Wright. Henry lived across from the church in what had gradually become a fixer-upper. The house had an overgrown backyard and a front porch that looked like it might fall right away from the front door if too many trick-or-treaters stood on it at the same time.

In contrast to his abode, Henry was an African American gentleman of 85 years, and always appeared wearing a slate-gray cardigan over a neat white button-down shirt, slacks with a crease and cuffs, and polished loafers over clean white socks. He loved to chat, and Fran loved to listen to his stories. Fact was, she was full of her own, and was uniquely able to make Mr. Henry laugh until he had to sit down and catch his breath. They became good friends on that rickety front porch.

Fran learned that he'd lost his wife of 54 years two years ago. Her name was Helena. The yard and garden areas behind the house were Helena's love in life, and he hadn't had the heart to tackle its upkeep. The ramshackle condition of Henry's front porch bothered Fran. A lot. As did the mess of a garden and backyard.

Three weeks later, Fran dragged Caroline and Joe (the 25-year-old former Lieutenant Junior Grade Navy Officer currently sleeping on their sofa), a couple of friends from the Norfolk women's rugby club who pulled an all-night drive to get there by eight in the morning, and Pastor Sue and her husband Bob over for a workday at Mr. Henry's place. By the time they were done, the brush along the back fence was gone, the fence repaired and repainted, the garden beds were weeded and planted with perennials that wouldn't take much maintenance, the stone walkways were reset, the lawn mowed and edged, the grass clipped close around the trees, and the screen door that led from the back of the house into the garden repaired. Mr. Henry stood on the back stoop leaning on his cane and looking down at Fran and her sweat-stained buddies grinning up at him and had to swipe tears from behind his glasses. The backyard looked beautiful.

Fran was just getting started. She and Caroline, Joe, Bob, and a carpenter from the retirement village named Harold fixed Henry's front porch the very next weekend. Fran finished the job by replacing the folding chair Henry had been using out on his porch with a cute little wrought-iron table and two matching chairs with sunny yellow padded cushions. Then she went back to her list of projects at St. Mark's, checking in on Mr. Henry across the street every day or two. She would bring her own coffee and call to him through the front door until he came out with his own and they'd sit for a spell at the table on his porch. Sometimes Caroline would send fresh flowers in a little vase to put on the table for an extra bit of cheer.

Fran learned that Henry still drove his berry-red Ford LTD down to the Village Inn every Tuesday morning at seven to sit and chew the fat with his old friends from Grady-White. Grady was the Greenville boat building company they'd all retired from after decades of service. More than half of them were veterans, as the company made hiring veterans and their spouses a high priority. Henry was not a veteran himself, but he had been proud to work for Grady-White for 42 years as a production supervisor. He knew boats. Which gave him even more to talk about with Fran. And he had good friends, still, from those years building boats. He talked about them often with Fran during their visits, and she felt like she had already met several of them, just from Henry's stories.

One fine Friday morning in September, Fran was over at the church for an on-site visit from Mr. Jim Lucas of the Coastal Plains Historical Society. She was trying to convince the man that the church building itself, built in the late 1800s, deserved some loving portion of the Society's new grant funding for architectural restoration. Fran had quickly assessed the church membership's capacity for tithing and figured out why the roof had been left to leak for so many years. She had subsequently determined that part of the foundation needed to be repaired because of a flood 40 years ago, and the brick in the bell tower needed to be rebuilt. All three projects were going to take some external funding. She was persuasive. And persistent.

This Friday morning visit was the third time she had met with Mr. Lucas, and this time Fran had Anna McAlister with her, Jim's mother's cousin, who just happened to be married to the president of the historical society board. The conversation seemed to be going more smoothly.

Henry Wright was watching the whole transaction with amusement from his new front porch chair, catching snatches of conversation that included some colorful and compelling arguments emanating from Fran's quick mind and mouth. That's when Henry decided to try to get Fran's attention after the man named Jim left. He had something he wanted to ask her on behalf of his best friend from the coffee club.

When Jim Lucas drove off, Fran walked Ms. McAlister to her car, thanking her for her time and influence. Fran spotted Henry waving to get her attention and waved back to let him know she had seen him. Fran had intended to visit with Henry, anyway, since Caroline had baked some apple tarts that Fran had promised to deliver before noon so he could enjoy them with his lunch. She pulled the plate of goodies off the passenger seat and grabbed a box of drill bits and a stud-finder from where she had left them on the hood. She headed across the street to visit with Henry before she started her next project, down in the church nursery. She had pitched a fit to Caroline when she discovered a bookcase that wasn't attached to the wall.

Henry invited Fran inside, which was different from their usual practice, and led her down the hall to the kitchen. It was a chilly morning, and he had a pot of coffee freshly brewed. Fran could smell dark roast heaven coming from Henry's old percolator before she even got to the door. Henry pulled out a chair for Fran at the little, white-painted pine table and fussed at the placemat on her side, straightening it before he walked to the cabinet and pulled out two mugs. Fran took those from him and set them down along with the tarts before she sat. Henry came back to the table with a glass bottle of milk and two spoons. He looked distracted and nervous, and Fran felt a bit of alarm. It wasn't like Henry.

Fran waited for Henry to settle, then pulled the wrap off the plate of apple tarts and told him that Caroline was worried he was getting too thin. She pushed the plate over toward him and nodded, waiting for him to take one. She watched his face and noted that he was avoiding eye contact, even as he selected one of the tarts and poured a little milk in his coffee.

Fran sat back in her chair, cradling her mug in her hands, and waited. When Henry still didn't say anything, she decided it was time to pull whatever was bothering him out onto the table.

"Henry. Spill it," she said, in a very firm but gentler version of her commander voice.

Henry looked up a bit startled. He rarely heard her use that tone of voice around him. His eyes met hers, which were steady as a rock and penetrating the space between them.

"Well, there is something," Henry said.

"Are you sick? Do you need money for a doctor?" Fran blasted past any semblance of Southern conversational delicacy, though she was familiar with it in all its forms.

"No, no! I'm fine. I'm well and truly fine," Henry replied. "It's just that, well, I have a friend and he needs some help."

Fran relaxed and took a breath. "Okay, what kind of help?"

"Well, I hate to ask, but I know it would mean the world to him…"

"Henry Wright, it is not like you to beat around the bush. You have a friend, he needs help, you think I might be able to provide that help, and any friend of yours is a friend of mine. So, what is it?"

"The thing is, he's Jewish," Henry replied.

Fran looked at him, confused, and could tell he was worried that it might matter to her. She just shook her head and smiled.

"I'm gay and a closet druid in Presbyterian clothes. Why does it matter? You still haven't told me what he needs," she replied, taking a sip of her coffee. "Damn, this is good coffee, Henry."

Henry finally smiled at her and took a big bite of the apple tart, sighing with satisfaction as he swallowed. "You tell your Caroline that she bakes an apple tart just as sweet and fine as my Helena's."

"I will do that," Fran replied, and waited.

"So, my friend, his name is Warner Jacobs. I know I've told you about him before. When his wife was failing from cancer, she told him to talk to their rabbi and find out what he most wanted done in the synagogue. It's old, and getting worn down, and she wanted to be remembered for something beautiful in their community. She told Warner it had bothered her for years that something behind the altar that holds their holy scroll, like a little cabinet, used to have doors that opened on the front, but one of the hinges broke. They'd replaced the entire front with a curtain. I don't remember what it's called, but she was thinking she wanted him to fix it, so it had the pretty doors again. But when Warner talked to the rabbi, the rabbi said what they really needed was to have the brick work and mortar on the building re-pointed and the woodwork around the windows repaired and repainted. He said they'd appealed to the historic society for funding to restore it, but in all the years that group had been giving out money, every penny had gone to Christian churches and old homes. Not a dime to any of the synagogues in the region. None of the members of the synagogue had the money to foot the bill, and they hadn't had any luck getting other grants from Jewish organizations. They're all getting older."

Fran's own life experience had left her with an extremely sensitive nose when it came to the smell of prejudice. She felt her chest tighten just thinking about the legacy of bias that must riddle the grantmaking history of the good Coastal Plains Historical Society. Her mind started to fly. She nodded once when Henry quit talking.

"So, the good white Christian people running the historical society think they've got the market on God and no one else deserves a sustained place in American history. Do I have that right, Henry?"

"Well, now, I'm sure they have some sort of priority list…"

"That's bull-crap, Henry, and you know it as well as I do. If I'm following you, what your friend Warner would like to be able to do is honor his wife's wish to repair their Aron Kodesh, so it has proper doors enclosing the Torah; and take care of the rabbi's need to see their synagogue building fixed up nice. The first, I think I can do if the rabbi will let me, along with a friend of mine who is a master woodworker. I'm going to have a chat with Sue about the rest. We'll make it right. Just you watch," Fran said, her eyes flashing hot across the table. "Give me Warner's phone number."

Fran finished her coffee in two swift gulps and reached across the kitchen table to shake Henry's hand. Then she left the house and strode back across the street to the church and marched down the back hall to Sue's office. The door was open. Sue had a Bible and an Old Testament commentary open on her desk while she frowned at her computer screen, one hand thoughtfully twisting a lock of her long brown hair. She was working on a sermon.

"Sue. We need to talk," Fran declared.

Sue jumped and knocked her phone off her desk and onto the floor.

"Dangit, Fran, I didn't even know there was anyone in the building!"

"There isn't. Just me. And I'm on a mission. Are you part of any cross-denominational or inter-religious clergy groups? Because if you are, we have a pitch to make," Fran blurted.

"Wait, what? Who's 'we'? And what mission are we on?"

Fran invited herself in and pulled out the guest chair next to Sue's desk. She plopped down and leaned forward, elbows on her knees. She summarized what she had heard from Henry Wright. Sue winced at the part about the historical society's funding record and tipped her head back to stare at the ceiling. Accustomed to checking for leaks, Fran looked up at the same spot. Sue noticed and started to laugh.

"Fran, it's not leaking. I was praying for patience and some fast help from St. Thomas," Sue said.

"Thomas?" Fran looked at Sue quizzically.

"Patron saint of architects. Remember, Bob, my beloved husband, is one of those. Architects, not saints, God knows," Sue said.

"Oh. I was hoping more for a connection to a good civil rights attorney, or some slack from the director of the county building and planning office. I know a dynamite brick mason, but he isn't licensed here in the U.S."

"Okay, okay, slow down," Sue said. "First, to answer your initial question, yes, there is a local interfaith alliance of clergy, and I'm a member. But the 'interfaith' part is just code for a noble effort to make sure the Methodists, all the Baptists, and the Presbyterians keep talking to each other. No Jews, no Muslims, no Hindus. The person I really have in mind to talk to is a friend of mine from seminary who works up at the Diocesan office of the Episcopal Church. She just led an effort to hire a rabbi as their internal consultant on actual inter-faith efforts around social justice. She might have some ideas."

"Good, let's call her," Fran said, picking Sue's phone up off the floor and handing it to her. "Put it on speaker."

"Now?"

"No time better," Fran said.

Sue sighed and glanced at her computer, which had just dropped into the rolling geometric pattern of her screen saver.

"God, you're bossy," Sue said.

"Professionally trained," Fran replied.

"Right. Lest I forget, Commander Solcati."

Fran smiled. Sue dialed. To her amazement, Sue's friend Janice Tollensby picked up her direct line.

"What? You're not in a meeting? It's Sue, down in Greenville, how are you?"

"I'm fine, Sue, and I have exactly eight minutes before the next one starts. What can I do for the Presbyterians today?"

Sue quickly explained the situation faced by Temple Emanuel and the apparent absence of interest in inter-faith support for historic preservation by the regional funders. She asked if Janice had any ideas for them. Janice did not, but she said she would make a couple of calls. One of her friends was a history professor up at the University of North Carolina. Privately, he was a serious geek about historic preservation, even though he laughed at what non-Indigenous Americans referred to as "historic," coming as he did from Iran. Janice said that the man was particularly interested in the local preservation of religious architecture from traditions that were more prominent in other parts of the world. He had recently told her about beautiful sculptures in an older Hindu temple in Morrisville that she had never visited. A little synagogue might intrigue him.

Sue hung up her cell phone and turned to look at Fran, who had been listening intently but was now staring vaguely into the middle of Sue's bookshelves, thinking.

"I worry when you think and don't speak," Sue said. "It's so unusual."

"Funny, Sue, you're so, so funny," Fran replied. It was true. In retirement, Fran very much enjoyed speaking her mind with little hesitation.

"Okay, I'll let you get back to sermon-writing," Fran said. "I'm going to call Henry's friend Warner and set up a time to take a spin over to the synagogue. I'll be back to work on the nursery bookshelves later." Fran pushed back her chair and stood to leave, picking up her box of drill bits and the stud finder she'd been carrying around.

Fran texted Caroline to let her know she was going to let the dog out in the yard for a few minutes and might be gone until suppertime. She knew Caroline had a class to teach at four o'clock and wouldn't be home until later that evening anyway, but they liked to keep track of each other. Then she climbed into her pickup truck, settled in behind the wheel, and gave Warner Jacobs a call.

Warner was a Grady-White retiree, just like Henry, and a Navy veteran.

Fran and Warner hit it off quickly on the phone. She explained why she was calling, then they spent some time chatting about the Navy and boats and how much it meant to work hard at something you cared about, and the importance of cherishing the loyalty of old friends. Fran was good at building relationships with relative strangers by gently steering conversation toward shared values and appreciating differences with curiosity and interest. It was one of the many skills she had cultivated in military leadership and in life. With Warner, it wasn't even a challenge. Within 15 minutes, Warner seemed completely at ease and Fran had him chortling. She felt fond of him already and could see how he and Henry had become so close. Warner said he was eager to meet her.

With her usual "life is short, so do the good thing now" attitude, she said she was free and wondered if he might be at the synagogue for Shabbat service that evening. Warner sounded surprised that she seemed familiar with Jewish tradition at all, and she explained that her stepfather was Jewish. Warner's voice warmed even more, and he quickly invited Fran to join him at Temple Emanuel as his guest for Shabbat. She agreed and confirmed their meeting time. Then she went home to let out the dog, shower, grab a bite to eat, and change into respectable attire.

After the service was over, Warner led Fran into the social hall next to the sanctuary, and they stood together as the Kiddush and Hamotzi blessings were said over the wine and challah. Friendly people greeted Fran with smiles and nods and welcomed her. Warner was beaming with pride as she responded to each in turn with a respectful "Shabbat shalom." In just a few minutes, Rabbi Larry Cohen approached Warner and invited him to introduce his guest. They chatted briefly, and Warner leaned close to the rabbi's ear and whispered, "This is my friend who wants to try to help with the renovations, and she has a friend who is a woodworker who might repair the old doors for the ark," he said. Rabbi Cohen's thick, dark eyebrows went up and he nodded appreciatively. He turned to Fran, held her eyes for a moment with his, and simply said, "Thank you," before inviting her to come back to talk further after the Sabbath. She discretely handed him her personal business card and he tucked it into his pocket.

When they left the building, Fran asked Warner to show her the parts of the building that the rabbi was most concerned about. She had already spotted several jagged gaps between lines of brick where the mortar had crumbled and fallen away. She could see where the white paint on the woodwork around the arched windows was fading to gray. In the back of the building, Warner showed her a set of windows facing the parking lot where the paint on the window frames had bubbled and peeled in spots. That told her there was water incursion, and the potential for some wood rot. She could fix leaking window frames, and the good news was that the unique curved glass panes were intact. Painting was easy, and she had ladders that would reach the upper windows. The brick repair needed expertise she didn't have, and money. Then she noticed that there were bands of decorative sandstone around beautiful, large stained-glass windows on the sides of the building. The sandstone had several fine, long vertical cracks around both windows. It was a softer stone, and the cracks could be the result of at least minor shifting in the foundation. Not good. A good engineering firm to assess for damage went onto her list.

Fran was making mental calculations for the growing budget and silently flipping through her personal Rolodex of people with useful skills as they walked slowly back to Warner's car. In her mind, the work was already underway. The fact that she didn't have a dime raised was a minor detail. She had faith in people most days and knew how to make a pitch, and a little guilt lit under the seats of a few well-placed progressives couldn't hurt, either.

The next week, Pastor Sue called Fran to say that Janice Tollensby had been able to reach her friend at the University in Chapel Hill. His name was Babak Amani, and he was connected in some exceptionally helpful ways. Janice learned that he was chair of the board for a university-affiliated entity called the International Center for Religious Art and Preservation. Mr. Amani had been working in the Middle East and in the United States, following the pathways of immigrants who came to the East Coast in the late 1800s and early to mid-1900s with their trades and artistic vision intact. For generations, some had retained affiliations with benefactors who wanted to test the promise of religious freedom in their "New World." These talented immigrants and their financial backers were steadily establishing prominent places of worship that reflected the glories of art and architecture back home in the Middle East, Asia, North Africa, and Europe. While most of their interest and funding were focused on preservation and restoration of the most extravagant buildings and art collections in the United States, there was one stream of funding that was dedicated to the rural diaspora. And that meant everywhere outside of the 10 largest American cities.

Sue told Fran she was nervous about taking the next step. Janice had told her that Mr. Amani was willing to talk. But Sue felt she was in way over her head already, and that it was a miracle she had been able to persuade Janice to reach out in the first place. Plus, she had already forgotten how Fran had talked her into this escapade to begin with. She remembered she had been working on a sermon when Fran busted into her office, but it all got fuzzy after that.

Fran recognized an introvert's terror when she saw it. Caroline, for example, could handle professorial duties just fine, but ask her to make a pitch to the junior league and she'd want to go hide. Fran told Sue that she'd be down to the church to talk to her in 10 minutes.

On her way over, Fran called Rabbi Cohen and left a message asking him to call her back. Then she called Warner and filled him in on the delicate tendril of opportunity that had presented itself with Babak Amani's invitation to talk. No promises, Fran said, but it was an opening worth exploring.

Fran walked into Sue's office to find her standing at her window, looking out at the trees.

"Hey," she said. Sue turned around and motioned Fran in.

"So, what's next?" Sue asked, her forehead lined with marginally controlled anxiety.

"Well, how do you feel about calling on all your buddies in the Christian Interfaith Council to see if you can convince them to join up in a special project? It'll be like a Habitat for Humanity project across Abrahamic religious traditions in North Carolina. I'm guessing Babak is Muslim, we've got a rabbi whose synagogue should qualify for historic preservation but isn't getting anywhere in this proud Southern state. You and I have a strong hunch that our local historic preservationists are tied to Christian philanthropists with short arms above their deep pockets when it comes to supporting people who aren't like them. That needs to change. They need to make some new friends. And then we've got you and your lefty friends. Who knows, maybe we can trade off, and next year we can take on a crumbling mosque, and the year after that everyone can turn up with hammers and chisels and fix up that old Gothic Revival church over in New Bern. You know the one, right? Brick, big tower, Baptist of some sort? I'm seeing a 10- to 15-year plan here. Big proposal. Millions. At least three cycles of investment in historic architecture celebrating North Carolina's diversity and the contributions of its immigrants from around the world."

Fran stopped to do a visual check on Sue's respiration and heart rate.

Sue's eyes had grown wide and were staying that way, her jaw slightly slack. After a long moment, she spoke. "Will you do the talking, please?"

Fran laughed. "Yes, Pastor Sue, I will do the talking. Let's get an appointment on our calendars with Mr. Amani at a time that also works for Rabbi Cohen. First, we need to listen to what his interests really are."

It took three days to juggle calendars, but they got a conference call on the books with Babak Amani. In the meantime, Sue had called her fellow pastors on the interfaith council and was thrilled to find that all but three were really intrigued. Only two thought they could put some money on the table from various lines in their ministry and community service budgets, but all the others knew parishioners in their communities who had skills that could help, and good folk who would always show up when asked to wield a paint brush or a hammer. Some of historic preservation and restoration required delicate, highly skilled labor—and some was plain hard work.

Fran took the lead on the call with Mr. Amani. She and Sue were sitting together in Sue's office. Sue chimed in briefly with information about the shared interest in the project among the members of the Christian Interfaith Council. Rabbi Cohen spoke passionately about the history of the Jewish community in coastal North Carolina and of Temple Emanuel's place in it. The story he told about the synagogue and the people who loved it as their gathering place in the wilderness was something Babak Amani identified with deeply. His parents had come here from Iran and were stunned to discover there were only five mosques in all of North Carolina. They were profoundly relieved to find that one of them was in Durham, where they lived.

Fran knew that Warner was sitting across the street in Henry's house, where they had dialed in to the call to listen in. What Fran didn't know is that both Henry and Warner were standing next to each other by the kitchen sink where they could look through his window at the church, knowing Fran and Sue were there on the phone. The two old men had their arms around each other's shoulders, heads pressed to either side of the old cordless phone gripped tightly in Henry's big hand, heads bobbing at every hopeful thing they heard. Fran had shown Henry how to set it to mute.

It took another six months of planning, but the proposal came together, invited with enthusiasm by the board of directors of the International Center for the Preservation of Art and Religious Architecture. It was the first time in the center's history that a proposal had been brought forward that embodied such deep community involvement from outside of those who owned a building or collection. What excited them most was the enormous set of letters of support that accompanied the proposal.

Each letter showed solid knowledge of both the spirit and content of what was being proposed and a personal commitment to do some part of the work, according to their talents. There were plumbers and carpenters, engineers and architects, a museum curator, professors, marketing professionals, hardware store and paint shop owners, and individuals who just wanted to help and meet new people along the way.

In return, the community collaborative asked for both funding and expertise that only the international council could tap to make sure that repairs to each building selected would deeply honor the religious traditions supported within it. They presented their proposed democratic governance structure and their fair selection process. Both would embody a commitment to making sure that an equal number of buildings from each religious tradition received a valuable and comparable investment of time, money, and effort. In addition to the physical restoration work, they outlined an equal commitment to education and social sharing that would build relationship connections and a deeper appreciation for one another across their respective faiths.

Fran was satisfied. It was among the most patriotically American things she had done since leaving the Navy. It was a bigger vision than anyone had initially held, and it had changed in important ways as everyone involved learned from each other. Fran made sure that Jim Lucas and Ann McAlister from the Coastal Plains Historical Society both attended the grant award celebration. Jim and Ann were given seats in front, where everyone could see them. And Fran waited for a handshake when she told them to expect a proposal for matching funding.

Two weeks after Temple Emanuel had its priority repairs completed as one of the first buildings selected for the initial cycle of renovations, Fran joined Rabbi Cohen and Warner Jacobs in the sanctuary to complete the finishing touch. She gently reattached the ornately carved and refinished doors to the Aron Kodesh and stepped back so the two men could see it. The Rabbi smiled and stood, turning as he set the Torah within its sacred cabinet, singing a quiet prayer of blessing in his lovely tenor voice. Fran beamed with satisfaction, watching the rabbi at work. She held Warner's hand and squeezed it when he rested his head on her shoulder—and turned quickly when she heard a soft sob escape his mouth. Fran held Warner's eyes in kindness when he smiled through his tears and spoke to her.

"She would have loved it. Thank you. Thank you so very much."

Fran knew that both Henry and Helena would also be pleased.

WORTH A SHOT

Stacy Brown lived on a steep side street that lacked a name but curled uphill beside the White Horse Tavern. Her home was a converted carriage house that sat beside a rambling old Victorian owned by Jeff and Suzy Katzenmeier, her landlords. They used the lower level of the carriage house as their garage. A wooden stairway around the back led up to a red door that opened into what used to be the hayloft. Now it was her very own unit of affordable housing, rural New Hampshire style.

Stacy loved it there. On calm evenings, she could open the windows and hear the water tumbling over the rocks in Willow Brook, just across the road; and the wind scuffling through the big pines and maples. The loft was topped with a glassed-in cupola that allowed the full moon to shine directly into her space. Some of the panes were cracked but didn't really leak much, which she thought was amazing given their age. The town was incorporated when the area was still under English rule, and the farmhouse was one of its original residences.

One awkward feature was the location of the bathroom, which was on ground level under the stairs and closed in. Sort of. It used to be a horse stall and was wired for lights and had a built-in space heater, for which Stacy was incredibly grateful in winter. But the heater had a non-negotiable safety feature that automatically turned it off after four minutes. She learned to get dry and dressed fast as a firefighter responding to a three-alarm call.

Stacy worked in Concord for the New Hampshire Task Force on Child Abuse and Neglect. It was a tiny non-profit with an enormous mission and exactly three staff. Stacy and Shirley Barrett, the executive director, shared a part-time administrative assistant who was the backbone of the whole operation. Lana Silva was a heavy smoker with a huge, rumbling laugh that made her round, polyester-clad belly shimmy from north to south. And she laughed a lot.

Lana and her laugh were the redeeming feature of all their days. She came from a huge Portuguese family, all still living in or near Providence, Rhode Island. Members of the Silva clan called her regularly at work for dire emergencies that were usually things she could do absolutely nothing about. This morning it was a tearful niece whose Pomeranian had escaped through the hole her rabbit had dug under the back fence. The rabbit came home. Princess the Pomeranian had not. Yesterday, it was her eldest son's latest need for her to sell something to get enough money for him to buy a new tool for his beleaguered home repair business. It had been a start-up for the last seven years. Things would happen, and Lana always knew what to do.

That was Lana's job description at the task force, too. When things happen, figure out what to do. If it involved programming, grab Stacy. If it required money, yell down the hall for Shirley. But invariably, Lana already had some idea about how to solve the problem and had taken the first steps.

It was Lana who had helped Stacy find a new place to live. A friend of a friend in Providence worked at the White Horse Tavern in Warner and told her the next-door neighbor was renting a cute little efficiency apartment. It was only a 25-minute drive from Concord, she said, and the rent was very reasonable. Stacy had jumped on it, since her current landlord had evicted her from her apartment outside Manchester when the maintenance guy discovered that she had a cat, which was against the lease. The landlord was not moved toward leniency when Stacy tried to make the case that the cat didn't really belong to her, per se, it had just come in the door when she was carrying groceries in from the car. And stayed.

Stacy had fallen impossibly in love with the tiny orange stray and named her Sherbet. Because the property management company had no heart and no flexibility about anything, Stacy and Sherbet were within a week of being homeless when Stacy turned to Lana in desperation. Stacy off-handedly asked Lana if she might have any leads on an apartment that was available for immediate occupancy and for rent that was anywhere under half of Stacy's monthly salary. Lana knew full well that Stacy's pay was about four dollars a month more than her own, even though Stacy had a master's in social work. Finding an affordable rental wouldn't be easy.

That's why Lana lived all the way out in Weare in an apartment above the Worth-A-Shot Thrift Store, which was on the same tiny strip of concrete as Worth-A-Shot Espresso and Worth-A-Shot Discount Liquor. It was affordable.

Lana had dated the owner, a long drink of water named Chet, for about a minute before she found out he was already married to the owner of the gas station two blocks over. Chet got an earful from both women, who became fast friends. Lana used the opportunity of the initial confrontation to negotiate a free month's rent. Six months later, Chet's wife filed for divorce, which went smoothly, with Lana serving as a witness in court. Chet moved away, selling the entire Worth-A-Shot conglomerate to Hank Marbury, who owned the Muddy Pond Market in North Weare.

Even though Stacy tried nobly to keep her tone light and casual, Lana knew a housing emergency when she saw one. In this case, the emergency was five feet two inches tall and standing in front of Lana holding a briefcase and a cellphone, ready to go downtown to testify on a child abuse prevention bill that was floundering in the senate.

Lana made some calls. In an hour, she texted Stacy about the place in Warner.

With Lana around, everything seemed to work out.

Which is why Shirley and Stacy decided together that a panic attack was in order one Tuesday morning when Lana didn't show up for work. No message from her had been left on either of their cell phones or the office answering machine. Lana's battered 2008 Chevy Impala wasn't in the parking lot, either.

Stacy ran over to the cafeteria on the campus where the task force rented office space. Called the Garden of Eatin', it was in the basement of the building next door and operated by patients progressing toward release from the hospital. One of Lana's good friends in Concord, Betty Serandon, managed the cafeteria.

Betty didn't know where Lana was, either.

At noon, Stacy sat down in Shirley's office. They still hadn't heard anything from or about Lana, from anyone.

Shirley dialed the Concord police.

The officer she spoke with explained, as kindly as possible, that a grown woman who didn't show up to work on time at a part-time job in a non-profit that paid next to nothing might just have slept in. There was no indication a crime had been committed, and they couldn't do much unless there was more to go on.

Shirley hung up, frustrated and still very worried. Stacy paced in front of Shirley's desk. There had to be some other people to call. Maybe Lana had taken ill or was in an accident. Maybe she had to make an emergency trip to Providence and was just too preoccupied to call. They batted around all the possibilities.

"Who's in charge of HR here?" Stacy asked. "You or me?"

Shirley thought for a second. They made all their hiring decisions together when there was one to be made.

"I guess I am," Shirley said. "Why?"

"Because I'm about to break some rules and I don't want the head of HR to find out," Stacy replied, heading down the short hall to Lana's desk. Shirley nodded and turned to check her email.

Stacy sat down at Lana's desk, scrutinizing the little stacks of paper and the Post-it notes in tidy rows off to the side. Lana still used one of those old desktop blotters displaying a giant calendar, and Stacy checked to see what was written on each of the days this week. There was a dental appointment coming up on Friday, but nothing else that wasn't related to task force business. Off to the side, she noticed some fun little doodles. One was a sketch of a unicorn riding a heart with a phone number inside of it with a Rhode Island area code. That might be worth calling. Maybe it was a niece. Stacy wrote that one down. Then she checked all the Post-its, finding nothing helpful.

The little red light on Lana's desktop phone set was blinking, indicating there was a voice mail. Stacy trotted back down the hall and asked Shirley to look up the administrative override code for the voice mail system. With the code in hand, she went back to Lana's desk and punched in the number to listen to the messages.

There was only one, from a friend.

Yo, Lana, it's Mar. You stood me up for coffee this morning. What's up girl, you get a good offer last night? Sleep in? Call me. I'll be at work at 10, so call me there. 746-2021.

Another connection, who might have some idea where to look for Lana. Stacy went back to her office with both phone numbers. Time to start networking.

The number from the unicorn sketch turned out to be Lana's niece, Cheryl, who ran an in-home daycare in Providence that was pushing the limit for toddlers, judging from the background noise. Cheryl didn't know where Lana was but agreed it wasn't like Lana at all to just not show up for work. Cheryl gave Stacy the phone number for Lana's brother Luke but said he probably couldn't answer the phone since he was an airplane mechanic down at TF Green International Airport. He'd be at work. Stacy thanked her and hung up.

Next, she called Lana's friend, Mar, who turned out to work as the business manager at a real estate office over in Hopkinton. Mar had no idea what had happened to Lana, either. They were supposed to meet for coffee in Hopkinton at eight o'clock, on Lana's way to the office in Concord. She just hadn't showed. No call, no nothing. Stacy asked Mar for Lana's home address, which Mar gave to her immediately. Stacy could have looked it up, but that would have required digging around in Shirley's file cabinets for Lana's employment record.

Stacy trooped back down the hall to tell Shirley what little she had learned. She checked her watch. She needed to free up a couple of hours to drive over to Lana's apartment and just knock on the door. Stacy was supposed to join Shirley in a lunch meeting with a prospective donor in half an hour, then go to a meeting at the attorney general's office. She was working with the AG on the next draft of new policy on how to handle sibling witnesses in child assault cases. That was going to be a lengthy process. She could reschedule.

Shirley agreed to handle the prospective donor on her own and told Stacy to get going over to Weare. Something was wrong.

It was a glorious early June day, the sun shining and the crocus popping up in the pocket garden in front of their building. Out in the parking lot, Stacy left her leather jacket unzipped and pulled her helmet on, throwing her leg over her motorcycle as she fastened the strap under her chin. In a minute, she was heading down South Street to pick up Route 13 west.

The cool wind in her face and sunny skies were a balm to Stacy's nerves. Maybe they were wrong. Maybe it was nothing. Lana was probably not feeling well and had just fallen asleep earlier and hadn't woken up to call in. At least she'd get a quick ride in, spinning over to Weare and back. Stacy normally headed north or out to the seacoast on pleasure rides, so the area over by Weare would be a change of scenery.

The trip went quickly, and she pulled into the parking lot in front of the Worth-A-Shot Thrift Store. Mar had said there were two apartments on the second floor, and both were accessed by a door in the back of the building next to a small loading zone. The door opened into a little vestibule at the bottom of the stairs. At the top would be a landing and a short hallway straight ahead, with doors opposite each other. Lana's apartment was #2. The other apartment was #3. There was no #1. In some prior decade, #1 might have been what was now the shop downstairs.

Stacy left her helmet hanging on the handlebar of her Harley and headed around to the back of the building. She found the right door and pulled it open. There were two mail slots in the wall on the left, and a small trash basket on the floor. The stairs were dark stained wood with worn carpet treads tacked into each step. It was dark. There was one lightbulb at the top of the stairs, glowing weakly through a cheap glass flush-mount ceiling fixture. The air was stale, and she noted a pine tree-shaped air freshener dangling from a loop of tape attached to the light fixture.

Stacy jogged up the stairs and down the hall to the opposing doorways.

The door to apartment #2 was ajar. Not open, just not completely latched. She tapped quietly.

"Lana?" No response.

"Lana, it's Stacy. You okay?" No response.

Stacy stood back a step, deciding how many more rules she was going to break today. She gave the door a shove to open it further when it gave way with a pull from inside.

"Oh!" Stacy was expecting to see Lana's stout form on the other side of the door, but instead, a man with a small potbelly wearing a worn New England Patriots T-shirt and jeans was pulling open the door and stepping aside. Given how short Stacy was, it was normally a man's mid-section she first encountered. She looked up to meet his eyes and noticed he had neatly trimmed brown hair, graying slightly at the temples, and glasses. His posture was relaxed, even a bit sad. Stacy assessed his behavior as decidedly not threatening.

"Lana's not here right now, sorry," the guy said, still holding the door with one hand, like he expected to close it again quickly.

"Um, who are you?" Stacy asked, with no manners whatsoever.

"I could ask the same," he replied.

"Right, sorry, I'm Stacy Brown, I work with Lana. She didn't show up this morning and we got worried. Is she around?"

"No. She just went for a walk. She'll be back," he said.

Stacy frowned a bit. Lana was not the exercising type. Stacy tried to surreptitiously peer into the room through the half-open door. All she could see was an old brown sofa with a coffee table in front of it, a magazine and a dozen balled-up tissues tossed on top of it next to an ashtray. A pack of Lana's cigarettes were on the table, too. Which Stacy figured she would have taken with her if she'd gone out.

"So, Mr. Mystery Man, is Lana okay? Is she sick or something? It's not like her to just not come to work and not let anybody know. I need to see her. And since you now know who I am, you mind introducing yourself? Are you related to Lana or something?"

Stacy knew Lana was single and figured she would have heard about it if she had started dating someone. She was working awfully hard to keep her face set in social-worker-neutral. It was looking more like whatever had gone on here at Lana's apartment last night or early this morning wasn't an experience Lana found pleasant. If she had just come down with the flu or a bad cold, she would have called.

The man sighed and stepped back from the doorway, waving her in.

"Look, come on in, I got nothing to hide from you. My name is Chuck. I just don't know when she'll be back and she'll probably want some space," he said. He turned away from the door and headed back over to the armchair next to the sofa and slumped into it.

Stacy looked around the apartment warily, but she wasn't feeling any sense of danger or threat from Chuck, and the place was stone cold silent. He was just staring at the floor in front of his feet, looking forlorn.

"How long has Lana been gone?"

"A little over an hour, I guess. Like I said, she just said she needed to clear her head."

"Did she say where she was going?"

"Out. Just out," Chuck replied.

"Did she take anything with her? Her purse, keys, smokes?"

Chuck looked up at Stacy, who was standing on the other side of the coffee table, feet spread shoulder width, arms crossed over her chest. This had clearly become an interrogation.

Chuck just shrugged.

"Chuck, man, this is not normal for Lana. What happened here? Tell me, because I'm getting suspicious and worried and you're not being exactly forthcoming with details, and that makes me get more suspicious about who you are and what you're doing here and why Lana is not in her apartment and you are." Stacy fixed Chuck with her best *answer me now* look. She used it on teenagers all the time. It worked on grown men most of the time, too.

"Jeez, lady, chill, okay? I'm an old friend. I showed up to tell her something she needed to know, and I had a hunch it wasn't going to be easy for her to take, so I wanted to tell her in person. I'm a little worried about her, too. I was hoping she'd be back by now, but I don't want to take off and have her just come back to an empty apartment."

"What did you tell her?" Stacy decided to take the direct approach.

"I'm not sure she'd want the world to know, okay? I'd rather let her tell you if she wants to," Chuck replied, a bit defensively, but finally looking Stacy in the eye.

Stacy thought that was an encouraging display of healthy boundaries, making the odds this guy was a criminal go down a notch or two. Plus, Chuck looked downright dejected. She relaxed her posture.

"Right, that's fair, I guess. Are you sure she just went for a walk? I don't see her purse. Is her car still in the lot? I didn't see it on my way in," Stacy said.

"Honestly, I don't even know what she drives these days. It's been a long time," Chuck said, his voice fading back into his chest.

Stacy took that tidbit of information on board and let it roll around in her head. Lana had owned that Impala since she bought it used in 2008. So, this guy hadn't seen Lana in at least 10 or 12 years.

She looked around the room again and took a few steps into the kitchen to scan the countertop. She was looking for Lana's gigantic rusty orange leather purse. It was the size of an award-winning pumpkin and weighed 20 pounds with all the stuff she hauled around in it. Stacy was a wallet-in-the-back-pocket kind of gal and teased Lana all the time about how she could furnish a small apartment out of that purse. She didn't see Lana's pumpkin. Chuck was just watching her with a quizzical expression on his face.

"I don't see Lana's purse. I'm going to look in her bedroom."

Stacy strode across the living room and down a short hallway. There was a small bathroom on the right with the light on. In a quick glance, Stacy took in the single-sink vanity cluttered with an assortment of makeup, and a pink-and-white crocheted Kleenex box holder on the back of the toilet tank. One towel hung scrunched on a bar, and the shower curtain was pulled closed, displaying its pale-blue seashell pattern.

On the other side of the hall was Lana's bedroom. The drapes were pulled, and it was dark. Stacy felt around the wall just inside the door and flipped on the ceiling light. The bed was unmade, and a well-worn terrycloth robe was tossed over a dark-green padded chair. There was a tiny desk in one corner and a four-drawer dresser with a picture of Lana and her two kids on top of it and some jewelry, nothing else. A crucifix hung on the wall next to the dresser. The closet door stood half open, enough for Stacy to see it was stuffed with clothes and shoes and boxes piled up on the shelf. The room was a little messy, but not torn apart, like someone might have left it if they had been packing in a hurry. Stacy still didn't see Lana's purse.

She walked back into the living room and stood, staring at Chuck again.

"What," he asked, flatly.

"Nothing. She took her purse with her when she left, which is a little weird if she was going for a walk. That thing weighs a ton. I'm going out to look for her car. Don't leave," she said.

"I wasn't planning on it," Chuck said, irritated. He hadn't moved from the chair.

Stacy trotted back down the hall and down the stairs. Outside, she did a quick circuit around the building. There were two other shops attached to the thrift store, in what looked like additions made at separate times. Next to the thrift shop was a liquor store, and attached to that, on the end, a coffee shop. She noted the names of all three and smiled. "Worth-A-Shot," she said to herself. Clever play on words. Worked for all three businesses. When she rounded the coffee shop, Worth-A-Shot Espresso, the smell of dark roast and fresh pastry drifted out, making her stomach growl. It smelled heavenly.

Stacy circled all the way back to the door that led up to the second-floor apartments. No Impala, no Lana. On a whim, she poked her head inside the thrift shop's rear entrance and peered around. No one was at the counter, so she went on in.

"Can I help you?" The disembodied voice called out from somewhere behind a row of metal shelves crammed with dinnerware, small kitchen appliances, and an enormous collection of coffee mugs. Stacy headed back toward the source of the greeting. A woman about Lana's age popped into the aisle as Stacy approached.

"Hi, there," Stacy said. "I'm actually looking for a friend of mine who lives upstairs. Do you know Lana Silva by any chance?"

"Of course, I do. Everyone knows Lana. She's a doll. And a hoot. She comes in on weekends and helps out sometimes, just for the hell of it. Sure makes a shift go faster when she's around. She's at work now, though. Works at that child abuse task force place over in Concord."

"I know, I work with her. She didn't show up today, which isn't like her. Did she say anything recently about needing to go somewhere, or anyone needing her help?"

The woman frowned and shook her head. "No, nothing like that. I haven't seen her in a couple of days, though. I was off yesterday. That's strange. She knows people count on her. And she cares about that place a lot. What's your name?"

"Stacy, Stacy Brown. I run the programs at the task force. Lana is my chief bacon-saver. Look, I don't know where she is. There's a guy named Chuck up in her apartment who says he's an old friend, and that she just took off for a bit to get some air. Everything is probably fine, but if you see her, tell her to call me, okay?" Stacy handed the woman her business card, which the woman took and examined before sliding it into the back pocket of her jeans.

"Yeah, okay, sure will. I'm Mona Davison, by the way. You can find me here most days. If you find Lana, tell her to check in, okay?"

Stacy nodded and left the store to go back up to Lana's apartment. She didn't like the fact that Lana's car was gone. And her purse. It looked increasingly like she wasn't off hiking in the woods but had taken off. Really taken off.

She let herself back into the apartment and told Chuck that Lana drove an old blue Chevy Impala, and that it was gone. She gave Chuck her business card, too, and told him to call her or have Lana call her the second she came home. Before she left, Stacy extracted a last name. Carlotta. Chuck Carlotta. Originally from Providence, now living in a small town in Ohio called Campbell, halfway between Cleveland and Pittsburgh. He'd done the 10-hour drive yesterday to talk to Lana after not seeing her in 20 years. Crashed on the couch. Told her shocking news, then stuck around.

Weird.

Stacy keyed the ignition on her bike and strapped on her helmet. The sun had disappeared, and it felt like it might rain. She eyed the sky, which had clouds coming up from the south. She pulled back onto Old Stage Road and headed back toward Concord.

When she got back to the admin building, she parked her bike as close to the building as she could and pulled out her rain gear in case it started to pour later. She trotted back up the stairs and through the door at the end of the first floor, into the task force offices. Shirley was standing outside of her office with two cups of coffee in her hands, headed into their small conference room. She made eye contact with Stacy and jerked her head toward the room, telling Stacy to join her.

Stacy dumped her jacket and gear in her office and hustled down the hall. Shirley was settling into a chair opposite a young woman with soft, shoulder-length brown hair that draped down along her face. Her hooded eyes were downcast, and her mascara and eyeliner were smudged. She had been crying. She had a worn manila folder in front of her on the table; her keys, a phone, and clutch-style wallet were on the chair beside her. She was holding the coffee mug in both hands, like it was cocoa on a 15-degree winter day.

Stacy looked down at her as she pulled out a chair and introduced herself. The woman responded in kind, telling Stacy her name. Donna Lombardi. It meant nothing to Stacy. Shirley was looking across the table at Donna with gentle sympathy.

"Donna, Stacy is our other staff person. She was just out in Weare, trying to find Lana at her home there," Shirley said. Shirley quickly looked over at Stacy. Stacy just shook her head to indicate she'd not found Lana at home. Shirley went on. "Do you want me to tell Stacy what you've shared with me, or would you like to tell her yourself?"

This entire day was strange and getting stranger. This woman must know something about Lana.

"I just got up here from Providence after making a trip out to Ohio a couple weeks ago to find my biological father. I was adopted, see, and a few years ago, I decided I wanted to try to find my real parents. When I turned 21, my adoptive parents agreed to give me the contact information for the adoption agency they used in Rhode Island. That's where I grew up, in Woonsocket. It took me a few tries, but I finally got someone to dig up my record. My bio-dad had been good about sending them his address every time he moved, just in case someday I might come looking for him. But my mother, she hadn't left any information at all. She was still a teenager when I was born, and her parents told the agency that no one was to contact her, ever.

Donna paused to take a sip of coffee. She grabbed a Kleenex from the box on the table and dabbed at both eyes. She looked across the table at Shirley, who just nodded, not saying a word, her eyes relaxed and kind, like there was nothing Donna could say that she hadn't heard a hundred times before. It was a highly refined skill when you worked around kids and parents in the child welfare system. Stacy was good at it, too. The two of them were like arms on a cozy sweater when they had someone in the office who needed to fall apart a little.

Donna glanced over at Stacy and then back down at her coffee cup.

"Lana Silva is my mother. Chuck Carlotta is my dad. He's a good guy. He told me the whole story, as much as he knew of it. They were madly in love the summer before Lana's junior year of high school. He was starting his senior year when his parents moved to Ohio and took him with them. He didn't know Lana was pregnant until after her parents made her give me up for adoption. Lana's parents called Mr. and Mrs. Carlotta when they found out Lana was pregnant and said they didn't want Chuck to have any contact with their family ever again. Chuck's parents told him that Lana would be better off if he let her have a fresh start with a guy who could be with her there in Rhode Island. It was all lies, but he didn't know that. He couldn't stop thinking about the fact that he had a child back in Rhode Island. So, when he was older, he tracked down the two private adoption agencies that did the most business in Providence and left his name and contact information with them, just in case it might get attached to a file on me or Lana. That's how I found him."

Stacy and Shirley gave Donna a minute to decide if she wanted to say anything more. She remained quiet. Stacy was rapidly putting two and two together. The Chuck at Lana's apartment must have been her long-lost high school love, come to tell her that their daughter was looking for them.

"Donna, thank you for sharing your life with us like this. It must be very painful to get so close and not find your mother. I wish we knew where Lana is right now, but we don't. All I can tell you is that even though she left you behind when you were a baby, she is a good person. She is probably upset and confused and full of a whole lot of emotions right now, wherever she is," Stacy said quietly. She was watching Donna closely to try to read how she was taking in the words. Donna nodded, slowly.

"It's a lot, I'm sure," Donna said. "But even though I'm an adult now, I was really hoping she might want to meet me again. I was hoping for that more than I was admitting to myself. Chuck didn't have her phone number, but to help me out, he called a bunch of people they knew in high school and found out where she was living and where she worked. She wasn't on Facebook or Instagram, so it wasn't that easy for him. He really went out of his way." Her voice drifted off into silence again.

"Donna, what do you need most right now, today?" Shirley asked.

It was one of those basic, non-judgmental questions that often worked well to help people who were distraught and lost in either the past or the future get focused again in the here and now. It was always a good thing to do with a distraught person before you let them get into a car and try to drive.

Donna looked past Shirley out the window, where the wind was kicking around in the trees. Then she looked back at Shirley and over to Stacy.

"Thank you both for being so kind to me. I know you've got to get back to work, and I don't want to take up more of your time. I guess, if you see Lana again, just tell her that I was here, looking for her. And that if someday she would like to meet me, I would like that, too."

Donna reached for her wallet and opened the main compartment. She fished out two personal business cards that were printed with stars and moons along the border, and her name and phone number in the middle. She handed one to Stacy and stood up to reach across the table to give one to Shirley.

Stacy saw Shirley suddenly look past Donna toward the door. Stacy turned to do the same.

Lana was standing in the doorway, tears streaming down her face.

"Donna, I do want to meet you. I want to do a lot more than just meet you," Lana said.

Donna's eyes widened and she turned in her chair to look at the source of the voice that sounded so much like her own. Their resemblance was undeniable. Donna pushed back her chair and stood up. Lana held out both of her hands, looking Donna straight in the eyes.

"In my mind, I always called you 'Sophie.' If I screw up and call you that, be patient with me, okay?" Lana stepped into the room and took hold of Donna's half-outstretched hands. "Can I give you a hug?"

Shirley stood up and walked around the end of the conference table, placing a hand on Stacy's shoulder. "We'll give you two some space. Take all the time you need," Shirley said, leading Stacy out of the room and closing the door behind them.

Shirley turned left to head into her office, and Stacy turned right to go back to hers. She could hear the old radiator against the wall start clanking softly. The temperature outside must have dropped. Stacy was hugely relieved to know Lana was safe, and the intensity of this personal life drama unfolding unexpectedly explained everything. But she still felt unsettled. She knew she needed to call the AG's office to reschedule her policy meeting, but was having trouble concentrating. She started tidying her desk instead, hoping a clean workspace would lead to a focused mind. It didn't.

Stacy sat back and stared out the window for a few minutes, trying to figure out why she was still feeling disturbed. It wasn't about Lana's old beau, Chuck. He had turned out to be legit. It wasn't about Donna, exactly. It was something about Lana. Stacy decided she was just feeling the aftershocks of Lana's realization that her daughter, whom she hadn't seen since childbirth, had reappeared in her life. And she was worried that it might lead to Lana reconsidering other things in her life. Stacy was worried about losing Lana.

She pushed back from her desk and walked down to Shirley's office, noticing the low sounds of Donna and Lana's conversation sifting through the conference room door. She tapped on the doorframe to get Shirley's attention. Shirley was on the phone, but waved Stacy in. She took the chair in front of Shirley's desk and waited for her to wrap up her conversation.

Shirley hung up and looked over at Stacy.

"What's up?" Shirley asked, as though the world hadn't just exploded down the hall.

"Is this going to change things around here?"

"Is what going to change things around here?" Shirley asked, a bit confused.

"Is the fact that Lana just found her long-lost daughter—who she abandoned at birth under parental pressure and after the loss of her first teenage love and the father of the child, who has also suddenly resurfaced—going to change things for Lana and her work with us here?"

Shirley sighed and sat back in her chair. She looked at Stacy, thinking. "I have no idea. Maybe. I hope not."

"Should we offer her some time off, maybe? Let her know we'll be flexible if she needs to spend some time with Donna, or go home for a while?"

"I don't know. She knows she can talk to us about those kinds of needs, if she has them; but sure, we can tell her proactively."

"Okay," Stacy said. "I just don't want her to go anywhere else. I'd be lost without her. For real. You know she's the only reason I can run our volunteer programs, do the advocacy work, and outreach education at the same time. She handles so much when I'm out of the office."

"I know," Shirley said, smiling softly. "I can say the same thing. My calendar was a disaster before she started managing it and screening my email and calls for me. Even part-time, she's almost made me a sane woman. Never thought that would be possible."

They heard the outer office door open. A guest. And no one was at the reception desk, obviously.

"I'll go see who it is," Stacy said, turning to leave Shirley's office.

Part way down the hall to the small reception area, Stacy saw Chuck standing awkwardly in front of Lana's desk, fiddling with his car keys. He looked up and saw Stacy walking toward him.

"Hey, Chuck," Stacy greeted him quietly.

"Is she here?" he asked.

"They both are. They're in our conference room talking," Stacy said. "I take it you drove all the way over here from Ohio to tell Lana about Donna?"

"Yeah, I just knew she'd be upset. Happy, sad, a lot of things. We were just kids, but I didn't think Lana would have changed so much that she wouldn't want to see Donna if Donna reached out. I know what a wild tailspin it put me into when Donna found me, and I wasn't even there when she was born," Chuck said.

Stacy was impressed. Chuck really seemed to care about both Lana and

Donna. Here he was, guessing that this is where Donna would have gone next, looking for Lana. When Lana didn't come home, he guessed she would have come here in case Donna did. Chuck had been looking pensively at the floor.

"Hey, Chuck?" Stacy's voice was gentle. He looked up to meet her eyes.

"Yeah? You want me to leave?"

"No, not at all. I just wanted to apologize for treating you like you'd kidnapped Lana. I was just really worried about her. One downside of being in my line of work is you see too much of the worst of what people can be and do. I shouldn't have been so suspicious of you," Stacy said.

"That's okay. I get it. You had no idea who I was. I'm glad Lana has people who care enough to look after her like that. She's a good soul," Chuck replied with a sad smile.

"Got that right. The best."

Stacy and Chuck just looked at each other for a moment. Another door in the hallway outside banged shut, and someone's footsteps faded, heels tapping on the old wood. She looked back at Chuck.

"Do you want to wait here for them? Or..."

Chuck just looked back at Stacy, a slight frown creasing his forehead. "I'm not sure. I'm not sure I even know what the right thing is to do. I know I'll see Donna again. Hopefully a lot. But Lana, well, there was so much she was told that just wasn't true about why I never called her or came to see her back then. It about killed me. I loved her so much. I was crazy for her. I'd planned to come back to Providence the second I turned 18 and could do what I wanted. She's the only woman..." His voice drifted off.

"You still care about her, don't you," Stacy said.

"I had no idea how much until I saw her again. She hasn't changed a bit. I mean, we're both older, wiser, life's done its numbers on both of us. But deep down? Lana is still just...incredible."

Chuck looked so torn. He had a ball cap in his hands and was snapping and unsnapping the clasp in back. He stared at the framed poster on the wall next to Lana's desk. It was of downtown Providence.

"That there," he said, nodding toward the poster, "still feels like home to me. Even though I've been in Ohio all my adult life." Chuck smiled sadly.

"Maybe it's time you came back," Stacy said. "I can't tell you what to do about Lana and your feelings for her, but I'd hazard a guess that lies and half-truths should be one thing you put behind you. This is a time for honesty and compassion, all the way around," Stacy said.

Finally, Chuck smiled at her. "You do sound like a social worker," he said.

"Busted," Stacy said, grinning. "Just take a seat, Chuck. I'll go let Donna and Lana know you're here."

Stacy and Shirley told Lana to take the day off. And the next if she needed it. When Stacy launched into her prepared speech about flexibility and family leave policy and how much Lana meant to the task force and to Shirley and Stacy most of all, Lana just stared at her for a second, confused. Then Lana pulled her into a big hug, told her to stuff it, and reassured her that she wasn't going anywhere. Stacy breathed a huge sigh of relief.

It took some time. And a few trips back and forth between Ohio and New England while the little family that had never had a chance to form found its knitting. It would never be what it might have been. But Chuck and Donna and Lana discovered each other and liked what they found. A lot.

Chuck turned up at the task force offices again several times, meeting Lana toward the end of a workday to take her to dinner in Concord or go to a movie. He'd moved back to New England and was renting a studio apartment in Lowell, Massachusetts. He figured it was halfway between his daughter, who still lived in Providence, and Lana.

Chuck turned up one day when Lana wasn't working and invited himself down the hall to Stacy's office. He tapped on the doorframe to get her attention, since she was pounding away on her keyboard in total concentration.

"Oh, hey, Chuck! Lana's off today. Can I do something for you?"

"Yeah, maybe," he said. "I guess I really just want to talk to you about something."

"Okay, sure, c'mon in. Take a seat. What's on your mind?"

Chuck took two steps into Stacy's office and pulled out the old wooden captain's chair that sat next to her desk for visitors. She'd found it at a garage sale in Warner for $8 and brought it into the office to replace the folding chair she kept borrowing from the conference room anytime someone came.

"Well, things with me and Lana, you know, it's going good. We had to really get to know each other again, get caught up on each other's lives and all. But Stacy, I feel the same way now that I did when I was in high school. I never married, after all those years. Just couldn't ever find anyone I could imagine doing life with the same way I knew I could with Lana," he said.

Stacy had a feeling she knew where this was going. A sly smile spread across her face.

"So, you gonna ask her or what?"

Chuck looked at Stacy, his eyes twinkling, one side of his mouth quirked up in a grin.

"Worth a shot, don't you think?"

About the author

Peggy Hill is a Midwestern American currently living in the mountains of western Colorado. After a long non-profit career advocating for children in poverty, the beleaguered environment, and public mental health, she is finding joy in simpler things. Her stories are inspired by people and places where she has lived and traveled, and by the magnificent complexity of the natural world. Bedtime Stories for Grown Ups is her gift to all those still hard at work in the difficult world where every plot line is blindingly complex and there aren't enough happy endings.

CPSIA information can be obtained
at www.ICGtesting.com
Printed in the USA
LVHW110839170822
726108LV00001B/1/J